Earl of Darkness

"A new trilogy . . . as dark, brooding, and chilling as a gothic novel and as startling as a paranormal tale while still maintaining the deep emotions and sexual tension of a romance."

—*Romantic Times* (4½ stars, Top Pick)

"This book is magic personified. . . . Watch out you other Grande Dames of paranormal romance, Ms. Rickloff just spun a winner that is sure to be nipping at your heels."

—Night Owl Reviews

"Secret societies, baffling documents, monstrous stalkers— Rickloff has studied the textbook thoroughly, then added more sex . . . the pages will turn breathlessly. . . ."

—*Publishers Weekly*

"A smart and exciting journey that will keep you enthralled until the very end."

—The Season For Romance

"An exciting and spellbinding book."

—Bitten By Books

The Heirs of Kilronan novels are
also available as eBooks

ALSO BY ALIX RICKLOFF

Earl of Darkness

Lord of Shadows

Available from Pocket Books

HEIR OF DANGER

BOOK THREE

Alix Rickloff

POCKET BOOKS

New York London Sydney Toronto New Delhi

Pocket Books
A Division of Simon & Schuster, Inc.
1230 Avenue of the Americas
New York, NY 10020

This book is a work of fiction. Names, characters, places, and incidents either are products of the author's imagination or are used fictitiously. Any resemblance to actual events or locales or persons, living or dead, is entirely coincidental.

First Pocket Books paperback edition January 2012

POCKET and colophon are registered trademarks
of Simon & Schuster, Inc.

For information about special discounts for bulk purchases,
please contact Simon & Schuster Special Sales at 1-866-506-1949
or business@simonandschuster.com.

The Simon & Schuster Speakers Bureau can bring authors to your live event. For more information or to book an event contact the Simon & Schuster Speakers Bureau at 1-866-248-3049 or visit our website at www.simonspeakers.com.

Cover illustration by Gene Mollica

Manufactured in the United States of America

10 9 8 7 6 5 4 3 2 1

ISBN 978-1-5011-0264-6
ISBN 978-1-4391-7060-1 (ebook)

For Jane, Georgette, Rosamunde, and Mary

Acknowledgments

Once more I send out a multitude of thank-yous to all who helped me birth another book.

To my agent, Kevan Lyon, who goes to great lengths to explain to me the business side of things. I'm hopeful that someday I might actually understand it all.

To my editor, Megan McKeever, and all the wonderful people at Pocket, who have done such a fabulous job on this series. It's been a joy to work with you from beginning to end.

To Maggie and Do, who are always there when my sagging middle becomes an insurmountable wall. This one almost got me, ladies.

To Helen McCarthy Goode and Pat Doody, for double-checking my Irish expressions. Any mistakes in the language are mine alone.

To the fabulous writers of The Beau Monde, who never leave me hanging when I'm searching for that last-minute answer and are always eager and generous in sharing their time and their expertise.

And kisses and hugs to my wonderful family, who smooth the path and keep me sane—even when they're driving me crazy. I love you all!

One

King Arthur's tomb lay hidden deep within an ancient wood. For centuries uncounted, the sheltering trees grew tall, spread wide, and fell to rot until barely a stone remained to mark its presence.

With a hand clamped upon the shoulder of his attendant, the other upon his stick, Máelodor limped the final yards through the tangled undergrowth to stand before the toppled burial site. The mere effort of walking from the carriage used much of his strength. His shirt clung damp and uncomfortable over his hunched back. The stump of his leg ground against his false limb, spots of blood soaking through his breeches. Every rattling breath burned his tired lungs.

"This is it," he wheezed, eyes fixed upon the mossy slabs. "I feel it."

He didn't even bother to confirm his certainty. No need. Once decoded, the Rywlkoth tapestry had been clear enough. Its clues leading him unerringly to this forgotten Cornish grove.

Excitement licked along his damaged nerves and palsied limbs, casualties of his unyielding ambition. The Nine's goals had been audacious, but Máelodor had known long before Scathach's brotherhood of *Amhas-draoi* descended like a wrath of battle crows that, to succeed, authority must be vested in a single man—a master-mage with the commitment to sacrifice all. To allow no sentimentality to sway him. To use any means necessary to bring about a new age of *Other* dominance.

He was that man.

His continued existence obscured within a web of *Unseelie* concealment, he'd called upon the dark magics to re-create life. Resurrecting an ancient Welsh warrior as one of the *Domnuathi*. A soldier of Domnu in thrall to its master and imbued with all the sinister powers that inspired its rebirth.

That first trial had ended in failure. The creature escaping Máelodor's control.

But he had learned from his mistakes. It would not happen a second time. Once resurrected, the High King would serve the man who restored his life and his crown. Would obey the mage who brought forth a host of *Unseelie* demons to fight for his cause. And would fear his master as all slaves must.

Mage energy danced pale in the green, humid air, mistaken by any who might stumble into this corner of the wood as dust caught within the filtered sunlight. Máelodor reveled in its play across his skin before it burrowed deep into his bloodstream. Melded and merged with his own *Fey*-born powers. Growing to a rush of magic so powerful he closed his eyes, his body suffused with exhilaration. The same uncontrolled arousal he usually sought in the bedchamber or the torture chamber.

His hand dug into the man's shoulder until he felt

bones give beneath his grip. No cry or flinch at such harsh treatment. He'd chosen Oss as much for his brute strength as his slit tongue. Máelodor's body jumped and spasmed as bliss arced like lightning through him. And it was he who cried out with a groan in orgasm.

Sated, he motioned Oss forward, the two moving at a crawling pace over the uneven ground until he stood at the edge of the toppled granite slab, close enough to lay his hand upon the rock. The mage energy leapt high, buffeting him as it sought to understand this intruder. Moving through him in a questing, studying twining of powers.

Arthur's bones lay only a mere stone's thickness away. Once he possessed the Sh'vad Tual, Máelodor would finally have all he needed to unlock the tomb's defenses. Triumph would be his at last, for who was left to stop him?

The *Amhas-draoi* had long ago assumed his execution. The rogue mage-warrior St. John doing much to turn the eyes of Scathach's brotherhood toward another and discredit any rumors of Máelodor's survival.

Brendan Douglas was their quarry. The treacherous dog could only hope they found him before Máelodor did. For once Douglas fell into his clutches, so too would the Sh'vad Tual. One would unlock the tomb. The other would feed Máelodor's unholy desires for months.

It was fascinating how long one could string pain out. An unending plucked wire where a simple tug anywhere could bring excruciating agony, yet death remained always just beyond reach. It would be thus for Douglas. The man who had brought the Nine down would suffer for his betrayal before joining his father and the rest in *Annwn's* deepest abyss.

Máelodor's *Domnuathi* had captured the diary.

Máelodor himself had stolen the Rywlkoth tapestry.

Brendan Douglas would hand over the stone as he begged for his life.

"We're close, Oss. No longer will the race of *Other* live in the shadows, fearing the mortal *Duinedon*. It will be our time again. We shall not so easily let it slip away from us again."

The bear-like attendant nodded, his empty eyes never wavering. His stance wide, his arms hanging ape-like at his sides.

"Help me back to the carriage. I'm expecting news of Douglas."

In silence, the pair—aged cripple and mute albino—stumbled through the tangle of brush, leaving the tomb behind.

But before the stones merged within the wood's defenses, Máelodor turned back. Whispered the words that would unlock the door: *"Mebyoa Uther hath Ygraine. Studhyesk esh Merlinus. Flogsk esh na est Erelth. Pila-vyghterneask. Klywea mest hath igosk agesha daresha."*

Trees shook as birds rose in a chattering black cloud. The sun dimmed, throwing the grove into sudden darkness. A faint chiming caught on a cold rush of wind. And refusal blossomed like a bloodstain in Máelodor's chest. The answer came back to him—

No.

Dun Eyre
County Clare, Ireland

"Stand still, Elisabeth. The woman can't do her work with you spinning about like a top."

Elisabeth subsided under Aunt Fitz's scolding. Inhaled

a martyr's breath, trying to ignore the burning muscles in her arms and the tingly numbness moving up from her fingertips. It was all very well for her aunt. She wasn't forced to stand with her arms spread wide, pins poking her in the small of her back, the feeling draining from her appendages. She rolled her neck, hoping at least to ease the tension banding her shoulders.

"Stop fidgeting. You know, if you didn't keep nibbling between meals, Miss Havisham wouldn't have to adjust the gown."

The modiste glanced up. "Mm. Phnnmp. Mnshph," she mumbled around a mouthful of pins.

"And that's very kind of you, I'm sure. But I'd rather Miss Fitzgerald refrain from extra desserts and late-night tea and biscuits."

Elisabeth glared at her aunt's reflection in the cheval mirror. It was a familiar argument between them. Aunt Fitz—her own figure rail-thin—had always viewed her niece's voluptuous Renaissance body with displeasure. Or perhaps with jealousy. Either way, visits by the modiste always ended in short tempers and long silences. And an overwhelming urge in Elisabeth to eat something tooth-achingly sweet just out of spite.

She risked smoothing a hand over the swell of one hip, the slide of the pale silk cool against her palm. "Perhaps you could simply throw a sack over me and save all this bother."

"Don't be pert, dear," came her aunt's response as she sank into an armchair by the fire with a tired rub to her temples.

Miss Havisham stood with an accommodating smile. "There now, Miss Fitzgerald. You can take it off."

With the assistance of her maid and the modiste, Elisabeth wiggled out of the gown.

"I'll have the alterations completed by tomorrow. Oh, it shall be absolutely stunning. You'll be a vision. Mr. Shaw will think he's marrying an angel."

Elisabeth stared hard into the mirror, doubting even the expensive and exclusive Dublin modiste could affect that kind of transformation. But it was pleasant to envision appreciation lighting Gordon's eyes upon seeing her in the creamy lace-and-silk confection.

Miss Havisham chattered on as she packed up her bags. "It must be so exciting. Having all your relations gathered together. The anticipation of starting a new life with such a respected and very handsome young man."

"It was exciting the first time," Aunt Fitz groused. "This time, it's simply tedious."

Elisabeth blushed, color staining her neck and cheeks. Eyes may act as windows to the soul for others, but in her case, all thoughts and feelings appeared pink and splotchy upon her face. Not a pretty picture when combined with her red hair. "You didn't have to make such a to-do over the wedding. In fact, I'd have been happier had you not."

Her aunt's lips quirked in a sympathetic grimace. "I know, child, but Aunt Pheeney would never have forgiven us. You know how she loves a spectacle. Let's just hope *this* wedding comes off without a hitch. I don't have the strength for a third. And neither you nor I are getting any younger. You'll be twenty-six this summer. Most of your friends wed long ago, their nurseries full."

Elisabeth stood still while her maid secured the tapes of her morning gown. "Thank you for reminding me of my approaching decrepitude."

"I'm only saying that once a woman reaches a certain age, it becomes more difficult to entice the—"

"I know what you're saying, Aunt Fitz. And you're right. It's just taken me this long to find a suitable man. Someone I could respect enough to build a life together. Gordon Shaw is that man."

"I hope so, or we've gone to a lot of bother for nothing—again," Aunt Fitz mumbled before plastering on a cheery smile at sight of Elisabeth's tart frown. "No, you're right, Lissa. He's a fine man and a suitable husband."

Lissa. Why had her aunt used that silly childhood pet name? Did she mean to confound her just when she most needed confidence? Or was it a slip of the tongue after an interminable day of wedding arrangements?

Only one other person had ever dared call her Lissa past her tenth birthday. One infuriating, exasperating, unconscionable, miserable horse's arse.

The dis-Honorable Brendan Douglas.

Music reached her. Even in her bedchamber, so far from the light and color and laughter of the drawing room downstairs, strains of Mozart floated round her like a ghost. The second movement of his piano concerto no. 27, of all things. She'd once thought it her favorite piece. But that had been many years ago. Now, just hearing the familiar chords set her teeth on edge.

First Aunt Fitz's use of that ridiculous pet name and now this. Memories hung heavier in the air tonight than they had in many a year. Like a fog, clinging to the back of her throat. Squeezing the air from her lungs. Though that might be her stays. Hard to tell.

She placed a drop of scent behind each ear. At the base

of her throat. Repinned a straggling piece of hair. Silly things. Inconsequential things. But they kept her safely in her chair while that horrible, incessant tune played below-stairs.

As a final gesture, she lifted a hand to the necklace Gordon had presented her at dinner. Amid a chorus of oohs and ahs from female relations and the menfolk ribbing him mercilessly about his besotted state, Gordon had fastened the opulent and conspicuously expensive string of sapphires about her throat. She leaned back into his hands, but he retreated with a singularly un-lover-like pat on her shoulder.

The necklace was stunning. Spectacular. A work of art. And completely not to her taste.

She reached behind, undoing the clasp. Laying the gaudy choker carefully back in its box. The music swelled as she searched her jewelry case. Lifted out another pendant to wear in its place. A plain gold chain. A simple setting. And a stone more breathtakingly dramatic than any she'd ever seen.

Large as a baby's fist and still chipped and rough as if it had only just been mined, the milky translucent crystal was slashed with veins of silver, gold, rosy pearl, and jet black. Depending upon the light, it could shimmer with flame-like incandescence or smolder like banked coals. Tonight it glimmered in the curve of her breasts. The subtleties of its colors accentuating the honey tones of her skin, pulling glints of gold into her brown eyes.

Would Gordon understand, or would he glimpse her neck and see only her refusal to wear his costly gift? Best to wear the sapphires tonight.

She started fumbling at the catch when the door burst open on the girlish round features of Aunt Pheeney.

"Are you still lolling about up here? My dear, everyone is beginning to think you've gotten cold feet. Even Gordon is concerned. You know what they say about time and tide. . . ."

"I'll just be a moment."

Aunt Pheeney would not be put off any longer. She dragged Elisabeth from her chair. "No more hiding away up here. This is meant to be a celebration. Not a wake."

"I know, I only need to—"

"No more delays, young lady." Aunt Pheeney had already bullied her halfway to the door. "Come downstairs now." Her usually cheerful features rearranged themselves into what, for her, passed as stern lines. "That's an order."

"Yes, ma'am." Elisabeth allowed herself to be led out, Gordon's sapphires abandoned upon her dressing table.

As they descended the stairs, the music rearranged itself into a proper country dance. Men led their partners onto the drawing room floor, the furniture removed for the evening, doors flung wide to create one enormous, glittering, laughter-filled expanse.

Elisabeth cast her eyes over the sea of guests. Most of them family, though neighbors and friends, some from as far away as Dublin, had come to be a part of the wedding festivities. The marriage of the Fitzgerald heiress had been a long time coming. Everyone wanted to be there to witness it. Or, a more cynical voice nagged at her, say they were present when Elisabeth Fitzgerald was jilted a second time.

Aunt Fitz and Lord Taverner chatted in one corner. Elisabeth's guardian no doubt discussing marriage settlements and jointures and land trusteeships. Aunt Fitz nodding thoughtfully, though she bore a hawkish scowl.

Cousin Rolf, dashing in his scarlet regimentals, and

beautiful Cousin Francis, in white and gold, whirled their way through the set while Cousin Fanny and Sir James grazed from the passing platters.

Uncle McCafferty deep in conversation with a gentleman she didn't recognize. Obviously one of the Dublin crowd invited by softhearted Aunt Pheeney, who felt anyone she so much as passed three words with merited an invitation.

Gordon and his half brother, Marcus, stood amid a group of sober-clad companions. Gordon's handsome features and athletic physique, as usual, drawing the eye of every woman in the room. She squared her shoulders. Plastered a smile upon her face. In a few days, this absurd spectacle would be over. She would be wed.

"Come along, Elisabeth. They're all waiting on you," Aunt Pheeney coaxed. "Behold, the bride cometh."

"I think that's bridegroom, Aunt Pheeney."

"Tish tush, close enough."

The music ended. But only for a moment before the scrape of violins began again. Different couples. Same pairings and partings to the steps of the dance.

She held back, slightly breathless, a strange tightening in her stomach. "Let me just collect myself for a moment and I'll be in." At her aunt's skeptical look, she added, "I promise," and kissed her soft, dry cheek.

Her aunt patted her hand. "Very well, child. But a moment only."

Elisabeth watched the scene below her as if she were a little girl sneaking down from the night nursery to catch a glimpse of her mother and father among the florid, laughing faces.

Even long after their deaths abroad, when Aunt Fitz

and Aunt Pheeney had been the ones hosting the lavish balls and jolly house parties, Elisabeth's gaze had always wandered over the tableaux below her as if she might spot her mother's Titian hair or her father's broad back amid the throng.

Taking a deep breath, she stepped from the comfortable shadows of the hall into the blaze of a thousand candles. Immediately, Gordon lifted a quizzing glass to his eye, studying her for a long moment before he lowered it, a question glinting in his eyes.

She tried smiling an apology, but he'd already turned back to the men in response to a chummy slap on the back that left them all guffawing in good humor.

But another had yet to look away. The stranger with Uncle McCafferty. The weight of his stare sent heat rising into her cheeks until she realized it wasn't her face he was fixated upon but her chest. Hardly the first man to be so bold, though it unnerved her just the same. Let him ogle his fill, then. What did she care? She lifted her chin to return his steady regard with her own.

He stood well above her uncle, perhaps even of a height with Gordon. But whereas her betrothed possessed a wrestler's build, this man's lean muscularity spoke of agility and nuance. A swordsman. Not a pugilist.

His gaze narrowed as he bent to sip at his wine. Tossing Uncle McCafferty a word while keeping her under watch. There was something familiar about him. The way he stood, perhaps. Or the slash of his dark brows. His eyes finally moved from her breasts to her face, a rakish invitation playing at the edges of his mouth. Warmth became a flood of scalding heat. No, she certainly did not know such a forward, insinuating gentleman.

And with a regal twitch of her skirts, she entered the fray.

The hours passed in a haze of conversation and music. She barely sat out a single dance. Traded from partner to partner as each man sought to compliment her beauty and impart his good wishes. Gordon spoke for her first, of course. Led her to the floor, his hand gripping hers as if she might try to escape. He made only one comment upon her choice of adornment. "I'm sorry you didn't like my gift. If you'd prefer, we can choose something more to your liking."

Guilt dropped into the pit of her stomach, and she smiled more brightly than she otherwise would have done. "I wouldn't trade it for anything in the world." He arched a brow which made her words spill faster. "But it didn't go with my gown, you see. Tomorrow evening. I promise. I have a new gown it will suit perfectly." She went so far as to bat him playfully on the arm with her fan.

Gordon offered a pained smile. "Wear your little bauble, Elisabeth. Among this company, it's quite beautiful enough."

"What do you mean by that?"

"No need to fly into the boughs, my darling. I only meant that I find you faultless in anything you decide to wear."

Her prickles smoothed, she gazed up at him in clear invitation. They could slip away for a moment or two. There were alcoves aplenty. And it wasn't as if they weren't going to be wed in a few days.

Unfortunately, Gordon stepped back at the same instant she leaned forward, almost unbalancing her. He cleared his throat, a decidedly proper expression on his face.

"Careful, Elisabeth. Your great-aunt Charity is casting dagger glances our way."

She straightened, smoothing her skirts. Tossed a demure smile over the crowd, all as if she meant to almost topple feet over head. "Oh, pooh for Great-aunt Charity. Glass houses and all that rot. If half the stories about her are true—"

"Still, my dear. It wouldn't do to antagonize her unnecessarily. I don't want her thinking I'm a scoundrel."

"What if I like scoundrels?"

"You're such a tease, my dear." He acknowledged an impatient summons from his brother with a wave. "Marcus is after me to make a fourth, dear heart. Will you be all right on your own?" He smiled. "Silly question. Of course you will. You're a natural at this sort of social small talk. And besides, it's family. Not a bunch of strangers, eh?" He chucked her chin as he might a child's before leaving without a backward glance.

She took advantage of the respite to snatch a savory and a glass of wine from a passing tray. Nibbled as she watched the crowd of parrot-bright ladies and dashing gentlemen. They laughed, danced, drank, and in one or two instances sang. Boisterous. At times rowdy. But always good-natured.

"Among this company . . ." What had Gordon been implying? And why did she feel she'd been chastised like a child? She shook off her questions with a sigh and a sharp flick of her fan.

"Abandoned at your own festivities?" came a voice from behind her, thick and dark as treacle. Definitely not Great-aunt Charity, who possessed a parade ground bellow.

No, Elisabeth knew that voice. That impudent tone.

She swung around to come up against an unyielding

chest. Her glass of wine sloshed onto his coat, staining his shirtfront dark red. He stepped back with a quick oath. And the moment burst like a bubble. The man from earlier. A stranger. Not him. Not at all. What was wrong with her that she jumped at shadows?

"Forgive me." She blotted at him with her napkin.

"Here, allow me." He eased it from her hand as she belatedly realized the unintended intimacy of her actions.

"I . . . Oh, dear . . . you don't think . . . oh, dear," she babbled.

He dabbed at the spot before crushing the napkin and shoving it into his pocket. "No matter. At least it's not blood this time."

What on earth did he mean by that?

He lifted his head, his veiled gaze finally meeting hers dead-on. Eyes burning golden-yellow as suns, the irises ringed in darkest black.

She crushed a hand to her mouth to stifle the sound choking up through her belly.

His lips twitched with suppressed amusement. As if this were in any way funny. Earth-shattering, more like. "Hello, Lissa."

two

Had anyone seen? Did anyone know? Surely such an event should be accompanied by a clap of thunder and the earth tilting wildly on its axis. But no. Gordon remained in company with his card-playing friends; Aunt Fitz and Aunt Pheeney chatted with the vicar and his wife; the rest of the guests remained wrapped in their own entertainments. Everything was as it had been a mere moment ago when she'd been happily, comfortingly unaware of the lurking catastrophe in her midst. Yet, all it would take was one curious family member or one inconvenient well-wisher to turn past notoriety into new accusations, insinuations, and speculation.

Miss Elisabeth Fitzgerald. From on-the-shelf spinster to an excess of bridegrooms in the space of a heartbeat.

"You'll excuse me . . . sir." The steady throbbing behind her eyes expanded until her whole brain hurt, and she'd trouble walking on shaking legs.

Instead of allowing her to depart gracefully, Brendan

Douglas accompanied her into the hall. And then some-how she found her hand linked with his. The contact firm, the callused palm at odds with his polished exterior as he steered her across to a small salon.

He turned to close the doors behind them, his coat stretching tight across his shoulders. And when he faced her again, she noted for the first time a hastily stitched seam. A worn cuff. Less polished than well patched. He hadn't changed as much as she thought.

"What have you done to yourself?" she asked.

This probably shouldn't have been her first question, but it was all she could manage as she saw her life flashing before her eyes.

"This?" He passed a hand over his face as if stripping away a mask, a tingle in the air lifting the hairs on her arms and the nape of her neck. Instantly his features shimmered and blurred, rearranging themselves before sharpening back into focus. "A *fith-fath* to keep from being recognized. I didn't think I'd be welcomed back with open arms other-wise."

"Don't do that," she snapped.

No matter how often she told herself there was noth-ing wrong with the race of *Other*'s *Fey*-born powers, she still flinched at the casual use of a magic that seemed like fairy-tale fantasy. Her grandmother had been *Other*. Elisabeth re-membered her as a dreamy old lady who spent every waking moment in her gardens, walking the paths, murmuring to the flowers and trees as if she greeted friends.

The neighbors called her mad. Elisabeth knew better, though she kept her mouth shut. No one must know. Better to be thought eccentric than *Fey*. And though none of her grandmother's powers had passed down to Elisabeth, she'd been raised knowing that alongside the normal *Duinedon* world she lived in, there existed another. A treacherous, beautiful, amazing world where anything might be possible and life held wonders brighter as well as evils blacker than any she could imagine.

Brendan grinned. "I forgot magic scares you."

"It does not scare me."

He lifted his brows in apparent disbelief. "Sour grapes?"

"It is not sour grapes. I don't care a fig for your ridiculous—"

His grin widened. Oh, if only she could wipe that annoying smile from his annoying face. A face that even undisguised sparked little recognition. The Brendan of her memories had been a skinny, awkward, bookworm with ink-smudged hands and girl-pretty features beneath a thatch of dark brown hair in perpetual need of trimming. Brilliant, impatient, sarcastic, conceited.

And she'd been head-over-heels smitten. Not that he'd ever noticed.

Almost no trace of that angelic attractiveness could be seen in this harder version of Brendan. Instead his looks bore the same rugged edges as her stone, as if both had been chiseled with a hasty hand, and his body, once thin and narrow-shouldered, had matured to a startling muscled athleticism. Hardly Herculean. More a rangy, quicksilver leanness. Years abroad in harsher climes were evidenced by the dusky tan of his face, the lines creasing the corners of his mouth and gathering by his eyes. Those startling, extraordinary eyes. The one feature he could never camouflage. Always they'd shone like molten honey-gold. Alive. Vibrant as the sun. And stunning as a horse's kick to the stomach.

"Why are you here? You've no right."

He sketched a flourishing bow. "Allow me to introduce myself. John Martin. Distant cousin to the bride, recently arrived from abroad. Amid the bustle of so many, none questioned one more relation among the crush already here for the wedding." A teasing smile hovered as he straightened. "Though I have to quibble with the room I was given. I'm practically under the eaves. A veritable garret. One would think I wasn't welcome."

That did it. They were alone, the drone of conversation and laughter and the gay strains of the quartet left far behind. No one to witness her confusion. No one to comment on her quaking limbs or the snapped sticks of her fan. She could finally give vent to the rage churning up through her. As if it had a will of her own, her free hand swung out. Connected with his cheek in a wrist-jarring, finger-tingling slap. "You stinking great, bloody-minded bastard!" She wanted to hit him again. Her hand curled into a fist. "Why couldn't you have stayed dead?"

Brendan ducked the second blow. It barely grazed his shoulder. But the third had seven years of bad blood behind it and took him full on the chin. He reeled backward more in shock than in pain, striking his head on the edge of a bookcase. Stars exploded behind his eyes, and he dropped half to his knees.

"Oh no, oh dear. I'm sorry. Are you all right?" Hands fluttered around him. Fingers brushing his scalp.

He winced on a grumbled string of profanity.

The hands retreated. "You needn't resort to such vile language."

He opened his eyes to Elisabeth's worried, angry visage.

Her arms wrapped about her midsection, face blanched of color. It made the carmine sheen of her hair all the more radiant. Living flame.

"You nearly cracked my skull open. What did you expect I would say?" He reached up, examining the point of impact. Already it swelled and stung like the very devil. "Thanks ever so for the great lump on my head?"

"Quit carrying on like a baby. If I wanted to—and don't think I'm not tempted—I'd have Gordon give you the thrashing you deserve. Or Aidan. That's what I should do. Send for Aidan. He'd—"

"No." The crack of his voice startled her silent. "You're not going to send for Aidan. You're going to keep your mouth shut. To anyone who asks, I'm John Martin."

"Why on earth should I keep quiet?"

"It's complicated. But believe me when I say doing anything else would be very unwise."

She crossed her arms. Eyed him with suspicion. "Aidan should know you're alive. Your brother—"

"When I'm ready, I'll go home to Belfoyle. Right now, I'm here and I plan on staying here for the time being."

He shouldn't be arguing with her. He shouldn't even have let her know of his presence. He'd told himself to keep his head down and his mouth shut while within five square miles of Elisabeth Fitzgerald. Jack had warned him at least a thousand times of the perils he'd face striding into the lion's den. Be sensible. Be safe. Get in and get out quickly and quietly. But spying her across Dun Eyre's drawing room had been too much of a temptation. He should have known she'd recognize him. And with that recognition would follow an ugly and awkward scene. Though he'd envisioned tears and accusations of abandonment rather than fists and fervent calls for his continued death.

Lissa had always been more than a little unpredictable.

"Please, Elisabeth."

"Give me one good reason."

"How about having your current groom involved in a brawl with your former betrothed? I can imagine the whispers, and whispers become scandals. And you certainly wouldn't want that. Not with the place crawling with relations and Mr. Shaw poised to lead you down the aisle. Your aunts would be humiliated. You'd be a laughingstock. Again. Think about it."

It was obvious she had already thought about it. And come to the conclusion he'd hoped for. She'd say nothing.

Still, her livid expression hinted at additional blows aimed in his direction, and if he remembered rightly, that spark in otherwise gentle brown eyes spelled trouble. "Very well. Your identity is safe, Mr. Douglas, for the reasons you so correctly spelled out." Her voice wavered, her hands closing into fists at her side.

He took a wary step back just in case, but it was unnecessary. She slumped onto a sofa, a hand rubbing absently at her temple. "But why? Answer me that one question. You were dead, Brendan. Dead and buried."

Why did he leave? No way to answer that didn't scare her to death. Why had he returned? Equally difficult to explain without revealing the depth of his past villainy. For some reason, it was easier to have Elisabeth hate him for a rogue who'd run out on his bride than know the far uglier truth.

His gaze flicked to the stone nestled between her breasts.

"Enjoying the view?" she asked tartly.

His attention snapped back to her face, which now wore an expression of resignation, as if she were used to men speaking to her chest. Something deep in his gut tightened at the thought of other men eying Elisabeth in such a bold manner.

"Perhaps like young Lochinvar, I came back when I heard you meant to wed another."

"If that was meant to be a joke, you'll have to do better," she answered breezily. "As you explained when you asked for my hand all those years ago, our marriage was one of convenience at the behest of your mother."

Had he said that? Damned rude of him. It's a wonder she'd agreed to have him if he'd carried on that way. More a wonder she hadn't smashed something heavy over his head for such impertinence.

He fought off a momentary stab of guilt, focusing his thoughts on the men hunting him, hardening himself against faltering resolve. "I'm here for one simple reason. Dun Eyre is the last place anyone will look for me."

The stubborn square of her chin pushed forward, her gaze narrowed in new speculation.

"Which is why I'll reiterate, the name is John Martin," he said.

She twisted her broken fan until the sticks splintered. "You're a right bastard, Brendan Douglas."

He grinned at the base language coming from that pretty mouth. She'd always been a contradiction of femininity and ferocity. "But you love me anyway."

"Once, maybe. But you've spent that coin." She closed her eyes for a moment as if trying to adjust to this new reality, and when she opened them, surrender dulled the heat of her gaze. It was almost worse than her fury had been. That he'd prepared for. This was different entirely.

"How could you come back like this and expect me to act as if nothing had happened?" she asked. "You left me, Brendan. No note. No explanation, though all and sundry were willing to supply one."

He turned to study the fire as if he might find answers written upon the flames.

"I didn't mind that so much," she continued. "I mean it was mortifying with Aunt Pheeney spouting proverbs like water and Aunt Fitz stalking the house, muttering threats on your person. But then afterward, your father's murder . . . that was so much more horrible. What was I supposed to believe after that?"

He swung around, a hand gripping the mantel. He noted the bloodless fingers as if they belonged to someone else. "What everyone did, I suppose. That I was guilty."

"There were some who refused to believe," she said softly. "Even then, they had faith in your innocence."

"I'm sure you soon set them straight." This was not a conversation he wanted to have. Being here cut too close to the bone for comfort. He hadn't thought it would. He'd thought those ghosts had long been exorcised. More fool he. Time had done little to salve that wound. "Take heart," he bluffed. "I won't inconvenience you for long, and you and your Mr. Shaw can gallop up the aisle with my blessing."

She too seemed to have shaken off her momentary confusion. She rose, adjusting her skirts in a show of indifference. "I'm relieved. I should have been heartbroken to know the man who threw me over didn't approve of the man honorable enough to hang about for his own wedding breakfast."

"Speaking of Shaw, where did you meet him? Last I heard, you were in London."

"Keeping an eye on me?"

"A year-old *London Times*. What's his background?"

"Are you my guardian now?"

"An interested party. I may not have married you, but that doesn't mean I don't want to see you happy."

Folding her arms over her chest, she huffed, "Fine. Not that it's any of your business, but Gordon has a decent fortune of his own. A solid position within the current government. And *isn't* you. All quality traits in a husband."

"Ouch. If I didn't know better, I'd say you were sorry to see me."

"Ughh!" She threw up her hands. "You're incorrigible. Go away, Brendan. Crawl back into whatever hole you've been hiding in, and stay there this time. You ruined my last wedding. You are not going to ruin this one. Do you hear me?"

"If you're not careful, the whole house will hear you."

Her dark eyes burned a hole right through him.

"Don't worry, Lissa. I'll not upset your apple cart. You and the respectable Mr. Shaw will wed and have respectable babies and lead a respectable life."

Instead of spearing him with a suitable scathing response, she lifted her chin, squared her shoulders, and swept past him to the doors. Throwing them open, she sailed back into the crowd as proud as any queen.

He let out the breath he'd been holding with an audible sigh. He'd jumped the first fence cleanly. He was in.

Brendan wandered the Dun Eyre gardens, reacquainting himself with the extensive grounds. Assessing terrain.

Studying the landscape. Seeing the parkland not as the masterpiece of tidy parterres and man-made wilderness, but as a means to hide, escape, or fight, depending upon circumstance. These skills had been the first things he'd learned while in exile. And had kept him alive more than once in the intervening years. By now, it had become second nature.

This should have been easy. Growing up close by, he'd spent countless hours running wild over this ground and knew Dun Eyre like the back of his hand. Coming upon a high hedge that ought not to have been there, he had to admit the back of his hand hadn't looked the same since being crushed beneath a boot heel last November.

He curled his fingers into an awkward, aching fist. The grinding of rough-healed bones a memento of those dangerous days when it looked as if his crimes had finally caught up with him.

The gods had smiled on that occasion. It remained to be seen if he'd be so fortunate again.

He backtracked, hoping to loop around the thorny barrier and come upon the house from the west. The cold penetrated his coat while the bones of his hand throbbed. A weather sense he could do without. It had been too long since he'd experienced Ireland's cold, damp spring. He'd grown used to sun and bleached blue skies and dry desert breezes.

The longer he remained close to his childhood home, the more memories surfaced like unearthed corpses. Every familiar landmark and well-known face brought those last horrible days back in vivid nightmare. Father's reproachful gaze piercing him with shame and guilt. Father's death playing out in eternal bloody violence until even waking there was no respite from the images.

Had it been quick and painless, or had the *Amhas-draoi* spent their vengeance in excruciating butchery? Had Father known in the end Brendan had been his betrayer? Or had he gone to his death ignorant of his beloved son's treachery?

He blinked, pulling himself back into the present. He could drown his sorrows at the bottom of a bottle for the rest of his pathetic life if he wanted. Now he needed to be cool, confident. Focus on his goal.

Retrieve the Sh'vad Tual.

Take it to Scathach for safekeeping.

And grovel as he'd never groveled before to save his sorry life.

Simple.

Hunching his shoulders against the chill, he trained his eyes on the path ahead, ears tuned to any hint of fellow wanderers. In the thick shadows away from the house, he'd shed the *fith-fath*. He was sorely out of practice, and the concentration it took to maintain the spell left little energy for aught else. Best to use his powers sparingly.

The hedge folded back upon itself, the path spilling out in a shallow set of stone stairs. Below him, the house stretched wing to wing from its foursquare central block. The ball had ended, guests leaving in a line of carriages or retiring to their quarters for the night. A few lights glittered from windows, but the blaze of candleshine and torchères lighting the entrances had been doused, night closing thick against the buildings.

He counted third-floor windows. Seven in from the right. Elisabeth's bedchamber. Light still shone behind the curtains. She would be undressing. Slowly untying her garters. Seductively rolling down the stockings on her long legs. Her luscious curves held tightly captive by stays and petticoats freed to fill the thin muslin chemise she wore to bed. The pins holding her chignon in place would be removed, letting that spill of dark red hair slide deliciously over her back to her hips. And last but not least, she'd lift her hands behind her neck. Unclasp the necklace that lay in the valley of her sweet, full breasts, and place it back in its box.

A wry chuckle escaped him. Gods, he must need it bad to be fantasizing about Elisabeth. She'd been close as a sister. A little sister. She amused him. She was smart, funny, daring, and rode a horse as if she'd been born in the saddle. But never had she been fantasy material. And yet now? If she'd been struck by the changes wrought in him, he'd been equally surprised.

He remembered Elisabeth as a little plump. A lot freckled. Hair a wild riot of dark red curls. And an impish gleam in her big brown eyes. Then he'd looked up and, instead of the girl of his memories, he'd fastened his gaze on a voluptuous woman tempting as chocolate with a body that made his blood rush faster. Seeing her made him light-headed and stupid with thoughts he never should think and ideas he daren't let take shape.

He should have joined Jack their last night in Ennis. His cousin had that scoundrel's knack for finding the perfect woman to scratch any itch. Brendan shifted uncomfortably, dousing his lust-filled imagination with more somber thoughts—the consequences if Máelodor gained possession of the Sh'vad Tual.

War between the *Fey*-born race of *Other* and their unmagical *Duinedon* neighbors. And the cataclysm for both sides should this come to pass.

". . . a king's ransom . . . what does she wear . . ."

". . . doesn't matter, Marcus . . . let it go . . ."

Men's voices rose up from the bottom of the stairs. Automatically, Brendan went still, his breath barely stirring in his lungs. No shoes scuffed the stone steps. They must have taken shelter in one of the numerous benched alcoves.

He delayed conjuring the *fith-fath*. Instead, he bent closer, letting the shadows glide up and over him until nothing moved to alert the men they had an audience.

"I'm going mad with boredom, Gordon. What the blazes do people do around here?"

"It's not London, certainly, but it has its own simple charms. I'm quite enjoying the escape from the mad crush."

Gordon Shaw. His brother, Marcus. Brendan's knees stiffened, his shoulders tightened, but he dared not move now.

"Charms aside, you can't convince me you're truly happy kicking your heels in this backwater while the London Season progresses at full swing. And what does Lord Prosefoot say about your absence during the session?"

"He was most agreeable. And it's not as if I didn't bring work with me. I've gotten quite a bit done too. Don't fret. A week more and we'll be on the packet for Holyhead. In London by the end of the month."

A dramatic groan. "I don't think I can survive another week tethered to this provincial idea of entertainment. I never told you, but yesterday at dinner I was caught by Miss Fitzgerald's cousin, Mrs. Tolliver of Bedfordshire. I had to sit through an interminable recitation of family connections between the Shaws and the Tollivers stretching back to the Conquest. Filial duty only goes so far."

"Yes, but at that same dinner I was in conversation with Elisabeth's guardian, Lord Taverner. He's offered to have a word about an ambassadorial posting with Stuart in France.

From there, who knows how far I might rise. I knew this Fitzgerald alliance would be the making of me," Shaw announced proudly.

"I'm not sure which you're more excited about—the wife or the political connection."

"Do you know? Neither am I."

Cynical brotherly laughter followed.

Poor bloody Lissa. She had horrible luck in picking husbands.

Elisabeth brushed her hair long after every tangle had been ferociously removed. Usually the steady even strokes soothed her. Tonight the jumbled tumult of her thoughts overpowered every attempt at relaxation. Why had Brendan come back from the dead? Who was he hiding from? Was he in trouble? Why did she care?

Placing the brush back upon her dressing table, she noted with a frown the slight tremble of her fingers, the riot of nerves jumping in her stomach. Wedding jitters. That was all. Excitement. Anxiety. A little fear. All of it normal. Expected.

Her anxiety had nothing to do with the return of a man she'd thought dead and buried.

She should have known better. He was far too clever to end unmourned in a pauper's grave.

Her fear was in no way connected to the surprising presence of a man rumored to have conspired in the death of his own father.

She'd never believed those stories. Brendan might be a lot of things, but not a murderer.

And her excitement was definitely not a surge of girlhood crush.

She cared for Gordon. Gordon cared for her. In an adult, mature, respectable way.

Carelessly, she reached up to finger the stone at her throat, resting dark and cool against her skin. Brendan cared for no one but Brendan. Never had. Never would.

Yet, when she slipped beneath the sheets and blew out her candle, it remained his gift about her neck. And his face imprinted upon her mind.

She didn't know who she hated more at that moment. Brendan for coming. Or herself for being excited by it.

Elisabeth's dressing-room door opened on silent hinges. Thick rugs muffled his every footfall. Thank heavens for the luxury of wealth. It made breaking and entering so much easier.

Her bedchamber door was closed, allowing him the freedom to light the stub of a candle. He sat at the dainty rosewood dressing table, her jewelry case conveniently at hand. Rummaging through the contents, he pulled free a heart-shaped locket containing miniatures of her parents, a small amber cross, two lavish strands of pearls, a topaz choker, and a dazzling necklace containing a rajah's ransom of sapphires. Earrings and bracelets. Gold and silver combs. Rings and brooches.

But no pendant.

Rifled drawers revealed jars of cosmetics and lotions, bottles of scent, packets of pins and ribbons. Handkerchiefs and boot laces and a broken embroidery hoop.

But no pendant.

He huffed an exasperated sigh. Where the hell had she put it?

He began again. Searching more carefully. Reaching

back into the corners of each drawer. Pulling piece by piece out of her jewelry case, then returning it in what he hoped was the correct place.

The room held a million places a woman could hide a necklace. Cabinets, tables, a desk. He searched each piece thoroughly. He even shoved his hand beneath the chair cushions and pushed against fireplace tiles, seeking a hidden panel.

If you didn't count two chewed-on pencil nubs, four missing buttons, a crumpled laundry list, and a handful of hairpins, he found absolutely nothing.

A faint thump from the bedchamber brought him up short. Blowing out the candle, he went still. Barely breathed. And surrendered the field.

For now.

three

The buffet table groaned with platters of eggs, sausages, thick slices of ham, cold tongue, and baskets of rolls and toast. Tea and coffee filled silver urns upon a sideboard. Brendan counted heads. Five other occupants still seated. He should have taken breakfast early when most were still foggy from last night's wine.

At one end of the table sat Miss Sara Fitzgerald, nose buried in the day's post. Across from her, Mrs. Pheeney eyed the sausage with heartfelt longing and heavy sighs. Between them, Elisabeth's great-aunt Charity, a woman Brendan had met once long ago and not on the best of terms. If he remembered correctly, he'd been holding a frog. She'd been screeching.

At the far end of the table, Shaw's and Elisabeth's chairs were pulled close together in apparent amity. Brendan's jaw tightened on a grimace of distaste that he transformed into a smile when Elisabeth spotted him. She wasn't as adept an actress. Her face flamed red, her fingers gripping her butter knife as if she might stab him with it.

And there was the stone, taunting him from amid the folds of her lace fichu. Brendan restrained the impulse to cross the room, rip it from her throat, and run like hell. Unfortunately, he'd not get twenty paces before someone brought him down. More than likely Shaw, who possessed the brawn to snap him in two.

"Mr. Martin, how nice of you to join us this"— Elisabeth made a great show of checking the mantel clock, which read half eleven—"why, it is still morning."

He pulled his watch from its pocket, snapping it open to confirm the time against the clock. "The same to the very minute." Shoved it back into his pocket with a smile and a nod toward Miss Sara Fitzgerald, who eyed him speculatively from the far end of the table.

"I'm afraid everyone else came and went ages ago." Elisabeth's smile stretched from ear to ear. More manic than cheerful.

"Good. I detest being jostled while I drink my tea." He drifted to the plates, heaping his high before dropping into a seat across from them, reaching for a clean cup and saucer, asking her to pass the salt. "Fabulous eggs. But then, your cook always had a knack. Do you remember when I visited in aught-three? Coddled to perfection, they were. Never had better."

Shaw regarded him with curiosity. "I don't believe I've had the pleasure, Mr.—"

"Martin," Brendan answered around a mouthful. "John Martin. Second cousin. Or is it third? Can't keep us all straight. There's more of us than a dog has fleas. Isn't that right, Lissa?"

Shaw offered him a placid nod while Elisabeth's stiff smile faltered around the edges.

"A little bird tells me you're moving to London soon. Be careful, Mr. Shaw. Elisabeth may bankrupt you once she's released on the big-city mantua makers and ribbon merchants."

"I never—" Elisabeth spluttered.

"I trust we won't need to worry overmuch about expenses," Shaw replied.

Brendan speared his sausage. "No, silly me. Elisabeth's rolling in the ready, isn't she?"

Shaw answered with a jovial laugh as if Brendan had made the funniest of jokes.

"London, Gordon?"

His attention flicked to Elisabeth. "I can't very well get ahead from the wilds of Ireland, can I?"

"I suppose. I—"

"London is a different place for a married woman than for a young maid making her come-out. Far more to do and see than you can imagine." He warmed to his subject, his voice rising in volume. "The invitations. Parties, dinners, balls. The *ton* will be clamoring to meet the newest jewel in their crown."

She straightened, shooting Brendan a dangerous stare. "Of course. I'd forgotten we'd discussed the move, and you're quite right."

Taken over by an imp of mischief, Brendan couldn't help himself. How much would it take to puncture that pompous self-importance? "I suppose your aunts are excited to move. Didn't Mrs. Pheeney spend a number of years near Richmond?"

"What?" Shaw and Elisabeth both began talking at once. "Aunt Pheeney and Aunt Fitz? They won't be—"

Shaw recovered first. "They're needed to oversee things here until a suitable agent is hired."

"But Mr. Adams?" Elisabeth's voice came uncertain.

"Is a frightful pushover. The tenants walk all over him, and he's so coarse. Not at all the way I imagine the land agent for such a fine estate should carry himself. Besides, I see a whole slew of improvements to the house and grounds, beginning perhaps as soon as the autumn. We'll need someone we can trust to see them through to completion."

Elisabeth's brows contracted in a frown. "Dun Eyre doesn't need improving."

Uh-oh. Brendan knew that look. He'd seen it most recently last night just before he'd taken a fist to the face. Apparently Shaw had yet to experience Elisabeth's temper. He barreled on, oblivious to her tight jaw and set shoulders.

"We'll start with the gardens," he said. "I've just the plan—"

"Not the gardens!" Brendan and Elisabeth spoke in unison.

Shaw cast them a sympathetic smile. "No one likes change, but when we're finished, Elisabeth, this old place will rival any of the great houses in England. Chatsworth or even Blenheim."

"Blenheim?" Great-aunt Charity roused herself from her dry toast. "Went there once as a girl. Got pinched by the late duke and slept in a horrid bedchamber smelling of camphor. Never went back."

"Probably weren't invited back," was Shaw's cool comment as he dabbed at his mouth with a napkin.

"That was Sir Wallace, Charity. And you married him," Miss Sara Fitzgerald corrected.

"Well, had to after that, didn't I?" Great-aunt Charity argued. "He was a rake and a cad, but oh, what hands." Her eyes went dreamy and vague.

Miss Sara buried her nose farther into her paper while Mrs. Pheeney flushed crimson. The rest of them shifted uncomfortably, trying to rid themselves of the picture created.

Brendan broke the awkwardness by waving his fork in Elisabeth's direction. "It's a lovely trinket you're wearing, Lissa. I don't believe I've ever seen a stone such as that one. Family heirloom?"

Shaw's gaze slid to Elisabeth's collar while her lips pursed thin and white. "This? A mere trifle."

Great-aunt Charity chose that moment to rouse herself from lascivious memories of her dear departed husband and remark in a voice loud enough to be heard in the next county, "Ain't that the necklace young Douglas gave you just before he murdered his father and ran off?"

Miss Sara stood abruptly, shooting Brendan a long, studying look. "We've all lolled about here long enough."

"But I've still half the paper to read," Mrs. Pheeney complained. "You know what they say: Knowledge is power."

"And no news is good news," her sister snapped, half-hauling Great-aunt Charity, who remained oblivious to the crosscurrents, out of her seat.

"A rogue, that Douglas boy was. Though he could charm when he chose. You were lucky to escape that marriage, Lizzie. This new lad's a much better catch. And handsome as the devil. I bet he's got a pair of hands on him like my Wally."

Shaw nearly choked on his piece of toast while the

family froze in various poses of mortification and horror. Poor Elisabeth's few remaining freckles were lost amid the furious red of her face.

"You're right, Aunt Charity," she stated. "I was extremely fortunate to have avoided marriage to Brendan Douglas." Her gaze held the scorching power of a lightning bolt. "Much as I'd love to stay and reminisce, I'm late meeting Fanny and the others for our outing. Are you joining us, Gordon?"

He focused a doting smile in Elisabeth's direction. "What? No. I'm afraid I'm going to have to stay here and catch up on my correspondence, and I have a horrible dull report to complete for Lord Prosefoot."

"Yes, I suppose you ought to stay behind, then."

He brightened. "When you return, come find me and tell me all about it."

"Perhaps I could assist with your report. I've spent hours with Mr. Adams in the office. He says I've a head on my shoulders the envy of any bailiff."

"I doubt you know anything of increased customs duties on Irish malt, dear," Shaw replied with an indulgent smile. "You go on and enjoy your little outing."

Brendan would have been overjoyed at being released from such servitude. Preparing reports on customs duties? Why not spend the afternoon jamming a fork into your hand? But Elisabeth didn't seem to see it in the same light. Her expression was crestfallen as if Shaw had denied her a trip to the jewelers' shop. It roused Brendan to speak when he probably shouldn't have. "An excursion sounds amusing."

"You're welcome to join us," she answered, the spark returning to her eyes when she turned to him.

He arched a brow. What was she up to?

"We're to visit Belfoyle. You remember Lord Kilronan, don't you? We were all children together."

Touché. "Kilronan? I believe I remember him dimly. Tall chap. Disgustingly accomplished at everything. It was a long time ago. I'm sure he wouldn't remember me."

"You'd be surprised. Come. He'd love to renew your acquaintance."

"No. No. Now that I think on the matter, I believe I'll kick my heels here and try not to get into trouble."

Her smile this time was genuine and glittered with victory. "There's a first time for everything."

Elisabeth grabbed Brendan's arm as they left the dining room. Hissed under her breath, "Ten minutes. The long gallery. Meet me." Just in case he didn't think she was serious, she added. "Or else."

Apparently her words held enough menace to sway him. Coming up the east wing's stairs, she found him. Still wearing the *fith-fath*'s pleasant but bland features, he waited, hands clasped loosely behind his back, staring up at a portrait of a stern-looking bewigged gentleman attired in gold brocade and lace, the woman seated beside him bearing a pale beauty like a January rose.

"As sour-faced an old prune as I ever saw," he commented as she approached. "Don't understand what your grandmother saw in him myself, though"—his gaze cut to her—"the attraction to bores seems to run in the family."

Elisabeth refused to be goaded or turned from her purpose. "I didn't ask you here to discuss my ancestors or my attractions."

"But look at him, Lissa. What a pompous stick-in-the-mud."

Was he insulting her grandfather or Gordon? "I don't want to look at him," she answered through gritted teeth.

"Suppose he couldn't have been all bad," Brendan conceded. "Could have locked her away once he knew her for what she was. Had her declared insane. Or worse." He frowned at the portrait. "Wouldn't have been the first to use witchcraft as an excuse." He paused, his frown deepening. "Nor the last."

Her temper snapped. "Enough. You can't come sneaking back here like a criminal and not expect me to demand answers. This is my home and my wedding. You're making a fool of me."

A muscle in his jaw tightened. "A century or two earlier your grandmother would have been tied to a stake and set ablaze for her *sorcery*." His last word spat from a mouth hard with anger.

She grabbed his arm. "Stop it. Do you hear me? Why did you come back? I want to know now."

"Told you. I'm in hiding."

"You could hide anywhere, Brendan. Why Dun Eyre?"

He finally turned his full attention upon her, his golden-yellow gaze alight and blinding, his expression severe. "It's Martin. Remember that."

She choked down a string of profanity. The foul words wouldn't have insulted him anyway. Brendan had taught her most of them. "I don't care if you call yourself bloody King George the bloody Third. Why are you here? And why now of all times?"

He regarded her for a moment as if considering how much to say. "I'm in a tight corner. I've angered a few people who'd like nothing better than to put a period to my existence. Very painfully, I might add."

"There's a surprise."

Amusement glimmered in his eyes. "They tracked me as far as Limerick before I shook them. I'd go to Belfoyle if it wasn't the first place they'd look. But who would imagine I'd dare hide out with the very woman I abandoned at the altar? No, I'm safer here than anywhere else. At least until I can contrive a way out of this mess. Now do you see?"

His explanation didn't add up, though Elisabeth couldn't put her finger on why. She stared at him long and hard as if the truth might reveal itself upon his face.

His gaze drifted to her throat. "Last evening and again today. Should I be flattered you're wearing the stone I gave you?"

Her ghost of a thought vanished beneath a renewed sense of outrage. "You knew"—she poked him hard in the chest—"asking about my pendant would stir up trouble."

"Ouch." He stepped back, rubbing his torso. "It wasn't me who blabbed the whole in front of Shaw. It was your aunt."

"You probably bewitched her." She tried emphasizing her point with a second good poke, but he caught her hand, his fingers linking with hers. They were warm and strong, his palm rough against her own.

"You flatter me." He laughed, which only served to make her fury grow. "Mind control would be a useful power. Alas, it's not one I can claim."

Elisabeth yanked her hand free. "It's still your fault for bringing up the pendant in the first place."

"Shaw's a dead bore, but I don't see him cutting up stiff over the gift of a dead man, do you?"

"You're not dead."

"Not yet, at any rate. Although"—mischief sparkled in

the depths of his eyes—"what do you think he would do if he discovered I was alive? Worse, that I'd returned to woo you away from him."

He reached out as if he might touch the stone, but she warded him off, color creeping up her throat, burning her skin. "You and I both know you're not."

His hand hovered before lifting to stroke her cheek. His gaze scalded a path over her face as if memorizing it. The very air between them charged with anticipation. She held her breath.

"No." His hand finally dropping away. "More's the pity."

How did he manage to make her feel hot and cold at the same time? To make her stomach swoop and dive and her throat close? It wasn't fair. It shouldn't be so. It was improper. Unseemly. Downright humiliating. She tore away from him to stalk the length of the gallery, arms crossed over her chest as if warding off a blow. "Gordon is everything a husband should be. He comes of a good family. He's responsible and trustworthy and safe."

"Sounds like a sheepdog I once owned."

"Tease if you like, but if you so much as hint at who you really are, so help me, I shall murder you myself."

"You're so bloodthirsty, sweet, fickle Lissa."

"Don't call me that. And I am not fickle."

He came up behind her, leaning close, his warm breath tickling her neck, his tone mocking and smooth and tinged with hidden laughter. "No? Then why do you wear a gift from one man on the eve of your wedding to another?"

Far from enjoying her outing, Elisabeth spent the hours worrying over what might be transpiring back at the house.

Visions of Brendan disrupting, delaying, or destroying her wedding crowded her head. What he might do remained foggy, but that he'd take pleasure in causing trouble, she didn't doubt. He was a monumental bomb-thrower. Delighting in mischief and reveling in mayhem. Should she reveal him, she'd be up to her eyebrows in both.

A trouble shared is a trouble halved, or so Aunt Pheeney would say. But there was no one to share her trouble with. Despite what she told Brendan, Lord Kilronan was away from home and none knew when he was expected back. Lady Kilronan had been Aidan's bride for less than a year. She might not know anything of Brendan. Aidan might have chosen to remain silent on those more sordid bits of his family's history.

No. Best to keep quiet. Brendan would leave. All would be as it was. She'd be married and leave for London as Gordon's wife.

London. They had spoken of it. Gordon had been so excited and energetic in its praise. His position as an under-secretary's assistant in the department of the Exchequer had been such a wonderful opportunity, and she had so wanted to please that she'd nodded and smiled and placed it aside to be worried over later. But later had become now.

She clenched her hands on her reticule. Replace Mr. Adams? What was Gordon thinking? The estate agent had served the Fitzgeralds of Dun Eyre since her grandfather's day. He knew every stone, stick, tenant, and servant. He could recite annual crop yields, recall to the penny what he spent in outlays during any given season, loved Dun Eyre as much as she did. And who would replace him? Some stranger who would renovate and improve the house until she didn't recognize it as her home? Someone who would supervise the destruction of her grandmother's beloved gardens in the name of the latest fashion?

She reached for her pendant before remembering she'd torn the odious thing from her throat with a half-sob and tossed it in her jewelry case right after leaving that disastrous encounter with Brendan. She should have worn it. She could have tossed it from the cliffs and been done with it once and for all. Anger with Gordon easily became anger with Brendan.

How dare he bait her? Ask her impertinent questions? As if it were any of his concern why she wore the pendant. Leave it to Brendan to assume she carried a *tendre* for him after all these years. That she wore the pendant as some sort of memento to a lost love. Just showed what a conceited, arrogant, vain, ridiculous man he was.

Still some small corner of her worried that Brendan was right. Was she fickle? Did her continuing to wear his pendant signify something she wouldn't even admit to herself? No. It was absurd. Brendan meant nothing to her, and his pendant even less. She'd prove it. She'd wear Gordon's necklace tonight. Make a great display of its opulence and expense.

Much heartened by her decision, she listened with equanimity to Fanny's recital of her last visit to Dublin. "We had dinner no less than three times at Dublin Castle. Once with the Viceroy himself."

Her children's superior intelligence. "Not yet four and little Bernard is reading."

And the bargain she'd haggled on the last gown she'd had made. "Ten yards of beaded brocade for four and six. I couldn't pass it by."

It took turning into the iron gates at Belfoyle to break

into her cousin's monologue. And only long enough for her to draw breath and declare as they crested the final hill to view Belfoyle's tangle of towers and battlements. "What a great heap! It must cost a fortune to heat."

Elisabeth had always loved the ancient stronghold of Belfoyle. It seemed to drift among the fog-shrouded cliff tops like a fairy castle. And the Douglas family had seemed like kings and queens. The old Lord Kilronan's imperious dignity, his wife's ethereal beauty. Their children, no less regal than their parents. Aidan's confidence, Sabrina's quiet gentility, and Brendan's smug charm. She'd counted the days until she could be one of them. As if marrying into the family would make her brighter, smarter, more clever.

With the old earl's terrifying murder and his wife's death following, that glittering future had shattered. Aidan had withdrawn to a hermit-like existence, Sabrina had departed for the sanctuary of the order of *bandraoi* priestesses, and Brendan—

Brendan had vanished. The implications and accusations of his disappearance swirling round both Belfoyle and Dun Eyre for months following.

Now he was home. A lit fuse. A primed pistol.

It only remained to be seen how many innocent casualties he took with him when he blew.

The courier arrived just after sunset. A bloody sky cast the walls of the study in crimson light and crawling shadows as Oss showed the man in.

Máelodor offered no food or drink. Nor asked after the state of the roads or of the man's health. Instead, he leaned back in his chair, heaving his false leg onto an ottoman to ease the pain, steepling his fingers as he regarded this latest messenger from Ireland.

He felt the man's discomfort in his shuttered sidelong glances at the glassy, expressionless features of Oss, the wetting of his red lips, and the destruction of his hat, which he scrunched in his hairy, sausage hands but made no move to ease his tension. He fed off the apprehension and thrilled to the fear. It had always been thus. And as his body's strength waned, it became all the more important to cultivate men's terror of him. It served to bind them to him when all other enticements failed.

"You've news?"

"Aye, Great One. Men in Cashell spotted Douglas heading west toward Limerick."

"I knew it. The stone is hidden at Dun Eyre. Just as his father's diary hinted. Did they lay hands on Douglas?"

"No. He evaded them."

"Never matter. It's the Sh'vad Tual that's important. Once we have it in our possession, Douglas will follow. I'm certain of it."

"And if the stone is hidden? The estate is a large one."

"The woman will know where it is." He directed the full power of his gaze onto the messenger, a taste of what failure brought as its reward. "She will be made to reveal it."

Well satisfied with the interview, Máelodor flicked his bony fingers in dismissal. "Oss, show the man out."

Once more alone, he surrendered to infirmity. Closed his eyes against a pain fast growing unbearable. So much he'd lost to his cause. Youth. Health. The powers needed for these darkest of arts draining him of both. But soon— when Arthur stood before him. When the *Other* marked their king's return and rose up as one—he would take the final step needed to secure victory in war and his own personal renewal. An alliance with the *Unseelie*. A loosing of the demons from their Dark Court.

With their legions riding at the side of this greatest of kings, even the staunchest of *Duinedon* armies would fall. His own bodily sufferings eased.

Worth it at twice the price.

For the man who controlled the Dark Court controlled the world.

four

It had taken Elisabeth most of the day, but she'd finally made up her mind. She would confront Gordon with her concerns about his plans for Dun Eyre. She didn't want her home to become a pale imitation of some Englishman's country house. Its charms were its own and not to be tampered with.

Stepping off the bottom stair, she followed the sound of men's voices to the billiard room. Peeking round the door, she spied Uncle McCafferty, Lord Taverner, and Cousin Rolf deep in play, a footman clearing away a picked-over platter of sandwiches. "Have you seen Gordon?"

Rolf took his shot, the balls cracking against one another. "I believe he and his brother drove to Ennis. Took a bag with him, so I don't expect he'll be back before tomorrow."

"Oh. He never said he planned on leaving."

Uncle McCafferty chalked his cue. "Not going to be

one of those kinds of wives, are you, m'dear? He's not under the cat's paw yet."

Heat rose into her cheeks. Grabbing up a sandwich, she ducked out of the room, followed by the sound of hearty laughter. Had her tone been nagging? She didn't think so. Disappointed, perhaps. Discouraged. Now she'd have to wait until Gordon's return to take up her case.

Left without a purpose, she couldn't decide what to do. Sit with the ladies in the drawing room, where gossip flowed freely as the tea? Join the younger crowd in the rowdy game of lottery tickets being played in the Red Salon? Perhaps a rummage among the kitchens to turn up some of Cook's leftover sponge cake?

But none of those choices appealed to her. Perhaps she should just retire. Put this entire horrid day behind her. At least Brendan had somehow managed to stay out of trouble. She'd not seen him since dinner and even then he'd been subdued, his gaze somber, his manner guarded. She'd almost thought to goad him into speaking before coming to her senses. What did she care if he seemed uneasy? It wasn't her concern. Against her better judgment, she'd kept his secret. Beyond that, his worries were his own and nothing to do with her.

The soft chords of a pianoforte slowed her steps as she passed the music room. Barely heard above the sounds of merrymaking elsewhere, the melody rose and fell in soft echoes before dying away. Began again. Clearer. Louder. And this time unmistakable. Mozart.

Pushing wide the door, she squinted through the dark. Shadows lay thick about the room, but for a branch of candles blazing upon the pianoforte. The light carved deep lines in the face of the man seated at the keys. Flickered over cheekbones and deep-set, heavy-lidded eyes before splashing across long-fingered, capable hands.

Elisabeth listened from the doorway, the familiar, heart-rending melody pushing against her anger like water against a dam.

He stumbled over a chord, his hands coming to rest still and gentle upon the keys.

"Try again," she murmured from the doorway.

He spun in his seat, scrambling to build his *fith-fath*. His eyes widened then narrowed, his disguise abandoned. It was Brendan before her. Not the man she remembered. But not the stranger with Brendan's golden eyes either.

His gaze fell to the sandwich in her hand. "For me?"

"If I gave you anything, it would be poison in your soup," she snapped, annoyed that a mere melody could wreak such havoc.

"I'd no idea you could hold a grudge so long. Were you always so resolute?"

"Always," she said, her feet guiding her farther into the room before her brain could counter. What harm was there in staying to listen? A few moments only and then she'd leave.

He began playing again. The music rippled and curled over her like water. Filled her ears. Sank into her blood. Made her heart race. She closed her eyes. Let this once-favorite composition sweep her back to a time when she'd been young and giddy and naive. Full of anticipation for a life with Brendan.

She'd understood it was a marriage of convenience, but in her fantasies she gained his undying devotion, their marriage rivaling the great love stories of history. Mark Antony and Cleopatra. Henry II and Eleanor of Aquitaine. Elisabeth Fitzgerald and Brendan Douglas.

What romantical claptrap.

The piece died on a sour note, bringing her back to earth with a thud. That was Brendan all over. Always the dream of him carried her along until the reality of him smacked her over the head. She opened her eyes to catch him watching her, a wry twist to his mouth.

He kneaded his left hand as if it pained him. "What's it like wearing a king's ransom in jewels?"

"Uncomfortable," she said, fingering her gaudy sapphire choker.

"Love often is." He chuckled. "I haven't told you yet, but you look stunning this evening."

His gaze scoured her, the candlelight making wicked flames of his eyes. She felt suddenly self-conscious. The way her gown clung to every curve. The tightness of her stays. The plunge of her neckline. "I look passable, which isn't the same thing at all."

"Now you're fishing for compliments. You know full well how beautiful you look. Always have. You used to spend hours primping in front of your mirror. I never knew a girl more taken with fribbles and furbelows than you."

"And yet, I could still outride you over any distance or ground."

His smile widened, losing the cynical edge. "I was being gallant."

She sniffed. "You've never had a gallant bone in your body. You hated when I won. Sulked for days and wouldn't speak with me. Said it wasn't seemly for a mere chit of a girl to beat you."

"Gods, did I say that? To your face? I really was a pretentious son of a bitch. How did you put up with me?"

"I could ask you the same. I was an awful tagalong. You couldn't turn around without stumbling over me."

He ran a hand through his hair. Thick and dark and overlong, though now it fit his rugged features. If he'd been porcelain pretty in his youth, age had hardened that delicacy to a knife-edge elegance. Dangerous in its perfection.

Nerves fluttered her stomach. If she weren't diligent, she'd be right back to head-over-heels infatuated.

He moved to make room for her on the bench. She hesitated before chiding herself for a silly gudgeon. This was Brendan. She certainly didn't have to worry about any predatory motives on his part. Not like most of the men she met, who were always trying to maneuver her into secluded corners or onto quiet balconies. Well, everyone but Gordon, who'd remained a proper gentleman throughout their courtship. Perhaps that's what drew her to him—a change from the usual. Certainly, Brendan had never shown that kind of admiring interest in her. Not even when they were engaged—much to her chagrin.

She slid in beside him, annoyed all over again. What was so wrong with her that he'd rather be assumed dead than marry her?

"You still play magnificently," she said, trying to fill the awkward silence.

"I've not had much practice lately. Nor have I been in much of a playing mood." He pulled free his watch to check the time.

Her eyes lit on the intricate scrollwork of the gold case, the enamel inside face painted with the Douglas spread-winged eagle bearing a crooked sword, and the complicated gadgetry of hands and dials. "You still have it."

He snapped the watch shut with a decided click, his lips thinning in agitation.

"Your father's watch. I'd forgotten all about it." A gift for his sixteenth birthday, Brendan had guarded it with his life. His most cherished possession. "Do you remember when I borrowed it?"

"Let's call it what it was." He chuckled. "You pilfered it."

"Your brother dared me."

"My brother was a nuisance and a bully."

"Only because you fought back. If you'd ignored him—"

"He'd have thrashed me twice as often and with double the ferocity. Thank heavens I could run faster than him." He grew solemn. "A lucky skill as it turned out."

"Where have you been all this time, Brendan? Aidan searched everywhere, but after years with no word from you, he finally gave up and believed you were dead. We all did."

"Right about now, Aidan probably wishes I'd stayed dead." He glanced over at her. Gave an offhand shrug, as he realized she'd not be put off with another non-answer. "Where was I? Let's see. The Low Countries. Spain. Italy. Though it was difficult during the war, and I finally fled farther south. North Africa. The Levant. Spent two years in Turkey before settling in Greece."

She envisioned Brendan attired in sultan's kaftan and turban, reclining upon a seraglio's carpets and cushions. Given his dark hair and tanned features, not a difficult image to conjure. Actually embarrassingly seductive. "Complete with your very own harem, no doubt," she scoffed, praying her face didn't betray her thoughts.

"Nothing that exciting. Actually, it was devilish uncomfortable. Staying alive can be a deuced difficult job."

"It still is, isn't it? You said you were in hiding."

He played a sad little run of notes before wincing, a grimace of pain passing over his face.

"You *are* hurt."

He shook his fingers out. "A disagreement with someone's boot heel. Staying alive doesn't always equal staying in one piece."

The darkness seemed to close in on them. A listening, watching hush, pregnant with stale regret. Elisabeth's skin prickled, though not due to mage energy this time, but to Brendan's diamond-edged charisma. He'd always possessed spellbinding self-confidence. It glittered off him. Sparkled the very air he breathed. Everyone who knew him fell under that strange mixture of cynicism and magnetism. It made him seem almost otherworldly. As if the blood of the *Fey* ran thick and icy just beneath his skin.

Tonight, that crystalline brilliance seemed tempered. That white inner light dimmed to mere humanity. Or perhaps the scales had finally fallen from her eyes and she saw him for what he was. Not glittering and silver perfect as the *Fey*. But a man chained by years and exile and events she couldn't begin to imagine.

She asked the first question that swam to the front of her mind. "Did you kill your father, Brendan? I never thought . . . but . . . you said you're hiding and . . ." Once the words were out, she wished to call them back. The stricken look on his face cut her like a whiplash.

His hands curled to fists. Dropping them to his lap, he flexed them loose before laying them palms down against his breeches.

"Forget I asked," she entreated. "I know you didn't have anything to do with his death. I should never have said. It was—"

"Long ago? Murder is murder, isn't it? Makes no difference whether the crime happened a week ago or an age hence. The stain remains."

"But the two of you were so close. He loved you. It was plain to everyone who saw you together."

"It makes the sin all the greater then, doesn't it?"

She chewed her lip. "Are you saying what I think you're saying?"

"No, Lissa. I didn't murder my father. But I didn't prevent it either. And isn't a sin of omission still a sin? Burying one's head in the sand is not a defense."

He began playing. The hop-skip tune of "The Girl I Left Behind Me" rang out. His idea of a joke? If so, she wasn't amused, but it did serve to snap them from the quagmire of this hushed room, these sinister broodings.

"Should I worry you'll turn me in for the bounty on my head?" he asked over the music.

"Is there one?"

"Oh, to be sure. I mean, as long as I'm to be hunted as a criminal, I may as well bring a high price. It's undignified to be worth any less than a thousand pounds." He joked, but a trace of unhappiness showed through his banter.

"You won't tell me what you're hiding from, will you? Or who hunts you?"

"Trust me, my love. You don't want to know. And wouldn't believe me anyway."

He finished the piece, the tension following almost palpable. It pounded against her ears. Throbbed in the air like the beating of great wings.

"This is all to do with magic, isn't it?" She caught herself peeking over her shoulder at every flickering dance of the candelabra's flames. Feeling the gaze of unseen creatures lifting the hairs at the back of her neck. "Something to do with the *Other*." She jumped at a breeze rattling the casement.

"Easy, now. There's no one there. You're tying yourself in knots."

She continued to peer into the corners of the room. "So you say."

"Believe me. After seven years, I can sense danger a mile away. But aye, my difficulties originate within that world. So, keep my secret, Lissa. And when it's safe, I'll vanish as fully as I did the last time. You'll wonder if I wasn't just a figment of your imagination."

"What if I told you I was happy to see you again?" The words caught in her throat, low and halting.

"I'd know you were lying. Shaw will whisper sweet nothings in your ear, and you'll remember why it was you wanted to marry him. And why I'm the last person you want in your life."

He was right, of course. What on earth had she been contemplating in the dark with the music in her head, the listening shadows surrounding them, and Brendan's dangerous magnetism working its spell? She shook off her fancies with a stern inner reproof. "Gordon *is* a good man, isn't he?"

"I'd say he's a typical representative of the male species."

"You don't like him."

"Does my liking him signify? It's *your* feelings that matter. Do you like him?"

Angry with herself for being taken in—even momentarily—by lost dreams, she straightened, scowling down at him as if he'd thrown her a challenge. "I love him as I ought to."

"Then marry him and be happy." He quirked a teasing eye in her direction, and the lovelorn strains of Mozart's concerto rang once more. "Sleep well, Lissa. If luck is with us both, I'll be gone from here when you wake."

She left him still playing. But alongside her relief, grief spiked her heart and hot tears burned the backs of her eyelids. She'd marry Gordon. And be deliriously, ecstatically happy. So take that, Brendan Douglas!

Brendan followed the riverbed from Dun Eyre, picking his surefooted way through stands of birch and willow, the pungent scent of ferns and boggy earth filling his head, the river a slow lap and gurgle against the muddy banks.

Joining the lane skirting the village, he climbed the hill leading away from the cluster of cabins to the far meadows. From here it was a short hike across the fields to Belfoyle's eastern boundary. Spring fragrance laced the night air, carried on the ever-present wind as it swirled up over the nearby cliffs, blew out over the wide, treeless meadows. The towers of the house rose up to his left, a roofline glimpsed between trees, a lighted window, a horse whinnying from the nearby stable block.

The sky burned with a million stars while a low moon rose up over the far hills behind him, casting its borrowed light out over the landscape, his shadow stretching long in front of him as he walked. His aim was true. Even now, his feet led him unerringly in the right direction.

Ahead of him, the ward stone stood like a sentry, moonlight glittering over the uncut ridges and folds within the ancient limestone. One of four set at each corner of Belfoyle's boundary, the stone released mage energy that flowed southwest and north in a never-ending invisible wall. No magic-bearing creature could pass through without first appeasing the silent guardian.

Still fifty feet away, he felt its power spreading outward within the earth, pushing up through him like an infinite vibration. Closer, and the mage energy coalesced into a constant pulse like a second heartbeat.

It had been years. Years since he'd exercised his powers. In the beginning, shock and revulsion and self-loathing had led him to deny his *Other* blood. Later, surviving meant leaving no trace. No trail of magic for any to follow. He had lived by his wits and his dagger alone as a *Duinedon.*

Only since returning to Ireland had he allowed himself to draw upon his *Fey* blood. And only then had he come to realize the wraith he'd become. Neither *Other* nor *Duinedon.* Neither living nor dead. A man of naught but shadows.

The way he needed to be if he was to remain free long enough to complete his task.

He placed his palm upon the standing stone and the mage energy burst in a flash of ribboning rainbow color. Numbing his fingers, singeing up his arm with a heart-stopping jolt before burying itself deep within him as it sought to identify in all ways who and what he was.

Closing his eyes, he focused on the space around him. The feel of the grass beneath his boots, the moon above, the wind upon his face, and the push of his blood through his veins. Braced himself for the blasting rip curl of denunciation and refusal.

Nothing.

The caress of welcome sank through him like a soft

weight, settling itself in the center of his chest. His name whispered in the oldest of ancient tongues.

Son of the house of Douglas. Son of Kilronan.

Breán Duabn'thach.

If he wanted to, he could follow the path down to the house. Cross the courtyard to the iron-hinged front doors. Wander the familiar corridors or stand as he used to at his bedroom window, staring out over the stretch of ocean below to the far horizon. The stones would not impede him.

Instead, he dropped his arm to his side, stepped back, the mage energy seeping away, leaving him hollow with renewed loss.

Once the Sh'vad Tual was in Scathach's possession. Once he'd been freed from the *Amhas-draoi* death sentence. Once the threat of Máelodor had been defused.

Would he go home then?

He turned away with a grim laugh.

Not even gamester Jack would take odds on that question.

Upon returning to Dun Eyre, Brendan waited until the house grew quiet. Then, to be safe, he waited an hour more.

Leaving his rooms, he crept down the nearby servant stairs, taking the long way through the gallery.

"As you were," he quipped, tossing a salute to the rows of long-dead Fitzgeralds as he passed.

Elisabeth's chambers stood at the far end of this floor. Sliding inside, he took up his seat once more at her dressing table. Opened her jewelry case, hunting for the stone that would set him free of the noose closing around his neck.

He needed to retrieve the Sh'vad Tual and leave.

Everywhere he turned, the past reached out to him with clawing, bony fingers. Naught would change for all his wishing. Those dead would remain dead. Their faces forever etched upon his brain like acid upon metal.

Lifting out an inner tray, he smiled his success.

There it was. The Sh'vad Tual.

As he palmed it, mage energy crackled up his arm. Buried itself deep in his brain. Words pounded against his skull in a tongue he, who had studied ancient languages with an academic's obsession, barely understood. A warning? A threat? Light flashed through the stone's milky iridescence like lightning against the flat of storm clouds. A scene surfaced as if rising up through black water. A man. A sword. Then the stone went dark. Silent.

"You," a voice hissed from behind him.

Shoving the stone deep into his pocket, he spun to face Elisabeth, frozen in a look of panic he knew mirrored his own.

He recovered instantly, his face breaking into a wicked smile.

"Is stealing into my bedchamber your idea of a joke, Brendan? Because I'm not laughing."

"Is it so difficult to understand why I'm here? Or have your aunts not had that talk with you yet?"

Her mouth snapped shut, her eyes murderous. She stomped to face him toe-to-toe, wrenching the sash to her dressing gown tight around her middle. Unfortunately that did nothing but emphasize the ample curves of breast and hip and buttock she tried to hide beneath the silken robe. She lifted her chin to him, the scent in her hair and upon her skin faint and lemony.

"Never mind what my aunts have told me," she

snapped. "You must think me ten times a fool if you're using seduction as your excuse."

He tucked a curl behind her ear, ignoring her flinch at his feather-light touch. "Never a fool, Lissa."

"I told you not to call me that."

Mere inches separated them. The heat and anger rising from her body stirred his blood. He had but to lower his head to touch his lips to hers. To kiss the full, soft mouth. Pull free the rippling tangle of her hair until it hung loose and wild about her head.

"If you leave now, we can forget any of this happened," she said.

"There hasn't been any of this yet."

The tip of her tongue flicked across her lips, her eyes so dark a brown as to be obsidian in the moonlight. Her breathing quickened, arousing a dangerous need. His blood pounded in his veins, and what had begun as mere improvisation deepened to something more carnal and exhilarating.

"This isn't heathen Istanbul where women swooned at your feet." Her words came harsh with recrimination. Or was it jealousy he detected?

"I wouldn't say they swooned."

"This is Ireland," she asserted. "Safe, normal Ireland where women do not entertain men in their bedchambers. Especially men who've proven they're not to be trusted."

"You talk too much." Assessing the situation, he chose to risk it. He couldn't stop himself if he wanted to. She was too close, his heart racing too fast. Cupping her cheek, he brushed his thumb over her lips. Lowered his head and kissed her. Her mouth as petal-soft and sweet as he imagined.

She didn't slap him. Or scream. Instead, she answered

his advances. Her lips moved on his with virginal timidity. Though not for long. Elisabeth might be innocent, but she wasn't naive. She caught on quickly. Her unschooled eagerness heady as any wine.

Her heat became his, a slow building pool. He pulled her closer, a fire fast rising through him. The kiss deepened, his tongue slipping within to taste, her breath mingling with his. Pulling loose her robe, he traced the curve of one beautiful breast, her nipple pebble-hard beneath the filmy fabric of her chemise. A whimper escaped her, her hand pressed over his heart.

That simple act of faith slid between the cracks in his armor. He shouldn't be doing this. Not with her. Better to spend his lust on an experienced woman who understood the game.

He'd no time to act on his gentlemanly impulse when Elisabeth wrenched free, a heady flush to her cheeks and a sparkle in her luminous, dark eyes. "No!"

He schooled his features into bland amusement, a corner of his mouth twitching. "Why not? Technically we're still engaged."

She shoved him away. Knotted her dressing gown with ferocity. "Now I know you're mad. And what of the last seven years when I thought you were dead?"

"We've been through that. I wasn't dead."

She dropped back into an armchair, drawing her feet up beneath her. "Please leave." She stared into the dying fire, shoulders heaving as if she sought to settle herself. "You were right to call me fickle. I've betrayed Gordon. I've kissed another man."

"*I* kissed *you*."

"Yes, but do you think I would have let you if I didn't

want it?" She covered her face with her hands. "What have I done?"

"Lissa—"

"I said don't call me that. You promised me earlier to-night you'd be gone from here by morning."

The taste of her still on his tongue, her smell still heavy in his head, he offered a brief nod. "And so I shall. Good-bye, Elisabeth. If the luck of the gods is with me, I won't trouble you ever again. "

Walking away was far more than difficult than he'd ever imagined. Yet staying was impossible.

five

Elisabeth cut a wedge of cake, licking the sugar frosting from the flat of her knife. A further rummaging through the kitchens unearthed a tin of gingerbread and a box of candied apricots. So much for the latest alterations to her wedding gown.

Carrying her plate into the front salon, where a fire burned high and bright, she sought respite from her whirl-wind thoughts in a comfortable wing chair with the final chapters of *The Baron of Falconberg* open in front of her. But no amount of drama between the pages or sugarcoated joy dulled her mind's mad spinning.

Tomorrow she would marry Gordon. No second thoughts. No backing down. She refused to experience the mortification of another broken engagement. She'd lived through the horrid tittle-tattle and sidelong stares once before. She'd not survive them a second time.

Yet, Brendan's unexpected appearance had exposed some ugly and uncomfortable truths. Pieces of her heart still belonged to the brilliant, mercurial boy of her youth. He'd exploded into her world again, stirring to life long-buried hopes, and just as abruptly vanished in an eerie duplication of his disappearance seven years ago. No word. No sign. As if he'd conjured himself away in a puff of black smoke.

Not out of the realm of possibility, given who and what he was.

Flames danced in the grate, a breeze sputtering her candle. Shadows moved over the walls, shapes tangled in the crowded midnight gloom. The feeling of spirits lingering just beyond her vision, and creatures living within the space between the candle's flickers quickened her heart until it thudded against her ribs. Her throat closed as she sought to catch the twitch of a gown or the flash of a wing. A pulling back of the curtain between the everyday world she inhabited and the fascinating impossibilities lying at the core of Brendan's life.

Had this awareness come from her grandmother's tales of *Ynys Avalenn*, the summer kingdom of the *Fey*, and the wonders to be found there? Was it a result of her family's straddling of *Other* and *Duinedon*? Acknowledging that world without accepting it?

Nervousness tightened her stomach, making her skin crawl as the breeze ruffled the collar of her robe. The candle flamed high then died in a thin stream of acrid smoke. The only light now coming from the fire. Her breath caught in her lungs.

In the ear-ringing tension, the shush of a footstep stopped her heart. The rattle of a knob and the soft creak of a door being opened froze her in her chair, breath held. But it was no wraith or faery who appeared at the door swathed in nightcap and wrapper.

"Aunt Fitz," she sighed heavily. "You nearly frightened me to death."

Her aunt eyed the plate at Elisabeth's elbow reproachfully but kept silent. "Having trouble sleeping?"

Elisabeth shrugged. "It's been a . . . trying . . . few days. But tomorrow, it shall all be over at last."

Aunt Fitz crossed to sit in the chair opposite. In her nightclothes, she seemed smaller, slighter, and older than usual, and Elisabeth's heart went out to her. Despite her prickles, Aunt Fitz had been everything to Elisabeth growing up. She would miss her sorely when she and Gordon relocated to London.

"You look dour for a bride on the eve of her wedding."

"I was thinking about how much I'll miss you and Aunt Pheeney. It's fine to say we'll see each other often, but we all know it won't be near as frequently as we'd wish. Gordon won't want to leave London and his work, you hate to travel, and remember Aunt Pheeney's last sea journey."

Aunt Fitz puffed out her chest, a martyred look in her eyes. "As Gilbert said, 'We are near to heaven by sea as by land,'" she quoted. "And we all know what happened to him."

"Exactly. You'll never get her back on a ship."

Her aunt waved away her worries. "Once you're married, you'll be too busy to brood over us old ladies. And we'll be fine. We have Lord Kilronan close by, should we need a man's assistance. I hear his sister is home, though none have seen her. They say she's ill." Her gaze slid sideways as if she might catch Elisabeth out.

"I don't know any more than you. I was told it was the measles, though I'm almost certain Sabrina and I had them the same summer."

"They also say His Lordship is away from Belfoyle right now," Aunt Fitz continued calmly. "The talk is that he might have heard from his brother after all this time."

Elisabeth stiffened, feeling the heat creeping up her throat.

"It would be an amazing thing to have Brendan Douglas back home after we all thought him long dead." She paused, clearly waiting for Elisabeth to comment.

Her cheeks burned. "It doesn't matter," she mumbled. "It was ages ago." In a desperate bid to change the subject, she grabbed up her book. Almost tossing it in her aunt's lap. "Have you read this one yet? Not nearly as thrilling as her last, but you might like it. That's the last volume, but the first two are in my rooms. I'll leave them for you."

Aunt Fitz regarded the novel as one might observe an ugly baby. A passive smile as she quietly handed it back. "That's fine, dear. I look forward to it." And without missing a beat, "If Brendan Douglas actually returns to Belfoyle, it's as well you're leaving. It would be awkward, as the families have always been so close."

She must be lobster red by now. "It's not Aidan's fault his brother is the worst sort of rogue. Besides, as Aunt Charity pointed out, it's a good thing I didn't marry him. Better to have been a jilted lover than an abandoned bride."

"A shame Kilronan traveled all the way to Dublin"—Aunt Fitz regarded her steadily—"when Brendan was here the whole time."

Elisabeth's stomach lurched. Her aunt's keen gaze seeming to pick the very thoughts from Elisabeth's head. At times like these, she wondered how much *Other* blood Aunt Fitz truly carried. "How did you find out? He tried so hard—"

"So he did. But at breakfast the other day, I recognized his watch. And he called you Lissa. Small slip-ups, but revealing."

"It doesn't matter. He's left again." Elisabeth added, "and good riddance."

"Has he? Then I suppose my worry was for naught. You worshipped him so when you were younger. In your eyes, he could do no wrong. I thought perhaps his return might spur you to . . . well, it doesn't matter now."

"Aunt Fitz! Really! I hope my judgment has improved."

"As do I, Elisabeth," she answered evenly. "Did he say why he came to Dun Eyre?"

Elisabeth flashed back to that first interview when he'd goaded her mercilessly, the twinkle in his eye, the tease of his smile. "He claimed, like young Lochinvar, he was here to steal me away for himself."

Her aunt's brows lifted. "Yet, he's gone and you remain."

"Does that surprise you? Brendan Douglas wouldn't know the truth if it bit him."

Aunt Fitz closed her eyes, cheeks gaunt, fine lines marring her brow. Her hands hooked around the arms of the chair, her breathing slow and even. Elisabeth could almost believe she'd nodded off mid-conversation. But then a frown touched her aunt's pale lips. "Or perhaps it was a truth so subtle, the tooth marks have yet to show."

As with so much else, the coffee room at The Goat's Whiskers in Ennis remained unchanged in the years Brendan had been gone. Even the landlord, old Ned Crowdy, looked as moth-eaten and bristly as ever. Brendan could almost make himself believe he was twenty-one again. Cocksure, obsessed, convinced of the justness of his cause. And equally baffled by those who could not see the rightness of what the Nine attempted for the good of the entire race of *Other*.

Freddie Atwood had been one of those unconvinced by his arguments.

Freddie's family paid the price.

Brendan stood by and did nothing.

At least, not then. Though his later attempts at atonement meant little to Freddie. Or any of his victims. After all, the dead can give no absolution.

With grim disparagement, Brendan conceded his inaction had cost Freddie and his family their lives, while his action afterward had resulted in the death of his own father. A sure case of damned if you don't and damned if you do. And if anyone could count on being damned, it was he.

His gaze rested on the row of decanters upon the sideboard, but he shoved the desire away almost as soon as it rose within him. Alcohol wouldn't help. It only numbed the guilt. Never erased it. And he'd emptied enough bottles to know.

The door burst open on a bluster of lung-clearing wind and rain, sending men scurrying to secure their cards and their newspapers with much cursing and many shouts to close the bloody door already. The newcomer shook out his dripping greatcoat, removing his hat to run hands through his damp hair. Scanned the room from beneath half-lidded eyes.

Brendan motioned him over at the same time he ordered himself a second pot of coffee.

Even now, nine months after a near-fatal attack, Jack O'Gara walked stiffly as if he'd been sprinting overlong. But he was walking, which was amazing. Hell, he was breathing, which was a miracle.

Leave it to Jack to be skewered like a pig on a spit and come away with nothing worse than the hollowed features of a languishing tragedian stage player.

The *Fey*-born O'Gara luck at work.

He slid into the seat, waving the maidservant over. "Brandy."

"That bodes ominous, coz," Brendan remarked after the woman went scurrying in search of Jack's order.

"It is." The brandy was brought. He downed it, eyes closed on a weary sigh of contentment, the deep lines carved either side of his mouth slowly easing. But when he looked again upon Brendan, fear sharpened his gaze. "You have to return to Dun Eyre."

"You couldn't pay me enough to go back there."

"And Elisabeth Fitzgerald?"

He pulled free his watch, checking the time with a smile. "Is even now dreaming of her trip down the aisle. By this time tomorrow, she'll be Mrs. Gordon Shaw."

"If she lives that long," was Jack's grumbling response.

Brendan frowned his confusion.

"Máelodor knows," Jack leaned forward, his words low and urgent. "Somehow he's figured out you gave the stone to Elisabeth all those years ago. His men are on their way to Dun Eyre as we speak."

"Where did you hear this?"

"From your contact in Limerick. After you and I separated, I headed there to see what I could learn about the *Amhas-draoi*'s intentions. No news on that front, but the story is that Máelodor has unraveled the stone's hiding place."

"How much time do we have?"

"Not long, I'd wager. If Máelodor knows where the

stone is, you can bet he's making all haste to get hold of it. You have to go back, Brendan. If Máelodor's men seize Elisabeth . . ."

He didn't need Jack to finish his sentence. He well knew Elisabeth's fate should Máelodor's men get hold of her. His sister, Sabrina, had barely escaped a similar grisly end after becoming entangled in Brendan's troubles.

Was he destined to bring disaster down upon anyone stupid enough to trust him? Was he a walking lightning rod? Get too close and suffer the consequences?

In an effort to safeguard their father's diary, his brother Aidan had almost died in a one-on-one battle with a conjured killer. Jack—another victim of Máelodor's obsession—saved only through his not-quite-of-this-world good fortune. The merest chance placing Brendan on that particular road that night. The craziest luck turning that blade from any vital organ. Could Jack be so insanely fortunate a second time?

Could any of them? Or would Brendan carry the burden of their deaths on top of his father's? On top of Freddie's? On top of the mountain of sins already weighting him down?

His eyes flicked once more to Jack's drink. It had been years since he'd felt such unbearable need.

Pushing away from the table, he shrugged into his coat. Pulled on his gloves. Gods, he'd forgotten how damned uncomfortable Ireland was.

"I need you to head to Knockniry. Find Daz Ahern. He's holding something for me. A ring. He'll know why I need it. Meet me back in Dublin. At Macklins on Cutpurse Row."

"So you still intend on going through with this mad

scheme? The *Amhas-draoi* seem the kill-first, ask-questions-later type. You show up among them, and they're liable to separate your head from your shoulders without pausing for breath."

"Which is why I'm going directly to Scathach with the Sh'vad Tual. With luck, she'll at least listen before she decides my fate." That was his hope anyway. The head of the *Amhas-draoi* was known to be just. She was also known to wrench out innards with a barbed sword but he conveniently put that aspect of her nature out of his mind.

"What will you do with Miss Fitzgerald?"

Brendan plowed a hand through his hair. "Hell if I know. She's never been exactly biddable at the best of times." He gave a resigned shrug. "No doubt something will occur to me."

"I can think of a few things," was Jack's cheeky answer. His normal roguish tendencies never far from the surface, even in the most hopeless of situations. "Here. You might need this." Jack pulled a pouch from his jacket pocket. "I won it off a lieutenant whose head for drink far exceeded his head for cards. Once he wakes from his stupor, he'll be a poorer but wiser soul."

Brendan scooped up the coins. He'd lived better in the past year than in the previous six thanks to Jack's skills at the card table. "Has anyone ever told you you're incurable?"

"My mother. Frequently. I'm sure she attributes my tragic killing to that very trait."

"Which brings me to my second errand."

"Aye, *mon capitaine*?"

He'd been trying to do this for weeks. Now was the time. "Once you've met me back in Dublin, I want you to go home."

"As in *turn up alive?*" He spread his hands. "Ta-da! And claim the stories of my demise were a tad premature? We've had this conversation before."

"Aye, we have. And until now I've allowed you to persuade me that your playing a corpse works to our advantage. But no longer. Let's call it even. I saved your life last spring. You saved mine this winter. We're square."

The amusement faded from Jack's eyes. "Máelodor has the diary and the tapestry, Brendan. If he captures you while you carry the stone . . ."

"I'll worry about that if and when it happens."

He'd grown adept at locking his fear away. He'd been on the run for seven years. The race to survive driving him deeper into the shadows as he fought to stay one step ahead of vengeance from both justice-seeking *Amhas-draoi* and Máelodor's bounty-driven assassins. If he was successful, that ever-present hand on his shoulder would lift. That nightmare would finally be over. If he failed . . . He forced his mind from that thought. He would not fail.

"My showing up alive will only fuel questions about you," Jack said. "They'll want to know where I've been all this time and, most importantly, who I was with."

"Tell them you fled to the Continent to escape your gaming debts."

"I don't have any gaming debts. Or at least none I'd be so silly as to fly to the continent to avoid."

"So pretend."

"And how am I supposed to have survived my unfortunate run-in with Máelodor's executioner? I imagine the question will come up."

"Do I have to think of everything? Use that famed O'Gara ingenuity."

"You can't do this on your own, Brendan. Admit it."

"I managed for seven years."

"No, you buried yourself away amid a bunch of foreigners and drowned your sorrows in alcohol and opium."

Brendan felt as if he'd been struck. His gut rising into his throat, a horrible sick churning as if he might be ill all over Mr. Crowdy's floor. "How?"

Jack's gaze dulled, jaw tightening as if he knew he'd crossed an invisible line. Still, he didn't back down. A sign of his dogged courage. "No one avoids alcohol the way you do unless they're blind scared of it. The opium I surmised by things you've said. Other things you took pains to avoid saying." He faced him straight-on. "Are you still . . ."

"No." It was all Brendan would allow himself to admit. It wasn't anyone's business how low he'd fallen during his years away. He repeated his avowal as if Jack needed convincing. "Not for a long time."

"Good. That settles things. I'll find Ahern. We'll talk about my resurrection once you arrive in Dublin safely."

"You're not listening."

"I'm older than you, Brendan. Think of it as your big brother speaking."

"Aidan wouldn't be so hen-brained."

Jack laughed. "It's surprising how hen-brained your brother can be."

"I won't let you—"

"You can't force me."

"It's better this way—"

"For whom?"

They spoke over one another until, exasperated, Brendan snapped, "Damn it, Jack. I don't want you."

His cousin gave a slow nod before downing the rest of

his drink. Slamming the glass upon the table. "Now we come to the crux of it. Typical Brendan Douglas arrogance. He doesn't need anyone. He can do it all on his own."

"It's not that," Brendan argued, stung by the accusation. "I can move faster and easier without worrying about you."

"Self-sufficiency's become a habit."

"It's safer."

Ice hardened Jack's blue eyes, a reminder his cousin's easygoing nature had its limits. "Aye, Brendan. But it's also lonelier."

Elisabeth woke with a vague unease she couldn't pinpoint.

No sound but the normal creaks and shifts of the house. A shutter caught in the wind. A fox's bark echoing lonely and distant. A thin gap in the closed curtains sent an arrow shaft of moonlight over the carpet and up the bed. A chill in the air drove her deeper under the covers for a warm spot. Twisting, turning, and sighing in an effort to get comfortable.

Was this restlessness the effect of too much gingerbread before bedtime? Last-minute wedding nerves? Or her troubling conversation with Aunt Fitz? Did it matter? She needed her sleep. She'd not managed more than a few snatched winks during the last few days, envisioning every Brendan-initiated, disastrous scenario her creative mind could conjure. If she didn't manage at least a few hours tonight, she'd risk falling asleep at her own wedding breakfast. Not exactly an auspicious start to marital bliss.

Rolling over, she punched the lumps from her pillow. Flopped back with a groan. Stared up into her bedhangings. Counted enough sheep to fill a small meadow. Her limbs grew lax, eyelids heavy. And just as she dozed, a light touch upon her shoulder jerked her awake.

She had a moment's horrified impression of hard-jawed, angular features, sun-bright eyes, and a finger pressed against full, sensual lips for silence.

She couldn't keep her eyes open. Couldn't feel her arms or legs.

So much for Brendan Douglas's damned luck.

Against her will, sleep finally dragged her under.

Six

She woke, heart pounding, nightmare vivid and alive in her mind. Cold raising gooseflesh upon her body. Arms clamping her middle. And an exotic spicy scent tickling her nose. She recalled them with perfect clarity. But . . . she took a ragged breath. Closed her eyes. Opened them again. Everything remained. The cold. The arms. The scent. Heaven help her! Not a dream, then.

She was being held tightly against an unyielding chest, her legs slung sideways across a horse's withers. Scrub and hedge enclosed a sunken lane, the gurgle of running water coming from nearby. A whirr of wings scraped the air above as some night prowler hunted. Beyond that, the only sounds were the horse's breathing, the creak of saddle and the jangle of bit, and the steady fall of each hoof on the muddy track.

She lurched, head spinning, stomach lifting into her throat.

"Careful. The mare's skittish enough carrying two."

No. Not that voice. It couldn't be. He wouldn't.

She went stiff, the top of her head connecting sharply with his chin.

"Ow, bloody hell." He jerked back, his grip tightening, the mare shying sideways in a dancing skitter of hooves. "Hold still, I said. You nearly made me bite my tongue off."

She looked up to see him rubbing his chin, annoyance in every disgusted line of his face. But just that slight movement caused her stomach to turn, and her head to whirl in a dizzy blur.

"What in blazes are you playing at, you stupid, selfish, arrogant bastard son of a damn bloody son of a . . ." Shaking with rage, fear, confusion, and a growing, belly-rush of nausea, she dredged up every expletive she'd ever heard, their palliative effect considerable, though they had absolutely no influence on their target, who remained frustratingly unfazed.

"You can thank me later," he growled.

"Thank you? For what? For destroying my"—she couldn't breathe—"for kidnapping"—couldn't stop the overpowering need to be sick—"put me down."

"I can't."

She beat against his chest, tears hot on her cheeks, stomach whirling. "Put me down. Now."

"What's wrong?" For the first time he sounded uncertain.

"Now. Or I'm going to throw up all over you."

He lowered her to the ground, where she immediately fell to her knees, digging her hands into the mud. Uncaring where she was or that she seemed to still be in her nightclothes. The dizziness made the world spin and lurch under her as she heaved until her throat burned and her stomach cramped.

She heard him dismount behind her. He put a hand upon her shoulder as she retched and wept and sniffled and coughed.

And though she fought it, once more the black well of unconsciousness claimed her.

"What are you looking at?" Brendan snapped.

The flea-bitten black-and-white mongrel cocked his head to the side, ears pricked, dark beady eyes filled with reproach. He'd slipped in as the owner had left, sniffing every corner, inspecting every stick of furniture. A process that took about five minutes in the shabby little cabin.

"I had to do it. That, or let Máelodor's goons have a go at her."

The odd little dog turned away, trotting across to the pallet. Climbed up, settling beside Elisabeth with a grunt of satisfaction.

"Get off there. You're probably full of fleas." He reached for the dog, which grimaced its teeth in a snarl.

Brendan backed off. "Fine. Let her itch. One more reason for her to despise me. As if she needed any more reasons."

He sat down, tipping his chair back against the wall. Crossed his arms over his chest and hunched his shoulders in an attempt to keep warm. The rain had begun again. A draft blew through what passed for walls, and the turf fire sizzled and spit with every drop from a leaky chimney.

The proud homeowner had vacated to a neighbor's for the night. Coins in his pocket and a knowing leer on his weathered face. As if dirty one-room hovels conveyed the perfect romantic ambience for a seduction.

Brendan wished it were that easy. But somehow he didn't

think Elisabeth would quite see her abduction with a rosy, starry-eyed glow. And he'd already experienced her wicked left hook. He rubbed his bruised chin. The last thing he needed was to transport a struggling, hostile female cross-country. They'd have Máelodor's men, *Amhas-draoi*, and an angry bridegroom breathing down their necks within miles.

He toyed with the idea of casting the sleep of the *an-farath* over her every time she looked as if she might wake. But toting an unconscious woman to Dublin held its own disadvantages. Normally it took the victim a few hours to overcome the nausea and dizziness. He'd never tried to keep someone asleep for up to a week. He couldn't be sure what the effect would be. Not a risk he wanted to take, especially as rusty as his powers had become. Hell, she might not wake at all at the end of it.

"Damn Jack and his altruistic tendencies. This is his fault. 'You have to go back, Brendan. You can't leave her. Máelodor's men are on their way,'" he mimicked. "If Jack was so bloody worried about Elisabeth, why didn't he go back and get her?"

The dog never even lifted its head, though its eyes remained steady on Brendan.

"Fine. Elisabeth's my responsibility, but let me nurse my grudge, will you? It's keeping me warm." It also gave him something to do besides wonder how the hell he planned to explain to Elisabeth what would seem like the most heinous of crimes.

"How can I make her understand it's for her own good? That the last thing I want or need is an unwilling companion? That I'd be more than happy to return her to Dun Eyre if it didn't spell her grisly death? That I'm not really the right bastard she thinks I am?"

The dog blinked and sneezed. Twice.

"Perfect. Now I'm asking advice from a mop with legs." Brendan leaned his head back to stare up into the tangle of cobwebs and shadows. Tossed a grim smile to the dusty rafters. He'd never make Elisabeth understand. He *was* a right bastard, among a host of other less charitable qualities.

Elisabeth rolled over, murmuring in her sleep, the greatcoat he'd spread over her sliding off onto the floor. Her night plait had loosened, wild red curls escaping to feather her cheeks. But her face remained white as her chemise, a frown wrinkling her brow as she groped for the lost warmth.

He dropped the tipped chair back to the floor. Stood to retrieve the greatcoat. This time, the dog allowed Brendan to approach. Even reached out a cold nose to nuzzle Brendan's fingers as he draped the coat back across Elisabeth.

Immediately, she snuggled into its warmth, a smile playing over her lips, a whispered thank-you barely audible.

A little late. And she probably wouldn't remember thanking him when she woke. She'd be as waspish and furious as ever.

Rubbing a hand over his face, he tried to focus, but concentration was impossible. He was cold. Damp. Uncomfortable. And saddled with a woman who would wake in hysterics. Enraged, upset, and sick as a dog—no offense. Not a good combination at the best of times. And this was far from the best of times.

He tried clinging to the one thing that mattered. The Sh'vad Tual was safe.

He pulled it free of his shirt, where it dangled from the gold chain. Such an unassuming gem. Crudely hacked edges. Neither brilliant nor beautiful. Yet, as he stared, gold and bronze and rose flickered and grew within the deepest corners of the gemstone's heart to become amber and citrine and brassy yellow. Dusky claret, light shell pink, and gold-red like good brandy.

Some colors surfaced and sank. Others flashed and twinkled only when he didn't look directly at them. And then there were the colors difficult to describe with any palette he'd learned. A brown possessing shades of smoky silver and carrot orange at the same time. A blue that in one shaft of light sparkled in a purply lilac and in the next instant sharpened to a jungle ferny green before darkening to sooty dull black.

He stared until his eyes stung and watered, the facets of the stone unfolding within his palm like a map. He saw caverns and caves. Sweeping oceans and skies alive with stars and streaming pennants of starshot gas. There were trees scraping clouds electric with lightning and a single drop of water sliding off one perfect veined leaf.

The clouds parted on a shaft of light. A man stood among the ruins of a battlefield. His golden head slick with sweat and blood. His sword broken. Death descending.

Pain lanced Brendan's skull as if someone had taken an ax-blade to the back of his head. The stone flamed against his palm, the colors pouring forth through his fingers in a ribbon of ebony and lavender and emerald and azure.

"Damn!" Shaking out his burnt hand, he dropped the stone. Once more cool to the touch. Dull and lifeless.

Shudders chattered his teeth, and he wrapped himself tighter in his coat. Waited for Elisabeth to wake.

And the true misery to begin.

Disconnected images. Jumbled, upended thoughts. They battered her mind with bizarre dreams, leaving her sick to her stomach, a horrid buzz in her ears.

Aunt Fitz's odd, mysterious smile. Gordon standing alone in the church, holding his sapphire choker. Flocks of cackling, sharp-eyed pigeons wheeling over Dun Eyre before streaming east toward Dublin and London. Brendan clutching her pendant, light seeping between his fingers. Herself, stuffed into her wedding gown, a piece of cake in each hand.

Images surfaced before submerging back into an endless twilight. She struggled to stay ahead of the encroaching dusk, but no matter how many strides she took, the shadows stretched closer. She broke into a run. Her fear feeding the gray nothingness just behind. Stumbling, she fell. Cried out for help from the one person she knew could stop the death waiting for her inside the void.

And came awake, sick and retching.

"Don't fight it. It only makes the nausea worse."

Fight it? Is that what he thought she was doing? No, she'd long since raised the white flag. She only wanted the floor to remain in one place and the walls to stop spinning. Then she could die in peace.

"You're not going to die," came the exasperated answer.

She went rigid. Had she spoken out loud? She didn't think so. "You mean this tenth circle of hell is going to last forever?"

"Of course not. An hour or two, and you'll be back on your feet." Added under his breath, "I hope."

He tucked her back under the greatcoat, the straw pallet crackling beneath her head. She shivered, curling into the heavy wool as she tried to piece together where she was. A peasant's mud cabin. Dirt floor. A few pieces of rough furniture. The odors of sweat and dirt and animals hanging low in the room. Rain puddling in a corner. Wind rattling the door, backing smoke down the chimney.

Brendan retreated to a chair, tipping it back against the wall. Arms crossed, annoyance and frustration clouding his gaze. As if he had any right to be annoyed with her.

She wanted to scream at him. Hit him. Beat him senseless for doing this to her. This and all the other this-es he was guilty of. Instead, the room swirled around her in a mad gyration, and all she could do was seethe and count the minutes until vengeance could be hers.

"Where are we?" she asked, through chattering teeth.

"On the road between Corofin and Gort."

That far? Even if they departed immediately, it would take hours to arrive at Dun Eyre. "How long"—she swallowed—"how long have I been here?" She couldn't bring herself to add, *alone with you, unchaperoned*. It would only serve to emphasize the catastrophe that already loomed greater than life-size.

"Twenty-four hours, give or take." Disgust clear in his voice.

A full day. She should be married by now. A respectable matron preparing to leave on her wedding trip to London. Instead, Gordon must be frantic. Aunt Fitz and Aunt Pheeney in a panic.

Or . . . She sucked in a horrified breath.

Aunt Fitz knew Brendan had been at Dun Eyre. Elisabeth had even joked about his ridiculous claim of stealing the bride away. Was it possible everyone believed Elisabeth had run off with Brendan? Could they imagine this had been an elopement rather than an abduction? Could her life get any worse?

Brendan rocked the chair forward with a thud. Stood to pace the cramped room, tapping a finger against his chin. "We can't stay here much longer. If you're not better soon,

I'm going to have to heave you aboard Onwen and take my chances on the road."

"Heave me . . . good luck with that. I'm not going anywhere with you, except home." Mayhap she could explain how she was called away unexpectedly, in the middle of the night, alone, in her nightgown . . . and mayhap pigs could fly. Who would believe such a ridiculous tale?

He faced her, a grim light in his eyes. An unfamiliar hardness to his features. "Believe me when I say I wish I could. But Dun Eyre isn't safe. Máelodor's bounty hunters are on their way there."

Anger overpowered the tiny frisson of fear rippling up her spine. "Isn't safe? What are you babbling about? Who's Máelodor?"

"Someone who currently wants to take me apart piece by piece. Preferably with a dull blade."

She clenched her teeth. "I know how he feels."

Still nervously stalking the cramped room, he rubbed his hands over his face as if trying to keep awake. Until then, she hadn't noted the deep shadows beneath his eyes or the grayness of his skin. Served him right if he was coming down with something. She hoped it was fatal. "Remember when I told you I'd angered a few people and needed to hide at Dun Eyre?"

"I'm surprised it's limited to a few."

A quirk of his lips and a bleak chuckle met her comment. "Hiding wasn't the only reason. I needed to retrieve something I'd left on the estate."

"And the reason you kidnapped me?"

"Dun Eyre was the perfect place to conceal the Sh'vad Tual. None would suspect such a treasure hung round my fiancée's neck. It would be safe until I needed it again."

"The pendant. That's what you came back for."

And why did she feel a tiny sting of disappointment at that bald-stated fact? She was ill and out of her head. That must be it. There was no conceivable reason on this good earth why she should wish for even one blink of an instant for Brendan to look on her as a desirable grown woman rather than a pesky nuisance only a few years free of the schoolroom. No reason at all.

"Somehow Máelodor's discovered where I hid the stone," he continued. "He knows you have it, and he's sent his men to Dun Eyre after it."

"So take me home, and I'll tell them they're too late. You've already stolen it." She arched a brow. "I assume you've stolen it."

He shot her an offended look. "I prefer 'collected' to 'stolen.'" Returned to pacing. "And that would be well and fine if Máelodor didn't have a tendency to kill anyone who stands between himself and the things he wants. His men won't accept you don't have the stone, and they don't handle failure well."

His incessant marching back and forth added to her a headache. "You stole me away from my family, my friends, and the man I was about to marry to—save me?"

"Exactly."

"Next time, let me take my chances with certain death."

"That's gratitude," he grumbled. "Look here, Lissa. Do you think I'm any happier about this than you?"

She had to admit he appeared as foul-tempered and frustrated as she. Belligerent jut to his jaw. Brows drawn low over eyes burning hot. Not exactly the disposition of a lover. Could he be telling the truth? Could she really be in danger? Or was this just his way of keeping her close while he wooed her? Although if this was his idea of seduction, he was extremely lousy at it.

She fixed him with a scowl she hoped speared a hole right through him. Unfortunately, the pain in her head slid into her neck and down her shoulders until her whole body hurt, and she closed her eyes before her brain oozed out of them. "I'm going to be sick again."

"It was a simple spell. How was I to know you'd have such a strong reaction?"

"Simple, he says," she muttered, turning her face to the wall.

She heard him moving about the room. The crackle as he stirred the fire to life. A scrape of a dragged chair. The grumble as he strove to make himself comfortable.

Helplessness did not suit her. If Brendan thought she'd simply allow him to toss her aboard his horse like a sack of flour, he was very much mistaken. But what choice did she have? She was in no position to argue or fight back. She didn't even have clothes, for heaven's sake. She was completely at his mercy.

For now.

She pulled the greatcoat tighter around her while she sifted through his explanation. Magic. Spells. The *Other*. They didn't belong to the well-ordered normalcy of her life. They were part of something strange and dark and forbidden. Whispers behind closed doors. Wondrous stories told by her grandmother, stirring Elisabeth's imagination with tingly, delicious excitement.

A bit of what she'd once felt when she was with Brendan. As if once they were together she'd finally discover that colorful, exotic, elusive world. That, as his wife, she'd finally understand the powers that drove him, shaped him, and glittered off him like diamonds.

She'd been granted that childhood wish with a vengeance.

But instead of wonder, all she experienced was a sense of standing upon the edge of an abyss, frightening beyond her ken. A held breath. A tense expectancy. As if her world and his stood poised upon a brink.

A single flinch and there would be no turning back for either of them.

"What is that hideous rag?" Elisabeth asked.

Brendan held up a shapeless piece of drab-colored fabric splotched with stains of unknown origin. "Your dress. Its former owner charged me an entire shilling, so treat it with care."

"Were the lice extra?" She gave a rude bark of laughter. "No, really. What is it?"

"It's that or your nightclothes until we reach Dublin." He dropped petticoats, an apron, stockings, and a sturdy pair of half boots upon the pallet. "There's no time to have the local dressmaker create something for you."

Wrinkling her nose, she studied the dingy gingham with disgust. That was a dress? Perhaps long ago in a previous life. Now it more closely resembled a burlap sack. An ugly burlap sack. She sighed. Things went from bad to worse. At least she'd recovered from the horrible, bed-spinning, stomach-whirling illness of yesterday. She'd celebrate the small victories. Besides, clothed—even in rags—she stood a better chance of regaining her freedom. She'd write to her aunts for help. Gordon would charge to her rescue. All would be well again.

"Fine. If I've no other choice." She snatched the garment from Brendan. "But once we reach the city . . ."

"I'll shower you with silks, I promise. Now get dressed, we've wasted enough time dawdling here."

Her gaze flicked pointedly between the dress and him and the dress again. She cleared her throat.

"It's pouring outside. I'll be soaked," he whined.

She shot him a look that spoke volumes.

"All right. Come on, Gordon," he said, gesturing to the dog.

"That's not funny." Tears choked her throat, but she refused to let him see her cry. That would be the final humiliation.

For a moment contrition surfaced in his gaze. "I'm sorry. Stupid joke. He doesn't answer to it anyway. Prefers 'Killer.'" The dog leapt to his feet, wagging his tail. "See?"

Elisabeth hiccupped and sniffed, a smile tugging at her mouth despite herself. Brendan wasn't supposed to be charming. He was supposed to continue being rude and bossy and arrogant. It made hating him so much easier. "Well, take Killer outside. I'll holler when I'm presentable."

"'Presentable'? We're not going to visit the queen."

"Out!"

Killer trotting at his heels, Brendan kicked open the door, growled an oath, and darted into the downpour.

Alone, she slid out of her robe. Studiously avoiding thoughts of its previous owner, she took up the cleaning rag posing as a dress and wriggled into it. Whoever Brendan had bought it from had been considerably thinner, flatter, and a good four or five inches shorter. The side seams barely held together, while the bodice threatened to explode if she so much as breathed deeply. And the whole thing smelled like sweat and stinky cheese. She wrinkled her nose, reminding herself it was a temporary evil. Once they reached Dublin, she'd burn it before scouring herself clean in a long, hot bath.

"May we come in now?" came an aggrieved voice. "Killer's floating away, and I'm growing gills."

She straightened from adjusting her stockings. "Killer's allowed. You can drown for all I care."

He squelched inside, drenched from head to foot, hair plastered to his head. "It's a bloody mess out there."

She bent to lace the worn leather half boots. Small miracle—they fit. Stood up, shaking out the skirts, adjusting the apron strings as if any amount of primping could turn this sow's ear into a silk purse. "Do I pass inspection?" She did a slow turn. "Grubby, sooty, and smelly enough for your unscrupulous, villainous self?"

A smile broke over his tired face. "That's my girl. When you stop insulting me is when I'll begin to worry." His gaze traveled over her new outfit with obvious skepticism. "Not exactly an *Ackermann's* fashion plate, but you'll do." He remained staring at her for long moments before quickly clearing his throat, suddenly spinning on his heel, agitatedly gathering up their scattered belongings. Stowing them in his saddlebag.

Grabbing up Brendan's greatcoat, she pulled it over her shoulders; the scents of travel and sweat and an exotic woodsy aroma clung to the wool. "When you stop insulting *me* is when *I'll* begin to worry."

He flashed her another wicked smile, and with a strange ache in her heart she turned away.

———o———

"Don't you dare," Elisabeth hissed as Brendan started to assist her onto Onwen. "Last I checked I was still able to mount a horse on my own."

He stepped back with a wave of assent. "Be my guest. Hoisting you about's not the easiest of tasks."

She flashed him a thunderous look as she gathered the reins and swung herself aboard. "I'll pretend I didn't hear that."

He mounted behind her, the mare sidestepping and tossing her head, but a firm hand and a gentle word quickly settled the horse. They hadn't left the farmyard but already rain soaked through the overcoat he'd scavenged. Dripped off his hat to slither down his neck. The calendar might have said April, but the cold felt more like February, and the rain pelted in torrents. Mud sucked at Onwen's feet, the road beyond a quagmire.

Killer watched them from the doorway with interest, his sodden fur spiky with wet. As Brendan urged the horse forward, the terrier followed.

"Stay," Brendan commanded.

The dog paused, its expression almost contemptuous before it once more began tagging behind.

"I think you've gained a friend." Elisabeth's amusement was evident.

"I don't want a friend. Or a dog. Or a woman." He shifted in his saddle. "Stay, Killer. Go home."

The dog sneezed but remained just behind them. Dodging puddles. Leaping over fallen twigs. Pink tongue lolling in a clever doggie smile.

"Too bad." Elisabeth chuckled scornfully. "Looks like you've got them whether you want them or not."

He glared at the back of her head, choking down a

properly sarcastic response. Tried not to notice the way she nestled back against him. Or the way her rear was dangerously positioned between his legs. Or the heady sway of her body in his arms.

It had been that damn dress. It was hideous. Probably the ugliest rag he'd ever seen on a woman.

And Elisabeth had never looked more breathtaking.

The snug fit emphasized every ripe, delicious curve, the bodice cut to reveal honeyed, freckled flesh. Add her wild tumble of dark red curls and those big brown eyes, and it was as if a come-hither sex goddess had suddenly appeared where an annoying little sister stood seconds earlier.

Disconcerting.

Onwen stumbled, Elisabeth rubbing against him, the back of her neck temptingly close.

Uncomfortable.

He gritted his teeth, trying to ignore his body's rising response. Lifted his face to the rain to quell the heat centered in his groin.

This was Elisabeth Fitzgerald. A pest. A nuisance. A spanner stuck smack in the middle of his carefully laid out plans.

And if he leaned forward just a little, he'd be able to kiss the soft spot right behind her ear.

Killer barked, tearing beneath Onwen's legs to dive into the brush after a rabbit. The mare leapt sideways in agitation. A flood of rainwater tipped from Brendan's hat's brim down his back in a freezing cascade.

"Son of a bitch," he snarled, shuddering.

But thankfully, the dash of ice water returned life—and Elisabeth—to normal.

Hellish, but normal.

Seven

The shine of Brendan's money overrode the publican's suspicions, and he ushered them into a tiny rear chamber with a searching look down his long, crooked nose and a recommendation to keep out of the way of the regulars.

Up to now, Elisabeth had clung with every ounce of willpower to a stony, unbridgeable fury until her chest ached and her head throbbed from the effort. Only in the last hours had she felt her anger slipping away. Too exhausted to maintain it, and besides, a cold shoulder only works if the person being pointedly ignored is aware of it. Brendan seemed completely oblivious. Another reason to be annoyed with him, and yet it only served to loosen that hard knot of rage even further.

Actually, laughter bubbled through her. A sign of approaching hysteria? Had Brendan finally driven her out of her head? If anyone could, it would be him for certain. He was a master of provocation.

No sooner had the innkeeper closed the door than Killer

wiggled free of Elisabeth's enveloping greatcoat, flinging himself nails skittering onto the floor. Shaking until his hair stood on end, looking like a black-and-white hairbrush.

Brendan rolled his eyes. "I can't believe you brought that dog in here."

"We couldn't leave him outside. He'd catch his death."

"He's a stray, Lissa. He's used to being outside in all weather."

"That doesn't mean he enjoys it. See?" Killer had curled up on a pile of musty sacks, giving a long doggie sigh as if he'd found nirvana. "He doesn't want to be out in the rain either."

She followed his lead, shedding her waterlogged outer layer before sinking gratefully onto the only chair in the room, a rickety thing with sagging cane and one wobbly leg. Yet still a pleasant change after being perched atop Onwen's knobby withers.

"Bloody Irish weather. I'm growing moss." Brendan peeled off his own sopping jacket. Plowed a hand through his wet hair.

"You sound as if you're surprised. You did live on this island for more than twenty years," Elisabeth responded, shaking out damp skirts. Peeling herself out of the wet shawl Brendan had purchased off a tinker in Gort.

He paused from rubbing warmth back into his arms, gaze somber. "That was a lifetime ago. I was another person."

Dun Eyre and the whirl of wedding preparations. A smelly roadside tavern and a man she'd thought dead mere days previous. Two halves of the same life severed cleanly down the middle. "I know exactly what you mean," she answered sourly.

Until now, she'd kept thoughts off the present by painting rosy pictures of her future. The happy-ever-after ending when Gordon reassured her that no mere scandal could tarnish what they had together. That he would still marry her. That the future they'd talked about was still possible.

She imagined the wedding, the smiles and laughter, the tearful farewells as they departed for London. After that, it all went blurry. She couldn't envision the house on Upper Mount Street. Couldn't fantasize about the life she and Gordon would have there. It was as if her imagination had stretched as far as it could. Beyond that illusory wedding, there was only a foggy unreality.

Instead, her mind seemed to fall back into the past. Showed her events she'd forgotten until now. As if Brendan's return had unlocked an entire part of herself she'd buried away after his desertion. The memories rose through her. Slowly. Steadily. Unstoppable as an encroaching tide.

"Do you remember when I fell out of the tree?" she heard herself asking. A day she'd not thought of in years, yet it sprang into vivid life as if only weeks had passed.

He brightened. "Do I? Of all the shatter-brained things to do. You're lucky I didn't leave you there for some poacher to stumble over."

She grimaced. "A gentleman even then. You looked so fierce, staring at me as if I were the worst sort of nuisance."

Just talking about it brought the memories flooding back. The crazy infatuation prompting her climb into the ancient, gnarled, walnut tree. The beautiful, young man pacing below her, muttering to himself in a language she didn't understand, though just hearing it made her skin crawl.

"Aunt Fitz didn't scold me as much as you did," she said.

Brendan relaxed enough to pull up a stool that looked as if it had recently been broken over someone's head. "It rained that day too," he grumbled.

"Buckets. I'd never been so happy to see anyone in my life as when you came striding through the wood like a hero to my rescue." Her young heart had done flips. She'd been sure he heard it thundering against her ribs when he scooped her into his arms to carry her to the house. She'd lived on that one moment for months.

His brows lifted in amusement. "Hero? Is that what you thought? Talk about off the mark."

"So it turned out." She sighed. "But at the time . . ."

She'd thought him magnificent. Proud. Haughty. And far superior to the raw young men she met at the assemblies in Ennis and Dublin. They were callow youths with no thoughts more weighty than the height of their shirt-points and the depth of her pockets. His intelligence and wit glittered. His looks dazzled. She'd fallen hard and fast for Brendan and paid for it dearly.

He'd left her heart in pieces. Abandoned her to ridicule and pity and murderous rumors. She'd learned the hard way how easily pedestals crumbled.

No man would make her feel that heart-galloping, hot and cold, tongue-tied, and quivery again. No man had. She'd accepted Gordon as much for the way he didn't make her feel as the way he did. Her calm affection for him the sheen of a tranquil lake after Brendan's violent emotional thunderstorm.

She blinked back tears. Focused on drying her arms and face with her shawl. Quickly changed the subject. "Aidan and Sabrina will be thrilled to have you home. They'd given up hope."

His face lost the glow of easy conversation. "My brother and I didn't exactly part on the best of terms. And Sabrina, well, I only hope . . . but it doesn't matter. The years have changed us all. It won't ever be as it was. Mayhap that's a good thing."

He toyed with the pendant, running his finger up and down its chain, though he never touched the stone.

Hanging her damp shawl by the fire to dry, she asked, "Why is Máelodor looking for the stone? What's so important he'd kill for it?"

His hand paused upon the chain, his eyes suddenly wary.

"After everything that's transpired, I deserve an answer, don't you think?" she asked.

"At least one, but deserving answers and wanting answers are two different things. Do you want to know? Truly?"

Again she had the impression Brendan ached to unburden himself, but feared it too. And perhaps with cause. For as long as they'd known one another she'd shied away from too much knowledge. Too much involvement. It's one thing to be conscious of the existence of the *Other*. Far different to embrace it.

She shuddered with sudden cold as if a goose had stepped upon her grave. "No. I don't want to know. I don't want anything to do with you or your stone or this man, Máelodor or magic or *Other* or any of it. But . . ." She paused. "My life has been torn apart because of it all. I have to know. Don't you think?"

For the first time he seemed at a loss for words, fiddling with the items upon a table. A bent brass candlestick. A chipped bowl.

"Brendan?"

He rubbed a tired hand over his chin. Stood abruptly to pace, hands behind his back. "Bear in mind it may sound slightly mad."

"You mean I haven't heard the mad part yet? What's happened so far passes for normal to you?"

"You're not making this any easier."

"Good."

"Do you want to hear or not?"

"Onward with the insanity."

He gave her a pained look before continuing. "The stone in the pendant is a key. With it, one can unlock the spells protecting Arth—You're sure you want to hear this?"

She folded her hands across her chest, cocking a brow in impatience.

"Very well. Protecting Arthur's tomb."

"Arthur who?"

"Arthur. *The* Arthur. You know, the High King and legendary Arthur. Defender of Britain. Scourge of Saxon invaders everywhere. His tomb is warded from intrusion by spells placed upon it at the time of his death. The Sh'vad Tual is the key to breaking those spells and opening the tomb."

"Arthur's a nursery tale. He's not a real person. He's a . . . a fable. A myth. The sword from the lake, the green knight, Morgan le Fey's evilness and Galahad's faith. They're stories."

"Are you through denying my history now?"

"*Your* history?"

"Arthur was the last great king of the *Other*. He ruled during a golden age. A period when carrying *Fey* blood was a wondrous gift. Magic needn't be hidden away in attics and cellars. We weren't persecuted. Targeted as freaks or witches or devils. Our families didn't pretend we didn't exist or refuse to acknowledge us as if we were crazy." His gaze landed squarely on her.

She flushed but refused to rise to the bait. "Why does Máelodor want to open Arthur's tomb? Is it full of treasure? Gold and jewels?"

"If only it were that simple. Máelodor is a master-mage. He's studied for years, every scrap of knowledge he could get his hands on. He begged, borrowed, and stole whatever he had to in order to further his understanding of magic and the *Fey* world. He delved into powers he shouldn't have and played a dangerous game with creatures from a nightmare. Arthur would be his greatest masterpiece. A feat unlike any ever undertaken." Brendan's eyes took on a feverish light as he spoke, his face transfixed. Almost as if he'd conjured the mask of the *fith-fath* to become once more a stranger.

"Unlocking his tomb?"

His gaze snapped back with knife-point intensity. The look of excitement dimming. "No. Bringing him back."

She must have shown her confusion, because he pressed on.

"With the bones of the king in his possession, Máelodor can resurrect the man. He can bring Arthur back to life. He would be all he was previously. A glorious warrior. An amazing statesman. Cunning. Wise. Courageous. Resourceful. Everything a leader should be. Everything one looks for in a ruler."

"I still don't see—"

"The *Other* are hungry for a return to that lost age. With Arthur to unite them, they could rally an army unlike any this world has seen. The superstitious *Duinedon* would fall before his power and a new reign of *Other* would emerge." He drew in a deep breath through his nose. Let it out on a defeated sigh. "That's the idea anyway. There aren't enough of us nor are we strong enough to take on the *Duinedon* and their armies, but Máelodor is beyond caring."

"That's why he wants the stone."

"That's why he wants *you*. He believes you have the stone. Or know where it's hidden. He'll stop at nothing to achieve his ends. Torture. Murder. He's obsessed to the point of insanity."

She sat there quietly, sorting through all he'd told her. Unable to take it all in. He was right. It did sound mad. And yet, why tell such an outlandish tale unless it was the truth?

"Lissa?" he asked gently.

She came to, throwing herself to her feet. "How dare you drag me into this? How dare you hide something like that with me? Are you bird-witted? What were you thinking? Didn't it ever occur to you I would be in danger if this madman murderer found out where you'd hidden it?"

"I was out of time and being hunted. I had to find a safe place for the stone. It was my insurance. It still is."

"Insurance against what?"

His gaze grew somber. "Against being murdered like my father."

Elisabeth made a nest among the pile of empty sacks, Killer's comforting weight in her lap. Brendan had stepped out. He'd given no explanation, only a terse command to stay put, followed by a more sympathetic "Try and get some rest."

Rest? She wished she could. She wished she could close her eyes and wake in her own bed with Aunt Pheeney's cajoling and Aunt Fitz's scolding and the sun streaming across her coverlet and the larks in the trees outside her window and a thousand other little moments that until she'd lost them had seemed inconsequential.

At every voice in the passage or approaching step outside, she braced herself for Brendan's return.

Murdered. Like my father.

His words had hung frozen in the air between them. She'd ached to push him further. To make him explain and yet another part had held back. Too frightened by what he'd revealed. Too afraid of what else she might discover. Already she felt as if she'd waded unknowing into a bog, the ground unstable beneath her feet. Every step taking her deeper into treacherous grounds where she might never find her way out again.

Through the walls, the soft chords of a harp broke through the babble of conversation and crude male laughter. A simple run of strings transforming into a sentimental melody.

She leaned her head against the wall, closing her eyes. Seeing once more the heroic figure of Brendan striding through the swirl of mist and drizzle to sweep her up into his arms. Muttering the entire time he'd carried her about the extreme silliness of females and his incomprehension of a sex possessing more fluff than brains. She'd laid her head upon his chest, listened to the steady beat of his heart, the warmth of his body against her cheek, and been in complete ecstasy.

The harper's tune changed. His voice joining in. Lifting in the melancholy longing of a soldier's song. The image of Brendan dissolving into bleaker, sadder scenes.

The fear and confusion following the bloody murder of Lord Kilronan. Aunt Fitz and Aunt Pheeney taking turns to stay with Her Ladyship in the weeks following when her widow's grief held a wild and unpredictable ferocity. Aidan, wearing his new responsibilities like a heavy chain about his neck. Sabrina, every day growing thinner and grayer and quieter until she vanished completely into the peace of the convent. The charmed glamour of the Douglas family disintegrating before Elisabeth's eyes.

And everyone asking the same question: Where's Brendan?

Now she knew. He'd been hiding. Running. Surviving.

He'd grown hard, dangerous, careful, and cynical. He'd become a man who guarded his words and trusted few. His gaze, once clear and bright as a summer sun, held deep and violent shadows. His formerly whippet-thin body had toughened to a rugged leanness.

And yet, for a few moments as they'd laughed over a young girl's folly, he'd been the boy whose smile broke hearts and laughter made her hurt for something she couldn't define.

The harper's tune changed again.

Killer sat up, ears pricked.

Whining, he jumped from her lap to scratch at the door, his whole body quivering. It had been quite a few hours. Perhaps nature called. Brendan had warned her to stay in the room and out of the way of the tavern's patrons, but Killer's whines grew in volume and intensity. He sniffed along the bottom of the door, pawing at the gap.

"Just for a moment and then come right back. Do you hear?" she ordered.

He barked once. Sat obediently as she cracked the door.

And was out like a shot, bolting down the passage, disappearing around a corner.

A half hour passed. Then an hour. Had he abandoned her? Had Brendan? Neither had come back.

A dog barked. A ferocious yipping and snarling. Then a sharp cry as if the animal had been kicked or hurt.

Elisabeth threw open the door. "Killer?"

Onwen drowsed, head down, back foot cocked.

Brendan brushed her until she shone. It gave him a task when he most needed to keep his mind and hands busy. A way to stop the eternal roundabout of what-ifs and regrets.

What if he'd spoken out—even once—against the growing madness infecting his father and the Nine?

What if he'd walked away as soon as he'd realized where the plan would lead the *Other*?

What if he'd intervened when Freddie lay dying amid the flames of his house and the bodies of his family?

What if he'd warned the *Amhas-draoi* himself instead of sending Daz Ahern in his place?

Would events have turned out differently? Would Father have come to the same realization as his son, or would he have seen Brendan's hesitation as weakness and his second thoughts as treachery? Would the *Amhas-draoi* have listened, or would they still have attacked blindly and savagely, seeing death as the only way to deal with such sinister evil as the Nine hoped to unleash? Had Father died cursing his youngest son's name?

There were no answers, no matter how many times he went round and round in his head. Only more questions. More pain. More voices infecting his sleep. More faces crowding his dreams.

But tonight new questions buzzed in his brain like sand flies.

What if he'd succeeded seven years ago in handing the Sh'vad Tual over to the *Amhas-draoi*?

What if he'd not had to escape retribution? What if Máelodor had died with the rest of the Nine?

Would Brendan have married Elisabeth as he'd intended? Would he even now be a sedate father and husband? His days spent playing the responsible landowner? His nights entwined with a passionate wife?

In the years of his exile, he'd refused to ask those sorts of questions. The future had been the next hour, the next day, the next week. There was no energy to spare to look deeper.

Only recently had he begun to envision an existence beyond that of fugitive. Yet it had been too long since he'd sought to dream. He could see nothing beyond his interview with Scathach. Beyond crawling from under the weight of his past deeds. If he tried reaching further, all was vague, indistinct, unknowable.

All but for a wild mane of red hair and a pair of bewitching brown eyes.

For some reason, he'd always thought she would be the one person he could count on. If all else collapsed around him, Lissa Fitzgerald's childlike faith would never falter.

Tonight, he'd attempted to put that theory to the test.

He curled and flexed his fingers, the ache of his injury a dull throb. The fear in Lissa's eyes had punched him hard. He'd not anticipated how hard. Elisabeth knew of the *Other* and still she shrank from them.

From him.

He gave a wry bark of laughter.

Smart girl.

Light

Thanks to Jack's gold, Brendan had planned to hire a chaise. Make the rest of the journey in comfort if not style.

He drew back into the alley beside the coaching inn.

So much for plans.

How he knew the three men standing within the circle of lantern light belonged to Máelodor, he couldn't say. Nothing marked them as such. No great "M" sewn upon their chests. No aura of death surrounding them. In fact, they looked rather ordinary. Unassuming expressions. Clothing neither filthy nor finicky. But Brendan had lived within Máelodor's sinister shadow for too long to ignore the warning bells going off in his head or the prickle of magic crawling under his skin, lifting the hairs at the back of his neck.

He retreated, already reevaluating his options.

Was their appearance here sheer coincidence? Unfortunate, but nothing to fear as long as he stayed out of sight until they departed? Or had they followed his trail from Dun Eyre and any movement on his part would be seized as a chance to capture him and the stone he carried?

He couldn't wait to find out. He was already behind schedule. Jack would be waiting for him in Dublin. The longer he delayed, the greater chance for something else to go wrong.

Ducking down the narrow passage between the posting inn and stables, he made his way back to Elisabeth. Prayed she'd stayed put as he'd ordered her and not gone wandering off. She seemed convinced the danger was real, but he couldn't stake all on her common sense. As he remembered, she'd never been a paragon of obedience. And from what he'd seen so far, time hadn't improved her.

The tavern he'd picked catered to the Irish scraping a living in the cabins and cottages clustered on the outskirts of the lakeside market town. They smoked and drank and cursed and fought in the two rooms making up the tap. Slept it off before a roaring fire, their breathing loud, their smell overpowering.

He'd slipped the publican a few extra pennies for the privacy of a chamber off the kitchen. Not exactly the best of accommodations, but at least they could relax out from under the suspicious, hostile glances of the normal patrons.

That had been the plan.

Once more, his plans had failed him.

As he ducked beneath the low lintel into the murky, smoke-filled room, his watering eyes fell immediately on a tableau he wouldn't have believed had he not seen it for himself. A crowd of men listening in attentive silence to a harper upon a stool in the chimney corner. Eyes closed in a gaunt, weather-beaten face, his fingers darted and slipped over the frets of the ash-wood harp in his lap. But the plaintive beauty of the music was nothing compared to the singer accompanying him, whose poignant longing was wrung from every note as she sang of love and loss and war.

"Siúil go sochair agus siúil go ciúin . . ."

What the hell was she about? Could he not leave her alone for two seconds without catastrophe following? He checked his impulse to drag her away by the hair. With Máelodor's assassins close, the last thing he needed was to draw attention. Nor did he particularly need twenty drunken farmers denied of their entertainment venting their anger on him. He liked all his limbs just where they were, thank you very much.

Across the room, Elisabeth's eyes lifted to his. Her face pale as moonlight compared to the ruddy, wind-chapped features of those watching her in rapt attention. Her red hair aflame in the low light from the fire.

". . . Siúil go doras agus éalaigh liom . . ."

Had she always possessed a voice like this? He couldn't remember. It made him wonder what else about the hoyden tagalong he'd forgotten. Or overlooked.

". . . Is go dté tú mo mhúirnín slán."

It took him a moment to realize her siren song had ended. Silence roared in his ears as he crossed the floor in two angry strides, grabbing her by the elbow, dragging her to a corner away from the others. "Am I wrong or did I order you to stay out of sight until I returned?"

She lifted her chin, face flushed, eyes shining and dark. "Killer escaped."

He drew up short. "What has that bloody dog to do with you singing to a bunch of drunken peasants as if you were on the damned stage at Crow Street?"

"When I went after him, they took me for a serving girl. I tried explaining, but it only made them more insistent." She flushed, dropping her gaze to her clasped hands.

Unexpected fury reddened his vision. "They didn't hurt you, did they?"

"No. Rogan"—she pointed to the harper—"stepped in before it came to that. He asked if I could sing, though whether he hoped I'd succeed and distract them or fail and make them more enraged, I'm not sure."

"If you'd stayed put instead of running after that blasted dog—"

"Well, if you'd been here—"

"I was trying to secure you a carriage. Onwen can't continue to carry both of us. Forgive me for chivalry," he said, glaring at her.

"Chivalry?" Hands on hips, she glared right back. Why couldn't he have been forced to abduct a nice biddable woman instead of this harridan? It would have made his life so much easier. "Is that what you call kidnapping me in the middle of the night, forcing me to wear putrid clothes, dragging me about the countryside, and making me sleep in a closet?"

"Let's not forget saving your ungrateful skin."

She flung herself away with a frustrated groan. "No, we can't forget that. Though I've yet to see hide nor hair of these villainous murderers you seem so convinced are after me."

The door opened. Three men shouldered their way into the room.

Furious, Brendan gestured toward them. "Elisabeth Fitzgerald? Let me introduce you to said murderers. Satisfied?"

———— o ————

Elisabeth's shoulder ached, a stitch cramped her ribs, and her heart pounded in fear.

Brendan remained oblivious to her labored breathing. Each time she stumbled, he yanked her to her feet. Never slowing. Unheeding of her pleas to rest. A moment only for her to get her wind back.

The men had barreled through the tavern, sending tables and tankards flying, hampered by the cramped room and the shoving and cursing of those they knocked over in the chase.

Grabbing her hand, Brendan had dragged her through the kitchen to the screams of serving maids and a cleaver-brandishing cook. Out the back door into the yard, careening through the mud and filth. Into the safety of dark alleys. Ducking in and out of empty lanes. Emerging near the lake, where the darkness gathered against the shoreline and every fish jump or ripple of wind-pushed water against the rocks seeming loud as a cannon blast.

Her legs throbbed and her chest was on fire. She couldn't seem to pull enough air into her lungs. She stumbled, her ankle twisting beneath her. Brendan's hold almost wrenched her arm from her socket as she fell.

"Just a little farther," he urged.

"To where?" she pleaded, hobbling and wincing. "I can't run anymore."

Bent double, hands on his knees, Brendan sucked in great deep breaths while casting a desperate look around. The lake on one side. High hedges opposite and a stone wall. He jerked his chin toward an iron gate. "Through there."

"And then what? On foot, we'll never escape them. We can't walk to Dublin. It would take weeks."

Weeks more time she'd be trapped with Brendan. Weeks longer she'd be unable to send word of where she was and what had happened. Weeks when Gordon would be assuming she'd run off with another lover.

The pain in her chest expanded.

Two men rounded the bend, slowing to a trot. The third stepped from the hedgerow farther ahead. Effectively trapping her and Brendan between.

Three on one. And they were a big three. Meaty. Broad-shouldered. Flat-nosed and squinty-eyed. Brendan didn't stand a chance by himself.

He shoved Elisabeth behind him. Slid a knife from his waist, holding it as if he actually might know how to use it. A reminder that the changes wrought by his years away weren't all visible. Brendan might act the joker, but it was only an act. Anyone who trusted too much in his nimble charm would regret it.

"Look, he's got himself a little knife."

"Oooh, I'm scared."

"Are ye thinking you can be stopping us all, Douglas?"

The men jeered, their faces empty of any emotion save contempt and brutality.

Brendan's response came too low to hear, but a flick of his fingers and the closest man went down in a heap of twitching limbs, eyes rolling in his head, a horrible gargling moan the only sound as he writhed upon the ground.

"Battle magic!" shouted one.

The two still on their feet rushed Brendan, causing him to spin out of the way, his concentration broken. One raised his arm, the night shattered by the crack of a gunshot.

Brendan went stiff before slumping, a hand clamped to his right shoulder.

Elisabeth opened her mouth to scream, but the best she managed was a strangled whimper. Her limbs went dead. She couldn't move. Couldn't cry. She could only stare, mesmerized, at the blood seeping slow and black from the ugly hole in Brendan's shoulder. Her stomach slammed into her throat, cold washing through her as if she'd been plunged into ice water. "They shot you," she gasped. "Brendan, they shot you."

"Did they?" he grunted through clenched teeth. "Hadn't noticed."

Then they were there. Rough hands grabbing her. Hateful words whispered in her ear.

Brendan spun at the final moment, his knife a flash of silver. A scarlet bib splashed across the shirtfront of one attacker as he dropped to his knees.

Still gripping her hard by the shoulder, the last man knocked the knife away. Slammed his fist into Brendan's jaw. Hammered a knee into his stomach. Punched his wounded shoulder.

Brendan toppled to the mud. Groans from a tight jaw, eyes squeezed shut.

"Damned bastard," the man snarled. "That's fer Keg and Perry." He kicked Brendan hard in the ribs. "Think ye be hurtin' now. Wait 'til the Great One's gotten his hands on ye."

The rattle of harness and a low whistle startled them all alert.

Around the bend, a canvas-covered wagon bumped and rattled, a pair of bony, short-backed ponies in the shafts, a tall, leggy chestnut tied at the back. Elisabeth recognized the tavern's harper at the traces.

"Here now, ladies," he spoke quietly to the ponies.

"Looks as if we've stumbled on what you might call a gang of Mohocks bent on mischief." He pulled up, staring at the gruesome scene before him, his eyes seeming to glow in his thin face. "Let the girl go now, friend."

"Fuck yerself, old man," the man snarled.

Rogan merely chuckled, laying his whip across his knees, a strange, focused expression upon his face. "I don't think that's humanly possible." He motioned toward Elisabeth. "Let her go, and be off with you. The sergeant and his men will be here soon." His voice came slow and even. No trace of fear or anxiety, just a rich endless sea of sound. "You don't want to explain yourself to them, do you?"

The man spit on the ground, his face drawn in stark lines, mouth a thin angry slit. "I've my orders."

"So you do," Rogan conceded, still in the melodious, fluid tones that warmed Elisabeth's whole body, relaxed muscles, and slowed her galloping heart. She wanted to wrap herself in his voice, where she would be protected and the fear wouldn't touch her. "But your orders didn't say anything about getting arrested by a *Duinedon* soldier and spending the next few nights in jail. Move along. Let them be."

The gentle persuasion seemed to be having the same effect on her captor. His grip loosened before falling away completely. His gaze confused as if he didn't understand why he was agreeing, but couldn't stop himself.

"Climb up, miss." The harper held out a hand. "Easy now. No sudden moves or you'll rouse him. The magic of the *leveryas* will bend him to our will, but its hold is fragile and easily shattered by a strong mind."

Her gaze fell upon Brendan's huddled, battered form. One pale hand flung out, the fingers long and beautiful. A musician's fingers. She remembered them upon her skin, the heady, quivery heat bubbling up through her at his touch. And the strength in them as he'd shoved her behind him, shielding her with his own body.

"I can't leave. Not without Brendan."

"Nor will you," Rogan agreed.

Just then, a streak of bristling, snarling fur and teeth broke from the trees. Tore across the road, needle fangs sinking into the villain's ankle.

He roared, eyes wide and round, face twisted in rage.

"Killer!" Elisabeth shouted. "Stop it!"

But the little dog hung on, his jaw clamped viciously upon the man's leg. Cursing, he drew his pistol.

"No!" Elisabeth leapt to grab his arm, but she was caught back by the harper.

Brendan took that moment to lurch forward, gather his lost blade, roll onto his feet, momentum carrying the knife up and into the man's throat.

Blood gushed. Elisabeth screamed. The man toppled soundlessly into the mud, clutching the hilt protruding from his neck.

Brendan fell back, panting through his teeth. Blood from his shoulder soaking his sleeve, his arm, dripping off his fingers. Gore streaked his face and chest like a savage's war paint.

Killer sniffed at him, his stump of a tail wagging with joy.

"Arrah, now," Rogan muttered, climbing off the box. "Helena! A little help, if you please?"

A woman appeared from the back of the wagon dressed in a short jacket and leather breeches, emphasizing a combination of lean strength and feminine curves. Dark hair pulled off a narrow face, firm jaw, lips pressed white. She sprang from the box, her gaze traveling over the bodies with barely a flicker of an eyelid.

"Is he dead?" she asked, nudging Brendan with the toe of her boot.

"Not . . . yet," came the raspy, painful answer as Brendan rolled over, staring up at the woman. His face broke into a cutting smile. "Out of the frying pan. Into the fire," he muttered just before he passed out.

The clack of beggars' cups in the square below the cathedral. Monsoon rains against a leaky roof in Algiers. A clatter of muted gunfire.

As he drifted awake, the noises coalesced to a steady creaking rattle, every jolt of the noisy, bouncing torture device sending pain scything its way from his neck to his fingers, flashes of it spearing his vision with streaks of brilliant light.

For a heart-stopping moment he was in the dilapidated cottage south of Glenlorgan where the traitorous St. John had held him for four excruciating days last winter, humiliation and degradation taking on many varied sadistic forms.

A hand touched his forehead. Without thinking, he lashed out, connecting blindly with the nearest body, his mind already plotting escapes, revenge, anything to keep the man away from him before . . .

"Ow!"

"He's awake!"

Voices. More than one. St. John's brutes? Did they come for him? He wouldn't go willingly. Not again. Never again. He lurched up, fists flailing. Pain arced through him, his shoulder burning, nerves raw and throbbing.

"Hold him before he hurts himself."

"Rogan!"

"He's torn the stitches. Be careful."

"Gods, that was a clean jacket."

Hands held him down. A knee across his chest. He couldn't breathe.

"Brendan, it's me. Elisabeth. You're safe. You've been hurt, but you'll be all right if you just hold still."

Was it a trick? Was he hallucinating? He surrendered, the price of fighting too high.

The dreams seeped out of him, first the panic and humiliation, then more slowly the despair, the boiling frustration when he knew Sabrina was in danger because of him, when he knew his sister would die because she'd cared enough for him to answer his summons.

She couldn't die. Not another corpse. Not another ghost. There were too many already. Their voices deafened him. Their eyes followed him in his sleep. "Can't . . . breathe . . . can't . . . talk . . ."

"You can get off him now, Rogan." A woman's voice. Confident. Cool.

The crushing weight on his chest was lifted, leaving him gasping and retching. He rolled onto his side, fresh needles of pain lancing from his shoulder into his brain.

Hands gentled him. A damp cloth wiped his face. "The bullet's out, but you lost a lot of blood. You need to rest quietly."

"Elisabeth?" The memories rushed in like water. The men in the tavern. The fight on the road. Being manhandled into the wagon where someone held him down while someone else dug into his flesh over and over and over until unconsciousness had claimed him.

"He's burning up."

"He'll survive. His kind always do."

He moved his head. So far, so good. No horrible, gut-wrenching agony. He was in a wagon, a canvas roof above him stretched over wooden ribs. Trunks, cases, blanket rolls, traveling valises packed neatly along the sides.

Elisabeth's face hovered above him, wearing a fearful, stoic expression, her hair pulled into a hasty chignon at the back of her head, though wisps of curls framed her gray, tired face.

At his foot, a second woman knelt, her mouth pursed in a disapproving line, her dark brows arched over eyes sparkling with triumph.

Jack's description hadn't been nearly as exaggerated as he'd thought. Miss Roseingrave was beautiful in a panther-esque sort of way. Lean, dark, graceful, deadly. She'd eat poor Jack alive and spit out his bones.

A laugh boiled up through his chest. Why not? The situation reeked of farce. Club-over-the-head, dangle-from-a-cliff-edge comedy in its most unsophisticated form. They both looked at him as if he'd lost his mind. Perhaps he had. He'd escaped Máelodor only to fall into the *Amhas-draoi*'s hands.

Poetic. Ludicrous. Just his typical rotten luck.

Nine

Upon opening his eyes, Brendan's hand immediately flew to his throat. Not there. The chain. The stone. Gone. "Son of a . . . !" He clamped his mouth shut, feeling around in the blanket. It would be here. Had to be.

Elisabeth looked up, a small line between her brows. "The usual salutation is 'Good morning, hope you slept well, lovely weather for a drive.'"

"Try having a blasted great hole in your shoulder and see how you greet the day," he said while riffling through the folds. Checking under the trunk by his head.

"There's laudanum." She started to rummage through a bag.

"No."

"But if your shoulder is bothering—"

"I said no, damn it!"

She flushed, her gaze uncertain. "I was only trying to help."

He glanced away, embarrassed at his outburst. His

weakness wasn't her fault. "Laudanum makes me ill. I stay away from it."

They were alone in the wagon. Who knew when they'd get another such chance to speak without fear of eavesdroppers?

"Where is it, Elisabeth?"

She gazed upon him, expression inscrutable but for a flicker deep in her dark eyes. "Helena says your wound is clean and no sign of infection."

She was going to play it that way, was she? Fine. He'd allow it. To a point. Whatever it took to get that bloody stone back in his possession. "Helena, is it?"

"It seems silly after all we've been through to stand on such proper terms. Who are they, Brendan? What do they want with us?"

"Remember when I said there were people angry with me? Roseingrave is one of them. She's *Amhas-draoi*."

Elisabeth frowned, shaking her head.

"They guard the divide between the *Fey* realm and the mortal world. Act as protectors. Warriors and mages of the highest caliber, they're both feared and respected by the race of *Other*."

Her lips pressed to a thin disapproving line. "You can't make normal enemies. Oh no. You have to fall afoul of cold-blooded murderers and a magic-wielding sorcerer army."

"I strive to excel," he joked before growing somber. "The stone, Lissa. Tell me you have it. Tell me Roseingrave didn't find it. That stone is the key to everything."

She looked away, fiddling with the buckle on one of the traveling cases.

"Do you want me to say I'm sorry? I will. I'm sorry. A

thousand times sorry. You don't know how sorry I am. I never thought it would come to this point, but you don't know what it was like back then. The chaos of those days. I needed to hide the stone. Just until things calmed down. Until I could figure out my next move."

She kept silent, her fingers worrying at the metal clasp.

"If Roseingrave took it—"

Her head shot up, an angry burn in her eyes, chin trembling with emotion, but no sign of crying. "I have the damned thing."

"You?"

"I kept it safe for seven years, didn't I?"

"Lissa—"

"Don't call me that. And don't look at me as if I'm some sort of simpleton who can't understand words of more than two syllables. I wept all over you like a watering pot long enough to slip it from your neck before Helena noticed. No doubt she thinks I'm a blubbering crybaby, but it worked. If the stone was so damned special, my life's destruction counted as nothing, then I knew it must be important. And I didn't trust them. Not completely. Not then."

"You do now?"

"Do I have a choice?"

A silence fraught with recrimination and regret on both sides blanketed the wagon. Gods, he hated this helplessness. Being at the mercy of others. He'd spent too long trusting no one to so easily put his faith in another's hands.

She reached beneath her gown, pulling free the simple chain. The stone hanging dark and lifeless. Unclasping it, she handed it to Brendan. "Here. If I never see it again, I shall count myself fortunate."

The stone barely touched his palm before the visions crashed through his brain.

A man picking among the fields of dead, cheeks blackened with dirt and sweat, streaked with tears. Finding one body among the hundreds, he dropped to his knees, cradling the corpse as if it were a sleeping child. Lifted his head to hurl a curse to the sky, his face caught by a bloody sun. Eyes burning hot and gold as molten steel.

"It can't be," Brendan whispered. "I won't let it happen."

Dropping the stone as if scalded, he dragged in a breath like a drowning swimmer. The defeated warrior and his fallen comrade, both fading beneath a pall of smoke and fog and gold-edged mist.

Once again he was in the wagon with Elisabeth. Somewhere on the road between Dun Eyre and Dublin. A distant ringing of bells still echoing in his ears.

"Did you really think you could return to Ireland and not be caught?"

"Let's say I was hopefully optimistic."

The wagon hit a bump, the jolt like an explosion of nerve endings from his shoulder to his fingertips. "Does he do that on purpose?" Brendan groused.

Helena Roseingrave gave a smile of half amusement. "Rogan's no member of the Four-in-Hand, but his other talents make up for any lack of skill at the ribbons. It was he who discovered your trail outside Gort and tracked you down. Lucky for you."

Luck? She called this luck? Lying in the back of a wagon with a hole in him that hurt like the devil at the mercy of a woman he knew by reputation as being driven, dangerous, and, according to Jack, the world's best kisser?

Though he doubted he'd ever be in a position to test that last quality.

"He's a mage-chaser?" He cast a respectful glance at the hunched back of his tormentor on the box. Many *Other* possessed the ability to sense mage energy. Those skilled enough to follow it like a hound follows a scent were rare indeed.

The wagon dropped with a rattling thud into another pothole, slamming his shoulder into the side of the wagon. Spots shot before his eyes, and he almost passed out at the pain. "Bloody hell, that hurt like a m—"

"Shh! You'll wake your captive."

Elisabeth lay rolled in a blanket, a folded coat as her pillow. In the narrow bed of the wagon, she'd curled uncomfortably close to him. A peep of red hair and the curve of a pink cheek was all he could see above the blanket, but she gave off heat like a furnace, and if he stretched his hand just a bit to the left, he'd be able to rest it on the swell of her hip. Not that he would. Of course not. This was Elisabeth. He needed to gain hold of himself.

"Is that what she told you?" Somehow he'd thought they'd moved beyond Elisabeth's initial fury. Knowing she still regarded him as the devil incarnate hurt more than he thought it would.

"That was the least insulting thing she told me. Though, for a prisoner, she seemed awfully concerned over your survival. Cried all over you. Rogan had to pry her away before I could sew you up. Let me guess, your incredible Douglas magnetism swept her off her feet."

"That's right. Nothing like a little mayhem and terror to get the blood pumping. Better than oysters and sentimental poetry."

Guilt gnawed at him. It was his fault Lissa had been dragged into this. His fault she'd almost been killed back there. "Elisabeth's involvement was a mistake. She's nothing to do with any of this debacle," he said.

"Another victim of Brendan Douglas? Shocking. You must be racking up quite a count of people who've paid for your errors." Her eyes bored into his.

"Why didn't you let me die back there? Or kill me yourself?" he snarled.

She gazed upon him coolly. "Perhaps you'd prefer that. A swift clean death at my hand to what waits should Máelodor recapture you?"

"You've made quite a study. Should I be flattered?"

"Warned."

"You haven't yet told me why you came to our aid? Was it merely so you can execute me at your leisure? The cat playing with the wounded mouse?"

She arched one sarcastic brow. "That's more in your line, isn't it?"

He breathed slowly as he sought to banish the memories. Or at least manage them. But illness and pain broke down his usual iron control. Images burned hot in his mind, whispering figures moved through his consciousness like ghosts.

"No, I'll not grant you your death wish, Brendan Douglas," she said smoothly. "If I'm not mistaken, your greatest punishment is living."

"No," he answered, "it's remembering."

Her gaze froze him with its malice. "Then may you live until you're old and gray and never forget. I know I won't."

They pulled the wagon off the road into a meadow. Unhitched the ponies to graze. A heavy sky threatened rain, gauzy mist threading the streambeds and bottomland. But the temperature remained pleasant, and Elisabeth shed her shawl as she crossed the grass to kneel beside Brendan.

"Miss Roseingrave's ridden ahead. Now's your chance."

Brendan fumbled with the plate of sausages on his lap. "My chance to do what?"

"Poof us out of here in a cloud of smoke. Turn Rogan to a toad. I don't know."

"You really do have an odd notion of *Other*, haven't you? And all along I mistook ignorance for hostility."

"It was not!" She lowered her voice when Rogan looked up from pouring himself a cup of coffee. "It was not hostility," she hissed. "I just don't . . . or rather, it's not as simple as that . . . that is to say I don't . . . Oh, bother, I'm not going to waste my time explaining to you."

If she couldn't articulate it in her own head, how would she make Brendan understand her conflicted fascination-repulsion with the *Other*? Easier to let him think her unreasonable, even if it reflected badly. After all, she didn't care what he thought.

Did she?

He juggled his fork and cup in his left hand, his right arm immobile in heavy bandages. "I bear *Fey* blood, Lissa. I'm not one of the faery folk myself. I don't poof. And as chummy as you and Rogan have become, I'm surprised you'd even entertain the notion of his being transformed into a toad."

"Just a temporary sort of spell. Nothing permanently scarring."

Brendan scowled at a sausage evading all his attempts to spear it. One-handed, he couldn't manage holding plate, fork, and knife. At every stab, the sausage wobbled and slid away from him. "The answer is still no. I can't cast a spell over Rogan turning him into a newt, a snake, or a flea on Killer's backside. He's Rogan, and Rogan he remains."

"But you said yourself they've been hunting you." Unable to watch his frustrated fumblings another moment, she took his plate and utensils and carved the offending sausage into bite-size pieces before handing it back. "That Máelodor and the *Amhas-draoi* are both out to kill you."

"Thank you." He speared a piece of sausage, popping it into his mouth with a vicious smile. "To clarify, the *Amhas-draoi* want me dead. Máelodor wants me alive. Torture's more fun that way. At least for the torturer."

She dropped beside him against the wall, the ground damp under her skirts and liable to leave a muddy spot, but in this dress, who'd notice? "Then Helena—"

"Is not playing by the rules, which generates all sorts of interesting questions." He finished his sausage. Sipped at his coffee. Leaned his head back against the wall, staring off into space with a sigh. "I won't draw on my powers more than necessary, Lissa. It would be . . . unwise." He blinked, and the anguish she thought she saw within his eyes vanished. "Besides, while I'm hampered with this damned shoulder, any escape attempt would end badly."

"So we do nothing?"

"So we're a 'we' now?" Amusement brightened his features.

"As much a 'we' as they are a 'them.'" She frowned. "You know what I mean."

"Which in itself should be enough to give us both pause."

He sighed again, adjusting his sling as if his shoulder ached. She shouldn't push him. His fever still came and went, the marks of his injury etched in every fresh line upon his already finely drawn features.

"Until I sort out my business with the stone, you're trapped with me, and while I'm vulnerable as a bloody kitten, we're trapped with them," he said. "Could be worse."

"I can't begin to imagine how." No, she shouldn't be insisting, but neither should he be taking this whole business as some sort of schoolboy lark. "You said you've spent seven years running from these people."

"Yes, but as I also said, Miss Roseingrave is behaving decidedly un-*Amhas-draoi*."

"Meaning you're still alive."

"Precisely. For whatever reason, she wants to keep me that way. Máelodor's men might find a wounded man and a young woman easy targets. Not so a battle-trained *Amhas-draoi* warrior. We're safe as houses for the nonce. I, for one, plan to enjoy the respite." He lifted his good arm behind his head. Closed his eyes.

"You are *the* most infuriating man," she huffed.

"Yes." He smiled, eyes still closed. "But you love me anyway."

Elisabeth sat on the box beside Rogan, watching the road unfold before them, the landscape to either side vibrant green with spring. She lifted her face to a weak sun moving in and out of low, thick clouds, scattering shadows over the fields to either side. Let the stiff wind give her mind a thorough sweeping as she inhaled the heady spring scents of turned earth and new growth. Birds chattered and sang in the hedgerows, and once or twice she caught sight of a fox, a red flash through shady woods strewn with wildflowers.

Brendan slept. Helena Roseingrave left them on their

way through Banagher with a promise to meet up with them later in the day. No explanation, though she and Rogan spoke quietly together for some minutes before she swung up into the saddle.

Passing the wagon, Helena reined in the gelding, her level black gaze resting on Elisabeth until she wanted to squirm. Horrid, smelly dress. Hair a messy tangle. She could well imagine the wonderful picture she made.

"He abducted you in order to protect you from Máelodor?" As if Helena found it hard to believe Brendan would act from a purely altruistic motive.

Elisabeth flushed. "That's what he says."

"He's not the way I imagined him."

"No. He isn't the way I imagined him either."

Elisabeth's initial terror had receded far more quickly than she thought it would. After the first night, when she'd started at every sound, she'd since slept like a log. She'd never realized how sheltered and protected she'd truly been. How privilege had insulated her from more than poverty. And how much she would enjoy this strange taste of freedom.

Long days of travel left her exhausted by nightfall. An inexplicable curiosity at the ever-changing scenery pulled her from her blankets at dawn. That and Rogan's breakfasts of thick slices of ham and eggs fried to perfection accompanied by crisp potatoes, which she shared with Killer.

The little dog came and went, sometimes disappearing for long stretches when Elisabeth would finally decide he was gone for good. Then, just as she'd given up hope, he'd turn up trotting along beside the wagon as if he'd never been away. Helena despised him. Rogan tolerated him. Brendan ignored him, but Elisabeth found Killer's company strangely reassuring and wouldn't hear a word against him. At times, she almost felt as if he knew what she was thinking and might at any moment open his mouth to tell her everything would be all right.

"Ah, Miss Fitzgerald. Twenty more points for me. Look there. A flock of sheep." Rogan's voice jolted her from her thoughts as he pointed to a meadow up ahead.

"You win." She laughed. "I'll never surpass you unless I'm presented an entire parade of post chaises and an old woman or two."

"Not your fault. I've more practice at travelling piquet. On the road as much as I am, I see what's about. Besides"—he glanced at her from the corner of his eye—"you've been a thousand miles away all day. We could have passed flocks of dancing pink sheep and you'd not have noticed one of them."

She ran her finger over the gnarled wood of the seat. "I've been thinking."

"A dangerous thing for a young lady to be doing," he teased, laughter in his voice.

"My family and friends must be worried sick. My aunts are probably out of their heads wondering what's happened to me. I shouldn't be here."

"No?" He shot her a crinkly eyed smile. "I'm a big believer in destinies, Miss Fitzgerald. Perhaps you're exactly where you need to be."

"Completely compromised, fleeing for my life, and heading who knows where for who knows why?"

"That about sums it up. Look on it as an adventure."

She gazed out over a lush green meadow, so beautiful it caused a pain low in her chest. "Catastrophe, more like."

He nudged her playfully with an elbow. "It's what you

make of it. You can let it beat you down or you can shape it into something better."

"Like taking lemons and making lemonade?"

"I prefer barley into whiskey." He grinned. "You drink what you like, and I'll drink what I like."

Chivied out of her melancholy, she returned to watching the unfolding of the road ahead, the sun warm on her back. Dwellings clustered close to the road, a scattering of cottages and storefronts. Traffic increasing so that Rogan had to slow the wagon, the ponies tossing their heads and whinnying their greetings. Two dogs ran from a yard, barking and racing after them. Killer responded with a series of yaps, the fur on his back in an angry ridge.

Elisabeth grabbed him by the neck. "Don't even think it. They would eat you alive."

The terrier didn't seem to take notice of her warning. He went on snarling and barking at the village dogs as if to say, *Back off. These are* my *people.*

Rogan chuckled. "If Helena sees that dog up here, she's liable to have my head on a platter."

"Miss Roseingrave isn't here and you won't tell her, will you?" She turned her best wheedling smile in his direction.

"Arrah, now, Miss Fitzgerald. Would I snitch on the little bugger? Not likely." He scratched Killer behind an ear, the terrier leaning against the harper with eyes half-closed in joy. "He's good company when he's not stealing the cheese from my lunch."

Rogan pulled up outside a blacksmith's shop, the ring of a hammer matching the thump of her brain against her temples. He leapt down from the box to tie the ponies and give them a rough scratch upon their heads. "You stay with Douglas while I purchase provisions."

Once he was gone, she drew aside the curtain to check on Brendan.

He slept on, his face chalk-white but for two vivid spots of color high upon his cheeks. Sweat damped his hair, sickness dulling the vibrant brilliance of him like a shade placed upon a flame. Where was his glittering *Fey* beauty now? Where was the rakish charmer who could twist her into knots simply by looking at her? This efficient killer possessed a savagery and a harshness she'd never experienced in the men she'd known. A dark heart to the diamond. A wolf among lapdogs.

So, why did her heart race remembering their one and only kiss? Why did she, even for a second, imagine the life she might have led if not for his disappearance? Why did Brendan crowd her thoughts to the detriment of common sense?

Her skin prickled, a fizz of excitement bubbling through her. Was this some cosmic plan in motion? Was Rogan right? She shook her head. Right or wrong, there was nothing and no one for her here.

He couldn't sleep. The air pressed cool and wet against his face. Killer pressed hot and furry against his ribs. Rogan snored and smacked his lips. Elisabeth remained a hump of a blanket across from him. Roseingrave? Who knew? She appeared and disappeared on a regular basis. No announcements of her departure. No sound to mark her returns. The *Amhas-drui* warrior elevated inscrutable mystery to an art form.

Her intentions toward him remained an unanswered question, though he was still alive, which boded well. Surely the fact she'd not executed him immediately meant she had other plans for him. Plans that did not involve a quick severing of his head from his shoulders. She wanted something. He could well imagine what that something was.

Brendan closed his hand round the stone. The jolt of its power kicking against his chest. A flash of fire pouring between his fingers.

Rose and orange and gold and bright white burst across his vision. Cleared to reveal the same field of dead. The same pall of thick, choking smoke. But this time, the defeated king lifted his head, and Brendan felt the connection between them like a current. The mage energy charging through his tired body.

Arthur pointed with the broken edge of his sword. Brendan's gaze following. One body among the hundreds and thousands. A corpse, bloodied and hacked, a mess of gristle and bone. The face, a little older, a little more careworn, but still recognizable.

Aidan.

His brother. A curl of auburn hair fell across a forehead blue-white in death. Sightless eyes staring toward a sky wheeling with crows.

Brendan slammed his hand against the side of the wagon, pain shooting up his arm. Shattering the vision into a million dancing shards of light.

Not a vision of past battles. But a prophecy of what lay in store for the *Other* should he fail.

Roseingrave, Máelodor, Elisabeth be damned!

He wouldn't fail.

ten

"It's not as grand as you're probably used to, but it's home."
Helena ushered them into her tidy comfortable parlor with
an imperious wave of her hand before sinking into a chair,
exhaustion clear in the tight lines beside her mouth.

After days on the road, Elisabeth's bones rattled and
road dust lay in gritty layers upon her skin and in her hair.
She couldn't wait to peel herself out of her gown and scrub
every particle of her body until it squeaked.

Rogan sauntered into the room as if long familiar with
its comforts. Despite the circumstances, Elisabeth had
grown to like the enigmatic harper. Over hours of conversation, he'd proven to be a man of many talents and many
faces. Cunning and resourceful. Always quick when spirits
flagged to play a tune upon his harp and jolly them along
with a song or two.

Brendan entered last. Thinner, paler, his molten amber
eyes overlarge in his gaunt face. Elisabeth could almost see
the wheels turning as he took in the *Amhas-draoi*'s lair from

the lack of fripperies or feminine dainties to the shelves of books, a vase of fresh flowers upon a piano.

"No chains. No whips. No torture devices of any kind. You're safe enough for now, Douglas," Helena said, motioning him toward a chair by the fire.

Suddenly the marks of his illness were erased in a breathtaking smile. "I'd say that hellish trip was torture enough for one lifetime, wouldn't you?"

"Oh no, not nearly enough," Helena replied maliciously.

They'd arrived in Dublin during a downpour, the soot-stained buildings and wet streets beneath a smear of charcoal sky a welcome sight. From outside, the tidy Duke Street town house with its bright green front door, marble steps, and gleaming black railing could have been any well-to-do merchant's home. Carriages and hackneys clattered up and down the street. Next door a costermonger stood upon the area steps speaking with a housekeeper. Two smartly dressed women hurried down the pavement, a loaded footman bringing up the rear. Life went on around them as usual.

Yet, within, the signs of *Other* were palpable. Almost as if the *Fey*-born could not completely hide what they were. Or, in Helena's case, took pride in that heritage. A book left open upon a table written in some sort of cryptic rune. An odd figurine upon the mantel, carved so that from any angle it took on a different aspect, the very atmosphere charged by the unseen.

A compact version of the same faery-steeped radiance Elisabeth had experienced upon every visit to Belfoyle. And, as at Belfoyle, she experienced the same combination of excited fluttering and cold dread in the pit of her stomach.

"Drink?" Rogan offered.

Brendan shook his head. "None for me."

Rogan shrugged. Took it for himself.

"Have a seat, Douglas. We're all friends here," Helena said.

"Are we?" He crossed to the fire, his gait careful, body bearing the stiffness of the recent invalid.

He'd shed his sling yesterday, claiming it was deuced uncomfortable. Shrugged off Elisabeth's warnings he was taking things too quickly with one of his infuriating smiles and a sarcastic comment that made her fists itch. She'd not experienced such violent urges since her tomboy childhood. Come to think of it, Brendan had been the usual reason for them then as well.

He warmed his hands for a moment before turning his attention back to the group. "I think it's long past time we stopped ignoring the elephant in the room, don't you, Miss Roseingrave?"

Wariness darkened her eyes.

"Am I prisoner or guest? I like to know where I stand."

"One would think it was obvious after all we've done to see you arrive in Dublin safely."

"One thinks all sorts of things, but I like to know."

The tension thickened. Even Rogan paused in the act of pouring another whiskey to watch the game of one-upmanship.

Roseingrave eyed Brendan as one might a recalcitrant child. "Máelodor's searching for you. And he's made sure the price on your head is exceedingly tempting. On your own, how long will you last with so many on your trail?"

"Long enough, I hope."

"And Miss Fitzgerald?"

Elisabeth stiffened, feeling the eyes of everyone in the room suddenly focus upon her.

"I'll protect her," Brendan answered. "She's no reason to fear."

"As you did in Loughrea? She may want more assurances than that. After all, it's her life we're talking about. Elisabeth? What say you?"

This was their chance to escape. What she'd urged Brendan to do days ago. And now? She'd run through the options in her head, counting debts and credits as she might balance a tally sheet. Her conclusion always the same. "I say we stay," she pronounced.

Brendan's face darkened, his body stiff.

Elisabeth plowed ahead, before she changed her mind. "You said yourself, like it or not, while your shoulder is poorly, we're safest in Helena's company."

"Safety might be going a bit far," the *Amhas-draoi* answered with a cold angry light in her eyes.

"If you wanted Brendan dead, you'd have done it already," Elisabeth replied smoothly. "We've nothing to lose and all to gain by remaining here as long as you'll have us."

"And if I choose to rid the world of Douglas perfidy once and for all?"

Elisabeth allowed herself a sly smile. "You'd have a hard time explaining away a dead body. Servants talk, Helena. Murdering one's guests just isn't done."

The three of them stared at her as if she'd grown horns, when all she'd done was point out the obvious. Digging her hands into her skirts, she pressed her lips firmly together and faced them all down. It didn't take a gift for *Other* magic to grasp the core of their current situation. Merely reasonable intelligence and plain common sense. And she was tired of being treated like the thick-skulled *Duinedon* among a bevy of *Fey*-born.

Brendan recovered first. Laughter sparking his luminous gaze, he eyed her as if seeing her for the first time. "I believe I have the answer to my question."

"Answers? Who looks for answers here?"

This new voice shattered the tension like a fist through glass. An old bent woman appeared in the doorway, her parchment fine face seamed with a million tiny lines, her hands bony and gnarled as they held the door handle. "Kilronan's heir has returned." She lifted her head as if spying something beyond the horizon, invisible to the rest of them. "The last battle has truly begun."

Brendan waited for Elisabeth to be escorted to a bedchamber by Roseingrave's grandmother before rounding on his hostess. Tired of being jerked like a puppet on a string. Tired of being at her mercy. Tired period. The *Amhasdraoi*'s enigmatic comments and sidelong, searching looks grated on already shredded nerves. "What do you want from me?"

Roseingrave answered with a thin smile. "It's been a most trying few days. Time enough for explanations once you've had a good night's rest."

"If you're waiting on that, we may never get to the crux. And I don't know about you, but I grow short of witty banter."

"So abrupt. So curt. Where's your gentleman's polish? That boyish appeal that so captivates an audience?"

"You've mistaken me for my brother. Aidan's the charmer. I'm the manipulative, sarcastic recluse. Ask Lissa. She'll tell you."

"Lord Kilronan charming? You *have* been away a long time, haven't you?"

What was that cryptic comment about? Had something happened to Aidan? He'd always been the happy-go-lucky rogue with the lively wit and the clever tongue. Brendan had envied his brother's carefree attitude. Friends flocked to him. Women swooned over him. Had Father's death wrought such devastating change?

All the years away, he'd ached for his lost family. It had been hardest to cut away those connections. His brother's confidence, his sister's faith. In his memory they remained unchanged. But reality was far different. Father's death and the destruction of their family had caught them all in its wake. None of them had been left unscathed.

"You didn't pull me clear of Máelodor's killers, dig a bullet out of me, and invite me into your home out of the goodness of your heart. What's in it for you?"

Rogan and Roseingrave exchanged meaningful glances, the mage-chasing harper giving a slight shrug. "You'll never know if you don't ask, Helena."

Her frown deepened as she made a slow turn about the room, hands clasped behind her back. She faced Brendan once more, decision cut into the delicate lines of her face. "The Sh'vad Tual—where have you hidden it?"

"Someplace secure."

Her gaze hardened. "Do you realize what will happen if Máelodor opens Arthur's tomb? If he summons the last king as a *Domnuathi*? Do you truly understand the scope of such an act of villainy?"

"Easy, Helena," Rogan said, a hand upon her shoulder. "We're all tired and short-tempered. Perhaps we put this off until tomorrow."

She jerked away. "You think a nice rest and suddenly Douglas will have a change of heart? He didn't give a damn then. Nothing's changed. He's as self-serving and calculating as ever."

"You're not very skilled at this whole persuading thing, are you?" Brendan commented.

She swung back to him with a snarl. "You think this fight will be a simple case of *Other* versus *Duinedon*? Hardly. It will be *Other* versus *Other*. Just like the dark times when the Nine set brother on brother. I refuse to let that happen again."

Brendan leaned forward, anger stirring deep in his gut. "Mayhap instead of hounding me all those years, the *Amhas-draoi* should have spent their time hunting the real menace."

"We were told Máelodor had been executed. That you were the only one of the Nine left alive."

"Gervase St. John had you all fooled, didn't he?" One of the many reasons sleep eluded Brendan. The traitorous *Amhas-draoi* warrior had known ways of destruction that left no visible mark, killing slowly from the inside out. A mangled hand had been the least of it.

Roseingrave flinched, a line appearing between her brows, her scarlet lips thinning. "St. John paid for his betrayal with his life."

"If one of you can be turned, so can others. Scathach is the only one I trust. She's the only one who can give me my life back."

Helena faced him with a scoffing laugh and a toss of her head. "That's your plan? Stone or no stone, she'll kill you."

Brendan's jaw tightened. "A chance I'll take."

"The last chance you'll take. St. John was a well-placed member of the *Amhas-draoi*. It hasn't been easy to overturn his influence or persuade the brotherhood of Máelodor's survival. Not without proof. Most are still convinced you're the mastermind behind this recent threat. You've been marked for death as the last living member of the Nine."

"So what makes you believe when your brethren don't?"

She slanted him a whip-thin smile. "I've seen him. A brief glimpse, but I know he's out there. Unfortunately, he's managed to hide himself away like a spider in his lair. No leads. No way to track him."

"Magic."

"What's that?"

"He's using forbidden magic to shield himself. He must be. That kind of power can only be generated through the dark energy wrought by *Unseelie* spells."

"That makes sense." She steepled her fingers against her lips, regarding him steadily. "So if we can't find him, perhaps we let him find us."

He arched a cynical brow. "And by 'us,' you mean me."

"He's determined to capture you as a way to gain the stone. Thus, we dangle you as bait and see if he bites."

"I don't think I like the sound of that."

"But it will work."

"It very well might, but it's my ass you're dangling."

"How secure is your ass now? Scathach and the *Amhas-draoi* will never let you live. To them, you're a conscienceless murderer with the blood of hundreds on your hands."

"I didn't . . . it wasn't like that."

But what had he told Elisabeth? A sin of omission was still a sin. He might not have struck the killing blows, but his handprints lay all over the daggers that had. His ideas fed the ambitions of the group. His arrogance blinded him to the mounting evil going on under his own nose. It had taken Freddie's death to finally make him see. And by then it had been too late.

"You want your life back? Help me find and capture Máelodor," Helena argued. "Force him to stand for his crimes. The *Amhas-draoi* will finally realize who's behind this new source of trouble. They'll have to listen to me—and you."

"What of Elisabeth? Máelodor thinks she knows where the stone is hidden."

"She's safe enough while she's under my protection, but surely that's another reason to assist me. As long as Máelodor is alive, Miss Fitzgerald is in danger. You dragged her into this. It's up to you to pull her free."

He didn't answer. Instead his gaze locked on the flames. The little frame house down the hill from the churchyard. Freddie's family. Freddie. The place had gone up like a box of tinder. He'd felt the heat upon his face like the fires of hell. And known, at that moment, there would be no escape from what he'd done. He'd tried. For seven years, he'd outraced the devil, but he'd finally been caught. It was time to pay.

Miss Roseingrave resumed her slow pacing, jaw flexing. Pausing now and then to slant an evaluating stare in his direction. "What do you say, Douglas? Bait to catch a killer? End this once and for all?"

Reaching out with the lightest of mental touches, Brendan sought to read the sincerity of her declaration. Slammed against a consciousness locked tight. Probing deeper, he met a tangled honeycomb of thought designed to thwart any intrusion. If she lied, there was no way for him to know.

If you wanted Brendan dead, you'd have done it already. We've nothing to lose and all to gain.

Elisabeth's words resounded within him. . . . *nothing to lose . . . all to gain.*

And he'd run out of choices.

Reaching beneath his shirt, he pulled free the stone on its chain. Light flickered in the rough-carved faces, a smoldering burn like the leading edge of a storm cloud or the flash and fire of a smoke-filled battlefield.

Gold eyes met black. Neither one willing to flinch.

"Agreed," he said.

Bath over and dress burned, Elisabeth stood at her bedchamber window in a dressing gown. Seeing little of what passed before her eyes. Instead her gaze drew ever inward, her mind a short cab ride away in Merrion Square at the Fitzgerald town house.

Aunt Fitz and Aunt Pheeney might be there now. Worried for her. Disgusted with her. Would they understand when she told them the truth? Perhaps. But there was no way to explain it to Gordon. In his eyes, she would be compromised beyond recovery. A ruined woman. Unfit to be his bride.

The pain accompanying that thought bit deep, though it didn't shatter her as she thought it might. She'd accepted Gordon, knowing him for the solid, dependable man he was. Knowing he didn't excite her or send her into raptures. Knowing he might be her last and only chance. So what did that say about her?

"Here, now. An extra blanket in case you get cold tonight, though it's warm enough now."

Elisabeth hadn't heard Helena's grandmother come in, but there she was, her winter pippin face creased in a welcoming smile.

Killer, who usually greeted all newcomers with a token snarl, remained snoring—belly up, paws in the air—in the middle of the bed.

"Some watchdog you are," she mumbled.

The old woman eyed the dog with a long, measuring stare. "You've had him long?"

"He sort of attached himself to us on the road."

"Did he?" She studied Killer long enough that the terrier opened one lazy eye to return the shrewd gaze.

"You're very kind, Mrs., uh . . . Mrs. . . . ." Elisabeth fumbled, not knowing how to address her hostess.

Laughter rustled in the old woman's chest. "Madame Arana." She draped the blanket upon a chair. "It is nice to have a house full again. Since *ma petite* Helena's brother died, the quiet has taken over. Too many empty rooms full of sad memories."

Petite Helena? That was taking things a bit far. The *Amhas-draoi* woman had the build of an Amazon. The looks too, come to think of it. Tall, dark, and cool as ice. Even bathed and changed into clothing that didn't resemble a charwoman's Sunday best, Elisabeth felt an absolute frump in comparison.

"I will leave you now. I must see to the young man. He is a poor patient, that one. Typical male. *Plaint toujours*—always fussing. Not trusting to my skills. I know much of the old ways. He would do better to allow me to tend him."

"I wish you luck. He's exceedingly stubborn."

"Ah, but then, so am I." Madame Arana smiled, her eyes lost in the creases upon creases of her face.

Elisabeth stepped away from the window, the thick carpet a luxury under her bare feet as she crossed to the bed. Sank into its feathered depths, the faint scents of lavender rising from the sheets. "Do you know why your grand-daughter wants Brendan? Why she's doing"—she spread her hands to encompass the comfortable, well-appointed bedchamber—"all this? The *Amhas-draoi* want Brendan dead, he told me so himself. Yet we're welcomed as guests. Why?"

"You *are* a guest, Miss Fitzgerald, if an unexpected one. At no time did we predict your presence. None of my scrying ever alerted us to this possibility. This makes you an unknown. Throws all possible futures into doubt." Suddenly the golden-eyed grandmother seemed less snuggly tea and biscuits than prescient *Fey*-gifted seer. "My visions are no longer helpful."

Why had Elisabeth asked? When would she realize questions only brought answers she didn't necessarily want and bred more questions that raced like rabbits round her brain?

"Helena has searched for Brendan Douglas since word first came of his return to Ireland. The whys are clear in *Amhas-draoi* duty. The brotherhood looks to stamp out the last vestiges of the Nine. Only the manner of her seeking has changed as circumstance changed. As the visions changed. Now do you see?"

She didn't but nodded anyway. "Who are the Nine?"

"That is not my story to tell. Better to ask young Douglas if you truly wish to understand."

Therein lay the rub. Did she want to understand? Or would it only pull her in deeper?

Elisabeth placed a hand upon Killer, letting his even breathing steady her own whirling head.

"What do you know of the young man?" Madame Arana asked, a sternness to her face at odds with her earlier cheerful ebullience. "What has he told you of himself?"

"I've known Brendan forever. His family's estates march

next to ours." She lowered her gaze. "He and I were be-trothed once. Long ago. Before . . ."

"Before the Nine's destruction." Madame Arana fin-ished her sentence.

"Actually I was going to say before he ran off for parts unknown, but—"

Madame Arana continued blithely on. "Terrible times, those were. Terrible for the *Other*."

Other. The Nine. *Amhas-draoi*. It was nothing to do with her.

"Kilronan led them."

That got her attention. "Lord Kilronan?"

Helena's grandmother smiled with an I-knew-I'd-pique-your-interest-sooner-or-later look. "*Oui*, the last earl was smart. Clever. A born leader. But the Nine's greatest hopes lay with the boy. The son of Kilronan. His heir."

"Aidan was Lord Kilronan's heir. Not Brendan."

"In lands and titles, the eldest inherited. In power and skills, young Douglas was all his father hoped he'd be." De-spite her frail appearance, she stooped to poke at the fire. Toss a new log among the embers, her hands roped and tough with hard work. She straightened, lifting her gaze to Elisabeth, a gemstone sharpness in her topaz eyes. "He's back. Let's hope he's not too late. And that he's no longer the true son of his father."

"What do you mean by telling me all this?"

"You can't fight what you don't understand."

"I'm not fighting anyone. I'm going back to Dun Eyre as soon as I can."

Madame Arana shuffled toward the door, glancing back over her shoulder with an ominous glint in her bright eyes. "Are you so certain of that?"

Eleven

The whiskey appeared unsolicited at Brendan's elbow.

"You look as if you could use a drink." Rogan poured one for himself before plopping into the chair opposite.

Brendan roused himself from his contemplation of the fire long enough to stretch. "That bad?"

"Actually, you look as if you could use three or four, but we'll start slowly and work our way up to complete inebriation."

"You sound a lot like a cousin of mine. You don't know Jack O'Gara by any chance?"

Rogan paused, giving Brendan an odd look over the top of his glass. "Why?"

"No reason."

He ignored the whiskey with great difficulty. To sleep without dreams was always hardest. His usual remedy was exhaustion. Any activity that would deaden his mind and body to a collapsing point. That outlet had been denied him. So he sat. Brooded. Avoided his bed as long as he could. The steady throb in his shoulder helped. Gave him something on which to concentrate besides the gritty, sandy burn of tired eyes or the intermittent flushes of heat followed by a wash of icy cold that left him wrung like a sponge.

At least he had Rogan for company. The harper had done much to break the glacial tension between him and Miss Roseingrave. As well as being easy company. Knew when to talk and when to keep silent.

"You and Miss Roseingrave are close." As sterling repartee it lacked, but Brendan wasn't up to maintaining appearances.

"You could say that." Rogan sipped at his whiskey, his long shanks stretched toward the fire. He scratched his knuckles over the salt-and-pepper stubble of his narrow face. "I've known Helena since she wasn't two hands higher than a duck. Second cousins on her mother's side." Leaned in closer. "I'm from the disreputable branch of the family."

"I knew there was a reason you and I got on so well. So, has she always been such an amiable creature?"

Rogan laughed. "She does come off all teeth and claws, doesn't she? Suppose it comes from being *Amhas-draoi*. Not exactly known for their soft, nurturing side, are they? Guess you'd know that better than anyone." He flushed an uncomfortable shade of red. "Sorry, lad. Didn't mean it to sound so callous."

"Can't quibble with the truth."

Rogan toyed with his glass, still looking sheepish. "An ugly episode, from all I've heard. How did you . . . that is . . . they're not known for leaving loose ends."

"It's amazing how fast a man can run when his life's on the line." Had he said easy company? This line of inquiry was definitely not helping his mood. He leaned his head back, shutting his eyes.

"Forgot you said you don't drink."

He opened his eyes to see Rogan reaching across to retrieve the whiskey. Brendan's gaze locked on the glass. Mellow gold as a late summer sun. The scent stinging his nose, burning his lungs. Inhaling, he tasted its essence soft and smooth on his tongue. One glass. Surely he could have one glass. Just to sleep. To hold the dreams away. To stop remembering. To stop thinking.

He turned away. "Easier to run sober."

Silence fell over the room, but for the snap of the fire, a breeze beyond the window.

Rogan stood to retrieve his harp. Settled back into his chair, the instrument resting in his lap. He strummed a run of scales, breaking the spring ice tension growing between them. "Since we're exchanging confidences, that Miss Fitzgerald of yours is a spirited lass. Facing you and Helena down as she did tonight"—he gave a low whistle—"the looks on your faces were priceless."

Brendan gave a soft, smiling shake of his head. "Couldn't fault her logic. A body would be a deuced hard thing to keep from the staff." He smothered a laugh. "She may look soft and sweet, but rile her and she's a force of nature. Have to say it was a relief to see her sinking her claws into someone else for a change."

"She spoke once of her betrothed. . . ."

Brendan grimaced. "Mr. Gordon Shaw. A young man of impeccable character and mediocre disposition. Bloody sod."

The harper chuckled, the tune arranging itself into a haunting lament. "Is that how it is?"

"Is what how it is? Lissa? And me? Not likely."

The music eased the whiskey's lingering temptation. Filling the empty parts of him with something other than alcohol. He'd forgotten the feeling of simple peace such moments brought. It had been long since he'd the leisure to listen. Longer since he'd enjoyed playing himself. It had once been his favorite amusement. A way to forget Father's mounting expectations. Aidan's guarded envy. Even Sabrina and Mother in their own quieter ways required something from him, whether it be love or duty.

He could always put that aside as he focused on the complicated twining melody and harmony of left hand and right. Lay aside the burdens of filial responsibility and the weight of fraternal confidence. No one counted on him. No one needed him. He could simply exist.

His final evening at Dun Eyre had been the first time he'd attempted the Mozart. Elisabeth's arrival in the music room had surprised him. Her questions dragging his old desire for freedom from shadow into light. But with it came something else. A remembrance of the girl who'd been the only one not to see him as either prodigy or threat. She'd never wanted anything from him other than friendship. Never offered him anything but quick laughter and a sure smile. The only one to see him as he saw himself in those brief naked moments while playing.

He'd hidden his shock at such a revelation well. Hell, he'd buried that split second's sentimentality beneath a ton of earth and sarcasm. She'd never guessed. Gone away assured of his patent bastardy. The earth remained turning upon an axis he understood.

Until tonight.

Tonight he'd looked on her and seen not the Lissa of

his memories but a woman completely unknown to him and utterly fascinating. Composed. Self-assured. And attractive as hell.

He leaned his head back against the chair. Closed his eyes. "Elisabeth hates me, and I can't say I blame her. I tore her away from said husband-to-be. Not sure how to put that one to rights, but I'll think of something. I usually do."

Rogan chuckled. "You care for her. It comes through in your voice. The way you drink her in whenever she's near."

"I've known her since she was dragging round a one-eyed doll and pestering me to let her play cricket with the boys. She's like a little sister."

Elisabeth's face swam before his scratchy, tired eyes. A wreath of wild red hair. Eyes dark and sweet. His heart turned over in his chest with a sharp, stabbing pain, grief finally pulling him under like one of the riptides off Belfoyle's coast.

A vision of past or future?

Or merely one more misdeed for which punishment still waited?

Shrugging out of his jacket, Brendan hissed at the jaw-clenching stab to the bone accompanying the simple gesture. Damned shoulder. He couldn't afford an injury now. Not with the hunters beating him toward the guns. It would take two good arms to escape the encircling net. A head clear of the fever fog. Perhaps let Roseingrave's grandmother have a look at it after all.

He sank onto the bed, unknotting his cravat. Unbuttoning his waistcoat. Trying not to jar his shoulder more than he had to. Pulling his shirt over his head brought tears to his eyes. Bending to remove his boots left him woozy as the pain in his shoulder moved up into his brain. He barely heard the knock upon his door—the faintest tapping followed by a whisper.

He rose to answer, taking care to plaster himself in the easy, roguish confidence Elisabeth expected. Anything less and she'd begin to doubt. Or worry. If he was to keep her safe, he needed her trust in him to remain secure and unshakable.

He wouldn't explore too closely why he desired her faith.

She stood in the doorway in a dressing gown of sheerest linen, collar and cuffs of lemon silk. Her plaited hair shining vivid red and burnished gold. Wisps and curls of deep mahogany and bright chestnut escaping to halo her head. A lock lying just behind her ear. Another across her forehead.

The dressing gown emphasized the rise and fall of her generous breasts, slid invitingly over her hips, the shadows in every fold following the long curves of her legs. "I'm up here," she said tartly.

Brendan let his eyes drift reluctantly upward.

He desired her faith, not her body, though that was a claim harder to deny.

And if she chose to come to his bedchamber clothed for seduction, he'd have to be a eunuch not to imagine.

He caught her gaze wandering over his chest and his blasted tattoo. Clearly her curiosity was damn near killing her, but she said nothing, and he gritted his teeth and allowed her to look her fill.

"Should I be flattered or concerned?" he asked lazily, laying a casual hand upon a bedpost. To her, it would look like the practiced move of a rake. She'd never know it was the only thing holding him upright.

She blinked, gathering her lost aplomb. "Let's try honest. What does Helena want, Brendan? She must have told you."

"She did, but it's naught to worry you." He gripped the bedpost more tightly. The pain in his shoulder came and went, but the fever clung. Hot and then cold. A sheen of sweat spreading across his back as his teeth chattered. If she didn't leave soon, she'd be treated to his spectacular collapse. Not a sight to inspire confidence.

"This is a prison for you, isn't it?" she asked, a steel gleam in her dark eyes. "Pleasant enough, but you're as trapped as if you were locked in a cell. Am I right?"

"I've known prisons, Elisabeth. I'll take Miss Roseingrave's hospitality, however grudgingly it's given, any day."

"That's not answering my question. Madame Arana spoke of the Nine. She said your father led them and that the brotherhood seeks to destroy them."

"Madame Arana needs to keep her mouth shut."

"It's true, then?"

"The Nine died with my father, Elisabeth. All but for Máelodor."

"He knew your father?"

He closed his eyes for a brief moment. The voices, the faces, the memories pounding in his brain with each throb of his shoulder. "Once upon a time, they were close as brothers. The two of them shared a great pride in their *Fey* heritage and the powers borne with that blood legacy."

"And then?" Her eyes shone black in the candlelight, deep midnight wells he could drown in. She shifted impatiently, the collar of her robe gaping to reveal the slope of her shoulder and the deep curve of one breast.

He needed to end this conversation and get her out of here before either he spoke of things best left unsaid or acted on urges best left unacted upon. "Father was murdered. Máelodor fled. The Nine were no more."

"And the Sh'vad Tual?"

His mouth curved in a suggestive smile. "Rested in the perfect curve of the perfect breasts of a beautiful lady for seven years."

He could almost feel the daggers shooting from her eyes. Exactly what he looked for. Yet instead of turning tail, she pressed further. A damned dog with a bone. "If both of you are out to destroy Máelodor, perhaps you and Helena could come to an understanding."

"Who said anything about destroying Máelodor? I'm out to stay alive long enough to deliver the stone to safety. Destroying Máelodor I'll leave to the professionals."

"But—"

"If we're going to exchange pillow talk"—his gaze drifted over her before traveling to the thick colorful blankets, the bevy of pillows—"I'm not up to outrageous gymnastics, but I could manage in a pinch."

Her face flooded with scarlet, full lips squashing to a prim line, chin lifting in a belligerent tilt. "I'm going to assume you're delirious with fever. That, or it's as I suspected all along, and you're raving bonkers."

His gaze slid over the ripe curvature of hip, torso, and breasts. The trace of girlish freckles almost swallowed by a scarlet flush. He gritted his teeth as parts of him went rock-hard. "Merely curious. Had things worked out differently you and I—"

"Would have murdered each other by now." She cleared her throat. "Can we please concentrate on the topic at hand? Helena Roseingrave? The stone? A way to untangle ourselves from this mess?"

"So we're still a 'we,' Lissa?" he asked softly. Invitingly.

Her eyes shone dark and luminous, the candle's reflection flickering in their velvet depths. Or did he imagine that ever-so-slight glimmer? That shuttered gaze trailing over his bare chest to linger for a moment upon the tattoo trailing over his shoulder? That taut pause lasting a beat too long?

He wanted to touch her. To feel that skin beneath his hands. To trace a path with his lips over the body he could imagine lay beneath the virginal white of her chemise.

He couldn't help himself. He risked releasing his grip on the bedpost to step toward her, clenching his teeth in what, to her, must have looked like a particularly wolfish smile, since she scurried back as if she thought he was about to fling himself on her.

"Stop it."

He leaned closer, his lips inches from hers, the scent of her skin filling his nostrils. She smelled of lemons and lavender and very faintly of desire and temptation. "Lissa?"

"Why do you ruin everything?" She shuddered, her voice almost a mew of pain. "Why are you such a beast?"

She threw open the door to escape, her robe dragging behind her like a train, her plait twitching like an angry cat's tail.

He fell wobbly legged into a chair, shoulder throbbing at the same rapid tempo as his heart. Leaning his head back, he squeezed his eyes shut, the imprint of that luscious hourglass figure burned into his eyelids. The sweep of heat washing up from his groin to his brain not completely fever-related.

Why indeed?

Elisabeth retraced her steps, angry with herself and furious at Brendan.

He was a horrid, annoying beast.

Couldn't he be serious for five minutes? Five bloody minutes! That's all she asked.

Are we still a "we"?

The way he'd said it as if he meant it. The way his stare torched a path over her body. The slide of silken muscles as he reached for her, the sensual curve of his lips as he smiled.

Why couldn't he return from the dead fat, bald, and wrinkled? Why did he have to explode his way back into her life like some fallen angel: all fire and ice and brutal good looks? On top of that, did he truly expect her to swoon at his feet just as if he'd never left? Never abandoned her all those years ago?

Fool that she was, that's exactly what she'd been about to do. One more second in his dangerous presence and she'd have crumbled.

She descended the steps to the second floor. Tiptoed down the corridor to her bedchamber.

"Douglas has agreed, Grand-mère."

Miss Roseingrave. Madame Arana. Their voices coming from the chamber beside hers, the door ajar.

Dismissing her ill manners as necessary, Elisabeth crept closer. If Brendan wouldn't tell her what was going on, she'd find another way to gain the information. Besides, if they'd not wanted eavesdroppers, they should have made sure the door was shut properly.

"And Mademoiselle Fitzgerald?" Madame Arana asked.

"As it stands, Douglas has ruined her. Among her kind, such a scandal will be all but impossible to overcome."

Not that she hadn't known it before, but to hear it spoken so casually sent panic fluttering up from Elisabeth's stomach into her throat. Inhaling deeply, she pushed the fear away. She would deal with the aftermath . . . after.

"That may be, *ma minette*, but I begin to believe there is a purpose behind her presence."

"She's *Duinedon*, Grand-mère. What possible help could she give?"

"In this fight, we do not know what will be the most useful bow in our quiver."

There was that word again—fight. What on earth could she do in a battle where magic gained and lost all? Helena was right. Elisabeth *was* just *Duinedon*, though for the first time the realization didn't comfort her as it had in the past.

"You said yourself the visions are unclear and cast all in riddles," Helena challenged. "Could it be it's not the Sight guiding you but your enjoyment of a houseful of guests?"

A raspy chuckle followed. "You do not go out as you used to. The invitations. The calling cards. I see them come, Helena, yet you shut yourself away. It has been a year, *ma minette*. Grieve, yes, but do you think he would have wanted you to stop living?"

Holding her breath, Elisabeth leaned closer in anticipation of the answer.

Below her, a door closed, steps crossed the corridor.

Someone was coming.

Scurrying the final steps to her bedchamber, Elisabeth closed her door. Leaned back against the panels, catching her breath. Helena's declaration pounding in her head with every beat of her heart.

Ruined.

Helena was right. That future no longer existed. There

would be no marriage. No life in London. No glittering parties or magnificent balls. Gordon would have to be mad to wed her after this. That, or madly in love. He'd never been either one of those things.

Ruined.

She waited for the panic to flood through her once more. Nothing.

Instead, the spark of an idea burst forth. An incredible idea. A ridiculous idea. An idea with disaster written all over it.

But then again, what choice did a ruined woman have?

twelve

"Let me make absolutely certain I understand you." Brendan tapped a finger against his chin as he paced back and forth across her carpet. He'd been engaged thusly for almost a full half hour.

"For heaven's sake, Brendan, you've been going round and round forever. It's not alchemy. I'm not asking you to turn iron into gold. Merely turn a lady of easy virtue into an honest woman."

"Iron into gold . . . easier," he muttered under his breath.

"What's that? I didn't quite hear you."

"Do you know what you're asking? I mean on the face of it, it sounds reasonable enough, but do you have any idea what marrying me would do to you?"

"Rescue me from a life riddled with humiliation and shame? Lessen the disgrace my disappearance with you has caused me and my family? Allow me to hold my head up in polite society? Make right your unconscionable behavior? Have I left anything out?"

"Align the planets and hold back the tides? As I said, iron into gold—ow!" He rubbed his left arm.

"And I'll give you a knuckler to your bad shoulder if you don't shape up."

"Why must you always resort to violence to win your arguments?"

"Why must you always joke? It's not funny, Brendan. Not in the least little bit. Even if I turned up today, Gordon Shaw wouldn't marry me. He's a good man, but he's no saint. He'll not jeopardize his future for me, and I wouldn't ask it of him. That leaves you, young Lochinvar."

He grimaced. "I was afraid you'd say that."

If you're half the man I think you are, you'll do the right thing and marry me."

"Dash it all, Lissa, I'm not even a quarter of that man. And marrying me . . . it's . . . well . . . it's more than likely you'll end up a widow within a week."

"A respectable widow."

He came to a sudden halt in the middle of the floor, wearing an odd expression that might have been contemplation or might have been sheer and complete panic. Hard to distinguish.

Shaking his head, he grumbled, "I'm an ass . . . be worse . . . dead and it won't matter anyway . . ." His attention snapped back to her, eyes bright as lamps. "You win. Miss Elisabeth Fitzgerald, will you do me the honor?" A twinkle gleamed in his eyes. Laughter in his voice as he added, "Again?"

"I still can't believe you managed to keep such a sacred relic hidden for so long." Helena Roseingrave leaned back in her chair, her stare like a razor as she sipped at her wine.

Brendan nervously tapped his thigh with one hand, guts in knots. He'd surrendered possession of the stone, but he didn't have to like it.

Roseingrave continued to study the Sh'vad Tual, though she made no move to pick it up. Perhaps sensing how close to grabbing up the stone and fleeing for the door he really was.

"Why did you do it, Douglas?" she asked calmly. "Why start such madness? Greed? Ambition? The Earl of Kilronan already had wealth and influence. Was it pride? Arrogance?"

A smile twisted the corner of his mouth. "It was power—pure and simple."

Her eyes widened, body tightening as she straightened in her chair to place her wineglass upon a table.

"It began as a noble lost cause," he continued. "*Other* and *Duinedon* coexistence, but it wasn't long before all those high-minded principles were stripped away, leaving the ugly truth. What could we do? How far could we go? Where would it lead us?"

"And?" she asked.

His nerves jumped beneath his skin, the stone's fire burning before his eyes. The battlefield. The corpses. His brother lying dead upon a mound of bodies.

"It's led me here," he said finally.

He stalked the room, feeling her steel gaze always on him. The mental push against his mind as she sought to see beneath the surface of his mind. He pushed back, no unschooled novice open to anyone who sought to read him. He might not be *Amhas-draoi*, but his powers were no less formidable.

She laughed. "You're as strong as they say."

" 'They'?"

"Your brother. Your sister. They didn't exaggerate your skills." She sounded almost impressed.

Pain slid like a knife into his heart. Aidan. Sabrina. It had been easier when half a world lay between them. When return had been impossible. Now? Hope only deepened the agony of his exile.

"A shame you chose to use such gifts for an evil purpose," she added.

"At the time"—he shrugged, refusing to allow her to see his weakness—"it seemed the only purpose."

Only after he'd fallen victim to the drink and opium had he realized the similarities between those addictions and his relentless need to master the forbidden magics. That his hunger for knowledge had become a seductive obsession riding dangerously close to madness. And like the drink and the drugs, complete and total abstinence had been his answer.

Until Ireland.

Until now.

Roseingrave drummed her fingers upon the arm of her chair, her expression grave. The fire reflecting in the black of her eyes. "You really think Arthur's resurrection is possible? That he might return to rule again?"

Asked quietly but with power enough to force an answer. Did she think to trap him into a confession? Was she looking for an explanation? Motivation?

"Máelodor's managed it once already."

"The creature Lazarus," she replied. "*He* managed to escape Máelodor's enslavement."

Brendan looked deep into the fire, remembering a cottage. A man in a desperate struggle for his soul.

Brendan's sister, Sabrina, had risked everything to help the *Domnuathi* fight free of his dark possession in order to gain a life with him.

"And in doing so, only hardened Máelodor's resolve," Brendan replied. "The man won't fail a second time. Should Máelodor get as far as opening the tomb—should the bones of the king fall into his hands—Arthur will return a slave-born soldier of Domnu. No woman's love will be enough to save *him*."

The question hovered at the edges of Brendan's mind: but could love save him, or would he destroy Elisabeth first?

No way to know.

There.

Brendan felt it again.

The numbing tingle just below his skin. The seeking brush of a mind against his own. A powerful *Other* by the focused thread of mage energy. A determined *Other*, as this was the third such tracing he'd sensed in less than an hour.

Every nerve bristled, every beat of his heart pushing him closer to a dangerous decision. How easy it would be to cast a cloaking spell and hide within its concealing folds as he obscured his trail before returning to Duke Street.

Instead, he tipped his hat past a chattering group of giggly young women being shepherded down Dame Street by an eagle-eyed doyenne, stepped off the pavement, threading his way between a coal man's wagon and a crested carriage driven by a pair of blood bays. Mingled into a crowd of shoppers headed east toward College Green until he reached the corner before the bank, where he swung out of the press of bodies and into the quiet side street.

Drawing up into a doorway, he concentrated on following the touch upon his mind back to its source.

He was not a true mage-chaser. The limited ability he possessed had been bought with much sweat and study, but at the least he might discover if he was still being followed.

The echoes rippled back to him on a sooty, foggy breeze. The mage energy surfacing up into his consciousness as a ribbon of curling, twisting pearl and gray. Clean. Pure. Diamond-brilliant. Nothing muddy or diluted. This mind had been trained by the best.

Amhas-draoi.

That changed everything.

There was no margin for error in a test of wills against one of Scathach's warriors. And no second chances. It was draw upon his powers or be killed.

Brendan threw out a cloaking spell as wide as he could. Exhausting, but it might buy him a few crucial minutes. At the same time, he passed a hand over his features, settling the camouflaging *fith-fath* over him, the itch and prickle of the magic burrowing into his facial muscles. Lengthening his chin. Blunting his nose. Darkening his hair and eyes. His skin now pouched and craggy with middle age.

His brain hummed with effort as he juggled the separate magics, his muscles taut and jumping. He smiled at the feverish eagerness igniting his blood.

Stepping back out of the shelter of the doorway, he followed the side street north. Ambling his slow but deliberate way north and east. No hurry. No rush. Nothing about him drawing attention. Sweat dampened his shirt to his back, his limbs tiring with every step as the magic drained him. He wasn't up to this. Not such a complicated dance of power. It had been too long and he remained annoyingly weak from the wound to his shoulder. A few more moments and he'd falter for certain. Already the cloaking spell's shielding destabilized to a hazardous point.

He rounded a corner and there it was—the answer to his prayers. In the middle of the block. Indistinguishable from the surrounding buildings. Just one more gentleman's club among a city that boasted a host of such elegant gathering spots for the elite, yet he could well imagine the reaction were that same city ever to discover what sort of elite congregated there.

Mages skilled in the art of war. Scathach's brotherhood. The order of *Amhas-draoi*.

Instant death if he was caught.

Escape if he were lucky.

He sensed the overwhelming confluence of magics as a deep drone vibrating at the base of his skull, saturating the air, rippling through the ground. Buffeting him in the cross-current like flotsam tossed upon a wave. A perfect storm of power to mask him. Better than the best cloaking spell. And enough mingled trails to throw off any determined chaser.

Just as he came abreast of the building, he slid into the adjacent alley, dropping his magics as if shedding a cloak. Instantly the weight lifted from his shoulders, the fog from his mind. From here on, he'd rely on street smarts and cunning learned in the sun-baked markets and winding streets of the Levant, where to hesitate meant the difference between life and death.

His smile widened to a grin.

It still did.

"So you're going to make an honest woman out of her. You're a good man, Brendan Douglas. I don't care what Helena says."

Brendan shot a sidelong glance at the long-shanked harper reclining with drink and pipe in front of the fire. "I can only imagine what ulterior motive she's attached to the idea," Brendan answered, scowling into his coffee. He'd been backed into a corner by Elisabeth, and while a part of him thrilled to the enticing idea, the bits not hard as a rock recoiled in abject terror.

Rogan plunked his brandy upon the table with enough force to rattle the accompanying decanter. "Should I be offering congratulations or condolences?"

Brendan rasped his knuckles over his chin, noting the dirt still crusted beneath his nails. The scrape across his palm where he'd jumped a fence.

A long soak in a hot tub hadn't been enough to completely erase hints of his afternoon's adventure, though at least his muscles no longer felt like wet noodles nor did he smell like a sewer. Unfortunately, the same could not be said for his clothes, which a horrified maid had retrieved with a pinched nose and much grumbling.

"Hold off on either for the time being. The shine may not be off her ring before she's pawning it to pay for my funeral. No doubt what she's banking on."

Rogan chuckled, eyes twinkling as if he knew a secret. "I don't think you need fear that. The two of you circle each other like two wary dogs, but it will only take one of you to unbend for the other to follow."

"Harper, mage-chaser, *and* love doctor extraordinaire? Your talents never cease to amaze me."

"I'm not blind. I can see what you both refuse to. She, out of pride. You, out of fear."

"Thank you for your expert analysis of the situation. If I'm not dead soon, I may even follow your advice."

"Dead? Who's dead?"

Elisabeth stood at the door. Her red hair upswept and backlit by candlelight, she seemed spun of fire and starshine. Brendan's breath caught in his chest, unable to peel his eyes from the seductive slide of fabric over her hips as she walked. The tantalizing curve of her breasts only emphasized by the silken shawl she'd draped over her shoulders.

Both gentlemen stood as she entered.

"No one," Brendan said. "Rogan and I were merely chatting."

She'd proposed. He'd accepted. Not the traditional order of things, but then, nothing about their relationship had ever been conventional. They'd grown up together, close as siblings. He'd agreed to their original betrothal out of duty not affection. And barely given a thought to the girl he'd deserted when he fled *Amhas-draoi* retribution. Like Belfoyle and his broken family, she'd merely been one more lost piece of a past he needed to forget if he'd any chance of survival.

He never could have imagined the frustrating, clinging shadow of his youth would mature into a desirable, alluring woman. Or his own intense reaction to that transformation. It was damned embarrassing was what it was. Lusty urges aside, he needed a wife like he needed a damned hole in the head. Though, at the moment, lust seemed to be winning the battle.

He hastily turned away from her, plunking himself down at the piano. The instrument very adequately hiding his awkward response to her arrival.

Rogan stretched, giving a broad fake yawn. "And we've chatted ourselves into a stand-off. I'll bid the two of you good night." He winked at Elisabeth as he passed her in the doorway. "I'd not waste a moment, pet. It may be all you get."

She frowned. "I wish he wouldn't say things like that. I don't need him to remind me we're hanging by a thread."

Brendan's hands found their natural way to the keys. The little run of notes a play for time. "You worry too much."

She entered farther into the room, glancing around as if expecting the buffer of others. Taken aback at their solitude if the slight hesitation was any indication. Still, it didn't stop her. She strode forward as if charging a cannon, eyes determined, hands gripped at her sides. "And you not enough."

"One can worry only so long before checking behind every doorway becomes a tiresome habit. I prefer to enjoy the semblance of life left to me. For as long as it's left to me."

"Are you saying I shouldn't be concerned at the current mess my life has become?" she demanded.

"Not at all. If I were you I'd be damned worried. After all, marriage to the Douglas family pariah may not quell gossip as much as it will veer it into new and titillating directions."

Her expression firmed to stubbornness. Her gaze flickered with something like challenge and she not only stayed but crossed to lean against the piano. He'd give her points for backbone. "A hasty marriage to a confirmed rogue is still a marriage. I may not be wed well, but I'll be well wed. As I've been told more than once, I'm not getting any younger."

He couldn't stop himself. His gaze traveled over her like a caress, sliding down the column of her slender throat to dip into the curve of her ripe round breasts before lazily retracing its slow, delicious course. "That's your only incentive for marriage to me? How lowering to my self-esteem."

A spark of either anger or desire flickered in the depths of her eyes. Impossible to determine, though the hitch in her breathing gave him a clue. "Somehow I think your self-esteem manages quite well."

Lost in the playing and his own salacious thoughts, he didn't notice her growing discomfort until she snapped, banging her fingers upon the keys in a crash of jarring notes. "Must you play that horrid piece of music? I'm sick to death of it."

He arched a brow. "Something against old Amadeus?"

"It . . . that is . . . of course not," she blundered. "I just don't like that particular piece. Play something else."

He thought for a moment before dropping into the simple, sweet notes of an old folk song. One that always reminded him of foggy cliffs, the growl of the ocean, and home.

Coming back to Ireland had unchained demons it had taken him years to shackle.

People he'd loved.

People he'd hurt.

The shades of his past moved freely now through the chambers of his mind.

When he'd fled Belfoyle, he'd tried armoring himself in cold, mocking contempt; his only weapon against the agony of having his life ripped out from under him. Scorn an easier emotion to swallow than bitter despair. And even that he'd only managed to choke down with copious amounts of alcohol and then opium in all its destructive forms.

He'd not choose that path again. Yet what release was left to him? How else to drown the voices?

He looked up from the keys to meet the dark heat of Elisabeth's eyes, a stray curl of burnished red hair loosed to fall invitingly against her neck. Did she know what she asked of him? Did she understand what he was? Would she be one more name on that bloody list of those he'd hurt? One more face haunting his dreams?

He stumbled to his feet and away from the piano. No, he wouldn't let that happen. He might have failed everyone else, but he'd at least keep her safe. If aught else blew up in his face, that was one thing he could do right.

"What's wrong?" She touched him, barely a brush of her fingers, but his nerves jumped, his heart pounding in his chest as if he'd been running. "Is it your shoulder?"

If only it were so simple.

This was Elisabeth. Freckles and curls. Hunting blennies in the shallows below Belfoyle and wild gallops across the high fields. He sought to cling to that vision he held in his head, but it was a memory fast fading beneath the glow of the woman standing in front of him. The long curves, the stubborn chin, the tangle of hair in a thousand shades of red.

Would she cringe from him if she knew the truth? Would she change her mind about marrying him if she understood who he was? What he was? What he'd done?

"This marriage, Lissa. Are you sure you want to go through with it?"

She stiffened. "Trying to wriggle off the hook? I'm not sure of anything, but you've left me no choice."

He opened his mouth to argue, the words hovering unspoken on a breath. The moment spinning out to a gossamer thinness of expectation.

Run, Lissa. Run as fast and as far as you can away from me.

That's what he meant to say. Instead, he lowered his mouth to hers, the warmth of her lips easing the ache beneath his ribs. The heat of her body soothing the steel grip of desperation.

She stiffened in his arms, her mew of protest becoming a whimper of surrender as his tongue skimmed her lower lip before dipping within. As he inhaled her gasped shock, arousal arced through him, the taste of her like the sweetest wine. The fragrance of her desire rising to mingle with the floral scent of her perfume.

She should be screaming bloody murder. Struggling. It was Elisabeth. He half expected a set of fives to the jaw. Not this enticing witches' brew of innocence and eagerness as she looped her hands behind his neck, the long soft weight of her pressed the length of him.

Had he called Elisabeth unpredictable? She was bloody irrational.

He should stop. Step away. End this before it went any further.

Instead, he kissed her cheek, the tender spot behind her ear, down her neck. Her hands were in his hair as she pressed closer. As she answered his assault with her own attack.

Inhaling the heady mingled scents of skin and perfume, he cupped the fullness of her breasts, rubbing the dark aureoles through the thin lawn of her chemise, her breath coming shallow and fast. Ribbons loosed. Fabric parting. His tongue teased the slope of her collarbone before dropping lower.

She needed to stop him. He couldn't stop himself. Instead, as had happened in her bedchamber back at Dun

Eyre, her timidity lasted barely the space between two beats of his heart before the sensual hoyden took over. Keen to follow his lead wherever it might wander. A dangerous trust that would end in trouble.

He took a nipple in his mouth, tonguing it until she threw her head back, her fingers threaded in his hair, quick inhalations rising and falling beneath him.

Rucking the sheer fabric of her gown up against her legs, he followed the swell of her thighs to the ribbons of her garters, the wet heat of her center.

She gasped, her eyes flying open.

He withdrew, just enough to leave her wanting. Her eyes grew black with desire, her face passing through a thousand expressions and emotions in a half second. The tightening spiral of arousal feeding his own desire.

She pulled free his shirt, skimming her hands up the line of his ribs over his chest.

Blood seemed to leave his brain for his groin, making him dizzy. Not the head-spinning effect of too much drink, but a wild exhilaration akin to mastering a half-broke horse or finally grasping an impossible piece of sorcery. It was the joy of discovery. A sweet marveling in the infinite.

His cock throbbed like a second painful heartbeat. Gods, he'd explode in another second.

She fumbled at the waist of his breeches, her fingers unskilled, her mind too absorbed to focus on the simple mechanics of buttons.

"Please," she whimpered as his thumb rubbed at her most sensitive flesh.

It would be so easy to have her now. To have her writhing beneath him as he took his pleasure. She would regret her easy compliance in the morning. She would hate him as she should. That would be the best thing he could do for her.

Instead, he tore himself free with a groan, his whole body crackling with unfulfilled desire. "Not like this, Lissa," he whispered.

She gazed upon him, dazed and glassy-eyed, her hair falling free of its pins to curl wild about her face. Her lips bruised and full from his kisses.

He bent to retrieve her shawl, wrapping her in its folds as he might a child. Kissing her brow. Smoothing her hair. His movements shaky and awkward as he fought back his desire.

"Brendan?" she asked softly, already a furious scarlet washing over her pale cheeks. "You left me once before at the altar. You won't do it again, will you?"

"No, sweet Lissa. On my honor, I won't."

It was only long after she'd left him and the fire had burned to cold ash that he realized the voices remained silent. The ghosts had receded. Only one face burned in his mind's eye—a tempestuous beauty with eyes dark and warm as oak. Only one voice called to him with touching uncertainty.

He closed his hand into a painful fist. Whispered, "On my honor," to the empty room.

For whatever that was worth anymore.

thirteen

Brendan browsed the Roseingrave library shelves. Not exactly a cornucopia of research material, but it would have to do.

He'd stumbled to bed close to dawn. Immediately fallen into a confusion of bizarre dreams. Not unusual. To sleep without the constant nightmares was a rare occurrence. But these dreams had been different. They'd not been the usual ghostly visitations leaving him drenched in a cold sweat. Instead, he'd wandered a field of corpses, a red sun sinking through a smoke-shrouded sky. Scattered bonfires raged, fed with the bodies of *Other*, while thieves and camp followers picked among the dead and dying. Smoke and gunpowder and the stench of burning flesh lay upon his tongue and burned his nose. His body ached, blood dripping from a gash in his head, but he held to his feet with a will born of fear. Aidan was out here somewhere. His brother lay among the fallen. He wasn't supposed to be here. This wasn't his fight.

Looked for or not, this will become his fight. He is Other. *And you are his brother. He will come for you.*

The king stood behind him, his usual flame of red hair plastered to his skull with sweat and blood. He pointed with the broken edge of his blade.

There. Among a pile of dead, their staring eyes and twisted limbs holding no hope. Brendan dropped to his knees, gathering his brother against his chest.

Did you think we could win? You should have known. The story of Arthur has only one end. It is my curse and my fate. The Fey *have spoken. What can mere mortals do against that? What can you do?*

Brendan woke shuddering and sick, the king's sorrow like a stone in his own chest. Had this been a premonition? Foreknowledge? Bad dreams brought on by food poisoning?

The sun had risen on a mind heavy with questions and sluggish with exhaustion. If he'd had to dream, why couldn't it have been about Elisabeth? The slide of her body against his. The glow in her eyes. The heat of her sex.

He scrubbed his face as if he could expunge the memory of her from his brain. He'd agreed to this marriage out of guilt. His name for her honor. But he refused to entertain notions of anything more. Not when his future remained uncertain. When just being in his company could destroy her.

He'd spelled disaster and death for everyone he'd ever loved. He'd not add Elisabeth to the list of those who'd gotten too close and been burned for their trouble. Alone worked for him. Alone meant no one got hurt. Alone meant safe.

Firm on that point, he pulled up a chair, opening the book, leafing the index for any Arthurian reference. What had he missed? Where had he gone wrong? And what more could he do to stop Máelodor?

"Something has happened." Madame Arana stood at the door, eyes gleaming strangely in a solemn face. "I feel the change."

He started up. "Lissa? Is she all right? What's—"

The woman smiled. "Miss Fitzgerald is safe. Whether she remains so resides with you. But you know that already, don't you? The safety of us all lies in your hands."

He'd had his questions about Madame Arana. Here was his answer. "What do you know of it?"

"I know that you search to leave the path your father laid for you. That there is a war inside you always. A struggle against your past, your guilt, your very power. This battle colors all you do."

"What the hell would you know of my struggles unless"—he arched a brow in question—"you scryed me. Clever old girl. Like what you saw?"

She drew herself up in indignation. "There is no need for scrying when all lies clear upon the surface for any to read. Your mask slips, son of Kilronan. The growing strain of these years is written in every line and every shadow upon your features." She shivered, her bony hands pressed against her stomach. "But I woke this morning with a new vision shifting the patterns like fingers stirring the water. Ripples that cloud the surface of my sight, making all unclear. A man. A sword. I will know what it means, or"—she folded her arms over her chest, lifting her chin in a look of defiance, her eyes throwing a challenge—"no lunch for you."

As if on cue, his empty stomach growled in protest. "That's hitting below the belt."

"I did not want to resort to such diabolical means, but you leave me no choice."

He pondered bodily lifting her out of the doorway and locking it behind her. Doubted Roseingrave would countenance manhandling her grandmother. Withholding meals would be the least of what she might do to him. And now Madame Arana . . . Fine. She wanted to poke her nose into his business? Why not? Serve her bloody well right.

"What do you know of the history of Arthur the king?"

"He is dead and must stay that way if our people are not to be drawn into a war we cannot win."

"But what of the man himself?"

A smile creased her eyes. "I may be old, but I'm not quite that ancient."

"Very funny. You asked what changed. I'm trying to tell you. I discovered something about Arthur I need to verify. Something about a *Fey* curse. A fate that cannot be changed."

"I know nothing of Arthur, but the *Fey* are known to play deep games with us. They do not define good and evil as we do. Nor does the race of man—*Other* or *Duinedon*—figure largely in their lives. Only when they see a threat to themselves will they notice us, and more often than not it is to our detriment. Tread carefully if you seek to tamper with a curse laid by the *Fey*. You may stir up more than you bargained for."

"Wouldn't be the first time. If you hadn't noticed, I'm expert at bringing trouble down upon myself and anyone else standing too near me."

"Yes, but Máelodor, for all his malevolence, still holds a human soul. We can understand the forces pushing him, even if they are repugnant to us. The *Fey* exist beyond our comprehension. We can no more know what moves them than we can know what moves the universe to spin. That is trouble of an unimaginable scale."

"I can imagine a lot more than you think."

"Search if you must." The far-seeing diviner shrank back into the wizened little old lady, but there was no stuffing that genie back in the bottle. He knew her for what she was now. He'd not underestimate her again. She patted him on the shoulder, chuckling as she left him. "I will keep your lunch warm."

Elisabeth lifted her face to the sun, warmth seeping through her chilled body, though the limpid breeze fluttering at her skirts was more redolent of coal smoke and cisterns than green fields and shaded glades.

Killer pawed at the flower beds lining the trimmed garden path, his little nose twitching with excitement. At least someone was happy with the odors.

"Stop that, you naughty dog," she scolded. "Miss Roseingrave and her grandmother won't let us out here if you insist on destroying their narcissus."

Was it her imagination, or did Killer pause in his digging just long enough to spear her with the same sneering contempt she'd seen on Brendan's face last night?

The poor narcissus didn't stand a chance.

She couldn't blame Killer. In another moment, she'd get on her hands and knees to join him. What else was there to do? Inertia was driving Elisabeth mad. Unable to leave the house without an escort. No occupation for her hands but needlework, which she'd always detested. Helena Roseingrave didn't even have a library to speak of. At least not the kind with books one would read for entertainment.

Boredom gave her far too much time to think. Never a good thing. Especially now, when thinking invariably led to Brendan. Then thinking about Brendan and last night. Then thinking about last night and her humiliating surrender. Thinking about the seductive kisses, caressing hands, a torrent of dizzying emotion and feeling that left her barely able to . . . think.

A circular roundaboutation bringing her right back where she started. The April sun wasn't the only reason her cheeks burned and her gown clung uncomfortably to her back like a damp second skin.

All this not thinking was driving her mad.

Throwing herself to her feet, she stalked back into the house. "Killer, come along."

The now-muddy terrier barely registered her command. He sneezed and lay down, squashing a bed of tulips in the process. Rolled over, exposing his muddy tummy. Eyed her in a way that said, *Try and make me.*

"Oh, fine, then. No one else pays me any mind. Why should you?" she complained before stomping into the house, her steps leading her toward the study. Even a dull book was better than this infernal aimless boredom and the questions that invariably filled the emptiness.

Brendan's actions last night could be interpreted in two ways: a noble withdrawal or a coward's escape. She certainly had offered little resistance. Had practically thrown herself at his feet like some cheap strumpet. And what had he done? He'd walked away.

Had she done something wrong? Had he decided she wasn't worth the effort?

No doubt in his years abroad he'd had women fawning all over him; dark, exotic, lithesome creatures with kohl-darkened eyes and dusky skin. She'd never been lithesome in her life, and her coloring was far more strawberries and cream than café au lait. She swallowed the annoying lump forming at the back of her throat. Brendan wasn't worth it.

She stutter-stepped to a halt just inside the library door. "Oh, excuse me. I didn't know the room was occupied."

As if conjured from her self-pity, Brendan looked up from his book, his stare seeming to cut right through her like a damascene blade before the light shifted and there was no more in his expression than mild surprise. "Come along in. I don't bite."

All as if last night had never occurred. As if he'd not shot her to the moon with a mere touch. As if she'd not made an ass of herself by letting him.

Butterflies big as vultures whirled through her stomach, warmth stinging her cheeks. If she wasn't careful, she'd make a fool of herself over Brendan—again.

"I came for something to read." Could she sound any more inane? As if he couldn't figure that one out by himself.

He cast a swift pessimistic glance at the few shelves of books. "Unless you're a devotee of Ogham's more inscrutable writings or the art of killing a man in ten easy steps, I'd say you're out of luck."

"You're busy. I'll leave you alone." She started to back out the door, happy to escape an awkward situation.

"Wait. You can help me. That is, if you're not doing anything else."

She didn't move. This was a trick. He would lure her in here, shut the door, and have his wicked way with her. Though he didn't look in a wicked mood. Not even in a very interested mood. More in a preoccupied, frustrated mood. And that irritated her as nothing else could.

"It won't take long, I promise and you can get back to whatever you were doing."

Which was nothing, though she wouldn't tell him that. "You want *me* to help *you*?"

"I asked you, didn't I? Here. Search the index in this one. I'm looking for anything to do with Arthur."

Fine. If he wasn't going to bring last night up, she certainly wasn't. Wrapping her shredded dignity round her, she crossed to where he sat, taking the book from him. Thumbing the pages.

Every time she'd sought to assist Gordon with his work, he'd patted her on the head—in much the same way she patted Killer—and told her too much reading would give her pretty face wrinkles and dull the sparkle in her eyes. As if the strain would simply be too great for her little pea brain to assimilate without exploding. All right, that might have been unduly harsh, but the sentiment had certainly been there, if couched in sweetness and consideration.

One thing she never had to worry about with Brendan was consideration.

"Are you certain you—" she began.

"If you don't want to, fine. I simply thought two heads might be better than one. Go back to checking your face for unwanted freckles or practicing fan semaphore or whatever it is women do when left to their own devices, and I'll look for it myself." He grabbed for the book, which she pulled out of his reach.

"I'll help. No need to be snippy about it."

She sat across from him, opening the book to the index. Running a finger down the page until she spotted a reference. Turned to the chapter in question.

"What, exactly, are we searching for?"

"References to Arthur's encounters with the true *Fey*. A curse, specifically. A *Fey molleth* placed on the king."

"Why would the *Fey* curse—"

He leaned over to tap on her open page. "Fewer questions. More reading."

If her book had been thicker, she might have been tempted to bring it down on his hard head. Instead, she gritted her teeth and allowed herself to be silenced. Simpler while she came to grips with her embarrassment over last night. Though Brendan's apparent unconcern made it easier.

They sat together in silence, flipping pages and taking notes, the clock's hands circling its face, sunlight from the open window moving over the floor. The noise of a fine spring afternoon an upbeat tempo to the companionable quiet within the study.

At one point, she glanced up from her reading. He sat bent over his book, long fingers plowed into his dark, unruly hair, the sweep of downcast lashes against his cheek. Girl's lashes. Thick. Black. He chewed the end of his thumb as he read. Shifted in his chair. His shoulders moved on a deep breath.

No tension in the set of his jaw. No silence fraught with bitterness. No shadows from the past dimming the beauty of those finely hewn features. It eased her apprehension. She could make herself believe all was as it should have been. This was where she was supposed to be. Who she was supposed to be with. That her life had not veered disastrously off course.

"Unless I have broccoli sprouting out my ears, you need to stop staring and get back to work," Brendan griped, never lifting his eyes from the page he was reading. "The answer won't jump up and bite you."

Elisabeth pursed her lips against a giggle. Considerate? Brendan? Hardly. Yet, there was something genuine about all his acerbic sarcasm that no amount of sugary sweetness could rival. It made her want to prove herself. Gain his grudging approval.

Either that or she'd simply lost her mind.

She dropped her gaze back to the book.

All this reading, no doubt.

Brendan stared with sinking heart at the roped-off ruin. A blackened chimney speared the gray sky, birds flitting in and out. Weeds sprang tall and scraggly amid enormous piles of debris. Broken tiles, heavy charred beams, the cracked and melted arms of a chandelier. Water stood in oily black pools. He dragged in a breath laden with a sour stench of soot and mildew.

Ducking beneath the rope, he kicked through the rubble. Plucked up the charred crackling remains of a book, its pages glued and soggy. Tossed it aside. Dug free a mud-caked shard from what might once have been a bowl or pitcher. A dim metallic shine reflecting off a bent and pitted candlestick.

Hours cooped inside, analyzing obscure essays by scholarly theorists with Elisabeth's tantalizing presence a few frustrating feet away, had finally driven him to clear his head with a long stroll. A few more seconds of breathing in that perfume of hers and he'd have completed last night's seduction on the library table. To hell with his noble intentions or Helena's furniture.

How he'd ended up here, he couldn't say. He'd never realized where his walk had led him until he looked up to see the charred lot. And then he'd been unable to simply pass by without pausing as if it meant nothing.

"You there! Can't you read? Sign says no trespassing!" A somber, official-looking character eyed him from the pavement.

"Just poking about."

The constable's scowl deepened. "No trespassing means no poking."

Brendan allowed himself to be shepherded away from the ruin. "Must have been quite a fire."

"Went up like a torch, it did. Lit the sky from the Liffey to Mountjoy Square. I was workin' that night, and seen it meself." Pride rang in his voice. "You know the family what lived here?"

"A long time ago."

"Word is they're accursed. Old earl murdered by his own son. New earl in queer street, with the creditors on his tail. I'd not be one of them for any amount of blunt."

Was it true? Were the Douglases cursed? He drew a breath, seeing once more Aidan's face among the dead, the king's warning carried on an acrid thread of wind, Sabrina's weeping as she fought to save the man she loved, and the imagined vision he carried with him always—Father's execution at the hands of the *Amhas-draoi*. The final moments when the truth of his son's betrayal was made clear. When love twisted in his chest with the same killing force as the blade that felled him and he died damning Brendan's name.

Would Aidan, like Father, go to his grave believing Brendan had betrayed them all?

He hurled the candlestick back into the blackened ruins, where it landed with a ping and a flash of gold before sinking out of sight forever.

Then, swinging away, he strode back down Henry

Street and away from the charred hulk that had once been Kilronan House.

"Madame Arana said you've been out here for hours."

Brendan's voice behind her slid along Elisabeth's nerves like a spark to a fuse. The flush of awareness simmering just below her skin. Her stomach tightening with pleasure.

She looked up from the book in her lap, relieved to put aside the brain-snarling confusion of the thesis she'd been reading. Something about time travel and the effects of past and future on the present. It might as well be ancient Egyptian hieroglyphs for all the sense it made. But she was trying. That should count for something.

Brendan stood haloed by a late afternoon sun, gold threading his dark hair, the rest of him left in shadow. All but his eyes which, as always, burned polished amber. He leaned down to slide the book from her hands, reading the title.

"Ouch. If you're trying to bore yourself to sleep, you couldn't have chosen better."

She snatched it back. "I'm not bored in the least. It's been highly informative. Did you know the *Unseelie*—those are *Fey* demons, by the way."

Amusement danced in his eyes "Yes, I think I may have heard of them once or twice."

She shot him a dirty look. "But did you know if one of the Dark Court possesses the body of a human host, they can gain permanent entry into our world?"

His expression hardened. "Yes, though I didn't know you did." He glanced at the pile of books beside her. "Have I created a monster?"

"Actually, all that searching intrigued me. I was hoping

you might explain a few things. There's a chapter in one of these"—she rummaged through her stack until she found the one she searched for, flipping pages as she spoke—"that sounds like it's talking of Arthur and the curse, but then it doesn't, and I can't make heads or tails of it."

He eyed her curiously. "Who are you, and what have you done with Elisabeth Fitzgerald?"

She slammed the book closed. "I knew you'd tease."

"I'm sorry, Lissa. I'm just a little stunned. You've never liked nor wanted anything to do with the *Other*. You seemed almost fearful. Why the sudden interest?"

She dropped her gaze to the book as she grappled with the question he'd posed. Difficult to explain, if she even could. After all, there had been no defining revelation. It had been a slow creeping awareness that between dread and wonder was a margin almost indefinable. Perhaps that narrowest of gaps had finally closed. Or perhaps she merely grew tired of being kept in the dark about events that impacted her in an intimate and life-altering way.

"It seems only sensible to try and understand what I'm getting myself into by marrying you."

He sank onto the seat beside her, and for the first time she noted the dust speckling his boots, the sour whiskey and smoky smell of him as well as the tired smudges beneath his eyes, the grim angle of his jaw. Her heart skipped annoyingly as he raked his hair out of his face. "Is that what this is about, Lissa? This marriage? You and I? I can say the words, I can put the ring on your finger, but it doesn't make us any more than we were before."

"Which is?"

"Which is two people trapped by circumstance. I may not even—" He broke off, massaging his damaged hand as if it pained him. "I just wouldn't expend a lot of effort in making this into anything more than a face-saving marriage of last resort."

He looked away, his hand lying upon his thigh, the fingers crooked, the joints swollen. She'd asked about it. Just as she'd sought to discover why he'd run, how he'd lived, what dark memories hugged the edges of his sun-bright eyes. Yet, now as always he pushed her away. Parried her questions like the ablest of fencers.

"I may be *Duinedon* but I'm not a fool, Brendan. And I'm tired of being treated like one."

His hand flexed and curled in agitation. "Never a fool, Lissa."

He'd said that to her once before, though she knew it was foolish of her to want more than he could give. To conjure a real marriage out of a few words spoken by a priest.

"None of this is to cause you pain, but to keep you from harm. I do it to protect you," he said.

"I'm not made of spun glass, Brendan. You should have noticed by now that I don't shatter easily. In this case what I don't know just might kill me."

He flexed his hand, scars standing white on his skin, but remained stubbornly silent.

"Forget I spoke," she said, annoyance and disappointment warring within her. "Forget this whole marriage. It was a stupid idea anyway. You go your way. I'll go mine and—"

She stood to leave, but he grabbed her hand. "Now you're angry."

She wrestled to free herself. "I'm not."

A smile twitched a corner of his mouth. "You're lying."

"And you're maddening. If you didn't want to marry me, why did you agree to it?"

"Your silver tongue and your winning ways?" he wheedled.

It was like boxing at shadows. She reasoned, argued, bullied, and yet he remained unfazed. She might as well be speaking to a wall for all the good that came of it. "Do you know how much I despise you right now?"

"I can guess, but I'll ignore it. You're overwrought."

She marched back toward the house, but he kept pace with her, not allowing her to escape. "If I was overwrought—which I most certainly am not—I'd have every right to be."

He lowered his head in sheepish submission. "If I apologize, will you forgive me?"

She refused to look at him, refused to be cajoled by his little boy charm. "Why should I?"

"No reason at all except it might make you feel better."

"It would take a lot more than that to make me feel better."

She spun around, coming up hard against his chest. When had he stepped so close? When had she forgotten how to breathe? She had but to lift her chin to touch her lips to his. To kiss the dimple at the corner of his mouth. Reach a hand to caress the stubble upon his cheek.

"How about this for starters?" he said, his voice dropping to a mischievous purr.

He did what she could not. Lowered his head to brush a kiss upon her lips. He touched her nowhere else, yet even that slight contact ignited a flame low in her belly. His breath came warm and soft and the flame roared higher, racing outward until every particle in her body simmered.

"You said you didn't want to marry me," she murmured.

His gaze traveled over her face as if he memorized her, sending the heat within her soaring before he stepped away, his practiced scoundrel's smile offering a promise of more if she dared. "One's got nothing to do with the other."

fourteen

"It worked like a charm." Elisabeth laughed. "By the end of the argument, Cook was fully on the side of Mrs. Landry, our housekeeper. And they were both dead set against me. Neither one answered me in anything but monosyllables for a month, but at least they didn't kill each other or quit altogether, which would have been far worse."

Elisabeth kept company with Madame Arana, who sat stitching away at her needlepoint amid the group gathered in the drawing room for the evening. All but for Helena, who'd disappeared after supper and had yet to return.

The ladies' conversation veered wildly from the price of wax candles and the proper wages for a housemaid who doubled in the kitchen to whether Helena's grandmother had ever tried the spa at Lucan for her digestion.

Elisabeth's eyes sparkled as she talked of accounts and economizing and how to stay on top of idle servants. She waxed poetic on sheep and wool profits, the use of turnips for winter fodder, crop rotation, and the school she'd begun at Dun Eyre for the education of the tenants' children.

It all sounded so damned domestic. Complete and utter drudgery. But she laughed, gesturing as she spoke, her hair escaping its pins to curl in ringlets against her neck. Her face aglow. Alive and excited and full of ideas. Her enthusiasm infectious.

"If you think Tom Newcomb will ever hear of you planting his fields in anything but potatoes, you're mad," Brendan interrupted.

She squared round, keenness still shining in her gaze. "That's the first time I've heard you speak of home like that."

He shrugged. "Like what?"

"Like you belong there." She cocked her head in a questioning pose, brows low as if she studied a bug beneath a magnifying glass. She must have found what she looked for. She smiled proudly. "Actually, Tom's talking round the others to try Mr. Adams's proposal. We hope to have them all on board by the next planting season."

Brendan sat back, rubbing his chin, watching her in conversation. At one point he caught Rogan's eye upon him, the harper giving him a wink and a grin as if he knew where Brendan's lascivious thoughts were leading him. Right off a cliff edge.

Brendan's watch said twelve before Madame Arana rose from her seat, exclaiming at the hour, Rogan lingering only long enough to tap out his pipe, take a final glass of whiskey, and wish the pair of them a cheery good night.

And then they were alone.

The night folded in on them, the candlelight softer, voices muffled, even the fire burned low and sultry in the grate. And yet, neither one made a move to leave. To pull themselves free of the clumsy awkwardness of this new awareness.

"I had no idea you took such interest in estate matters," he finally ventured when the silence stretched too thin.

Elisabeth played with her empty wineglass, eyes downcast. "I assist Mr. Adams in his office. We discuss his plans and read over the latest articles on husbandry together." She looked up, a challenge in her gaze. "He listens to what I have to say. Respects my opinions."

"Yet Shaw wanted to replace him."

She flushed. "Gordon didn't understand. He saw Dun Eyre as a stepping-stone to better things. I see it as the only thing. I didn't understand that before. It took almost losing it to make me see how much I love Dun Eyre." Sadness colored her once-animated face. "Gordon was suitable in so many ways, I should have been a ninny to have refused his suit."

"Did you love him?"

"You asked me that once before. Do you remember?"

The music room at Dun Eyre. "I do. Has the answer changed?"

She took a deep breath as if she had to think about it while he unconsciously held his. "I loved the idea of him. I wanted a husband. Children. A life with someone I could rely on. I thought Gordon could give me those things."

Brendan crossed to take her hands. His fingers lacing with hers as he drew her up. She smiled, a spray of freckles across her nose, her mouth soft and full and berry red.

A beautiful woman. A quiet night.

So far nothing out of the ordinary.

A thousand times he'd done this and a thousand times he'd walked away.

"You never talk about Belfoyle," she commented.

"As if I belong there?" he teased, wary of this conversation's path. Home was a topic off-limits and had been since he'd left. If he didn't think about it, it didn't hurt.

She gave a toss of her head. "Ever. Or not as I thought you would after being away for so long."

"I'm a second son, remember?" he answered caustically. "Pride of ownership belongs to Aidan now."

Again there was the sense she was searching for something within him. If she wasn't careful, she'd find more than she bargained for. "It's not ownership I'm speaking of, but loving a place. Carrying Belfoyle and all that makes it special inside you."

"What are you trying to do, Elisabeth? Wring a confession from me? Have me tell you that I wept for my family every day I was gone? That every night I closed my eyes and saw the towers of Belfoyle?" He grabbed her by the arms, a slow burn beginning behind his eyes. "Life boiled down to survival. Food. Shelter. Safety. There was no freedom for regrets or tears or maudlin wretchedness."

She braved his anger. "And now?"

"You've seen what I face," he argued, his grip tightening. "My life is not my own until Máelodor is dead and the stone is secure."

Anger became arousal. He wanted to punish her and devour her at the same time. His lips found hers in a kiss born solely of the need to shut her up. Stop her mental assault. The slow degradation of all his defenses. He didn't want to imagine or hope or dream. He didn't want to see Elisabeth as anything other than a hindrance. "Even if we marry tomorrow, I can't promise you the future you want."

Then he tasted the sweet heat of her luscious mouth.

The wine-tart tang of her on his tongue. He palmed the perfect firmness of a generous breast. Inhaled the comforting scents of lemon and lavender. And he could no longer deny his body's craving.

"Perhaps not," she murmured, threading her hands into his hair, "but you can offer me the hope of *a* future. That will have to be enough."

The swooping plunge of her stomach, the roar of blood in her ears, every muscle jumping with excitement. Elisabeth could have been riding neck-or-nothing over the rocky heath and cliff-top meadows of home. The sensations were exactly the same, including the feeling of careening out of control toward a dangerous jump.

Brendan had guided her up the stairs to her bedchamber, the darkness wrapping round them, drawing them close as conspirators. He closed the door behind them, just the snick of the latch raising gooseflesh on her body, spreading heat low across her belly.

He pulled her hair loose of its pins. She was so used to the constant fight to confine its wildness, the heavy curling weight of it against her back felt both unfamiliar and oddly sensual. As if he were seeing a secret part of her. Peeking beneath the tamed sensible woman she'd become to the hoyden tomboy she'd been when he knew her.

He ran his tongue over her bottom lip, nipping and sucking until she opened to him, her tongue darting out in naive exploration. He dipped within, teasing and tasting. Carrying her along on a river of rising need, yet spinning out every touch and every kiss in an infinite dance of discovery.

Her arms lifted to encircle his neck, the fringe of his

hair against her bare skin. His lips moved over her cheek, each eyelid, behind her ear. She threw back her head as he caressed his way down her throat, along her collarbone, before lowering into the valley between her breasts.

Her heart thundered. It pounded against her ribs as his hands skimmed her sides, folding around her to stroke the length of her spine.

She shucked him free of his jacket, her trembling fingers working at the buttons of his waistcoat as he backed her toward the bed. Struggled to free her from the restraints of too many layers of clothing. Ribbons, buttons, laces. Finally, her gown slithered to the floor. Her stays following after.

She should be embarrassed or apprehensive—at the least she should mutter a few maidenly protestations to prove her virginal innocence—but Brendan didn't make her feel innocent. He made her feel wicked and wanton and reckless and passionate. She couldn't breathe when he was near. And forget thinking. Her brain turned to mush as soon as he locked that hungry golden gaze on her.

He encircled her waist with his hands, grazing the lines of her ribs, the curves of her torso, taking the chemise with him as he massaged his way up.

She shivered, leaning into his embrace, loving the capable strength in his work-roughened palms. The feel of every stroke upon her sensitized skin. Off went the chemise, tossed to the floor with the rest of her clothes.

He thumbed her nipples, the dark buds hardening beneath his touch. He bent to take one in his mouth, swirling the softness of it with his tongue, sucking it taut while kneading the pliant flesh of the other. No amount of dream-spinning had prepared her for this tantalizing heart-pounding hunger. Aching between her legs, she moaned, pressing herself against him, needing him closer. Skin on skin.

And then they were on the bed, Brendan above her, leaning upon one elbow, eyes scorching a path over her body, his hand following lazily after.

She'd waited seven years for this. She would memorize it. Imprint it upon her brain where nothing that followed would erase it. The curve of his wrist. The line of his jaw. The dimple at the corner of his mouth and the slash of his brows. The flop of hair over his forehead and the slow bliss of his caress.

She closed her eyes, picturing him as he was right this instant. Knew she'd remember always.

"Forget the silks I promised you. I prefer you just like this," he murmured.

Her eyes snapped open on a smile. "That's right. You did promise me, didn't you? I should have known they were so many empty words." She lifted her head to nip his chin.

He skimmed his hand down over the flat of her stomach. "I've warned you more than once, I'm an unreliable, selfish bastard, but I'm beginning to think you like the bad boy." His eyes gleamed with mischief, that devilish dimple aching to be kissed.

Words were lost as sensation took over. As Brendan rose up on his knees to pull free the ribbons of her garters. As he rolled her stockings down over her calves, his hands gliding over the exposed flesh before he retraced his way up her inner thighs. To the junction of her legs. The feather-light touch there sent lightning shooting through her like a live charge. Her hips rose off the bed in an unconscious response to his seduction. Her center hot and wet and throbbing for him, every second the pressure building low within her.

And then he was gone, rolling off the bed and into the shadows. She heard the thud of boots, the shush of discarded clothing as breeches and shirt came off. And then he was back, his weight upon the bed, the fierce heat of his naked body like an inferno.

He came over her, the lean muscles of his hard-packed body perfect against hers. His right shoulder still wrapped in a thin bandage, he held himself awkwardly, but like a coiled spring still managed to radiate strength and power. He paused above her, his body between her legs, his sungold eyes stabbing her straight to the heart.

So close, she felt him just there. The torment of his sudden hesitation agonizing.

His gaze dimmed. "Say the word, Lissa. Say the word, and I can still leave you." He ground his teeth. "It'll hurt like the devil, but I'll do it," he moaned.

"No words. Not tonight." Smiling, she lifted her hips, taking him into her. He entered slowly, stretching her inch by excruciating inch. Letting her adjust to the sensation of their joined bodies, the thrill of him inside her. To this mind-bending exhilaration sweeping her along now, the river in spate.

She gasped at a sudden sharp sting, Brendan hovering unmoving over her in the dark. Clearly letting her make the first move. Take the first step forward. Slowly, tentatively, she rocked forward, the only feeling now one of longing as Brendan silently exhaled on a slow, ragged breath.

An inexorable headlong weight built inside her as he withdrew. Entered her deeper. She arched into him in a slow building rhythm, digging her nails into his arms, her breath coming fast, her vision dancing with fire and light and color as waves slowly built behind this tightening quickening urge.

His kisses deepened as he drove harder, faster, her breathing becoming a pant and then a moan as every thrust sent her spinning closer to that cliff edge. And then it was there. In front of her. She felt herself tumbling. Up and up, the rush of her heart drowning out her cries. Her body alight with a pleasure-pain she never knew existed.

As he shuddered, his eyes squeezed shut, his body taut as a cocked bow, she ground once more against him, and the two found release together.

They lay spooned together, their bodies cooling in the breeze from an open window. Brendan's arm slung over her hip, his fingers tracing a lazy path up and down her side.

"That wasn't supposed to happen."

"You mean I did it wrong?" she asked.

"Oh no, my dear. You did everything exactly right. Too right. I shouldn't have allowed it to go as far as it did. We're not married yet."

His chest pressed against her back, his breath tickling her neck. "I know you're only marrying me because you have to," she said.

"Is that what you know?" he teased, tickling her side until she screamed, writhing to escape him.

"Stop. No, Brendan. Don't——" she pleaded. "I surrender. I surrender."

"That'll teach you"——he dropped a kiss at the nape of her neck——"to try to tell me why I'm marrying you."

"Well, you obviously weren't too thrilled about it the last time. And nothing's changed. I'm still me. And you're still you."

"How profound we become after sex. I'll remember that." He squeezed her tight.

That wasn't what she wanted to hear. She wanted to hear *I love you*. Fool that she was.

She rolled over, his chest hard against hers. The sleek lines of his shoulders melting into the lean, corded muscles of his arms. "I didn't hurt you, did I?"

He chuckled, dropping a kiss on the tip of her nose. "That's supposed to be my line."

She blushed. "I meant your shoulder."

He gave a look of sudden comprehension. "Ah, the shoulder." He flexed his bandaged arm, windmilled it up over his head, wiggled his fingers. "That dried monkey tongue Madame Arana gave me really did the trick."

"Monkey tong—Brendan! She gave you no such thing."

His eyes danced with laughter. "No, but I had you for a minute there." He pulled her close. "The arm's better. Stiff, but still attached. I'll live to fight another day."

Flying high, she'd been unprepared for the sudden belly-punch of fear. Brendan joked, but it was the kind of grim humor people resorted to when the truth was too awful to contemplate. She glanced away, not wanting to show him how his words frightened her.

It didn't work. He knew.

"Lissa?" he asked gently, tipping her chin back to him, worry in his gaze. "Are you truly all right?"

She didn't want to talk about it. Didn't want to have to explain her feelings when she didn't completely understand them herself. She would revel in what she had of him. Try not to yearn for what he could not give.

With a brave smile and a shrug, she quickly changed the subject. "What's this mark?" She traced the outline of a broken arrow bisecting a crescent. It began at the junction of his neck and left shoulder before curving down over his chest. "I noticed it before."

Brendan's stare seemed to reach right inside her. But instead of pushing for answers, he merely reached up to cover her hand with his own, slowly drawing it away from the tattoo. "Momentary insanity."

"Did you have it done in Greece?"

"In the back room of a Paris brothel. Father was furious. Called me—well, I'm too much of a gentleman to repeat what he called me, but he vowed I'd regret it." He closed his eyes for a brief moment, his jaw jumping. "He was right."

She leaned up on an elbow, searching his face for some hint of the man behind the mask he wore so deliberately. The façade he created to keep everyone out. "Why did you leave Belfoyle? What really happened to make you disappear so completely? We all thought you dead, Brendan. Your family—" She dragged in a steadying breath before meeting his gaze. "—I—mourned you."

He pushed her hair back from her forehead before pressing a kiss there. "It doesn't matter anymore. It was a long time ago."

But it did matter. She could see it in the shadows of his eyes. The strain of his body. Whatever had driven him away and destroyed the Douglases haunted him still.

Why wouldn't he tell her? What could be so horrible?

Was it because she wasn't good enough? Not smart enough? Didn't have that invisible aura of power she felt in the presence of all those gifted with *Fey* blood?

Resentment licked along limbs so recently alive with passion's fire.

"In other words, impossible for a *Duinedon* like me to understand," she huffed.

He chuckled. "You may not have inherited the gifts of the *Fey*-born, but that doesn't make you any less a part of our world."

"But I'm not, don't you see? I never have been. My father always said the *Other* were cursed to remain apart. To hide who they are. To stay within the shadows. And he was right. My grandmother was always seen as a madwoman by those who didn't know."

Brendan rolled onto his back, hands folded behind his head, his expression serious. "Yet, to those who knew her and what she was, Elisabeth, her affinity for growing things wasn't seen as a curse but as a great gift. She chose to shower that gift upon Dun Eyre, making it a magical place."

He was right. Dun Eyre was magical. Travelers from all over visited to see the magnificent gardens set among the rugged moors and rocky cliffs. Aunt Fitz would proudly show them round the house and grounds while Aunt Pheeney awaited them in the drawing room, where paying guests were offered refreshments and a cheerful welcome.

"I miss Dun Eyre. I miss my aunts." She laid her head upon his chest, the steady beat of his heart calming the sudden ache in her throat. "I miss my dull, quiet life."

He pushed her hair off her face, his smile wistful. "I miss mine too."

It was the closest he came to a confession.

He closed his eyes, though he didn't sleep. His body remained too taut, his breath too shallow. Gods, he was beautiful. The narrow chiseled lines of his face, the curve of sensual lips, strong patrician nose, and those sinfully long lashes. His broad chest tapering to a ridged abdomen, a narrow line of hair disappearing beneath the sheet covering his waist. Even the swirl of the arrow-and-crescent tattoo only added to his raw masculinity.

Her chest tightened, her hand reaching to caress him.

A smile hovered at the edge of his mouth. "Describe it to me," he whispered, almost a plea.

"What do you want to know?"

"The look. The smell. Is Aidan well? Is he happy? What's changed since I was last there? Tell me everything so I can see it."

"You said you didn't care. That you couldn't look back and survive."

"I never said I didn't care. I said I couldn't care. There's a difference."

And so she told him. Curled with him in the night, she spoke of the house upon the cliffs, the way the mists came down to curl silver gray and damp against the walls. She described the winds that never ceased, the way they held the bite of the ocean as they swept across the wide cloud-chased sky, the way the sun threw light and shadow over the moors.

She talked about Aidan—the wild young man who'd become a brooding recluse as he faced the possibility of financial ruin. Of the late nights and long days as the new Earl of Kilronan had struggled to hold the estate together. Of the grief he held tight within him for the family he'd lost. Of the shock among the neighbors that followed his impetuous marriage to a woman of unknown pedigree and scandalous rumored past.

"He's not the Aidan you remember, but he's happy again. He loves her. It's clear the way he follows her with his eyes whenever they're together. Almost as if they're connected by some invisible cord."

She spoke of Sabrina, gone away shortly after her parents' deaths. Gone to Glenlorgan and a life as a *bandraoi* priestess. "Aunt Fitz said she's home now, though none have seen her and none know why she's come back. Some say there was a man involved."

"Was? But he should—" Brendan shook his head. "Oh, Sabrina."

"When you go home, you'll see it for yourself. You'll see all of them. The prodigal son returns. They'll welcome you with open arms."

"More likely with daggers drawn, if I know Aidan. No, your words will have to do. I can't go home, Lissa." His words bit sharp and deep like a knife. "Not after—" He closed his eyes. "Not ever."

Elisabeth slept, a tangle of red-gold hair above the covers, a soft whisper of even breathing.

Brendan leaned over, brushing a kiss upon her forehead, inhaling the enticing lemony floral scent of her creamy skin. He closed his eyes, imagining a life with her. Waking by her side. Finding her at day's end when they could sit together and laugh and talk and enjoy each other's company. Taking her in his arms at night with no fear clouding her gaze.

He opened his eyes on a sigh. A beautiful dream, but daylight would bring reality. He ran a hand over the broken arrow and crescent needled into his chest. A permanent reminder that his past made that life impossible.

Rising from the bed, Brendan padded across the room to the fire, his naked body chilled by the cool night air.

Lissa had given him a great gift tonight. Not just her body, which had been perfection in his arms, but her reminiscences. He'd not been able to help himself. He'd needed to know. Suffered with a homesickness that left him dry mouthed and shaking. And in those brief moments when she had spoken, Belfoyle had come alive for him. He'd seen once more the barren rocky cliffs, walked through the waist-high grass down to the thin stretch of beach, galloped along the orchard road chased by the salty wind, and talked and laughed late into the night with Aidan, trading stories and boasts and secrets like brothers who've nothing to hide.

Shoulders hunched in defeat, he braced himself against the mantel. Closed his eyes, seeing once more the vision of Aidan lying dead among the scores of battlefield corpses. The copper sheen of his hair. The blue-white pallor of his face. The splash of crimson across his chest.

He will come for you.

Arthur's denunciation to the man bowed and broken as he crushed his brother's mutilated body to his chest.

A vibrant single image burning through the gray, mist-shrouded wraiths he'd lived with for the past seven years. The heartrending cry to the heavens drowning out the poisonous whispers echoing in his ears since Freddie Atwood's failed last stand.

fifteen

Mr. McKelway didn't look old enough to shave, much less perform a wedding ceremony, though by the leering glances he kept stealing at Elisabeth's breasts throughout, he was plenty old enough to have his ears boxed.

It was one thing to marry in such a helter-skelter way. Another to have the priest ogling her as if she were a side of beef at Fleet market. She speared the cleric with a ferocious stare that had him tugging at his collar as if he were in sudden need of air and hastening through the rest of the service in double time.

Not the wedding of her dreams. Madame Arana and Miss Roseingrave were the only witnesses to her honor's restoration, Rogan pleading an aversion to churches in general and marriage in particular. And in place of Miss Havisham's expensive confection of cream-colored silk and yards of silver lace, Elisabeth wore a modest gown of white muslin. One of the few outfits in Helena's wardrobe that needn't be let out or taken in.

Brendan stood beside her, pressed and polished and looking as mouthwatering as she'd ever seen him.

The Douglases possessed looks to draw every eye. Aidan bore an austere elegance and a confident swagger that left no one in doubt of his noble bloodlines. Sabrina's winsome flashing smile and sparkling blue eyes more than made up for her inherent shyness. But Brendan outshone both of them with his sun-bronzed, square-jawed face, the dagger gleam of his gold eyes, and the taut balance of his swordsman's body.

Until now he'd been a million miles away, his expression unreadable in the dim interior of the church, but when the priest asked, "Do you take this woman?" he finally looked at her, his eyes a darkened bronze like ancient coins, face uncharacteristically solemn.

"I do," he said, his fingers tightening on hers in a gesture she chose to interpret as encouragement rather than dread.

It didn't take nearly as long as she'd expected to change the course of her life forever. A few words spoken over them. An exchange of chaste kisses for the spectators, and a marriage seven years in the making was finally accomplished.

There should have been bells. A parade. Perhaps a few fireworks. Instead, Madame Arana blew a great honk into her handkerchief and Helena's bark of brittle laughter echoed along the rows of empty pews. "Hunted by armies only to be caught in a wee parson's mousetrap."

Elisabeth heaved a sigh. So much for celebration.

Brendan must have taken her sigh as one of sad regret. He whispered in her ear, his soft breath against her neck shooting butterflies through her. "It's not the wedding you deserve, nor am I the man you wanted. For that I am sorry, Lissa."

Not the man she'd wanted? You couldn't have told her that while Brendan's lips had been trailing shivers of sensation over her skin. While he'd stroked her body to a fever's pitch and she'd responded with a raw frenzied hunger.

Shame settled like lead in the pit of her stomach. Surely she should have felt some remorse at so quickly shedding one man to tumble into marriage with another. Surely she ought to be crimson with guilt. It was only proper. To be expected.

So why then did becoming Mrs. Brendan Douglas, awkward as it was, seem so much better than worse?

Elisabeth was disappointed. Brendan could tell as soon as they emerged from the church this morning into a steady downpour, the streets gray, the wedding party grayer. She'd put on a brave, cheerful face throughout the improvised wedding breakfast, had sat through Rogan's litany of "horrible marriages hath I known" without batting an eye before retiring to her room to refresh herself. Code for escape before she drowned the harper in his tea.

Brendan had let her go without comment. It was best to give her time to gather her thoughts. After all, she must be imagining her lost life with Shaw the sheepdog. Probably wishing Brendan to the devil. Screaming her fury into her pillow.

It wasn't until late afternoon when he finally couldn't stand the suspense anymore and went in search of her. She wanted to brood? He'd written the book on brooding. Gordon Shaw was not worth wasting good brooding time over.

He found her in the study, head buried in an accounts ledger, receipts and bills of lading spread out around her, twirling her pen between ink-stained fingers. And not looking in the least bit gloomy or pensive or sad. Rather, she held a distracted, harried eagerness like a child in a confectioner's shop.

"Have they put you to work earning your keep?" he asked.

She looked up with a smile that had every nerve ending in his body jumping to attention. "Madame Arana asked if I could sort through the household finances. I've spent the last hour just organizing. A pile for incoming. A pile for outgoing. And a pile for miscellaneous." She grimaced, lurching to contain the largest of the three stacks before it slid onto the floor. "Helena may be able to wield sword and magic with cutthroat precision, but she's a mess at finances."

"You can finish later. I brought you a gift," he announced.

She cocked her head up at him, her eyes almost black in this light, brows scrunched, lip caught between her teeth. The gesture caused his chest to tighten with an unexpected ache. "I can't leave it now. I've only just started."

"Do you want to spend the afternoon locked in here with your abacus?"

Hesitation as she studied the muddled accounts in front of her. "Not particularly, but they have been very kind and it seems only right to try and assist if I can."

"Come with me now, and I promise later you can file and categorize to your heart's content."

She tossed her head, eyes dancing with mischief. "Another promise you don't intend to keep? The number grows exponentially."

"Quit your scolding, woman, and come along." Chaining his runaway libido, he drew her up beside him.

"Where are we going?"

"The gifts are in my room."

A brow arched in devious excitement, a tiny flame alight in the dark of those deep brown eyes. "Your room? And calling it a gift now? That's hubris for you."

He shot her a look. "I'd no idea what a filthy little mind my wife would have." Let his gaze wander. "I like it."

She laughed. "So what is this gift?"

"You see . . . well, I had told you . . . oh, just come see for yourself." He grabbed her hand, pulling her after him. "You women talk everything to death."

She allowed herself to be led up to his bedchamber, hanging back for the slightest of moments at his door.

"Come along," he said. "You can hardly stand on maidenly protests now. A bit like guarding the barn after the horse has been ridden." He quirked her a scoundrel's grin.

"Brendan!" she exclaimed in mock horror. Another flash of something unreadable in her eyes.

He hadn't expected his eager anticipation upon presentation of his purchases. But as he stepped away from his bed, revealing the pile he'd had the maid bring up, he couldn't help the impatient smile or the sweep of nervous excitement. Would she like them? Would she throw her arms around his neck? Would they make her happy? Would he have done something right where she was concerned? He shouldn't care. Couldn't care. But he did. More than he'd admit.

"Remember when I promised to shower you with silks?"

She blinked as if she didn't understand what she was seeing.

"You didn't think I'd do it, did you? Tell the truth." He drew a bolt of fabric from the pile. "It's"—he glanced at it with a frown—"well, this isn't silk. It's muslin. But there's silk among the lot."

She stepped forward. Held out a tentative hand to touch the cloth.

"I made a promise and I kept a promise. I don't make a habit of it, but every now and again." He dropped the bolt into her arms. "I bought enough to make up a half dozen gowns."

She flushed, the sprinkle of freckles fading into the dusky pink of her cheeks. "They're all lovely, Brendan. Thank you."

"To give credit where it's due, Madame Arana helped. She knew the best warehouses and linen drapers and what colors and fabrics were in fashion. I've never been much when it came to that sort of thing. As long as you're not exposing anything that ought not be exposed, I don't see what all the fuss is about."

"You don't say." She pursed her lips around a smile, making him acutely aware of his borrowed coat, his haphazardly knotted cravat, and a pair of broken-in boots. So he wasn't Beau Brummell. He was comfortable.

"I'll never be a pink of the *ton*. Never had aspirations to make a splash. But that doesn't mean I don't appreciate those who do."

The curve of her cheek. The curve of her body. When had his room grown so small? When had Elisabeth Fitzgerald changed from millstone round his neck to fire in his blood? He cleared his throat. Snatched the muslin back from her to lay it with the rest.

"One more thing. Spin around."

Her eyes widened. "Excuse me?"

"Quit yammering, turn around, and close your eyes."

She did as she was told, shivering as he brushed her neck, the smell of her and the sight of the tender skin just behind her ear sending the blood rushing from his head to his groin.

"No peeking," he barked, furious with himself for behaving like a lust-crazed simpleton. "Very well, you can open your eyes now."

Her gaze dropped to the necklace gracing her throat, the shimmering opal teardrop upon a thin gold chain.

"This one is just a stone," he admitted. "Nothing more. Nothing less. But it's yours to keep."

She turned, throwing her arms about his neck. "It's perfect."

He ducked his head, not completely able to hide his joy at her response. "I don't know about perfect. Shaw's sapphires probably cost twenty times what this little trinket did."

Tears shone in her eyes as she stepped back to stare up at him. "But this is worth twenty times more. How on earth did you afford all of this?"

"Not married a week and already harping over my spendthrift ways?" He shifted uneasily. "I managed to pawn a few things."

Her gaze dropped to his waistcoat. "Your watch," she gasped. "You loved that watch. Brendan, you didn't have to. Not for me."

Loss twisted his innards, but only for a moment. "I didn't have to. I wanted to. My felicitations, Mrs. Douglas. You are now officially un-ruined."

The scent of her filled his nostrils, that lemony lavender spring bouquet of hers that never failed to catch him unawares. Like the flash in her dark eyes or the way she had of tossing her head or the rousing way she moved, every curve an invitation to sample.

She leaned forward, kissing him at the edge of his mouth. "It's our wedding day. What say we ruin me all over again?"

His whole body went rock hard. "I hope someday I might look back and say marriage was the best thing I ever did."

"Let's make someday now."

Still floating with a dazed sense of satisfaction, Elisabeth bent over Brendan, kissing his rippled abdomen, his sculpted chest, the side of his neck where his pulse thundered against his skin. He tasted salty, smelled of soap and man and some faint exotic scent she couldn't place.

So much for calm, placid waters. She'd landed smack in the eye of the hurricane.

Brendan embraced her, pulling her down on top of him, tucking her head beneath his chin, his hand skimming up and down her spine, sending trills of delicious pleasure jolting through her.

"Am I squashing you?" she asked.

A rumble of laughter beneath her ear. "I think my frail body can handle you." He caressed her ribs, cupped her backside. "You're hardly a stoning weight."

She snuggled into him, already feeling signs of his renewed desire between her legs. "No, but nor am I a skinny twig who can live on air."

He dropped a kiss upon the top of her head. "Twigs are overrated. And I've never been fond of air as a main course either."

Crushing her in his arms, he rolled her beneath him, settling himself between her legs, a flop of dark hair falling across his forehead, his smile as full of sinful promise as ever.

She fought to maintain hold of the wild blaze of emotion engulfing her. She repeated over and over in her head, *This cannot last*, as she kissed him. The danger remained. It may have retreated into the shadows. She might not feel as if she was running for her life, but she was. They both were. She needed to hold tight to that thought. "Until death do us part" might mean tomorrow when survival hung by a fraying thread.

This wasn't about making a life together or a home or a family or any of those pretty pictures she held in her mind. This was about Brendan putting right his mistake. If she pretended it was anything more, then that was her fault. Not his.

Driving away her second thoughts with a slow, deep kiss that shot quivers of anticipation straight to her center, he slid his hand up her calf, skimmed her inner thigh. The kiss deepened as he nipped and tongued and teased her senseless while his hand caressed her woman's place, the wicked play of his fingers making her push up into him in a desperate bid for more. She heard her pleading whimpers, his seductive chuckle as he played her closer and closer to her edge. She threw her head back, rocking up into his hand and then his erection as he sheathed himself inside her.

She moaned his name, the lush subtle cords of desire binding her tighter and tighter. Tremors of building need began at their joining, slowly moving through her veins like honey, an intoxicating erotic abandonment as she locked her legs behind him, moving with him, their rhythm as relaxed as if they had lifetimes to enjoy one another. But there was no link between the subtle possession and the volcanic eruption as she convulsed against him, every muscle down to her toes contracting. The fires still swept her away with devastating ferocity. Tears still stung her eyes, and she still caught herself imagining forever.

"You said you'd found mention of Arthur. Show me," he said.

They sat up in bed together, though she'd donned a nightgown and bundled her hair into a messy knot at the back of her head, and he'd thrown on a pair of breeches— thank the gods or she'd never be able to concentrate.

At his request, she rolled out of their nest of quilts to retrieve the book. Handing it over as she slid back in beside him.

He checked the title page, widening his eyes in appreciation. "Gilles de Clercq in the original French. You are ambitious," before turning to the page she'd bookmarked.

Brows drawn low, he scanned the paragraph.

She drew her knees up to her chest as she reread the passages over his shoulder. "It's the only place I've even seen a curse mentioned, though I'm not sure if it applies."

"Hard to say," he said without taking his eyes from the page. "So much of what's been written has been twisted by *Duinedon* who want to discount Arthur as myth. They've pulled threads from the truth and woven them into a story to fit their need. A way to discount the *Other*. Relegate us to fantasy. Or persecute us as witches."

His voice took on a bitter edge she'd never heard before, his body growing rigid.

"So the passage doesn't mean anything?"

He glanced over at her, his gaze troubled, a finger tapping his chin as he considered. "I didn't say that. I've never heard of this Merovingian warlord the author speaks of, but the similarities to Arthur are certainly eerie, aren't they?

Right down to the messy end." Stretching, he put the book aside with a sigh. Plowed a hand through his hair, unkinked his neck, his gilded muscles rippling beneath his skin, making her itch to caress the warmth of his back.

"It doesn't matter what I find," he said, fury threading his words. "I already know how it all turns out. I've seen it again and again. A war with the *Duinedon* will leave the *Other* broken and scattered at best, hunted and slaughtered at worst." His hand found hers, their fingers linking. "We're not immortal. We bleed and we die. And unless I can stop it, we'll be dying by the thousands."

"Surely Máelodor knows this. He may want *Other* dominance, but he must know it can never succeed."

"He thinks he holds the trump card." He paused, his jaw jumping, gaze hard as steel. "The *Unseelie.*"

"But the book said they can't survive in our world without a human . . ." The truth dawned with a sickening churn of her stomach. "He can't possibly."

He shot her a harsh grimace. "He's convinced they'll accept his leadership in order to escape their captivity, but they won't remain subservient for long. They may have been cast out of *Ynys Avalenn*, but they're still *Fey* and no less powerful for being imprisoned."

Fear cruised her skin in icy waves before sinking into her bones with a panic that chattered her teeth, tumbled her stomach until she wanted to be sick. Her hands fisted under her breasts as if she could calm the ugly jump of her heart.

Máelodor's defeat by the armies of the *Duinedon* would destroy the race of *Other*. His victory, if it came with *Unseelie* aid, might destroy the world.

She hugged herself, unable to stop the splash of nausea rising into her throat. "How could he even contemplate such a thing? What kind of man comes up with such madness and evil? What kind of monster would conjure such sickening malice?"

Sorrow stabbed his tawny gaze, a flash of grief quickly shuttered as he inhaled on a quick ragged breath. "A man blind to everything but his own abilities and his own pride. But for all that, Lissa, I swear to you, still just a man."

"You risk much with this interruption." Máelodor pushed himself up against his pillows, running a hand over his scalp and the strange scaly patches there.

The woman beside him slept on, the straggling black of her hair and one bruised cheek the only bits of her not hidden by a hump of blankets. He ached from the evening's exertions, but already his cock throbbed for more. Once he dealt with Oss, he would rouse the woman. She'd learned her lesson. She'd submit this time without a struggle. A shame. It meant he'd have to find a different way to prolong his pleasure.

Oss crossed to the bedside, handing over a letter. As usual the albino's impassive milky gaze barely registered the discarded garments, the tangle of bedclothes or the sleeping whore. Nor with even a flicker of an eyelid did he react to the slow transformation of his master's body as the *Unseelie* magics took Máelodor over.

Oss too had learned his lesson well.

Máelodor ripped open the letter, scanning the contents. Exhilaration burned along his twisted limbs, shook his palsied hands. Victory was near. "Prepare my traveling coach. We leave for Cornwall. The stone's been found."

Sixteen

The dram shop smelled of sweat, urine, and stale whiskey. Brendan wrinkled his nose against the stench and played at drinking the hell broth, though he'd yet to have the grimy cup touch his lips.

On the face of it, he'd come here as a way to draw Máelodor's hunters, though to be honest Brendan had simply needed to free himself from the never-ending spin of his thoughts. Impossible to do while cooped within the closing walls of the Duke Street town house. Not much easier here with every new arrival throwing his pulse into a gallop, his hand involuntarily closing around the dagger hidden beneath his jacket.

Experience told him he tempted fate. He should follow his own rule and stay as far away from Elisabeth as possible. Between Rogan, Roseingrave, and himself, they'd laid trails, dropped hints. Nothing obvious, but surely word had leaked in all the right places. Máelodor would know by now Kilronan's heir had resurfaced in Dublin. An easy target for his bounty hunters. Which meant time grew short and nothing was certain. For every step he took to secure his freedom, circumstance chose to snatch it from his grip.

He'd come here in company with Rogan, though soon after their arrival the harper had disappeared into the back with a woman of soft curves and hard eyes.

"I'd appreciate it if you keep Lyddy to yourself. Helena's got high-minded ideas and she doesn't take to my women," Rogan had said with a sheepish smile.

Brendan raised his cup to the man's success, and the couple ducked beneath a curtain stretched over a doorway at the back of the room with much giggling and pinching.

Reaching for his watch, he suddenly remembered its present location at a pawnbroker's near Arran Quay. Ah, well, he'd take it on faith that at least a half hour had passed. Where the hell was the lover boy?

As he waited, a man entered. Of medium build with shaggy black hair threaded with silver, he took a seat in the corner. His shabby clothes looked as if he'd stolen them from a beggar. An old threadbare jacket, breeches that barely covered his knees, and a pair of shoes with cracked soles bound with twine.

Brendan tensed in sudden anticipation of approaching trouble. He dropped a careful hand to his dagger. The plan might be to draw Máelodor's assassins to him, but it wasn't easy to put aside years of discipline. And he refused to go without a fight.

The shop door opened again, this time on a group of laughing, shouting men, their faces bearing signs of more than a passing familiarity with the crippling effects of cheap whiskey. Red-veined noses, jaundiced eyes, skin lying slack on brittle bones.

One of the newcomers pulled aside the curtain, shouting for Lyddy, his friends egging him on. Apparently this had not been the first stop on their tavern-crawl.

Immediately, Rogan was there, his long, thin body seeming to fill the doorway, his normally placid face dark with an emotion Brendan had never seen in his eyes. He'd yet to put on his jacket, his shirtsleeves rolled to his elbows to reveal the dark curved edge of a tattoo.

"You speak like that again and I'll have your tongue from your head," he threatened.

The drunk looked cowed for a moment, but his boldness returned as his friends joined him. "I pay good money. I expect good service," he brazened.

Rogan's gaze flicked down to the man's groin back up to his eyes, contempt twisting his features. "Why don't you and your friends stick to goats?"

The men surged forward as one, Rogan disappearing beneath the crush of bodies.

Devil take it. Did the man have to play knight errant for a damned doxy?

Brendan shoved up from his chair, sliding his dagger free. Drew to a halt before he'd gone two steps.

One rascal had fallen to his knees, a second came away with a bloody nose. But the last two fell back as if they'd been stunned by a hammer blow between the eyes.

Rogan laughed, throwing his arm around the bully who'd first called for the woman. "Arrah, now, you don't want to be bothering my girl Lyddy. She's a good lass. She doesn't do that sort of thing anymore."

Mage energy shivered the air, flickering against Brendan's skin before sinking into his bones, running with his blood.

"No?" the man said, still with a look of dazed amazement. His companion following after with a glassy acquiescence.

"You want to take yourselves off and find another shop," Rogan offered. "The one in Braithwaite Street, or try Martha above the skinners in Marrowbone Lane."

"I've been there. Martha's a ripe one," the man said, nodding stupidly.

"Of course she is," Rogan purred. "She'll be just the thing. Go on and take your friends with you. And we'll forget about our little brangle."

Rogan's gaze concentrated upon each man in turn, the persuasive power of the *leveryas* settling over the turbulence of the dram shop. It pulsed along Brendan's muscles like a drug, the calm easing the tension banding his back. He released the dagger and dropped his arm to his side as the men filtered out, subdued under the influence of Rogan's subtle yet unbending mental pressure.

"Come, Douglas." Rogan motioned toward the door. "We'll follow to be sure they're headed toward Marrowbone Lane."

Anything to get the hell out of here.

Brendan tossed a coin on the table, casting a swift glance at the corner table, but the strange man with the black and silver hair was gone. No sign of him in the shop anywhere. He must have slipped out during the commotion.

Brendan joined Rogan outside. They trailed behind the foursome as they made their way down Bridgefoot Street and away from the river.

"You're lucky they didn't beat the hell out of you. The *leveryas* is a dicey thing to control."

Rogan laughed. "If they'd been sober, I'd say you were right to be nervous. But the stench of whiskey rising off them was enough to drop a bull in his traces. No fears they'd have broken free."

"You must care for the woman to risk mob dismemberment."

"Lyddy's a good girl, Douglas. She doesn't like working there, but she's not had much choice. She ran away from home when she was a wee thing. The first time she worked the mage energy."

Brendan sucked in a quick breath. "She's *Other*?"

"Aye, mind ya, she's no master-mage, but she carries the blood of the *Fey*, no doubt of it. Her family sought to drive the devil from her." His voice hardened. "Bolloxy *Duinedon* sons of bitches damn near killed her."

"They don't understand."

"And that gives them a right to go about murdering young girls? Burning out whole families? Driving people from their homes just because they're *Other*?" Rogan spat in the gutter. "It might not be such a bad thing to have Arthur back. Show those ignorant bastards we're not a bunch of demon spawn."

Brendan grabbed his arm, spinning him roughly around. "That's dangerous talk. It could get you into trouble."

Rogan pulled free. "And what's doing nothing got me?" He looked past Brendan to where Lyddy stood in the doorway, a hand shading her eyes. "Or any of us?" He raked a hand through his salt-and-pepper hair, defeat in his rounded shoulders. "Here, now, I'm sorry for gabbling on at you like that and I know you're right, Douglas. It's just"—he sighed—"sometimes I wonder: Can the world get any worse for us than it is now?"

Brendan gave a harsh bark of laughter. "That's a question to bring down Armageddon if ever I heard one."

"Yet you don't answer me."

"You want an answer? Then yes, Rogan." Brendan kneaded the throbbing muscles in his hand. "Take the word of one who knows: Should Máelodor succeed, hell will be the refuge."

"More pigeon pie? Cold mutton?" Madame Arana asked.

Elisabeth allowed the platter to pass her by. Not that she couldn't have eaten another helping, but already her stays bit into her sides and the borrowed gown she wore clamped around her middle. One more piece of bread and she'd be relegated to a sheet and a smile.

"Grand-mère!" Helena snapped.

Madame Arana jerked her head up, a guilty smile quirking her lips.

"I've allowed that walking flea hotel the freedom of the house. The least you can do is not feed him from the table."

"He's hungry, *ma minette*," she replied, unmoved by Helena's scolding.

Killer, obviously realizing he was the topic of conversation, moved to Helena with a soulful look and a wagging rear end before dropping to the rug to roll over in a love-me pose of abject patheticness.

"Don't even try your canine wiles on me. If you're not careful, I'll use your bony carcass for a throw rug," she warned.

The dog knew when it had met its match. It slunk under the table to lie like a hot, furry lump across Elisabeth's feet. He'd been missing since last night with none to say when or how he'd gotten out. And now here he was, as if he'd never left. Did he have a girlfriend? Was he hunting rats in the mews? Taking in the city's sights? Impossible to say with Killer. Sometimes he almost seemed human.

As dinner progressed around her, she sank into a pensive silence. She'd risen this morning to an empty bed. Brendan gone. She'd have almost doubted her own memories had she not smelled the musky foreign spice of him in her sheets and on her skin. Seen the marks of their marriage upon the flesh of her breasts, her stomach. A love bruise high upon her thigh. She hid her blush behind her wineglass, sipping slowly of the fine French claret.

"You look like a woman in love, *ma puce*. Marriage with young Douglas agrees with you."

Madame Arana's knowing grin deepened Elisabeth's flush. Heat flamed her face.

"You've been waiting for him many years, I'm thinking."

"Since I was ten and put a toad down his shirt," Elisabeth admitted. From the corner of her eye, she caught Helena shaking her head, mouth pulled into a disgusted frown.

She'd been this way ever since the wedding. Locked in her own thoughts. Surlier than usual.

Madame Arana didn't seem to notice her granddaughter's dark mood. Either that or she was used to it. She beamed as she buttered her bread. "Ah, a young girl's first love. And now you have him. No more waiting at the altar. It is done. *Tout de suite*. Just like that."

Elisabeth had him, all right. A tiger by the tail.

But had marrying Brendan been less about saving face and more a drastic last-ditch effort to hold on to him? A desperate measure meant to force a pledge made out of duty by a callow twenty-year-old? If so, she was a simpleton.

Oh, he'd given her all she asked for. Had awakened a wicked craving within her and then sated it with delicious thoroughness. He'd even allowed her a glimpse of more than his usual icy cynicism. But what did it mean if duty still drove him and nothing else? Fulfilling the letter if not the spirit of their vows? Could she live with that?

Was she insane to want to dare the deep waters when sense told her to remain satisfied with the shallows?

Did it matter when all hung upon such a precarious knife edge?

"You mustn't fret. Helena knows what she is doing. She would not ask it of young Douglas if she did not think their bargain would work out."

"Grand-mère!" Helena snapped again.

Nerves fluttered Elisabeth's stomach, making her relieved she'd not taken that helping. "Didn't think what bargain would work out? What have you asked of Brendan?"

Helena put down her wineglass. Crossed her arms in front of her, her gaze steady and inscrutable. "Douglas is Máelodor's only hope of finding the Sh'vad Tual. We're using this to our advantage. Luring Máelodor out from the shadows where he's hidden for so many years. Once he's exposed, the brotherhood can no longer dismiss his existence. We can move against him in force."

"You're using Brendan? He's spent the last seven years running from Máelodor, and now you want him to stake himself out like human bait?"

Helena's lips pursed, her body shifting ominously in her chair. "And why shouldn't he? It began with him. It's only fitting he should end it."

A sliver of fear seeped in to join Elisabeth's stomach's nervous dance. "What began with him?"

"Douglas has told you nothing of his past?"

Helena sounded surprised.

Feeling herself on the defensive, Elisabeth met bold gaze with bolder. "He's told me enough." She didn't like where this was headed. "I know Brendan's powerful among his race. That he was a source of great pride for the old earl, much to the chagrin of Brendan's older brother, Aidan."

"But not what havoc he wrought with that great gift." Contempt riddled Helena's tone. She pushed back from the table to stand, leaning her arms menacingly upon the table. "Did Douglas tell you he was part of the Nine like his father? Like Máelodor? That's why he ran. That's why he hid. And that's why he agreed to our bargain. Because if he didn't, he knew I wouldn't have hesitated to fulfill my duty and execute him for the cold-blooded, ruthless murderer he is."

The word hit Elisabeth like a punch to the stomach.

Murderer? Was it true?

I can't go home. Not ever.

Now she knew why.

"I want the truth, Brendan. All of it—not just the bits and pieces round the edges, but the whole stinking heap."

"And good evening to you too." Hair still damp from a bath, Brendan looked up from pulling on his boots, his cravat hanging loose against the open collar of his shirt. His jacket lying on the bed beside his waistcoat. A dab of paper stuck to his chin where he'd nicked himself shaving.

Ridiculous as it sounded, it wasn't the glittering, lynx-gold stare he fixed upon her that sent heat flooding her cheeks. Nor the sudden bunch of his muscles that made her stomach tingle. Not even the slow, dangerous smile creasing the tiny sun lines at the corners of his eyes that set her heart galloping.

No, it was that dratted bit of sticking plaster on his jaw. Evidence of his vulnerability. His humanity.

Her stupid, self-destructive, jelly-kneed infatuation.

"Answer my question," she snapped. "For once."

He dropped the boot to the carpet with a thud, creases deepening either side of his mouth, a guarded look instantly entering his gaze.

"I thought this was just about keeping that stone of yours safe, but it goes far and away beyond that, doesn't it?" she demanded. "No evasions. No snappy repartee. Clear, simple answers."

He bent to pull on his other boot before straightening slowly, spreading his hands palms up as if to show he had nothing to hide.

"Helena says you're going to set yourself up as a decoy to lure Máelodor out," she said.

His body tensed, a chill descending like a knife between them as he resumed dressing.

She'd pushed too far to surrender now. She'd never get a better chance. Brendan would not allow himself to be cornered again. "You said your father and Máelodor were part of the Nine. That the *Amhas-draoi* executed the members of the group. You never said why. What did they do, Brendan?" She swallowed. "What did *you* do?"

The sticking plaster had fallen off. And whatever she'd taken for vulnerability had vanished in the grim-edged contours of a face carved in stone. His mouth ringed in white, furrows in his brow. Eyes ablaze.

A man who frightened her with such a concentration of intensity, he seemed to radiate like sun off sand, yet despite everything made her feel and yearn as the Brendan she knew had always done.

"Lissa—" He spoke hoarsely, as if holding himself together by the barest of threads.

"Don't call me that." She drew in a shaky breath. "Tell me Helena lied and I'll believe you, but I want the truth."

As if she'd touched a nerve, the blaze in his eyes flared like oil thrown upon a fire.

"Shit." He lurched away with a sickened groan. "Isn't it obvious? The truth has been staring you in the face for weeks. Father spent his life searching for the relics, but to him they were merely artifacts. Pieces for a museum. It was me. I devised the damned plan. To use the Sh'vad Tual to break the wards shielding Arthur's tomb. I unraveled the spell that would resurrect the king as one of the *Domnuathi*. And when the violence escalated and the deaths began, I didn't care. As long as I could dig as deep as I wanted into the forbidden *Unseelie* magics, it didn't matter who was hurt along the way. I turned a blind eye to all of it. Now do you see?"

She shook her head, hearing the disgust in his voice. She would deny his words. It wasn't Brendan. No matter how many sins he'd committed, this was not the man who'd carried her home through the rain. Who'd allowed her to tag after him from the time she was old enough to escape her nurses. Who'd agreed to marry her when it would have been easier to walk away. And whose kisses seared a blast of heat straight to her dazed brain and whose touch melted her to sweet liquid ecstasy.

"You'd have done better to hold to your ignorance," Brendan said. "Knowledge is dangerous. It can blow up in your face."

She couldn't fit these pieces together into any puzzle

that made sense. "If your goal is the same as Máelodor's, why didn't you give him the stone years ago and be done with it?"

He didn't answer.

She latched onto his silence as a brief hope within the maze of her confusion. "Could it be because you're not the criminal they think you? It's been seven years. People change in seven years."

"People may change. They may wish with all their heart they could undo the things they've done, but the crimes remain. The stain of that legacy never leaves."

"You spoke once of your part in the murder of your father. What did you do, Brendan? What happened to him?"

Again he did not answer.

"That's why you came back to Dun Eyre. That's why you've agreed to this insane scheme of Helena's. To make amends." Terror fluttered up from her stomach into her chest. "Don't do it, Brendan. It's too dangerous. You said yourself Máelodor wants you—"

"Alive." His expression softened to one of sorrow. "And he'll keep me that way as long as I know where the stone is. And as long as I keep scream—" A shudder of his body. "As long as I entertain him."

She grabbed him as if she might hold him back. Keep him here with her in this room where they were warm and safe and where *Other* and *Duinedon* didn't matter. Where evil couldn't touch them. "Tell Helena you won't do it. Tell her to come up with some other way."

"There is no other way."

"You can't do this alone."

He shook her off. "I like alone."

"Then why did you marry me?"

Hand on the knob, he turned back, face graven with scorn. "Why indeed, Lissa?"

Brendan descended to the parlor. Voices rose and fell and silverware clinked from the dining room across the hall, but, thank the gods, this room was empty. He couldn't face any witnesses to his dance so close to the razor's edge.

He eyed the piano in the corner, deliberately turning his back on the instrument. Music wouldn't be enough to drive the devils from his mind tonight.

His temples throbbed as he lifted the decanter. His hands shook as he poured, whiskey sloshing over his fingers. He sucked it off, the bite of the alcohol lying sharp on his tongue. Falling into a chair, he clutched the glass before him, rolling the smoky gold whiskey around and around. Unable to drink, though he shivered uncontrollably, his gut in knots.

His body craved a different temptation. A tall, voluptuous figure filling a gown to distracting perfection. A wild riot of red hair meant for a man to run his fingers through. And dark, velvety eyes hinting at secrets a man would want to tease from a pair of full, pouty lips.

He shook his head, cursing his folly. He'd spoken the vows, signed the license, but his marriage with Elisabeth was as much a sham as ever. And now that she knew his criminal past, there was less than a blizzard's chance in the Sahara for the two of them. And that was a good thing. He'd only cause her grief. He excelled at hurting those closest to him.

But had he confessed his guilt in order to frighten her away, or had it been more a desperate bid to test the strength of her faith?

A question he couldn't answer that only showed him

how pathetic he'd become since returning to Ireland. The only thing he knew for certain: Lissa Fitzgerald couldn't be trusted to do what any normal, sane, levelheaded female would do—run like hell. No, she analyzed, scrutinized, re-arranged him into the hero of her wild imaginings.

He rose to toss the whiskey on the smoldering parlor fire, flames leaping high and bright in the grate, then dying back.

Shadows banished for the blink of an eye before crowding closer and thicker than ever.

Seventeen

"Killer, where are you, you naughty animal?"

Elisabeth peeked in and out of rooms in her search for the dog. If she didn't find him before Helena did, he'd be mincemeat. "I know you're hiding somewhere. I saw that gnawed table leg in the drawing room. How could you?"

No sign of him yet, and she'd hunted through every room from the ground floor up. Only the attics left to explore. The temperature dropped as she climbed the stairs, a whisper of a breeze scented with a woody sweet tang like cedar or patchouli lifting her shawl about her shoulders. "Killer?"

She'd expected the barren mustiness of a servant's garret. Instead, she stood in a long, slope-ceilinged chamber. North-facing windows along the back tossed clear afternoon sun in great puddles over a floor strewn with carpets and rugs like an Oriental bazaar. Furniture cluttered the far end of the room. Sofas and chairs, long buffet tables and delicate side tables—even a bed—stood crammed into a corner beneath the eaves, all as if someone's entire house had been packed into a few square feet.

The rest of the space resembled an apothecary's shop. Books stacked upon a desk. Others crammed willy-nilly into a tall case. Rows of tiny drawers lined one wall, neatly labeled, the contents alphabetized. Shelves containing jars of dried herbs, aromatic oils, spices, and scents. She picked one up, half expecting eye of newt or tongue of dog. Perhaps even a good dose or two of dragon venom.

Whale oil. Smelly, but hardly the stuff of witchcraft.

Replacing it upon the rack, she sighed.

It would take her hours to search the attic for one misbehaving mutt.

"Killer," she hissed. "Come out this instant."

She checked under tables and behind boxes. Even opened a wardrobe's doors, finding an abandoned mouse's nest and a few hungry moths, but nothing else. Rising from an investigation of the space beneath the bed, she felt the back of her neck prickle. A queer trill of nerves up her spine as if she were being watched.

Spinning around, she froze. No one was there. The chamber remained empty. Yet the feeling persisted. A strange watching presence lifted the hairs on her arms, prickling the back of her neck. She was picking her way back toward the stairwell when she caught movement from the corner of her eye. A flicker of gold. A drift of gray. She paused, and the movement stopped. She started, and it began again.

There behind that highboy. She laughed, her voice sounding shrill in the quiet room. Of course. A mirror.

The cheval glass stood apart from the rest of the furniture. A piece of cloth draped across its speckled surface. An old mirror, then, the silver backing coming away in spots. Woodland animals twined with flowers and leaves around the frame. Perfectly rendered in the dark, polished cherry.

Unable to help herself, she caressed each carved detail, drinking in the blunt, suspicious features of a badger, the long twitching nose of a fox, a kestrel's wing outstretched as if it might catch the next updraft. Skimmed her fingers lightly over the curved petals and wide leaves of a king cup, the delicate grace of a wood anemone, a fern's intricate fronds.

Her hand barely touched the glass when the mirror's surface clouded, the light within dimming to obsidian, but for a slash of silver lightning.

She shouldn't look. This was *Other* magic. Trouble in every sense of the word. Hadn't it been proven to her over and over? But even as the thought burst in her, she pulled aside the cloth, letting it slither to the floor in a pile. The boil of storm-cloud black rippled over the mirror, the lightning charge off its surface prickling her skin.

"Elisabeth?"

A voice startled her heart into her throat.

Madame Arana stood wiping her hands upon a towel at the far end of the room, a door behind her open on some kind of storeroom or office. She wore a long snowy apron and a mobcap to cover her wispy white hair. "I thought I heard someone wandering about up here."

Elisabeth fought to keep the giddiness from her voice. "I apologize, but Killer . . ."

The dog trotted around Madame Arana's skirts to sit at her feet, his pink tongue hanging from the side of his mouth, wearing a wide doggie smile.

"He's been keeping me company while I work." She

threw a critical gaze around the clutter. "You must excuse my lack of order. When I moved my household, I could not bear to part with my things. So many memories, you see. Some pieces I brought all the way from my homeland in Provence when I fled the troubles. Helena, she lets me store them for when I am homesick for the old days." Her smile vanished, her mouth folding into a deep frown, her eyes scalpel-sharp. "But you don't want to hear an old woman's stories. You worry over young Douglas." She laid aside the towel. "Has he yet to return, then?"

Madame Arana's otherworldly insight was unsettling yet comforting. It was almost a relief to Elisabeth not to have to explain herself to someone who seemed able to pull the thoughts right out of her head.

"No, Helena's not seen him all day. I . . . he finally told me what happened. Everything."

"Did he, now?" Madame Arana rubbed her chin in thought. "His mask crumbles more quickly than I thought."

That was exactly what he wore. A charming, seductive disguise to keep everyone at arm's length. Peel one away and there would be twenty more layers behind it. The man was virtually armor-plated.

Again, as if reading her mind, Madame Arana nodded sagely. "He's locked much inside him. Unable and unwilling to face the things he did while under his father's influence. Such denial can fester like an untreated wound. Cause great suffering. The spirits do not like to be ignored. They will find a way to be heard."

She approached Elisabeth, the deep wells of her eyes an infinite spinning of the heavens. Her hands as they caressed the rim of the mirror like those of a tender lover. "You've found my scrying glass. It shows me things when I ask. Not always, but when the mood strikes."

"It's alive?" For a moment, Elisabeth had forgotten the presence of the unnerving mirror, but now it seemed to crackle behind her as if acknowledging the compliment.

"Not as you and I are alive," Helena's grandmother replied, "but like all things born of *Fey* magic it bears a will. And it is aware. It is how I knew Douglas had returned to Ireland. It is how I know there can be no return of Arthur without great suffering." Her gaze moved between Elisabeth and the mirror. "You have seen something."

"I didn't . . . that is, I felt someone watching me. Or thought I did, but that's absurd."

Madame Arana's gaze narrowed. "The glass would not have spoken to you if the need were not great. You must accept the invitation and learn its secrets."

"I don't want to learn any more secrets. I know them all."

"But you do not believe. Not completely. You think Helena lies or that Brendan exaggerates. That there must be a mistake somewhere."

"Brendan wouldn't do such awful things. He's sarcastic and intense and arrogant and at times downright infuriating, but he's not a murderer."

"Perhaps you choose to see only the parts of him you want to see. The man who makes your heart flutter and your blood heat. To know the man for who he truly is, you must recognize the best he can be and the worst he is capable of. The mirror will reflect both if you are strong enough to face the truth."

The challenge in Madame Arana's stare set Elisabeth's hands back upon the glass. Instead of the heat she expected, an icy chill raced up her arm. Buried its frozen needles deep into her center. Gasping, she sought to break free, but the mirror held her. The contact between them unbreakable. A scene surfaced as if rising from the deep of an ocean's tempest. A heavy drone like a hive of bees pounded in her ears.

As she watched, the cloudy glass focused upon nine figures becoming nine men. A tenth prostrate within the circle. The drone expanded to become words. Words chanted over and over. Words in a language she'd heard only once before in her life. In a clearing at Belfoyle. Spoken by a boy whose life had always seemed charmed and whose love she'd long ago given up on.

"*Yn-mea esh a gwagvesh. A-dhiwask polth. Dreheveth hath omd-hiskwedhea.*"

As she watched, a cloud formed over the man on the ground. Coalesced to become a monstrous creature. Teeth. Claws. A body squat and ungainly.

The chanting rose in pitch and excitement. "*Skeua hesh flamsk gwruth dea.*"

The man on the ground shuddered.

"*Drot peuth a galloea esh a dewik lya. Drot peuth a pystrot esh a dewik spyrysoa.*"

The creature hovered for an instant above the man before the two seemed to merge. The process causing the gorge to rise in Elisabeth's throat as the victim screamed and fought his transformation.

At the end, what had once been human now stood facing its creators.

Two men stepped into the circle. The elder, his bearing regal, solemn as a graven image. The younger, his face a mask of horror, but his gold eyes wild with excitement.

"Ana daraa ymesh'na igosk," he said. "The Nine welcome the Dark Court."

The creature's mouth drew back in a razored snarl, more grotesque as it bore the features of the victim it had possessed. *"Ana N'thashyl hyghtyesh, Erelth."*

With a cry, Elisabeth tore herself free. Heart thrashing against her ribs, throat sore as if she'd been screaming. She could barely breathe, as if the air within the room had thickened to smoke. Bitter. Acrid. It stuck to her throat. Stung her eyes. She trembled against the splash of icy awareness then the wash of heat that followed. Felt the lancing tightness of a headache clamp her skull.

What kind of man comes up with such madness and evil? What kind of monster would conjure such sickening malice?

Brendan. The Nine. The true son of his father.

She wrapped her arms around herself as she shivered, sickened by what she'd witnessed. "He's as monstrous as Máelodor. This is his fault. All of it."

"Is that what you think?"

"Can you tell me it's not? Look what Brendan's madness has unleashed. His father's death. His family's ruin. And if Máelodor ever captures the Sh'vad Tual, the atrocities could begin all over again. I knew I should never have asked. I didn't want to know. The world of *Other* is cursed. Magic and the *Fey* and the rest of it. It's nothing but misery and trouble."

"Ah, but there is misery whether we live our lives as *Other* or *Duinedon*. And trouble will find us no matter whether we hide from it or meet it head-on. You have seen young Douglas's past. His shame. His crimes as Helena might deem them. But have you not seen his bravery, his honor, and his love as well? He braved capture to return to

Dun Eyre for you, he has offered the honor of his name when his actions caused your ruination, and his love?"

"He doesn't love me. He cares for me. He worries over me, but he doesn't love. Not in the way I once hoped he might."

"Does he not? I would say it is his love for you and again for his family that has caused Brendan to agree to Helena's scheme. He is willing to risk all for love. Can you not see your way clear to do the same?"

Brendan walked. He couldn't say how many miles he wandered nor what he saw. Lanes merged into one another, crowds jostled him, the sky opened, drenching him to the skin with a miserable cold rain.

He slept for a few hours in the shadow of Kilronan House, the ruin a fitting backdrop for his mood. Was prodded awake by a constable who found himself backed against a wall, a hand pressed across his throat until the dreams receded and Brendan realized where he was. The next hour he spent eluding capture, his street skills kicking in as he moved silently and expertly through the close, dirty alleys. Crossed the Liffey at Essex Bridge, the brackish brown river gliding beneath him.

He paused for a moment, dismissing the inspiration almost as soon as it entered his head. He'd never been desperate enough to contemplate that way out, even when he'd been numbed by opium and stupid with booze. If arrogant pride was his greatest sin, it was also his greatest strength. There was always an answer. Always a way. One simply needed to attack the problem from all angles. Use all available tools at hand. Persistence and a dogged unwillingness to surrender.

Still, Elisabeth's face haunted him. Her expression as she fought to hold to an ideal he'd known from the start he could never live up to. Now she knew it too.

On impulse, he shoved his way toward Cutpurse Alley and Macklins in case Jack had arrived. Spent an hour or two crammed into a corner, watching the door. No luck and no message. What the hell had happened? Had the *Amhas-draoi* found Jack? Had Máelodor? Was his cousin lying dead in a ditch or had he merely lost track of time as he fleeced the last coins from some naive patsy?

Back out on the street, Brendan pulled his coat collar up around his neck against the renewal of this afternoon's storms. With no destination in mind, he skirted Saint Patrick's and the tangled alleys nearby. Turning off Lower Coombe, he sensed his first stalker.

Two streets later, a second joined the chase.

By the time Brendan reached the yards behind Elbow Lane, the hunt was on.

His body vibrated like a wire. His awareness expanding as he sank into a role he'd played across countries and continents. The rabbit running before the hounds.

Were these Máelodor's men looking to capture their quarry or *Amhas-draoi* determined to assassinate the Nine's last member?

His answer came all too soon. In a blind alley behind a tanner's yard. Nowhere to step into the deeper shadows until danger passed. No way to double back and lead them on a false scent. The *Amhas-draoi* warrior straddled the roadway, his features granite-hard and inscrutable, mage energy scalding the surface of Brendan's mind with a blast of numbing power.

Drawing his knife, Brendan lunged forward, hoping

to thread his way between the giant and the nearest house. Jinking sideways, he threw himself in the gap, rolling back to his feet with a yell of pure excitement, the knife still clutched in his hand.

And just as suddenly he dropped to his knees, his cry becoming a stifled scream as mage energy crushed him.

The man stood over him, victory in his impassive eyes as the battle magic knifed through Brendan, a horrible scything of joint and tendon. He curled into a ball, unable to breathe without a stabbing pain cutting into his lungs.

Spots and pinwheels burst across his vision, blood pounding in his ears, but he fought back. Raw instinct taking over as he unleashed his own powers upon Scathach's gloating warrior.

The man reeled, his expression one of shock, then pain, as Brendan slammed his knife hilt-deep into the fighter's gut.

The *Amhas-draoi*'s battle magic receded like an ebb tide, leaving Brendan shaky and sick but whole. He scrambled to his feet, heart thrashing in his chest. Ducked a wild blow. Lurched away from a second. Gauged his situation, trapped as he was between Scathach's soldier boy and the mouth of the alley.

Without warning, the *Amhas-draoi* charged like a bull. "Filthy murderous pig," he spat from a twisted, white-lipped mouth.

"Stubborn jackass," Brendan shot back, dancing on the balls of his feet, keeping the man at arm's length as he sought to steal along the wall. What the hell did it take to bring one of the brotherhood down? The man pressed a hand to his abdomen, his face going pale as a winding sheet, yet he continued to fight with amazing ferocity.

"You think this wise? Anyone could happen on us. Scathach won't be happy with questions."

"No one's going to happen by, Douglas. And there won't be enough of you left for anyone to question."

"How did I know you were going to say that?" Brendan parried a knife thrust, hammering the man a blow to the chin that should have knocked him cold, but only seemed to enrage him further—if that were possible.

With lightning speed, the *Amhas-draoi* swept out, catching Brendan a slice across his chest. A shallow, stinging gash, but enough to break his focus. Instantly, a numbing chill stole over him as the man sought to use the opportunity to bind Brendan in a web of mage energy. Already his limbs grew unresponsive, his muscles freezing over. Much longer, and he'd be unable to dodge a thrust through the heart.

Thank the gods for all those years of rote study. The counterspell swam up out of his hazy memory, released on a gasp of breath as the bonds of magic tightened across his chest. With a shout, he threw himself under the man's clumsy swing, blood loss finally taking its toll. Another parry and roll, and Brendan was out. Nothing else stood between him and the street.

Once beyond the alley, all he would need was a moment to bend his concentration toward a cloaking spell. The invisibility of the *feth-fiada*. Anything to buy him running room.

Just as he hit the corner, a blast of battle magic pummeled him from behind, flinging him forward into the gutter, his knife spinning away.

It was like being struck by lightning. Mage energy lanced through him along fried nerves, his brain shocked into whirling confusion.

He stumbled into a stack of crates. Scraped his hands as he fell to his knees. Sweat stinging his eyes. Escape screaming in his ears.

A shout. His own or someone else's? He didn't stop to look. To answer.

He ran.

"Wake up, *ma puce*. You must dress quickly."

The voice yanked her from sleep. Dropped her to earth with a dull thud.

She tried pulling the covers over her head, but the voice persisted. "Elisabeth, it is important. It is young Douglas. You must come."

The thread of fear running beneath the words did more than the hand on her shoulder to drag her up and out of the quilts. She rubbed the sleep from her eyes, a tremor shaking her hands. The danger had finally caught them up.

"What's happened?"

"Rogan has come with news. The *Amhas-draoi* found Douglas."

Elisabeth forced a calm she did not feel. "Is he . . ." The words caught like glass in her throat.

"He is alive, but hurt. Helena tells me to let you sleep, *mais vous êtes son épouse*—you are his wife. It is for you to be there as well." Madame Arana dragged her out of the quilts. "Come. We leave soon. Dress and be downstairs in ten minutes."

And then she was gone, leaving Elisabeth shaking with cold and dread and a knowledge she wished she could wipe clear from her mind. She sat on the edge of the bed, hands braced on either side of her, staring at her toes.

She closed her eyes. The vision she'd seen in the mirror

rising in her mind's eye as the gorge rose in her throat. Madame Arana's admonition scraping across her heart. Her own denials pounding in her head.

Had she meant what she'd said when she'd tried to convince him of his redemption? Or had she merely been hoping to convince herself?

A thought occurred to her there in the dark with the memories thick as wraiths around her. Would this attack convince Brendan that Helena's plan was futile? Would he decide survival meant losing himself again? Living amid strangers in a foreign land? A man with no past. And no future.

Could she let him go without a fight?

Again?

With shaking fingers, she buttoned herself into her gown. With a heart pounding unsteadily in her chest, she dressed her hair. And in nine minutes fifty-nine seconds, she was downstairs, ready to go.

Eighteen

He tried opening his eyes, but they seemed weighted shut, just as his arms and legs barely held the strength to move and every breath came as a struggle. Piecing together the scraps of memory, he recalled a filth-strewn alley, pain enough to fell an elephant, and a man strangely familiar to him warning him to be silent as he shoved Brendan beneath a tarpaulin.

So where the blazes was he now?

Scratchy, smelly wool beneath his cheek. A steady drip of water from somewhere nearby. The sour odors of stale alcohol and old sex.

"*Shhh*, rest easy." A cool hand on his forehead. A woman's voice, but not one he recognized.

He tried turning his head toward the voice, sending a sizzling twist of pain shooting down his neck into his spine, squeezing his ribs as if they might snap. He moaned and retched, the hand falling away with a tiny cry of surprise.

The curved edge of a glass was pressed to his lips, liquid running down his throat. Thick and sweet, though a medicinal bitterness lingered. A taste he recognized, though it had been long years.

"To help you sleep," the voice comforted.

He struggled to open his eyes, to warn her about what she'd done, to heave up the viscous poison seeping into his system. Yet even as he tried to open his mouth, his weighted body seemed to cave in on itself, his breathing deepened, his guts twisted, and he knew nothing more.

"What happened?" The first words out of Helena's mouth upon pushing open the door of the dingy dram shop. "You were supposed to be following him."

Rogan rose from a chair, pipe clenched between his teeth, his gaze flicking over Elisabeth. "Should she be here?"

Helena's dark eyes flashed. "My grandmother thought it best for her to be at her new husband's deathbed."

Elisabeth caught back a gasp, her hand tightening on Madame Arana's.

Rogan shot her a comforting shake of his head. "Here, now, it's not as bad as that. Lyddy's in with him. He's sleeping."

"What happened, Rogan?" Helena asked.

He rubbed a tired hand over his face. "Douglas slipped his leash. I spent a half day crisscrossing this blasted city before I picked up his trail. He'd hidden his magic well. There was barely a trace to follow. I finally found him near Meath market covered in blood and out of his head with battle magic. Said he'd been set on by an *Amhas-draoi* but managed to knife him before he escaped."

"Devil take it!" Helena muttered. "All I need is Douglas

killing one of the brotherhood for this whole scheme to unravel."

"Let me see him," Elisabeth interrupted, lifting her chin, squaring her shoulders.

Rogan hesitated.

"Now, please," Elisabeth asserted with chilly authority.

"Aye, of course. He's upstairs."

Rogan led the way, pushing through a curtain at the back of the room, the rest of them following. Down a narrow passage, out a back door, up a rickety flight of stairs.

"How did he get away?" Helena demanded.

"He wasn't up to much talking, but I caught the word 'chase' and what I thought sounded like 'naked man,' at which point he passed out."

"Did you say 'naked man'?"

"Could have been 'baked ham,' or mayhap 'wicked plan.'" Rogan scratched his head as Helena sighed.

"You did well," Madame Arana said, a gentle hand upon the harper's shoulder.

He shook his head. "If I'd found him before the brotherhood, we'd have saved ourselves a peck of trouble."

He tapped at a door that opened on a tiny young woman, her eyes darting from face to face, her hands wrenched into her apron.

"I've brought the help I promised, Lyddy." Rogan motioned to Elisabeth. "And the man's wife."

Relief visible in her face, the woman opened the door, ushering them into a shabby little room. The only light coming from a tallow candle upon a battered table. Beside it, a plate held a gristly piece of fat swimming in grease and some burnt potatoes. "I tried feeding him, but he wouldn't take nothing, so I gave him a sleeping draught. It seemed to help for a bit, but now he's moaning and thrashing as if he's got the devil after him."

Brendan lay restless upon a straw-filled mattress, a grimy blanket over him. Sweat plastered his hair to his head, his shirt to his chest where he labored to breathe as if he were running. He was awake, his staring bloodshot eyes locked on some invisible scene, neck muscles taut as he hissed, "Freddie, damn it, just do as they ask."

Freddie?

A memory nagged at the back of Elisabeth's brain as a shiver of apprehension licked over her skin. "It wasn't laudanum, was it?"

"Aye, it was. I'd a little from an apothecary what . . ." Lyddy's words trailed off as she noted Elisabeth's troubled expression. "Was that not right to do?"

"Laudanum makes him ill," Elisabeth explained, crossing to crouch beside Brendan, a hand upon his forehead.

Lyddy's brows snapped low, her chin jutting forward in a belligerent frown, hand on one hip. "Well, how was I to know? Rogan shows up with a man half dead and says nurse him. I did what I could. I did my best. What do I look like? A surgeon?"

Helena studied her with a bloodless twitch of her lips. "I don't think anyone would mistake you for that."

Not to be outdone, Lyddy eyed Helena with a sharp, catty gaze. "At least I've got me a man. From what I've heard, you've naught but cobwebs between your legs since that fellow of yours up and died."

Helena stiffened, a strange expression passing over her features, steel entering her gaze. "Charming young lady, Rogan. Wherever did you find such a pleasing creature?"

"Lyddy, I'll be having words with you." Rogan grabbed her by the arm. "Now."

He hustled her out, justifications trailing behind her. "She's no right to talk to me that way. I done the best I could. Who does she think—" A door slammed below.

Madame Arana bent beside Elisabeth.

"Can you do anything?" Elisabeth asked, taking Brendan's hand in her own.

Madame Arana placed a freckled hand upon his chest. Closed her eyes, her seamed and wrinkled face alive with concentration. "If it is battle magic, there are ways. But if his sickness originates with the drug, it is best to let it run its course."

Brendan's eyes locked on Elisabeth's, the gold of his irises a dull muddy bronze. "Not such a good bargain after all." His laughter came tinged with bitterness. "Should have married your sheepdog."

Freddie's eyes haunted Brendan. Disbelief to shock to terror to sightless in death. He relived the sequence of expressions in an infinite loop. Freddie's murder playing again and again in his fevered mind.

The confrontation turning ugly. The men in Brendan's company growing first impatient, then violent. Threats. Ultimatums. And the murders one by one of Freddie's family before his horrified eyes. His death coming when it finally did, almost a mercy. A heedless ride away from the scene, fire raging at Brendan's back. Eyes red with smoke and weeping, hands gripping the reins slick with a cold sweat, sickness chattering his teeth, souring his stomach.

Freddie had trusted him. Father had trusted him. Elisabeth had trusted him.

Two out of three dead. His fault. All of it was his fault.

He heaved his guts up, throat raw, muscles jumping.

Calm words soothed the howling cries of the dead. Hands gentled him. He rolled onto his side, squeezing his eyes shut, praying for relief. He didn't want to relive it. Not again. Not the imagined murder of his father. Not the real memory of Freddie's butchering.

Why wouldn't they leave him alone? What did he have to do to send them away? To live without them in his head?

As if to taunt him, a new face swarmed up out of his nightmares. A monster of fangs and talons. A creature born of smoke and brimstone and keen with malice. It hovered above him. Waiting. Watching. Knowing its time drew close.

Its mouth opened on a bloody maw, its tongue thick and forked and slithering with snaky words. *"Ana N'thashyl gorloa agasesh gelweth. A'sk beuewik perthyana, Erelth."*

Agony drove the breath from Brendan's lungs, seared the blood in his veins. He jerked awake. The *Unseelie* vanished. Freddie gone.

But as if his old friend had pulled him aside and whispered the answer in his ear, Brendan knew what he had to do to end the nightmares. To end the threat.

Máelodor must die.

And Brendan was the only one who could do it.

Elisabeth kept vigil from a chair by the door. She'd propped it open, hoping to air out the musty room, though nothing seemed to dispel the heavy, fetid atmosphere. Smoke from cook fires mixed with the stench of latrines and animal dung from the nearby alley floated in on a sour breeze. Shouts and cries and rude laughter rose from the close-winding maze of nearby streets. A beggar snored in the shade of a torn tarpaulin. A hollow-eyed woman picked through a refuse heap beside her child while chickens pecked among the dirt at their feet.

Elisabeth wrapped her shawl closer around her, turning her face away from the distressing sights beyond her door to the man sleeping beside her. An arm lay outside the blanket, the shoulder pink and shiny with recent scarring, the curve of the crescent-and-arrow tattoo, a dark ribbon against the gray pallor of his skin.

He rested peacefully this morning. Earlier he'd called out to the mysterious Freddie. At first begging him to surrender. Later, pleading for his forgiveness. A hazy memory nagged at the edge of her mind, but as his outbursts grew less frequent and then stopped altogether, her thoughts turned to more immediate concerns.

Would the *Amhas-draoi* still be searching for him? Would they track him here? Was their refuge fast becoming their trap? What if Máelodor's men took this moment to attack?

Elisabeth forced her mind off problems for which she had no solutions. Instead she watched as Brendan fought a sickness Madame Arana said was cured only by time. Another facet to a man she once thought she knew.

Only now was she finally coming to realize that man had never existed. He'd been a mirage. Smoke and mirrors. A *Fey*-glittery delusion she'd clung to long after she should have known better.

But what about the Brendan who fought tooth and nail to make up for his crimes? Who risked his very life to undo the horror he'd unleashed as part of the Nine? Who wept for a lost family and a home he feared he'd never see again?

No fantasies shaped her knowledge of this man. She saw him for what he was. Desperate. Lonely and alone.

And as real as the warm muscled flesh beneath her fingers, the wicked gleam in his eyes, the spicy foreign scent of him that clung to her hair and her clothes and her skin as he pleasured her senseless.

Daylight faded, leaving the room gray and cold and colorless. His hand flattened out upon the blankets. His breath became a sigh, his eyes fluttered open. Dazed at first before sharpening hard as diamonds.

Throwing himself up against the wall, he let the sheet slither to his waist. His gaze sliced over the room as if searching for something, landing on Elisabeth, confusion slowly replacing his wild-eyed trapped look. He settled back, wary but calmer. "Where am I?" His voice came cool and brittle as glass.

"In rooms above a tavern off Bridgefoot Street."

Understanding dawned as his gaze cleared. "How long?"

"Three days."

"Shit," he muttered, kicking free of his blankets as he tried to rise. "A damned sitting duck." His glance slanted toward her, the cautious light still blazing in his eyes as he swayed dizzily. "I'm surprised to see you here. Come to finally make good on your threat? Poison in my soup, I believe it was."

She flinched, remembering that long-ago confrontation. It seemed like another Elisabeth Fitzgerald who'd sparred with him over his shocking return to Dun Eyre. She'd changed. Become a different person since then. Or perhaps she'd simply reverted to the woman she'd been before he vanished, taking her dreams with him.

"If murder's your goal, you'll have to take a number," he grumbled. "The line of people who want my head on a pike is growing longer by the bloody hour."

Could any man drive her more insane? Elisabeth returned his glare, the urge to throw her arms around him warring with an equally strong urge to beat him over the head. "That's gratitude for you. If you must know, I've spent the last days making sure you didn't turn up your toes. Fat lot of thanks I get."

His eyes widened as he staggered against a wall, throwing out a hand to steady himself. Shook his head as if trying to clear it. "We didn't exactly part on the best of terms."

"I had a right to know, Brendan."

He grimaced. "And now you do. Happy?"

"Ecstatic," she shot back. Men!

He dragged a hand through his shaggy hair as he padded over to the table and the pitcher set there. He lifted an eyebrow in question. She answered with a nod.

With a weary sigh, he upended the pitcher over his head, gasping as the water spilled out over him. He heaved a sigh, slapping the hair off his face. "Much better. I feel almost human," he said with a wry twist of his lips

She swallowed around her caught breath, trying not to stare at his muscled chest or the way the water tracked over the sculpted elegance of his face, slid down over the ridges of his stomach into the waistband of his breeches. He certainly didn't look like any convalescent she'd ever seen.

His eyes flicked toward her, a strange glimmer in their depths as if he knew exactly what she was thinking. "You were here throughout?"

She blushed an uncomfortable scarlet, hating herself for doing so. What on earth did she have to blush about? They were married. They'd seen every embarrassing inch of each other. So why, then, did she feel as if a new and impenetrable wall had risen between them? "Since Rogan came to Duke Street with word of the attack."

Sagging onto the pallet, he dropped his head in his hands. "Gods, that must have been pleasant."

"I can think of more suitable adjectives."

He lifted his eyes, his expression unyielding. "As can I. Let's try 'foolhardy' for starters. 'Cork-brained.' 'Utterly and completely out of your pretty little head.' If they'd found me here—" His jaw jumped, his mouth set in a grim line. "How could Helena let you stay, knowing the danger?"

Elisabeth folded her arms across her chest. "Helena doesn't *let* me do anything, and I don't have to ask her permission. I stayed with you because I wanted to and because you're my husband."

He gave a disgusted snort. "You know, I almost thought we could—" He shook his head. "Too late now for that."

Too late for what? She wanted to shake him by the shoulders and force him to explain himself. But the space between them seemed strewn with obstacles. Until Brendan stepped out from the shadow of his past, there could be no future for them. Not for all her wishing.

He opened his eyes, casting a rueful look up at her. "Have you ever wished you could turn back time? Wake up one morning and know you've your whole life ahead of you, clear of any mistakes?"

Was she one of his mistakes? She didn't ask. The answer would be too demoralizing. Instead she said, "You were barely more than a boy, Brendan. Your father never should have brought you into his schemes."

"Don't make excuses for me, Elisabeth. They were my schemes. The Nine never would have grown so powerful without my wholehearted involvement."

"So what changed?"

"Freddie Atwood."

She sucked in a quick, sharp breath. Of course, the nagging question tickling the back of her mind. "What has Freddie to do with any of this?" She asked the question, yet a spreading ill feeling told her she already knew the answer.

"He was *Other*. Did you know? His whole family possessed *Fey* blood, but in Freddie it flowered to a strength that brought him to our attention."

She hadn't known, but then, why would she have? Freddie Atwood had simply been one of the neighborhood boys: a bruising rider, a good-natured partner at dances, a laughing, jolly fellow with a twinkle in his blue eyes. Never a hint there was more to him than that.

"I recruited him into the network. And for a time, he and I worked well together, but he soured on the group. Decided to get out." Brendan paused, his body rigid, his breathing coming faster, his gaze focused on his linked hands.

Elisabeth felt her own tension increase, a throbbing at her temples.

"There was too much at stake by then. We couldn't allow deserters. They gave me the task of persuading him to remain."

Her mouth had gone bone-dry. She wished Brendan hadn't used all the water. She could really use a drink right now. "The fire was blamed on the peasants as retaliation for an increase in rents. You were there, you never said——"

He eyed her as if she were daft. "That the deaths of Freddie and his family were my fault? Of course not. But after that, it was never the same between my father and me. I saw the truth of what we were doing. How it couldn't possibly succeed without the deaths of thousands like Freddie—innocents caught up in our madness." He gave a grim quirk of his mouth. "Here's where you tell me I'm a heartless murdering bastard. That I deserve the death Máelodor wants to mete out, and that you hate me and wish you'd never married me."

She flinched. "I don't wish that."

His laugh was rough and cruel and like a nail through her heart. "Though you don't deny the rest."

Brendan's stomach remained fragile, his nerves raw and jumping, but the worst had passed. The hell of gape-mouthed, eyeless dead had faded. Their grasping hands receded into the twisted strangulation of soaked sheets. The hiss and snarl of their curses no more than rain against the window.

In the early days of his withdrawal from the opium, he'd spent weeks pacing the floor as images crashed through a brain afire with insatiable need. Pausing only to take a few drops of water or a foul piece of bread before heaving it up, his stomach unable to handle nourishment.

That had been years ago. His body no longer craved the poison. His mind had been freed from the constant hunger. Or so he thought until he woke from sleep with violent cramps, sweat bathing him, the bittersweet aftertaste of opium upon his tongue.

Had the ministering been purposeful?

None knew of his affliction. None but Jack and those who'd dragged him free of the drug the first time in a grimy set of rooms over a Turkish souk.

A mistake then. But it only underscored how little it would take to bring him to his knees. How easily he could be pulled from his current path. How close to the surface the demons drifted.

Yet something had changed. It had happened so gradually he couldn't pinpoint the exact moment, but the certainty of the difference was tangible. He'd not spoken Freddie's name aloud in years. Had done all he could to push the events of that day as far down within him as possible. Yet never was he able to eradicate completely the shame and the guilt of his crimes.

Until today. And Elisabeth.

Always a surprise. Always unpredictable. Never doing what he expected. Or what any rational female might do when confronted with her husband's infamy.

Brendan had awakened to that light, citrusy floral perfume of hers, her scent tearing through the fog of his fever. Not truly believing until he'd opened his eyes to see her watching him, her gaze a troubled mix of worry, fear, and affection.

For an instant, he'd known pure happiness. A stab of hope and pride and desire and love so fierce his chest ached with it. He'd almost told her. Almost taken her hand in his and dragged her down beside him where he might show her; the need to wrap himself in these feelings had been almost undeniable. But cooler heads prevailed. Practicality had trumped sentimental dreams.

There was no future for him there. He knew that now. He had given her the dubious protection of his name and the benefits of his ragged honor. To offer anything more would only make the end that much harder. Best to sever this tie now before he changed his mind. Before he drowned in those deep brown eyes or tasted the ripe sweetness of those lips.

So Freddie became the weapon.

A lethal blade he'd mercilessly turned upon himself.

Only somehow it hadn't been the killing stroke he anticipated. Instead, it had felt as if something had broken loose inside him. He closed his eyes and saw—nothing. No jagged pieces of anguished memory etched upon his brain. As if slicing open the old wound had finally cleansed it of its power.

"Like a cat with nine lives." Helena Roseingrave stood within the doorway. No knock. No hesitation. She gave him her usual glacial stare, her gaze lingering upon his tattoo, a flicker of some lost emotion in her eyes. "I've seen that before."

He pulled his shirt over his head. "The mark of a lost cause," he growled.

She entered the room, closing the door behind her. "Your *bride* sent word you wanted to speak with me."

The contempt in her tone sent an impossible fury lancing through him. "You can say what you want about me, but I don't ever want to hear you say one goddamn word about Elisabeth. Do you hear me?"

The flicker became a flame. "Playing at the besotted bridegroom? How noble of you." She stiffened. "What do you want, Douglas? I'm busy mopping up your mistakes, so excuse me if I don't swoon like the rest of the female race at your feet. You'll be relieved to know the fellow you knifed is recovering nicely."

"Should I send him flowers and an apology?" Helena Roseingrave might be a coldhearted bitch, but she was exactly what he needed to drive Elisabeth from his head. Hard to mope while trading barbs with a woman who'd be more than happy to see him drawn and quartered. "That was the second time one of the *Amhas-draoi* tried murdering me."

"And that surprises you? I warned you there was a standing order to kill you on sight. Did you think I exaggerated? If Máelodor's men have learned of your return, so have the *Amhas-draoi*. You should have followed orders and stayed close to Rogan."

"I'm not a child who needs minding. I managed for years without the use of a mage-chaser to keep me out of danger."

"Even the luckiest lose now and again," she answered bitterly. "Listen and listen well, Douglas. Had you killed that *Amhas-draoi,* I'd have butchered you myself, plan or no plan. I may be stretching the rules for you, but if this blows up, you go down alone."

"How noble of you," he answered her scorn with his own. "Has the brotherhood discovered we're working together?"

"Not so far as I can tell, but that could change. Just in case, you can't return to Duke Street. You can come to gather your things, but then you'll have to lay low somewhere in the city." She opened the door, scanning the yard before turning back, jaw set. "It shouldn't be much longer. I hear the bounty on your head has gone up. You're quite a catch these days."

"Máelodor's growing desperate. The summoning of the *Domnuathi* nearly destroyed him. Soon he'll be too ill to work the magic."

"Alive, he remains a lethal threat. Dead, and any hope of clearing your name is gone. Quite a conundrum."

"I'm glad you can call it such. I call it a devilish great nuisance."

Her gaze passed over the squalid ruin of the chamber. "It still amazes me how far you've fallen. From the pampered son of an earl to this."

"The location's not much but the service is excellent."

"Always the wit, Douglas, though I think after the last few days I'm in on your little secret."

"I sleep in the buff?"

Her look shot daggers. "Your guilt almost killed you."

"Fortunately shame isn't fatal. It just plays havoc with your free will." He offered a casual shrug and a flash of a gallows smile before sobering. "What will happen to Elisabeth once I leave the town house? You have to promise me she'll be taken care of."

"She's welcome to stay with Grand-mère and me until this is over and you return for her."

Brendan concentrated on knotting his cravat, eyes downcast. Over and under, his hands fumbling with the knot, muttering under his breath.

"You're not coming back, are you?" Helena ventured. "This marriage of yours. It was all a sham. You plan on skipping out on her just like last time."

He tossed the damned cravat on the pallet. "My marriage is as legal as I can make it. And you'll see that Mr. McKelway trumpets his part in matters to the heavens when the time comes. But no, I don't think I'll be coming back." He lifted a brow. "And you don't either. So between us, let's stop pretending."

She smoothed her hands down the sides of her skirt, lifting her chin high, her face a mask of *Amhas-draoi* determination. "Máelodor has to be stopped, Douglas. The *Other* are scared and nervous, the tension between the races thin as spring ice. All it will take is the rise of a leader on the part of our people to solidify their discontent into rage, and the world won't know what hit it. Already there are reports of *Other* vengeance and *Duinedon* retaliation. The *Amhas-draoi* are working to contain them before it escalates beyond our control, but we're stretched thin. It won't be long before the rage spreads like a torch set to a dry field."

"It's what the Nine counted on."

"You said yourself Máelodor wants you alive." Her voice almost conciliatory. "His malice might be your best protection."

He buttoned his waistcoat. Shrugged on his jacket. "I'll choose death over Máelodor's version of alive any day."

"Let's hope you get the choice, then."

Perhaps his brains had been addled. Perhaps he looked to shed Jack once and for all. Or perhaps he simply felt sorry for Helena, who'd probably come as close as capable to being compassionate. Come to think on it, perhaps it was her brains that had been scrambled. Whatever the case, he heard himself saying, "I believe you knew a cousin of mine. Jack O'Gara? Tall fellow. Strapping. Frightfully blond and manly."

She stiffened, giving him a thunderous glare. So much for sympathy. "I did. Is there a point?"

"Well, you see, there's something you ought to know about Jack—"

"He's dead, Mr. Douglas. That's all I need to know." Eyes like chips of obsidian, she strode out with a swordsman's swagger, leaving him to sink upon the chair. He should have known any kindness on his part would be rejected, but no one could say he hadn't tried.

Closing his eyes, he let out a whoosh of spent breath.

What the hell his cousin Jack saw in that woman was completely and utterly beyond him.

Nineteen

"Madame Arana? Are you up here?" Elisabeth called. "I've calmed the butcher down enough so that he's not quite foaming at the mouth, but you'll need to pay him by next week or he says he'll come back with his brother, which I believe is meant as a threat. It certainly sounded ominous, and it's probably not wise to anger men who wield sharp knives for a living."

Elisabeth topped the attic stairs. Once more struck by the clarity of the northern light, the rich jeweled vibrancy of the rugs upon the floor, the tiny shelves, the neat rows of bottles and jars, the clutter and crush of a woman's life kept hidden away like a wonderful secret.

Her gaze rested on the mirror, but no clouds moved within its surface today. No lightning-flecked images burned their way up through the roiling darkness. Instead, it reflected not on Helena's grandmother but Brendan, his golden gaze locked upon a stone she'd last seen hanging about her own neck.

The Sh'vad Tual.

In Brendan's hand, it took on a new and almost frightening aspect. The blunt, rough-carved broken edges, the light captured deep within its heart, the way it seemed to flicker and burn with a thousand separate colors. His stare deepened as his body went rigid, shoulders braced, face iron-jawed, unmoving by even the twitch of a muscle.

The stone pulsed, the colors writhing as if a storm raged within it.

Brendan squeezed his eyes shut, a shudder running through him.

"Esh-bartsk Breán Duabn'thach. Mest Goslowea ortsk."

The bloodcurdling rasp and slither of his words caught her breath in her throat.

"Ana N'thashyl bodsk nevresh boa dhil warot."

A headache burst against her temples as she dug her nails into her palms and a tiny moan escaped her.

Brendan whirled around, the stone going dark and empty as his eyes.

"If I can't stop Arthur's resurrection, Lissa"—the pain in his voice fluttered against her heart—"he'll die."

She crossed to his side. Sweat gathered at his open collar, his pulse rapid at the base of his throat. "Who? Who'll die? Arthur?"

She pried the Sh'vad Tual from Brendan's fingers. As with the mirror, a numbing icy tingle raced up her arm. Shimmered for a moment at the base of her brain.

Brendan scrubbed his hands over his face, his eyes no longer foggy with confusion. "Aidan. I see his death in my head. He almost died once because of me. He still carries shards of the *Unseelie* within him. A temptation and a darkness that will haunt him forever."

Like the man in the scrying glass. Bloodied and dying upon the turf. The creature possessing him in a gruesome agonizing assault. She closed her hand around the stone, the pain dragging her free of the memory. Had Aidan suffered this horror?

No. She'd seen the Earl of Kilronan a month ago. He'd been preoccupied. Distant. But quite recovered from last year's horrible injuries from his fall at the cliffs. "You're mistaken. Aidan is safe and well. There's naught wrong with him. When this is behind us, you'll see for yourself."

"I told you already, I can't go home to Belfoyle."

"That's ridiculous. Of course you can. You must. You have a life waiting for you there. Your family needs to know you're alive."

"You don't understand, Lissa. I'm the one who destroyed my family."

Brendan watched from the attic window as the coldhearted Helena Roseingrave hugged Killer to her chest, the terrier nuzzling her wet cheeks, though his thoughts remained focused on the still, pensive figure seated behind him.

"*You* sent the *Amhas-draoi* to Belfoyle. That's what you meant when I asked you about your father," Elisabeth said. "Brendan, you can't hold yourself responsible. You tried to do what was right."

Brendan's gaze lifted to the tangle of rooftops, smoking chimneys, low clouds falling into dusk. "And only managed to wreak more devastation. You're a prime case in point."

He turned from the window. The setting sun sent bars of light over the floor. Shot sparks into the flame of her red hair. His gaze fell to her left hand, the simple gold band resting on her fourth finger.

Despite Elisabeth's assertions, he'd not seduced his way through country after country, leaving behind a string of discarded beauties. He'd sought relief when he needed it and offered it on occasion. Unsullied by any emotion deeper than lust and a hunger for mutual comfort. At first appalled by the emotionless coupling and the solace he found in strangers' arms, then inured to it. But never had he let his heart be touched. There was a risk in letting someone in. It opened one to weakness. To danger. And, worst of all, to loss.

He'd lost too much already.

So, why, then, did the sight of his ring upon Elisabeth's finger shoot a zing of excitement rather than panic through him? Why did he want to cross the room, grab her in his arms, and kiss that damned sweet mouth of hers until she begged for it?

When had he been fool enough to let her touch his heart?

"Damn it, this wasn't supposed to happen, Elisabeth. I came back to Ireland for one simple reason. To reclaim the Sh'vad Tual before Máelodor got his hands on it. You didn't figure into it other than as a faded memory."

Her face stiffened, eyes darkening. "And now?"

"I let my guard down and you walked in like some ocean wind, reminding me of a past I'd done my best to obliterate. You're home, Lissa. You're wide, cloud-filled skies and green fields and cool mists and the sound of pounding surf."

She brightened. "Then, that's a good thing."

"No, it's the worst possible thing."

"All right, now you're just confusing me."

"When I'm with you I'm forced to see how much I've

lost and what I can never have. Not if I want to finally end the threat I initiated."

"It won't get to that point. Helena will be there. She and Rogan—"

"I can't count on them. Máelodor's not survived so long without knowing the odds and working them in his favor."

"You forget. You survived too."

"An answer for everything."

"You weren't going to tell me any of this, were you? What were you going to do, Brendan? Leave today and never look back?"

That's exactly what he'd planned on doing. "It seemed best."

"For who? You? Why not? You've been running for so long, why not keep going? Leave me behind to pick up your pieces. You did it once before. I imagine it gets easier every time." Her words grew sharper. "But mark this: From what you're fleeing, no amount of distance can save you. So go ahead, try and forget. I dare you."

"Bloody hell. This is just what I didn't want. An argument with a hysterical female."

"I am not hysterical."

"How about delusional?"

The fist came out of nowhere.

"Damn it, woman," he grumbled, clutching his upper arm. "Can you refrain from beating me senseless until after we've stopped arguing?"

She put a hand on her hip. "I don't know. Can you refrain from being a horse's ass?"

He smiled in spite of himself. Typical Elisabeth. No feminine tears or blubbering all over his waistcoat. She went straight for the jugular. A stupid sense of pride grabbed him. This one-of-a-kind, intoxicating, infuriating, radiant, bullheaded woman belonged to him.

He took her gently by the shoulders. Her gaze still shot fire, but the fight seemed to have ebbed from her body. "That's what I'm trying to tell you. I'm finally going to face the devils I've loosed. I'm not running anymore. And I won't forget. I couldn't if I wanted to."

Again she didn't react as he expected. She didn't fill the deafening silence with false hope or denials. She didn't curse fate. Didn't throw herself into his arms with pleas for him to stay that would embarrass them both.

Instead, she regarded him steadily, tiny creases between her brows, her mouth pursed in the slightest of frowns. Long seconds ticked away, the weight of her stare an increasing burden.

What the hell. He'd risk it. He reached for her hand, nerves jumping. Tension banding his shoulders. Terrified of how easy it was to tell her things he'd never revealed to anyone else. Of how much he'd come to rely on her for that.

Of losing her so soon.

And just like that, her fingers slid against his, her palm cool and soft upon his own. She took a step closer, lifting her face to his. Her kiss as gentle as her words had been harsh. Her scent filling his head.

He returned her kiss, probing delicately until she opened to him, the flick of his tongue deep within her heat igniting a reckless hunger. A need to mark her as his own. To brand her with his touch. To set his stamp upon her soul.

Máelodor's men closed in. He sensed their coming as a weight deep in his bones, a sizzle along his nerves, a questing whisper in his head.

But until then, Lissa was his.

He would taste that honey flesh. Cup those round, firm breasts. Kiss his way down the length of that soft throat. Bury his face in the wild tangle of that hair. It might only be for a few hours; still, he would leave her remembering him.

Before she was widowed, she would be very, very married.

Twining her arms around his neck, Elisabeth answered Brendan's impatience, hoping to lose herself in the luscious thrill of his lovemaking. Hoping to forget for a few precious moments the reality behind his terrible admission. He was leaving. And, without a miracle of epic proportions, would not return.

He'd tried to make her understand. He'd done everything but spell the truth out for her in big red letters, but in her desperation she'd ignored him. Taken his dire warnings as a last attempt to escape the fetters of an onerous marriage.

Nothing with Brendan was ever that simple.

Faced with his implacable determination to confront Máelodor, she'd been too shocked to respond at first, and then too numb. Arguing would be pointless. Brendan might call *her* stubborn, but a more mule-headed man did not exist, and she knew that bullish jut to the jaw all too well.

"Aren't you going to tell me I'm a fool?" he murmured, his warm breath against her neck sending shivers fluttering down her spine and into her belly. "Or mad? Or both?"

"Would doing so change your mind?"

His gaze grew dagger sharp, his hands tightening around her waist. "No."

"Then love me, Brendan," she whispered. "That will have to be enough."

His lips brushed her forehead, her temple. Behind her ear. Down her throat. Everywhere he touched, her skin tingled. Every kiss sent sharp jolts of heat straight to her center until she burned with wanting him. His hands fumbled with the buttons at her back until her gown slid free to her waist, her breasts bared. Nipples puckering at the first blast of cool air.

Palming their soft weight, his thumb skimming over the taut pink buds, he lowered his head to take one in his mouth, the swirl of his tongue delicious agony against her tender flesh. She threw her head back, a low purr escaping her throat as she dragged free the tail of his shirt to slide her hands over the sinewy hardness of his packed muscles. She rubbed against him, inflamed by the hard length of his arousal nestled in the junction of her legs.

Dropping to his knees, Brendan slid his hands beneath her skirts, dragging the fabric around her hips, exposing her stockings, garters, and quaking legs. A wash of embarrassment stung Elisabeth's cheeks, but only for a moment before recklessness and a wanton craving overpowered all lesser emotions. Her stomach clenched, her heart thrashing against her ribs as he climbed with mouth and fingers toward the throbbing, wet heat between her thighs. The slow march of his seduction pulling her into a whirlpool of sinful desire until she gritted her teeth to keep from begging him to never stop.

His hands skimmed and stroked her swollen, aching flesh. She jerked, choking back a cry as he licked and sucked the sensitive nub hidden there. Her legs buckling as she melted into the lightning shock of pleasure generated by each expert flick of his tongue. Her nails dug into his shoulders, and without his arms about her waist, she'd have melted into a puddle onto the floor.

Pressure built low across her stomach, an insatiable longing expanding with each swirling thrust of his tongue. Tremors vibrated her limbs until she pulsed with a brutal, painful need, her breathing ragged as he assaulted her senses. As the riot of mind-stopping ecstasy exploded through her like fireworks, she bucked and cried out. Her inner muscles contracting in wave after wave of crashing, shuddering bliss.

Brendan drew himself up, the pulse in his neck throbbing as rapidly as the space between her legs. And as easily as if she were naught but featherlight, he tossed her onto the old four-poster, the scents of camphor and dust rising from the lumpy mattress. It could have been a granite slab for all she cared.

He raked her with a look, his glittering eyes as dangerous and full of desire as she'd ever seen them. This was no gentle lover. This was a man ready to devour. A predator. A conqueror. Shucking himself free of his breeches, dragging his shirt over his head, he kneeled above her, his greedy gaze searing a path over her body until sweat damped her skin, and she quivered with renewed anticipation.

She kissed him, licking her taste from him even as she wrapped her hands around his shaft, guiding him into her, rocking upward until he groaned against her lips.

They stayed this way for a long delicate moment, neither one willing to end the fiery, devastating torture. Finally, he drew out before plunging deep into her again. She wrapped her legs around him, meeting each thrust, their coupling frenzied and ardent and stormy with loss and grief and a love struck down before it ever had a chance to bloom.

Movement caught Elisabeth's eye, and she turned to catch a glimpse of their joining reflected in the dark of Madame Arana's mirror. Elisabeth's hair falling loose across her shoulders in a scarlet ribbon, Brendan's sleek, muscled body driving into her in a raw, urgent assault. Watching him pleasure her awakened a new sexual thrill. She smiled, feeling her passion coiling tighter and tighter until she peaked, writhing against him as scalding rivers of volcanic heat slid through her veins, drawing a shout of exhilaration from her kiss-swollen lips.

He gasped her name like a prayer, his neck muscles taut, back slick with sweat as he thrust once more, shuddering his climax, spilling his seed inside her. He lay unmoving, still sheathed within her, as he pressed a kiss upon her cheek and each eyelid. "If that's your idea of a farewell, I should leave more often."

He joked, but there was no humor in his tone and shadows crouched dark at the corners of his gaze.

Elisabeth closed her eyes as twists and eddies of lingering pleasure pooled and swirled through her. "You should see what I do for a homecoming."

A chuckle rumbled low in Brendan's throat. "I'd like that, sweet Lissa."

She swallowed back bitter tears, refusing to send him away with weeping. Cradled his face in her hands to stare deep within the *Fey*-born beauty of his eyes and smiled through her heartbreak. "So, my love, would I."

"*Mon dieu!* There you are. I have been looking everywhere for the two of you."

Brendan and Elisabeth broke apart like guilty children

as Madame Arana caught them on the landing outside Brendan's door, her crinkled, wizened face pulled into frightened lines, alarm edging her tone.

Brendan's transformation happened in an instant. From desirous to deadly between one beat of her heart and the next.

"Downstairs. The *Amhas-draoi*. Helena's out, but they have said they will wait for her return."

"Shit." Brendan positively vibrated, the air charged with an invisible current. It prickled Elisabeth's skin, lifted the hairs at the back of her neck, slid shivering along her bones. "If they discover me here—" he growled.

"Go." Elisabeth pushed him away, her heart pounding in her chest, panic knifing up through her stomach. "Grab what you need. Madame Arana can take you down the back stairs. You'll be able to slip out through the kitchen into the yard and down the alley. I'll see to the *Amhas-draoi*."

"Are you sure?"

"No, but it's that or allow all my nursing to go for naught."

Brendan pressed a kiss to the palm of her hand. "Careful, Lissa. Helena's a pussycat compared to most of them."

"I'll be fine," she assured him, putting on a brave face. "After all, I'm a simpleminded *Duinedon*; what could I possibly know?"

His bad-little-boy smile did crazy fluttery things to her insides. Or perhaps that was a residue of mad panic. Difficult to tell. "I'll take your *Duinedon* brains over any amount of *Other* magic any day."

"Which just goes to show you're still not feeling well," she scoffed. "Right now I'd pay ready money for the ability to fly like a bird to the Outer Hebrides for a very long, very peaceful holiday."

"You really do have an odd idea of *Other* abilities," he said, amusement and excitement glittering in his eyes.

Good heavens, was he was actually enjoying himself? With both arms, she shoved him away. "Stop gabbling at me and go already!"

He crushed her in an embrace that drove the breath from her lungs and left her dizzy and reeling. "You'll be fabulous. Five minutes is all I need. You can keep them busy for five minutes. I know you can."

She squared her shoulders. "Five? I'll give you a good half hour. It's amazing how chatty I can get if I put my mind to it. As Beaumont would say, 'Women should talk an hour after supper. 'Tis their exercise.'"

"You sound frighteningly like your aunt."

She wrinkled her nose. "I'll take that as a compliment."

"You would." He laughed.

And then Brendan was gone, leaving her to face the indomitable ferocity of Scathach's brotherhood alone. Her last sight of him as the door closed, his bent head, back arrow-straight, fists clenched at his sides.

She would not break down. She would not dwell. And she would most definitely not snivel.

Descending the stairway to the drawing room, Elisabeth channeled a century and a half of Fitzgerald hauteur. She flung open the drawing room doors, gliding into the room on a frigid wind. The pampered heiress on full display.

Her visitor stood at the hearth with his back to her. He bore a wide-legged stance and broad shoulders, his auburn hair barely brushing his collar. As she watched, he took a shaky drag on a lit cheroot before tossing the whole into the fire.

"Miss Roseingrave is out at present, sir. Perhaps I may

assist you?" she asked, hoping the wobble in her voice didn't betray her.

He spun round, bronze eyes wide, the color draining from his face. "Elisabeth?"

Her head spun as a roaring filled her ears, her heart crashing against her ribs. She sagged against a chair, one hand strangling her skirts as she fought to understand. "Lord Kilronan? Aidan? God in heaven, is it really you?"

twenty

Elisabeth gripped her hands tightly in her lap, willing a cool, elegant pose as if the events she'd just related were not the outrageous stuff of fantastical nightmare. Magical stones. Máelodor's bounty hunters. *Amhas-draoi* attacks. Arthur's summoning. And, oh, by the way, her marriage to a man everyone thought was dead.

Completely humdrum and not worth getting into a pucker over.

"He's been carrying that guilt around with him like a damned great anchor all this time? The stupid sod, he should know I'd never think . . ." Lord Kilronan's words trailed off. "If I'd only come an hour sooner."

I see his death in my head.

Brendan's words repeated in her mind, but was the vision of Aidan's fall a future that must come to pass? Surely not, if Brendan continued to fight to prevent it. Or was his growing desperation born of knowing the fate he feared was a fate inescapable?

Lord Kilronan closed his eyes, uttered a very ungentle-manly "Thrice-damned son of a bitch," before stalking the length of the room, hand beating a rapid pulse against his lame leg. "The last I heard, he was in the north. Why the hell would he . . ."

"Aidan?"

"Gods, if the *Amhas-draoi* find him . . . or Máelodor. Bloody sod all. He's mad to even contemplate such a scheme."

"Aidan!"

Startled, he spun on his heel.

"You knew he wasn't dead. You knew and never said."

A corner of his mouth turned up in a dry smile, for a moment the family resemblance between the golden Lord Kilronan and his dark-featured brother more than obvious. "Thought you'd be the last person in the world to want to hear of Brendan Douglas's continued existence."

"It would have been nice to have a bit of warning."

"Can't say his turning up at Dun Eyre ever crossed my mind, though had I known that blasted stone was there—" A dumbfounded expression clouded his face. "Hell and the devil, what a bloody great mess."

"Did you know Brendan was alive all this time?"

Aidan dropped heavily into a chair. "No. Like you, I'd long ago assumed his death. It was only last spring I learned of his return to Ireland." He drummed his fingers upon the chair's arm. "I've spent the past year searching for him. Hoping to find him before the *Amhas-draoi*."

"How did you know to come to Helena's?"

"I didn't." He pulled a much-folded letter from his coat pocket. "This arrived at Belfoyle from an old friend of my father's. Mr. Ahern said he'd irrefutable evidence that

Brendan was in Dublin. I left immediately, hoping to speak to Miss Roseingrave. I thought she might have knowledge of Brendan's whereabouts." He shook his head, a rough bark of grim laughter. "Apparently she did, though I can see why she kept the knowledge to herself. She knows I'd have tossed a spanner into any plan that involved using Brendan as the lure to catch Máelodor."

"But Madame Arana said you were *Amhas-draoi*. Why did you lie?"

He dropped his head, rubbing the back of his neck. "Miss Roseingrave and I aren't on the best of terms. I thought I'd have more luck seeing her if I introduced myself as one of the brotherhood than as the accursed Lord Kilronan. Had I known Brendan was here . . ." He pulled a cheroot from a case. Bent to light it off a candle, inhaling a long, steadying drag. "Where's he gone, Elisabeth?"

Her hands shook. "I don't know, but, Aidan"—she paused, trying to swallow back the lump in her throat—"I don't think he plans on coming back. I think Brendan believes this can only end in his death."

His brows drew into a frown, a shocked stillness descending over him.

"I think he knew even before he married me he'd not much time left."

Every word she uttered drew Aidan tighter, hardening his already austere features. Her own body tensed, shoulders up near her ears, an arm across her stomach to hold the sickening ache in check.

Then, just at the moment she thought she might run screaming from the room, Aidan snapped. Leaping to his feet, an awkward smile brightening his somber expression. "What am I thinking? I should be offering you my felicitations on your marriage. Brendan couldn't have chosen better."

He embraced her in an enormous brotherly hug, his jacket scratchy against her cheek and smelling of smoke and brandy and dust and man.

Not precisely the reaction she'd been expecting. It took the wind from her sails, leaving her confused and empty and dazed; and yet, in a tiny way, she wanted to throw her arms around Aidan for seeming to understand how desperately she wanted to be a normal bride with a normal husband and a normal life.

He took her by the shoulders, stepping back to gaze down at her. "This is the best news I've had in ages." Exhaustion smudged the skin below his eyes, frustration tensing his square jaw. "Your aunts will be ecstatic. They've been seeking word of you everywhere; actually, part of my business in town was to see what I could find out about you."

A cannonball dropped into the pit of her stomach. Her aunts. How on earth was she going to face them after this? Somehow in the mounting chaos of her days in Dublin, that question had gotten lost in the shuffle. Aidan's arrival drove it front and center. "Are they all right?"

He released her to once more prowl like some great hunting cat, his hand tapping at his thigh. "Mrs. Pheeney has taken to her bed with hartshorn for her nerves and magnesia for her upset stomach, but Miss Sara has been stalwart in containing the scandal. In fact, she was the only one unsurprised by your elopement."

Elisabeth took a seat upon the edge of a settee, her queasiness resuming double force. "She knew Brendan had returned. She recognized him, you see." Elisabeth rubbed her temples as if trying to keep her brains from oozing out her ears. "And I think somehow . . . some way . . . she sensed what would happen."

"Did she?" He grunted. "Fancy that. Don't doubt it. Your grandmother carried the blood." He scraped a knuckle along his chin. A gesture she'd seen Brendan make a million times. The cannonball moved up into her chest.

"Was it . . . as bad as I imagine?" she ventured.

"I wasn't there during the ruckus, but Lady Kilronan told me the place was pandemonium, with everyone accusing everyone else. One group wanted to charge out after you and drag you back by the hair. The other faction washed their hands of the debacle."

"I can imagine which side Gordon came down on."

"Apparently Mr. Shaw and his brother left Dun Eyre three days after you did following an argument between the pair of them and Lord Taverner. Your guardian was quite the bulldog, I'm told."

"Oh, dear."

"Not to fear. I believe your great-aunt came ably to your defense with a raking that had the entire household in an uproar and both Mr. Shaws resembling a pair of startled codfish. My wife's opinion, not mine."

Bless Great-aunt Charity. Elisabeth well knew what sort of tongue-lashing might issue from that plain-speaking mouth. But poor Gordon. It hadn't been his fault, though it was a relief to know his heart had been as little touched as hers. He would find his glittering political hostess just as she had found the man she needed. Who turned her legs to jelly and her blood to fire. Who'd dragged her into the deepest, most treacherous currents and then left her to sink or swim on her own.

Aidan straightened, decision settling easily over his broad shoulders. "Come with me tonight. I have my traveling coach in town. You can return to Belfoyle. You'll be safe there, and Cat and Sabrina would love to discover they've a new sister-in-law."

She looked around at Helena Roseingrave's stylish yet simple drawing room. The snapping fire. The thick Turkey carpets. The indescribable sensation of otherworldliness that seemed to permeate even the most mundane items.

"I'm tempted, but no." She shook her head. "It sounds like madness when all I've wanted since waking in Brendan's company was to find a way home again, but I think I need to stay here for the time being."

His gaze narrowed with obstinacy. She'd forgotten how stubborn he could be. A Douglas trait, apparently. "As Brendan's wife, you're my responsibility now. He would want you safe. Your aunts will want to know what's become of you."

Elisabeth straightened. "I'll write straightaway to Aunt Fitz and Aunt Pheeney, but Madame Arana has offered me a home here as long as I have need of it. I want to be here when"—she refused to say "if"—"Brendan returns."

A flash of something dark and furious boiled up through Aidan's eyes, a glimpse of his wild *Other* blood. As if a monster surfaced for a moment before descending back into the deep. "And if he doesn't? Máelodor's obsession with *Other* supremacy has twisted him until he's naught but evil shaped in the form of man. He's barely human anymore. Brendan's powers are strong, but are they strong enough?"

Elisabeth gazed into the fire, seeing in the glowing embers a pair of yellow-hot eyes. In its heat a warm touch upon her face. And still she felt frozen, the blood washing cold and sluggish through her veins. A fear she could not push away.

"What do you think?"

Aidan tossed his lit cheroot on the fire with a trembling hand. "I've lost Brendan once. I refuse to lose him twice over."

Elisabeth's smile came tinged with sadness. Her sentiments exactly.

After Aidan's departure, Elisabeth went in search of Madame Arana. Found her, as she knew she would, in her attic studio, seated in a deep, tapestried chair, her needlework in her lap, though she wasn't sewing. Instead, the old woman stared serenely out the window on a night scraped low with rain, lights washing up from the streets below, a breeze hissing through the casement gap to lift the curtains. Killer lay upon a rug nearby asleep, his whistling, whuffing snores comforting in an otherwise delicate peace. She seemed to tear her gaze from the window with great difficulty, a strange shadow passing over her face. "Lord Kilronan has gone?"

Refusing to glance over at the old bed she and Brendan had shared only hours before, Elisabeth sucked in a sharp breath. "You knew he wasn't *Amhas-draoi*. Why did you pretend otherwise?"

Madame Arana rose stiffly, her body bent as if the mounting trouble bore her down. "There is much confusion within the mirror. All is in flux and nothing is certain, though I have scryed the glass every day, hoping to make sense of the images. The only thing I can say with confidence is that Douglas must face this challenge alone. Only in this way will he succeed against Máelodor and against his own private demons. Kilronan's presence would have changed events. Perhaps even tipped the scales in a different direction. I could not allow that."

"'Not allow'? Who are you to move people about like pieces upon a chessboard?"

Madame Arana's grandmotherly persona slipped, her eyes blazing, a strange unearthly brilliance glowing beneath her skin. "I do what I must to ensure my race's survival in a world all too quick to condemn. Just as Brendan Douglas does what he must. We all have a role to play, Elisabeth. Perhaps even you. Though you are not of our race, you are of our world."

"Show me," Elisabeth demanded. "Show me what you've seen."

For the first time Madame Arana seemed wary, her gaze slanting between Elisabeth and the long mirror half-hidden in the shadows. "I do not understand."

"You said the mirror is aware. That it will reveal what it knows if I'm strong enough to accept it. I'm strong enough. Let me see the future."

"Very well." Madame Arana crossed to the mirror, pulling free the slippery silk covering its surface, caressing the polished frame. Immediately the glass darkened, the rolling thunderclouds pushing thick and angry. The border of woodland animals and twining greenery alive and writhing under her *Fey*-born touch.

"Come close, *ma puce*. If the mirror wishes, it will reveal what it knows. But do not be disappointed if it chooses to hide its wisdom, or if it shows you something you do not want to see. It answers my pleas, it does not follow my commands, and I cannot force it to show you anything if it believes it would be best to keep its secrets."

Now that she was faced with the crackling, hypnotizing scrying glass, Elisabeth's feet became lead, her heart beating erratically, her breath coming fast. What on earth had she been thinking? Knowing the future was not a good idea. Not even a little bit.

Yet her legs seemed to propel her across the floor without her brain putting up a fuss. One minute she was at the top of the steps, the next she stood in front of the scrying glass, mesmerized by a rainbow's prism rising and falling within the flickering, black-bellied clouds.

Unsure of how to proceed—she'd never made a conscious decision to read the future before—she emptied her mind of anything but Brendan's face as she'd seen it last. Laughing. Wild. Eager. Placed her palms flat upon the surface. Tried to cast her silent question out to whoever or whatever might answer.

Immediately it felt as if ice crystals formed inside her veins. Her heart glazed over with a frosty coating so that each breath drew forth a white winter cloud. Her teeth chattered, her stomach clenched with cold, and numbness spread from her fingers up her arms toward her chest, but she did not break free. She stared within the mirror to the rainbow's dancing hues as the clouds parted here and then there, a glimpse of color, a flash of movement that changed or disappeared before she could focus her gaze.

"The mirror may reveal past events or future possibilities. Or it might reveal only what is written in your own heart. There is no way to predict."

Madame Arana's voice echoed from far away, her words fading into the noises of Elisabeth's body—her blood moving through her arteries, her lungs filling and collapsing, her joints' slow click and grind as she moved, the pulse of her brain as it struggled to make sense of the nonsensical.

An image. Caught for an instant. Long enough for Elisabeth to catch a glimpse. A man and a woman pleasuring one another. His golden body sleek with sweat, her head thrown back amid a river of red hair. Aflame with embarrassment, Elisabeth's stomach plunged as she watched the man drive himself deep into the woman. Felt a throbbing pull between her own legs as the cresting of their need played out before her.

She blinked, and the image was swallowed back into the clouds, replaced by a second. A man crippled and stooped, his grotesque face aglow with greed and desire and success. He turned to speak to someone barely discernible in the fog but for one pale eye, hollow of emotion.

"Does the mirror answer what you ask of it, or does it play the coy lover and wrap itself in veils to entice?" Madame Arana asked.

Elisabeth tried swallowing, but her throat closed, her mouth dry, her tongue swollen. She couldn't blink. Couldn't move. It was the only reason she caught the final fleeting image—the broken body of a man amid a bleeding, smoke-smeared sky. A cry of pain shouted to the heavens that ripped through Elisabeth like a knife.

With a retching, gagging moan she tore free of the mirror, flinging herself into Madame Arana's waiting arms. Her sobs cracking the icy shell encasing her, her tears scalding her cheeks, leaking hot and bitter into her mouth.

"What, young one? What has the mirror revealed?"

"Brendan won't be alone." Elisabeth closed her eyes, but the image seared her brain like fire. "I'll be with him when he dies and Máelodor claims victory."

North. South. East. West.

Earth. Air. Water—Máelodor cast flame to wick—fire.

All was set to draw upon the mage energy bound within the combined strength of compass and element. To tear the fabric between this world and the *Unseelie* abyss.

Stepping into the circle, Máelodor immediately sensed the power of the forbidden magics seeping into him. Pain no longer touched him. Uncertainty no longer weakened him. He was no longer bound only to one universe. Instead, his awareness expanded to other worlds, other planes of being, as he traveled on a current of thought. The attainment of this power had cost him—some might say the price had been too high—but he knew better. Knowledge involved sacrifice. As did victory.

He sought both.

As he cast the blood runes upon the floor, his lungs struggled to fill, air and light swallowed into a pinhole stretching outward as if someone had stabbed a knife into the world, ripping downward in a violent rift. Beyond the tear loomed a horrible gaping emptiness, a chasm of freezing, eternal nothing that was the Dark Court's abode. And a voice rising from that wasteland like Lorelei's call—pure and soulful and full of pain. "Is it time, son of man? Are we at last able to prove to you our gratitude and loyalty? Your humble servants yearn to join ourselves to you."

"Patience," Máelodor replied. "The stone is found. It will not be long now before Arthur stands by my side and I open the gates to you. Together, we will overcome any opposition. The *Duinedon* will have no chance."

There was a long silence when all that could be heard was a crackling roar, the infernal emptiness of the abyss beyond the rift roiling with a million shades of black.

Then: "The *Fey* do not suspect? They would stop us if they could."

"They remain ignorant of our contract." Máelodor felt his very essence being pulled into the hole, the *Unseelie* feeding on him like maggots upon a corpse. But in this case, they replaced what they stole with bits of themselves. Dark for light. Power in payment for a soul. They understood it was their only chance at freedom from their prison. "Your spells of concealment, combined with my own manipulations, have kept their eyes turned elsewhere, and I have been left to proceed in peace."

"We wait only on you, our master and liberator. When the gate is opened, we will come. We will fight. It shall be as you command."

He smiled, his tongue running over his lips in delicious expectation. "Then go and prepare your armies and await my call."

Bending down, he wiped a hand through the runes, smearing the blood in which they'd been written. Immediately, the rift shrank, the howling, vicious chasm fading back into four corners marked by four objects—a candle, a pile of earth, an eagle's feather, a shallow dish of water.

As the tear in the world healed, a final voice rose like the dying shriek of millions. "*Erelth, skoa.* Soon."

twenty-one

Macklins stood halfway down Cutpurse Row, the bow-front window fogged over with a half century or more of smoke and grime. From across the street, Brendan watched the crowds of vendors bearing carts of fish, crates of chickens, a knife grinder, a beefy-armed gentleman with stained teeth bearing what seemed an entire half a cow across his broad shoulders. The cries of the street merchants mingled with the screams of children shoving their way through the throng. A shout for a thief to stop. The bells of a nearby church. Beggars' moans from dark doorways. The rattle of a noddy as it rumbled down the narrow street.

A buxom young woman winked at him from a nearby alley, bending over to retrieve a dropped handkerchief, allowing him a good long look at her bountiful wares. Hitched her skirts to her knees to give him a taste of what could be his for a few coins and a few minutes.

He tipped his hat with a smile, but remained where he was.

A blade pressed cold against his throat. "Tag. You're it."

For one heart-exploding moment, he thought it was over; then: "A little up and to the left and you can put us both out of our misery," he replied, feeling the strength of Roseingrave's hand behind the steel.

The knife withdrew. "Too easy, but if this is how you manage, it makes me wonder how you survived for so long."

He'd never lost focus. He'd never let down his guard. And he'd never let himself indulge in stupid fantasies. That's how he'd survived. Until the last few weeks. Until Elisabeth had tumbled back into his life.

He glanced once more up and down the street for signs he'd been followed. The young woman had retired into the alley with a sailor. The thief had been caught by a gang of enthusiastic youths who kicked and punched him as he rolled on the ground with his stolen loaf of bread.

"You're here, make yourself useful. Any *Amhas-draoi* out there? Am I walking into an ambush?"

"Seems to me you already have."

He shot her an evil look as she scanned the street, a small line between her brows. A tightness to her mouth. "None that I can sense. Now, suppose you tell me—"

"Let's go." He gave a sharp jerk of his head, forestalling further conversation. Stepped out of the alley without once looking back to see if she followed.

Crossing the street, he pushed open the door of the tavern. Smoke lay over the tables like a cloud. A maidservant yelled an order to the bar. A gruff shout came in answer. Men hunched over their tables, liquid escape hoarded between gnarled, work-hardened hands. The stench of spilled alcohol and the fug of unwashed humanity stung his eyes as he sought through the murk for sign of his cousin.

A hand lifted in weary greeting. A call to the maid for another beer. Brendan smiled. Success.

Threading his way through the tables, he grinned on hearing the dirty propositions and drunken catcalls following in his wake. At one point, a hand reached for Roseingrave. A startled yelp, and it was withdrawn in haste while she muttered warnings about what body parts would be stabbed next if the miscreant didn't mind his beer and keep his hands to himself.

But it wasn't the threatened man who answered with a startled oath but Jack O'Gara, whose face even in the tavern's half-light drained to white. "Fuck all. What's she doing here?"

"I still can't believe my eyes, lad. It's like staring at a ghost. I mean, here you sit. Alive. Barely changed from when I saw you last."

"You need to clean your spectacles if that's your opinion, Daz." Brendan handled his untasted pint.

The old man pushed his glasses onto his forehead, blotting his bleary eyes with an enormous square of linen. Wiping his shiny forehead. Honking loudly into it before shoving it into the pocket of a gold-trimmed, once-scarlet, now-pink velvet coat.

Daz Ahern might have been of the opinion that Brendan remained unchanged in appearance, but the same could not be said of the great bear of a man Brendan remembered. He had a deflated look, as if the years had punched the life out of him. Shoulders hunched, hollowed chest, skin sagging on a once enormous frame. His hair had grown sparse and lank, his face ruddy with drink, and his gaze behind enormous spectacles held a myopic absentmindedness. To top it off, he seemed to be attired in a stained, threadbare suit at least two decades out of fashion.

Daz had been Father's closest friend. A jolly, happy-go-lucky mountain of a man who carried peppermints in his pockets and would pause in whatever he was doing to play with the children of Kilronan. A game of tag. A round of blindman's bluff. Hide-and-seek. He'd been a favorite uncle. A doting, laughing adult in a childhood bracketed by a demanding father and a meek, inattentive mother.

Never allowed to breach the inner sanctum of the Nine's meetings; still, he'd been an active participant in much of the group's work. Assisting Father in his experiments. Helping him search for the Rywlkoth tapestry and the Sh'vad Tual when everyone called the old earl mad for investing his life in chasing legends. An adoring confidant who always felt privileged to be included.

It was only as Brendan had grown in years and in what he thought of as maturity that he had begun looking on Daz's lively amiability with contempt and his unquestioning willingness to do whatever was asked of him with a cheery smile as a sign of weakness.

Yet Daz's good-natured affection for Brendan had never wavered. And when events began spiraling out of control; when intimidation became a tool and murder a weapon; when the Nine's influence spread like a disease and Father's dreams of coexistence changed to a mania for supremacy— when Brendan could no longer ignore the voices invading his sleep and the guilt twisting his bowels—he'd turned in desperation to Daz and been surprised and relieved to discover his traitorous thoughts were shared by at least one other.

Together they'd sought to make amends. To halt the

encroaching madness of a march toward a war the *Other* could never hope to win. To satisfy the clamoring dead.

Daz rubbed his bulbous nose with one sausage finger. "When O'Gara arrived on my doorstep, I almost shot him."

Brendan spun his pint round and round in circles upon the tabletop. "He gets that reaction a lot."

And where was Jack, anyway?

He'd gone a rainbow of colors in the moments following Brendan's arrival with Miss Roseingrave. White, then red, then a decidedly pucey shade of green. Brendan feared his cousin might be in danger of poisoning until he'd glanced at Helena Roseingrave and seen a matching multicolored display crossing her visage. Though she also looked as if her head might explode any second.

"You!" she'd hissed. At which point Jack had leapt to his feet, taken her by the arm despite her murderous glare, and hustled her away. The two had been gone for a while, necessitating a decision. Should Brendan remain here or start an alley-by-alley search for his cousin's dead body? Would there be enough of him left to find?

"Thought the young gentleman was one of them come after me at last," Daz commented, starting Brendan back to the matter and the man at hand with a heavy sigh.

He'd sent Jack to bring him old Archie's ring. Not the whole bloody man. He wasn't up to a frolic through old memories.

"Aidan says they won't come now. Aidan says I'm safe from the *Amhas-draoi,* but I told him they remember." He stuffed a hand into his pocket, a worried expression upon his features. "They won't let it go. Not until we're all gone. Until we've paid with our lives for what we did."

"You've spoken with Aidan?"

Daz paused in his pocket-rummaging. "Aye, he came last spring with the diary and the girl." Withdrew a cherry stone, a duck's pinfeather, a small bent stick. Laid them out on the table. "Sweet thing, she was, though I don't know if I believe the story of how they met. Apparently he caught her burgling his town house. Prettiest arch doxy I ever saw."

Brendan gave a rough bark of laughter. "Aidan always did have a way with women."

"He wanted to know about those days. Wanted to know about"—Daz lowered his voice—"him." He stole a worried look over his shoulder. "I told him, Brendan. Told him all of it, even the worst bits. The parts we didn't want to think about. The things we'd done. You and me and the others. Took it hard, he did. Don't think he knew how far things had gone."

"No, he hadn't known any of it. Father and I agreed it was for the best."

Though Brendan had wanted so many times to confide in his brother. He'd started so many letters to him in London before tossing them on the fire. At first afraid and then unable to involve his brother in what was growing to become an explosive situation. Best to keep him in London and safe out of the way.

Brendan's hand tightened on the pint, the beer sloshing over his hand, but his voice remained calm. "His discovery of the truth was inevitable once Father's diary came to his attention."

"His Lordship's more like the old earl than I imagined. Got his temper, for certes. He called me names. Cursed me for what I'd done. Threatened to kill me himself. I don't blame him. I deserved that and more."

Brendan swallowed around a sharp lump in his throat,

a tremble in his fingers. His older brother's fury wasn't unreasonable. He had nearly died for Brendan's crimes. Still, it only emphasized Brendan's isolation.

"It's why I came with Mr. O'Gara. He didn't want me to come. Said I'd slow him up, but I wouldn't let him leave without me. Locked him in a cupboard until he promised to bring me to you. Can you ever forgive me, Brendan?"

"For telling Aidan the truth?"

"Not about young Kilronan, no. For telling"—another furtive glance around the room—"them. For betraying your trust. My fault. All my fault."

"What are you talking about?"

Daz shoved himself back from the table. Slammed to his feet. Throwing the lapels of his coat open to reveal a grimy shirtfront. Squeezing his eyes shut. "Kill me! I deserve it!"

More than one startled fellow drinker looked up.

"Shhh, Daz. Sit down."

"It's no use, Brendan. I betrayed you to them. I deserve to die for what I did. Drive a dagger through my heart. Hilt-deep!"

Brendan laughed it off, casting a smile at the curious spectators. "It's all right, everyone. An actor, you see. New stage production. Rehearsing his part. Jolly good, don't you think?" Before turning his attention back to Daz, whispering, "Dash it all, man. Shut up and sit down before I gag you."

"You're right to be angry, Brendan. I sold you out. Offered up your life for mine. I was weak. But no longer. I'm here to pay my debt to you. A pistol. A knife. Choose your weapon."

"Sit your bloody arse in the chair, man, and get ahold

of yourself." Brendan shoved him back in his seat. "Here. Drink this." He pushed the tankard in front of him.

The old man gulped it down, rivulets seeping over his sagging cheeks. He wiped his mouth the back of his hand. "Ta, son. I needed that. Good of you. A last drink before the end."

"Daz, I am not going to kill you. Why—"

Daz reached across the table, grasping Brendan's hand in both of his. Pumping it up and down. "You're a great lad. Always knew it. Better than all of them. Didn't have the madness in you. Not like the rest of them."

"Debatable, but now's not the time to—"

"A weight off my old chest. I've carried the guilt so long. Thought I'd sent you to your grave. Thought the *Amhas-draoi* had tracked you and killed you like the rest of them. My conscience wouldn't rest. Then Aidan turned up telling me you were alive. Made up my mind then and there to face you and take my punishment."

Brendan had the odd impression of wandering into the middle of a conversation or the end of someone else's story. Though as Daz rambled a picture emerged. The answer to a question he'd carried for seven years: Why?

Why—after he'd sent word with Daz of his willingness to surrender the Sh'vad Tual into their hands—had they attacked him? Why had the *Amhas-draoi* hunted him with such persistence over the ensuing years?

He'd assumed the answer lay in the depth of his crimes. That Scathach and the brotherhood had proclaimed his death and would see anything less as failure to destroy all vestiges of the Nine.

"Slow down, Daz. What happened after I sent you to the *Amhas-draoi*?"

Ahern's face crumpled, great leaking tears rolling down his blubbery jowls as he arranged and rearranged the feather, the stick, the cherry stone. Moving them this way and that. His gaze locked upon the strange patterns. "Went like we agreed. Did just as you said. None suspected me. None stopped me."

"Did you speak to Scathach?"

"Aye, the warrior queen is as fierce as they say, Brendan. She just had to look at me and I felt as if she were picking my brain apart particle by particle. Seeing every guilty secret." He whipped free his handkerchief, giving another horrid honk. "That's when I failed. So many questions, all talking one over the other. Scathach never taking her eyes off me. I grew confused. Muddled in my thinking. Never meant to hurt you. Never meant to betray you. My fault, though. I claimed your information as mine. They never knew you'd sent me. . . ." Daz's voice trailed off into a horrified, strangled whisper. "Never knew about you at all."

Brendan rubbed his injured hand up and down his thigh, working the kinked muscles loose. Pictured Daz's confrontation with the *Amhas-draoi*. The circle of stern, angry faces. The drawn swords. The threats. It made perfect sense. Hell, he'd probably have done the same if standing at such an epicenter of warrior-mage fury.

Laughter started low in his gut. Worked its steady way up through his chest, loosening the taut muscles across his shoulders, the bands clamping his back, the stiff neck and the pain in his temples.

He roared with the irony of it all.

Did he blame Daz? No. The time for that was long gone, if it had ever been. The blame lay squarely at his own feet. If he'd gone himself to the *Amhas-draoi* instead of sending Daz as emissary . . . But he'd hoped still to salvage the disaster to come. Still had visions of reasoning with Father. Of making him see where the Nine had lost their way. Of the grim conclusions he'd come to over hours and days and weeks of planning.

Such a conversation had never happened.

He'd never been able to work up the strength or the courage needed. Father had always seen him as his golden son. The pride of his house. Against Aidan's athleticism and charm, it had been a source of delight to be seen as superior in any way to a perfect brother who floated through life on a cloud.

To confess his fears or reveal his treachery would have resulted in the loss of that prized status. So, in the end, Brendan had said and done nothing.

Father had died beneath an *Amhas-draoi* blade.

Brendan had run for his life.

He laughed until he cried. Chest aching, ribs throbbing and bruised, breath coming in unsteady gulps. A feeling he'd not experienced in years too long and dark and painful to dwell on.

Hope.

twenty-two

"What do you think?"

Elisabeth held the gown in front of her, turning this way and that while Killer watched from his permanent spot on her bed.

"I know. I'm so glad I followed the dressmaker's advice. It looks much better than I thought it would from the illustration in *La Belle Assemblée*."

The mirror reflected a printed muslin in the first stare of fashion, ribboned in apple green at hem and collar with cap sleeves. The style drew attention to her height while minimizing her less-than-waifish shape. And the color brought out hints of green and gold in her brown eyes.

In a desperate attempt to keep herself from reliving the scrying's indelible images, she snatched up a second gown, a beautiful silk in apricot that gleamed in the late afternoon light streaming through her window. Swirled it around her, posing again in front of the cheval mirror. Loving the feel of it against her skin. The way it threw gold and bronze and copper highlights into her hair. She'd never take nice clothes for granted again.

She smiled, recalling Brendan's eager gaze as he'd revealed his gift. The almost shy way he'd offered her the bolts of fabric. As if she'd reject his present. As if what she thought mattered to him. It had been a heady realization. Brendan had never cared what she thought. Or felt. Or did.

Elisabeth clenched her jaw, refusing to let the bitter tears swimming at the backs of her eyes gather force. She would not weep. She would remain positive. Madame Arana had said the scrying glass showed possibilities. No way to know how the tiniest twist in events might affect the future. Brendan would not die. He would return to her. They would travel to Dun Eyre as a couple. If she believed it strongly enough, she could make it happen.

She tossed the gown across the bed. Threw a worried glance out the window. *Please, whoever might be listening. Keep him safe. Watch over him. Don't let him vanish out of my life again.*

Today had passed in murmured conversations and worried looks. Madame Arana had departed. Then Helena. Both had been gone for hours. Both had assured Elisabeth before they left that Rogan would remain in case there was trouble. She was safe.

As if on cue, a strumming chord shivered up the stairs to her bedchamber. It grew into a lively bouncing tune, one where feet had no choice but to tap. It brightened her somber mood and she caught herself humming along before branching off into a harmony that seemed to augment the sweet laughing melody. Even Killer wagged his stump of a tail, his beady black eyes alert, his nose twitching.

The music changed. The harp's song growing quiet and sad and full of pensive longing. Her own song altered to match the new tone. A bride's fears. A woman's desire. A life unknown.

So engrossed in her own confused jumble of thoughts, she at first didn't notice the harp breaking off in a sudden disparate jangled chord. Didn't note the ominous listening silence. The creak of a house that wasn't as empty as she'd imagined.

It was only Killer's low-in-the-throat growl that started her from her musings. He scrabbled to his feet, a ridge of raised fur down his back.

Men's voices belowstairs. Raised. Angry. Arguing.

Amhas-draoí? Máelodor? A quiver of fear raced up her spine, cold washing through her. Heart slamming against her ribs.

She would not panic. She would not swoon. She would not curl into a ball and pretend to be invisible. Gazing around the room, her eyes lit on the heavy iron poker leaning by the chimney. Perfect.

Plucking it up, she clutched it like a cricket bat. Crept toward the door to await any intruder stupid enough to try and enter her room.

Killer's nose lifted to the air, hackles raised, growl ominous, teeth bared. He followed her to the door, glancing up at her as she pressed her ear against the panel.

She strained to catch any more sounds, but there was only a muffled shuffling from belowstairs. A quiet murmur.

Where was Rogan?

She squeezed her eyes shut against the vision of the harper spread-eagled dead upon the parlor floor. Surely he'd have gone to his grave with more struggle. Perhaps silence was a good thing.

She'd no time to relax before the stealthy scrape of

a boot sounded upon the stairs, accompanied by hoarse breathing. A creak outside in the passage.

Killer whined, scratching at the door, every muscle in his little body quivering. Every muscle in her body was quivering too. She caught her breath, lifting the poker in as threatening a manner as she could.

The knob turned. The door cracked. A dark head appeared in the gap. She squinched her eyes shut, took a breath, and swung. The connection of iron poker against skull trembled up her arm. A man fell across her threshold like a sack of wet sand.

Killer nosed the body, licking the all-too-familiar face.

She no longer had to imagine Rogan lying lifeless upon the floor. Here he was in stomach-lurching authenticity.

Blast. She'd clobbered the wrong man.

Where the hell was Jack?

After waiting . . . and waiting . . . and waiting . . . at Macklins for over an hour, Brendan gave up. Helena had either fed his cousin to the fishes or the two of them were catching up on the last year in orgiastic excess. Brendan didn't care which. He just wanted to know what he was supposed to do with Daz. And finally get hold of Archibald's ring.

Jack must still have it.

Jack damn sight better still have it.

But where was the lump-headed clodpole?

When Brendan asked Daz about the ring, the man fished around in his pocket before pulling out a piece of looped and knotted twine. Handing it over with a beaming grin. "Not much to look at, but she'll do you in a pinch."

Brendan knew he'd been away a long time, but the last

he'd seen of the *Fey*-wrought treasure, it had been silver and pearl, not—he eyed the limp bit of cord with raised brows—hemp and dirt.

He accepted the twine, placing it in his breeches pocket with a gritted smile of thanks.

If Jack weren't dead, Brendan might just kill him himself.

Shepherding Daz into a passing hackney—difficult to do with the old man addressing the horse as his cousin Bridie and tut-tutting about her poor dead husband—they drove as far as Stephen Street, where the pair disembarked—after an exceedingly generous tip to the bemused driver—and walked the last remaining streets to Roseingrave's house. Easier on foot to assess the risk. To approach with vigilance. If need be, to fade away quietly.

He glanced over at Daz, whose round-eyed, childlike gaze and odd attire were sparking curious looks from passersby.

So perhaps fading away was being a bit optimistic.

From a corner across the street, Brendan searched for indications the town house was being watched. No sign of surveillance. No tracing brush of mage energy against his mind. He decided to take that as a sign the brotherhood remained ignorant of Helena's rogue activities.

His mouth curled in a smirk as he stepped off the pavement. Perhaps Jack and she were more alike than Brendan had first thought.

Climbing the steps, he paused just before lifting the knocker.

Was it the subtle hint of the front door hanging slightly ajar?

Or the follow-up smack over the head of a dog snarling and barking ending in the crash of shattering glassware?

Either way, Brendan drew his knife free of its sheath before he tipped the door wider. Motioned Daz to remain behind.

The entry hall was empty. A glance to the right into the parlor and a left into the dining room showed him nothing out of place. The noise came from the floors above. Killer's frantic yaps, a pained yelp, and then nothing more. Not a promising sign.

Where the hell was Rogan? And more importantly, where was Lissa? Damn it, if anything happened to her . . .

He restrained the impulse to take the stairs three at a time, death in his heart. Instead, he crept step by interminable step, praying to any god that might hear him to keep her safe until he could get to her.

A shadow fell across the upper corridor. "Get the girl. She'll tell us what she knows or we'll have the tongue from her head."

Máelodor's men. But how had they tracked him to Duke Street? He and Helena had been meticulous as they laid their trail that none could track him back here.

A sharp stab of laughter followed. "Aye, Croker. She's a luscious little peach. Any chance of—"

"Keep your prick buttoned up, lad. Time enough for that if we have to get rough."

Rage burned along Brendan's veins like acid as he tightened his grip on the blade's handle. Felt for the comforting bulge of the pistol in his pocket.

A man appeared around the door.

Brendan never hesitated. He sent his dagger on a whistling arc, knocking the would-be rapist back against the wall, a blade buried hilt-deep in his chest.

The man called Croker shoved his way into the passage with a curse. "What the hell?"

No time for finesse, Brendan drew his pistol, cocked the hammer, and fired.

This time his aim was not quite so true. The bullet exploded into the plaster to the right of the man's head, spraying him with chalky dust.

He swung around, his gaze narrowing in concentration, words already whispering the curse that sent Brendan to the floor in a twitch of fried nerves.

Mage energy sizzled through him like lightning. Shredding muscle. Knifing tendons. He howled against the agony even as he focused long enough to parry the curse with his own spell.

The man froze for a moment, an odd confusion marring his features as the pain eased in Brendan's chest. He could breathe again. He could stand.

But it was a short-lived victory.

A second figure stepped from the parlor, adding his strength to the fight. Two against one. The pair of them working in tandem to overwhelm his defenses. Even as he staggered to his feet, an insidious curdling cold infected him. A teeth-chattering arctic burn pulled along veins toward his heart.

He clenched his jaw, limbs as unresponsive as if he'd been plunged into a frozen sea. There was nothing to break the icy grip upon him. His mind seemed to divorce itself from his body. He couldn't concentrate. Couldn't think.

Upstairs, a woman screamed. A man shouted. There was the sound of breaking furniture.

And not a damn thing he could do about it.

———o———

Elisabeth would have been far more successful if she'd been wearing half boots. All she'd managed to do in slippers was bruise her toes against the man's shin, making him angrier than he already was. His pistol jammed against her temple, he leaned into her face. So close the onion smell of his breath nearly knocked her out. "You do that again and I'll—"

The barrel of the gun was cold, yet sweat trickled between her shoulder blades and down her back. The lawn of her shift seemed to have plastered itself to her body like a damp, uncomfortable skin. "You'll what? Kill me? I don't think so."

Elisabeth found her gaze fastening on the bit of lunch caught between his teeth. It was that or look up into his eyes and see her terror mirrored back at her in those dark irises. She didn't need to know how terrified she looked. She was well aware. But she would not let that paralyzing, lung-squeezing, stomach-knotting fear take over.

The man ground his teeth together so hard, his jaw looked in danger of shattering, but his pistol was withdrawn to a jacket pocket, his grip loosened. "You're damned lucky I'm a gentleman, bitch, or your brains would be all over this room by now." His notion of gentlemanly behavior definitely left much to be desired if his leering smirk and roving hands were any indication.

She cast a look at Rogan's inert body, willing him to rouse and come to her aid. But he remained frighteningly lifeless, the blood in his hair altogether too red for her taste. Heavens, what if she'd killed him?

The blast of a pistol shot broke the momentary stalemate. The man's head came up like a hound upon a scent, his divided attention easing the death grip he had on her arm.

Now or never.

She tore herself free with a shout. Lunged for the dropped poker. She'd barely touched it when he spun back to her, eyes widening for a fraction of a second, mouth curled in a snarl of animal rage. His first hit backhanded her to the ground.

She never felt the second.

The son of a bitch bent to take up Brendan's knife. Eyed it for a moment, a gleam of a smile on his ruddy features.

"Brendan Douglas as I live." He placed the knife along Brendan's throat. Slid it achingly slow along his neck, the incision igniting a stinging fire. "Máelodor's getting desperate. His price has risen over the last months. We'll be able to retire as gentlemen on what you'll bring us."

Brendan could almost feel the frost layering him over. He stared up into eyes hard as stones, the cold encircling his heart. Slowing it. Every beat sending color bursting across his vision. He would not pass out. He would not give this bastard the satisfaction.

He refused to let his mind wander to Elisabeth's fate upstairs. Blind fury would only kill him quicker. He needed an icy clarity. And he had the icy part of things well in hand.

The knife moved again, this time slitting open one cheek.

Wonderful. He had to be caught by a man who saw himself as some kind of macabre body artist.

A door slammed open upstairs, a woman's cry.

To hell with the plan. To hell with Roseingrave and the stone. Elisabeth wasn't a part of this. He'd vowed to keep her safe. If it meant giving up a chance to save his sorry ass, so be it.

"Brendan?" A voice floated up from downstairs. "I know you said to wait outside, but"—Daz's head poked above the banister, eyes growing round behind his spectacles—"oh, I say! That's not playing fair."

The distraction he needed. The moment he'd prayed for.

The man's head snapped around, the power of the curse receding.

Brendan forced his body to obey, thrusting his arm up, clamping fingers around the man's knife hand. A sharp twist, and the bones snapped.

The man screamed, the knife sliding free.

A shadow fell over Brendan, but his vision had narrowed to a scarlet pinprick. He saw only his opponent, knew only the surge of the struggle.

Instinct overruled all else.

He rolled out from under the man's weight with a snarl of animal rage. Took up his knife, intent only on the space between the villain's ribs.

"Douglas!" A man's shout. "We've got the girl! Don't do anything stupid or she's dead."

Oh gods. Elisabeth. They had her. Did they know what a weapon they held? He could do nothing. He was trapped.

Brendan fell back sick and shaking, his vision no longer scarlet but black with killings, old and new. Beyond the rush of wind in his ears, he heard only Daz's surprised voice.

"I have to say, I didn't see this coming at all."

twenty-three

Elisabeth woke with a raging headache, one whole side of her face sore, her jaw throbbing. It didn't help that the room rose and fell, sending her stomach into her throat.

Brendan. That dratted sleeping spell again.

She tried to sit up, nearly braining herself on a beam inches from her face.

No squalid cabin. No dog licking her nose. No sarcastic comment meeting her awakening. Not Brendan at all.

Worse. Much worse.

Memories flooded back, making the pounding of her temples triple in power until she had to put her head between her knees to keep down her dinner. She sat this way for a few minutes, wallowing in misery and muttering a few choice oaths before lifting her eyes to try and decide where she was and what in blazes she might do about it.

She sat beside a stack of lashed barrels. Darkness enveloped the space, but for weak spears of pale light from a grate above. Water slapped beneath her ear, booted feet tramped back and forth over her head. There was the squeak of rope and the snap of sail.

Máelodor's men won't accept you don't have the stone. They don't accept failure.

Fear splashed up her legs into her stomach, setting her bowels quivering. Pride and practicality coming a distant second to the primal animal terror sending her reeling to her feet.

Climbing the ladder, she pounded against the grate until her fists stung. Until the breath was driven from her lungs and she couldn't swallow for the ache in her throat.

And no better off than before.

Giving up, she huffed the hair off her face. Wiped her scraped and bleeding palms upon her skirt. What would escape achieve anyway? Unless she planned on swimming for safety, she was caught well and good.

She slumped back to the floor, eyes squeezed shut, afraid to give in to the terror lurking at the edges of her consciousness, though it was tempting to slide into mind-numbing hysteria.

Was Brendan dead? Had he been taken when she was? And if so, where was he? What did they want with her? The obvious answer made her queasy and she quickly thought of something else. Had Rogan survived? Her stomach rolled ominously. So maybe that wasn't the best thought either. Had she committed murder today? She clenched her jaw, glancing up at the hatch above her. If she got the chance, could she do it again?

As if wishing made it so, the hatch opened, light from a lantern blinding her to her visitor. She scanned the hold for anything to use as a weapon, but it was difficult to see in the inky, oily blackness, and other than the barrels and some rather large unwieldy bits of ship that looked too heavy for her to lift, there was nothing at hand.

Heavy steps and the scents of whiskey and pipe smoke coalesced into a familiar figure. A woolen greatcoat with the collar pulled up. A hat jammed upon salt-and-pepper hair, and as he raised his lantern high, a telltale purple bruise marring the side of his face, sticking plaster covering a cut across his left cheek.

She blinked in case she was hallucinating, but no. It was him. Rescue had come quicker than she'd hoped.

"Rogan!"

"Where is she?" Brendan sat at the table where they'd shoved him, eying his captors coolly, revealing nothing of the rage coiling round his heart. "I want to know she's well."

He'd not seen Elisabeth since they'd bundled them out of the house, her body lifeless in the arms of a brute big enough to snap Brendan in half. She'd been placed into a carriage, the horses set to with a sharp slap of the reins.

It had only just disappeared around the corner when they'd shoved him into a second carriage. He'd sensed the presence of someone in the corner, there'd been an explosion behind his eyes, and he'd known nothing more until he woke to find himself aboard this smuggler's lugger. The sounds of a ship newly under way dashed any hope he might have held of a swift rescue.

Freedom was up to him alone.

The man called Croker circled behind him, the sour stench of his breath hot on Brendan's neck, while the other remained, hands on hips, legs planted wide against the roll of the ship. "She's well enough for the time being. Up to you if she stays that way."

Brendan placed his hands flat upon the tabletop, letting the rough wood anchor him. A way to focus his scattered mind. "You touch her and I'll see you in hell."

A knife caught him under the jaw. "Tough words," Croker jeered, "but it's that soft spot for the girl what's going to keep you in line. Long as Sams and I have her, you won't do anything, will you?"

Brendan kept silent. The dirty bastard might look stupid, but he had it exactly right. As long as Elisabeth remained hostage, Brendan was powerless.

"Though she's a savory morsel, ain't she?" Sams said with a dark chuckle, grabbing his crotch. "Mayhap we ought to give Captain Quick's sailors sport for the journey. A little morale booster."

Brendan lunged from his chair, only to be struck on the back of the head. Pain crashed through his skull, a ringing in his ears like the clang of a thousand church bells. He fought free, getting in at least one good punch before a fist slammed into his jaw. Another doubled him over, the air smashed out of him. He bit back a groan as he sank into his seat.

Sams shoved his face into Brendan's. "Try that again and we'll let you watch," he growled.

They left, taking the lantern with them, the room plunged into darkness, nothing to pull Brendan's mind from the death spiral of his thoughts.

But in their gloating, they'd made a fatal error. They'd left him unbound. Free to move and free to work the mage energy if he could stop the ringing in his ears long enough to concentrate.

He paced the tiny aft cabin. Explored by touch every board until he memorized his prison. The steady creak of rigging and the cradle-like rise and fall of the ship work-ing against the fevered savagery in his mind. The door was locked, but if he . . .

Closing his eyes, he reached with his mind. Pictured the mechanism. Whispered the words like a prayer. *"Daresha di-alhwedhesh."* The clink of the sprung lock echoed up his hand into his brain.

Now what?

Find Elisabeth. Free her. Take the captain and turn this hostage situation around. Foolhardy. Absurd. The best he could come up with at short notice. Otherwise, he might as well sit himself back down and await dismembering. And Elisabeth . . . no, he'd not dwell on what would happen to her once she was no longer needed to keep him compliant.

He stepped into a narrow companionway, opening onto a larger gun deck. A row of four cannon to either side. A ladder ascending to the upper deck. A passage narrowing farther forward to a grilled hatch leading down to the hold.

Could she be topside, where they could more easily keep an eye on her? In the hold? He crept forward to the ladder, a hand upon the rung, eyes searching that narrow square of overcast sky. Wind dragging the dank odor of his fear away with it.

With nothing left to lose and no reason to hide what he was, he cast his mind out as if he might sense her on a ribbon of energy. A wild hope. As *Duinedon*, she would be difficult to trace. It was doubtful he'd be able to sense any-thing about her other than perhaps whether she breathed or not, but there was always a chance. After all, she held some *Fey* blood from her grandmother.

He cast his power like a net upon the air. The salt-laden breeze washed cold and clear over his cheeks, a ripple of mage energy bound within its currents, enough to make him sure the smuggler captain was an *Other* with a developed weather sense. There would be no helpful wind to slow them down or steer them off course.

At the farthest edge of his mind, there came a faint echo. A dusky red shimmer that drew his attention. He locked on the tracing, slight as it was. Headed toward the hatch and the hold below. Had taken only a handful of steps when a man appeared from the shadows of that far companionway at the other side of the gun deck. His beady eyes afire with surprise, the sailor drew up, muttering an oath, a hand going to the knife at his belt.

Unhesitating, Brendan released a writhing coil of battle magic with viper speed. The blast crumpled the sailor like a broken doll, Brendan on him in an instant. Wrenching the man's knife from his hand, he slit the rogue's throat. His blood splashing hot and sticky. The iron tang thick and biting in Brendan's nostrils.

Wiping the knife on his breeches, he continued down the passage to the grille. A heavy iron bar had been drawn aside, the grate pulled back to reveal a cavernous opening, the first few damp, slimy steps down into the ship's forward hold.

Had the dead sailor just come from there? Were others waiting below?

Brendan adjusted the knife in his hand, a wild keenness firing his body. He would never say he reveled in bloodshed, but the kick to his heart and the sharpening of his senses had its advantages. The kill-or-be-killed survival instinct had saved him more than once.

He placed a booted foot upon the first riser, a familiar buzz of magic zinging through his head.

It couldn't be. Not him. Not here. Not unless . . . *Shit, shit, shit.*

Shouts followed by the running stamp of feet and the ship made a sudden heel to starboard. He stumbled, biting the inside of his mouth to keep from voicing the howl of fury burning up through him.

And then chaos broke loose. The ship lurched, his foot slid on the damp stair, and a rake of cannon fire sent splinters and debris flying as he slithered and dove into the dark hold.

"Why?" Elisabeth pressed as far back into the corner as she could. As if through sheer willpower she might disappear through the decking and float away with the froth.

Sitting on an upturned bucket, Rogan clasped his hands between his knees, regret and defiance battling it out.

"It's not my fault," he whined. "I never meant for you to be hurt. I only wanted the stone. The Sh'vad Tual for Arthur's rebirth. I tried to talk Croker and Sams out of it. Tried to convince them to leave you both behind."

"So, what went wrong? Why kidnap us if you have the stone?"

"They wouldn't listen to me. The bounty on Douglas is triple what a normal man can make in a lifetime. Máelodor wants him, stone or no stone."

"And me?"

Rogan shook his head. "They took you as security. If Douglas tries anything, it'll be you that suffers."

Elisabeth swallowed. Somehow she'd known that already, but hearing Rogan say it only cemented it like a weight in her chest, pinning her to the floor, feeding the whirl of her thoughts. More than anything, she wanted to burst into copious amounts of weeping and wallowing, but she refused to give Rogan the satisfaction.

Clamping down on the impulse to blubber, she asked, "Do you know where they're taking us?" hoping the squeak in her voice wasn't audible.

"Cornwall. We'll be there by dawn tomorrow."

A roar of sound exploded the night. Screams and running feet and shouts of command followed just as another whistling explosion pummeled the air, knocking her hard against the hull, sending dust drifting into her eyes.

Rogan threw himself to his feet as someone came half falling, half leaping into the hold, righting himself at the last instant to land crouched, ferocity washing off him in waves.

Brendan. Awash in blood, his eyes seeking her like blazes of wild light. A thin slash began at the top of his left cheekbone, ending by his chin. A second, uglier score marred the side of his neck.

"Lissa!" he shouted.

A cannon's bellow, this time coming from above. The captain was firing back at their attackers. Could it be Helena? Could she have found them so quickly?

The ship seemed to shake with exertion, sails cracking like gunshots, the hull creaking threateningly. Brendan used the distraction to throw himself at Rogan, who leveled his gun at Brendan's chest, startling him to a halt. "Kill me, you lose your best hope for keeping Miss Elisabeth safe."

"The stone?" Brendan demanded with an icy menace even Elisabeth found chilling, and it wasn't even directed at her. "Where's the damned stone, Rogan? Tell me it's safe. Tell me Helena has it still."

Rogan flinched but did not weaken, the rightness of his cause trumping his obvious fear. "I have it."

Elisabeth hadn't thought Brendan could grow any more frightening. She was wrong. Something bloodthirsty entered his gaze. Something that held nothing of humanity, as if the *Fey* in him had taken over. Yet this was no shimmery, ethereal splendor but a heartless, implacable brutality. Elisabeth was reminded of the image in the scrying glass—the heir of Kilronan watching as evil was unleashed. This was a man capable of murder. Of malice.

"You son of a bastard—the Sh'vad Tual is all Máelodor needs to open the tomb and complete the summoning."

Rogan's eyes darted wildly in the flickering glow of the lantern, both his gun and his voice shaking as he responded. "Exactly. The king will finally return. The *Other* will have the leader they need to defeat the *Duinedon.*"

"It won't happen, Rogan. It's impossible. I've seen it. Arthur doesn't succeed."

A boom, and then another. This time the echoing crack of thunder, the slice of lightning. Above the din rose what must be the captain's voice in a slow, chanting lilt. Winds rose. The ship lifted up and over before dropping into the trough of undulating waves.

Elisabeth banged her head as she fought to hold herself upright. Grabbing hold of one of the ropes lashing the barrels to keep from sliding in the murky sludge rolling back and forth over the floor of the hold, she sidled a step closer toward Rogan. With his attention all on Brendan, she might find a chance to grab the gun or at least turn its aim from the center of Brendan's chest.

Brendan's words cut the air like a blade. "The *Other* will fail, and when they do, *Duinedon* vengeance will be swift and merciless. They'll not allow such a threat to continue to exist."

"A risk I'll take if it means the chance for a life lived free of harassment," Rogan argued.

Elisabeth inched her way forward, palms burning every time the ship heeled over and her hands slid painfully along the rope. Three feet. Two. *Keep him busy, Brendan. Keep him talking.*

"And Daz?" Brendan growled. "The old man. Did you kill him? Can we add his life to the list of those you've torn apart?"

Rogan's face tightened. Brendan was losing him. It wouldn't take much for him to pull the trigger. "The old man's alive. At least, he should be. I left him unconscious but breathing. More mercy than he'd have received at *their* hands."

Elisabeth was there. She need only lunge to her right and she could knock Rogan off balance.

She never got the chance.

Brendan's face seemed to shine, his eyes shimmering burnished gold and bronze and amber. Hard. Pitiless. He lifted a hand, flicking his fingers forward.

Rogan doubled over, retching. His body jerking as seizures tremored through him.

Brendan's gaze swept toward her, the horrible power in his eyes stripping her raw. "Come. Quickly."

Letting go of the rope, she crabbed her way around Rogan, making it halfway to the ladder before the harper grabbed her ankle. Her feet slipped out from under her at a heaving rush of storm waves, and she felt herself falling. Her head slammed against the barrels, her side hit the edge of a crate, her knees banged hard on the floor.

In the wild swing of the lantern, she glimpsed bodies, heard shouts, a gunshot. Someone grabbed her around the waist, another slapped her hard enough across the cheek to throw spots into her eyes. She heard the thunk of fist meeting flesh over and over, and by the time she wiped the tears away, Brendan was on the floor, and a knife had been pressed cold against her throat.

Rogan struggled to rise over Brendan's slumped and bloodied body, voice hoarse, hands shaking. "You say hell will be the refuge, Douglas. But you're already there."

Brendan looked up through one glittering eye, the other one swelling shut. "No, Rogan. You've no idea. My hell hasn't even begun. Nor has yours."

"Get him out of here," shouted one of the men.

The winds had dropped from a hurricane scream and the nauseating pitch and roll of the waves had eased. Thunder still rumbled and bounced over the water, but no longer did the bark of cannon fire sear the air. The storm must have separated pursuer from pursued. The hope of rescue vanished.

Two sailors grabbed Brendan beneath the arms, dragging him up and out of the hold.

The man watched before turning back to Rogan and Elisabeth. "That happens again and I don't care what you say, Rogan. I'll let Quick's boys do whatever they wish with her. Do you hear?"

The harper nodded sullenly, following him out. The heavy scrape of the grille pulled across the hatchway like the closing of a coffin.

Alone, Elisabeth curled once more into her corner, unable to stop the slow leak of tears.

Her whole life, she'd avoided asking the questions.

Yet the answers had come.

And there was no going back for any of them.

———o———

Croker had come twice with his knife. Each time leaving Brendan shaken and bloody. A hairline slash down his neck. A razored scoring of his upper arm. Death by a thousand cuts.

The last visit had been a few hours ago, or so it seemed. He'd closed his eyes in a vain attempt at sleep, but his mind spun through plot after plan. He'd have a small window of opportunity once they came ashore. He needed to be ready when the time came.

The ship remained taut, the water slapping and curling against the hull. Winds steady and southwesterly. No return of the mage storm. They must have outdistanced their attacker to the point the captain felt safe in resuming only subtle nudges to the weather. Enough to keep them on course. Not enough to exhaust him should he need to call the power down again.

Brendan's heart lurched at the sound of a key turning in the lock. Croker back for more?

He fought at the cords binding his hands behind his back, his ankles to the chair until his wrists burned and his bones felt as if they'd been pulled loose, but there was not even the slightest give in the knots. They'd not risk his escape from the cabin again.

The door swung open on the shuttered flame of a lantern. The light splashing up onto Rogan's drawn and tired features, his eyes bleary and uncertain.

Brendan's gaze narrowed, his jaw clenched against the curse forming on his lips. Whatever his crimes, Rogan was right. He was all that stood between Lissa and the crew's lust. Brendan needed the harper alive. Better yet, if Brendan could convince Rogan of his mistake, perhaps he'd be a powerful ally at the moment of decision.

Rogan hung the lantern from a peg above the table. He sat across from Brendan, his eyes widening at Croker's handiwork, his Adam's apple bobbing nervously as he ran a finger over the scarred tabletop, clearing his throat. "Elisabeth is well. I wanted to let you know I've seen to it they stay away from her."

Brendan had tried closing his mind to what might be happening to Lissa, but at Rogan's assurances, he felt the throbbing pain in his temples and the tightness in his chest ease.

"You said you'd scryed what the future held," Rogan continued, his voice thready in the tense silence between them. "What Arthur's return would mean for the *Other*. What have you seen?"

Brendan closed his eyes, the backs of his lids dancing red with flames. A spreading, suffocating pressure building up through him as the stone drew closer to its destination. "Arthur is cursed, Rogan. His reign fated to fail. I've seen the battle's end. Arthur is defeated. The *Other* lie scattered and destroyed. There is no return of a golden age. Only fire and death and ruin."

Rogan's lips pressed to a thin white line. "I don't believe it. Arthur was a great and glorious king. His power almost rivaled that of the *Fey* themselves. He couldn't possibly fail against a horde of weak and powerless *Duinedon*. They won't have a choice. They'll be forced to live with us in peace."

"A peace bought with so many innocent dead is no peace. It's tyranny. With Máelodor at its head. And Arthur his slave-born puppet."

"You lie."

"If you're so certain, why did you come? I don't think you're as confident of your convictions as you pretend."

He paused, trying to gauge the man's mood. "Does Lyddy know where you are?" Brendan ventured.

"Leave her out of this. She's not involved."

"Neither was Elisabeth," Brendan answered quietly.

Rogan blanched. "Enough talking." He rose, fumbling uneasily with his pipe. "We'll be arriving off Cornwall in a few hours."

Brendan nearly choked on the request he was about to make, but he'd had too long to dwell on the possibilities to leave this one unaccounted for. "Then time runs out. I would ask a favor from one I thought of as a friend and one whom I think still could be."

Rogan turned back, the lantern swinging wildly in his hand. "I won't free you."

"I don't ask for myself, but for Lissa. See to it she's kept safe after. You understand what I'm trying to say: after. And if you're able to, escort her to Belfoyle. She'll be sheltered there if the worst should happen and war begins."

Rogan's face seemed to sag, and he looked as if he might speak, but he merely nodded before departing, the key once more scratching in the lock, the darkness crowding back in on Brendan like closing walls.

He swallowed back his fear. He'd been here before. Surely nothing could be worse than St. John's repulsive advances, his degradation, his power-mad sexuality that had left Brendan retching and sickened with his own body.

He closed his eyes, willing a calm he did not feel. The words burned up through him. Buried themselves in his brain. A whisper on the wind. An echo in the water.

It is my curse and my fate. What can mere mortals do against that? What can you do?

He lowered his head. His curse and his fate.

What could he do?

Alone had meant safe. Alone had meant deadly. But alone had also meant alone. He'd weakened and this had been the outcome. He'd sought to outrun his curse and his fate. Had only succeeded in pulling his ruin down on Elisabeth as well.

twenty-four

A rough shake of her shoulder dragged Elisabeth awake. Rubbing her sticky eyes, she peered up into Rogan's anxious, sweating face. Milky gray light spilled from the open hatch, the air damp and drizzly. The ship rocked softly, no sound to break into the quiet birdsong and murmured lap of water against the hull.

"We're going ashore," he said.

"Where's Brendan?" she asked. Anger holding her fear in check—barely.

"Topside."

He pulled her to her feet, skirts sodden, stockings clinging uncomfortably to her legs. She tried pinning her hair up in a quick knot, but the damp had caused her curls to frizz into an untameable mess and a crick in her neck made turning her head painful.

Rogan gave a grunt of impatience, and Elisabeth surrendered, shoving the heavy wild mass back over her shoulders.

"How is he?"

"A bit the worse for wear, but still ornery as an ox. If he's not careful, Croker'll forget and stick him just to keep him quiet."

"Maybe that's what Brendan's hoping for."

Rogan's expression darkened. "Enough talk. It's time to go."

She scrambled up the ladder. Passed through the companionway beneath the gaze of sullen, hard-eyed sailors. Climbed to the upper deck, where mist floated like smoke over a narrow estuary, trees rising thick and black to either side of them in the somber gray of predawn.

A dory had been lowered over the side, two men at the oars, two others seated in the bow. One in the stern. They moved like ghosts in the gauzy veil of morning fog.

"Down the ladder. I'll not leave you with them." Rogan glanced over his shoulder at the men still on board.

It didn't take a mind reader to understand the danger to her if she remained. The crew stripped her with their eyes, whispered comments passing from sailor to sailor like an infection.

"Thank you," she said, holding to her shredded dignity.

Rogan looked startled. Rubbed the back of his neck as he motioned her before him.

She stepped upon the first rung of the rope ladder, gripping it tightly as she swung out over the black water. Her slippers sliding against the wet footholds, her skirts getting in her way as she descended.

At the waterline, hands grabbed her about the waist, hauling her aboard the dory, where she was tossed into the stern beside the same pugnacious, jowly faced man she'd confronted yesterday, his pistol jammed hard in her ribs.

Brendan sat between two others, hands bound behind him, hair silvered with damp. Ugly purple and black bruises marred his sun-bronzed face, thin bloody slashes crisscrossing his face, and one eye was swollen shut. A dark red stain damped his shirt to his left shoulder.

She couldn't help it. She started to tremble. Locking her knees together, she clamped her elbows against her sides to stifle the growing tremors. She hated being afraid. Being powerless. If only there was something she could do. Some way she could fight back.

Rogan stepped into the boat, taking a seat across from her, never once looking Brendan's way, as if he didn't exist. Dropping his coat around Elisabeth's shoulders, he murmured, "Won't do you getting a chill on top of everything else."

The man with the gun gave a snort of crude laughter. "Such a gentleman. A chill's the least of the bird's worries."

Rogan speared the man with a stony gaze over the top of Elisabeth's head, a jackknife appearing in his hand as if conjured. "You keep your comments to yourself, Sams," he snarled, "or I'll see you regret them."

Sams bristled, his face reddening. "You think so, Paddy? I'll fucking blow your head off."

"English bug!"

"Shut your yobs, the both of you," Croker growled from his place beside Brendan. "If the excise tumbles to us, you can finish your arguing in Bodmin jail awaiting the assizes."

The dory shoved off, the oarlocks muffled in cloth, the water sliding in swirls and eddies with each stroke as light spread somber and gray across the sky. Rain took the place of mist, speckling the water as the boat ground against the rocky shoreline.

Croker took command of Brendan while Sams grabbed Elisabeth, his fingers digging into her shoulder as he propelled her out onto the slimy rocks and up into the trees. Rogan trailing behind.

The group pushed through the scrub and deeper into the spinney. Ahead, a narrow lonely track. A closed coach. And an enormous, barrel-chested man, his wispy white hair barely covering the gray skin of his head, his eyes pale as marbles.

Elisabeth peered over her shoulder, but the river had vanished back into the swirling fog. Nothing to show a ship lay hidden only yards away. No sound but the crunch of trodden leaves, the mournful call of a nightingale from a nearby tree, and the pounding of her frightened heart.

The cottage sat back off the road in a shallow valley, green, rocky hills rising up behind it. Brendan took in hasty impressions as he was hustled from the carriage to the door. The isolation. The number of guards lounging about in various poses of idleness. The way the trees closed in to the west. The narrow track into the hills that lay out of sight of the guards in the yard. And finally, the magic saturating the air. Buzzing up through his center. Not just the dark energy he expected congealing like sludge in his head, but a force outside the cottage walls that singed his mind with war and fire and images of death.

He glanced at Rogan, the focal point of the energy, standing a few yards away with Elisabeth. He must still carry the Sh'vad Tual.

Brendan felt it whispering to him. It was as if he was

expected. As if someone or something beyond Máelodor awaited his arrival.

Oss shoved Brendan forward, a guard moving to open the door and usher them through into the cottage's surprisingly clean and comfortable interior. A tiny entry hall leading to a room at the back. A narrow set of stairs. Two front rooms to either side. One closed door. One open, from which someone called in dubious welcome.

"Back already, Oss? Do you bring us company?"

Like a knife along slate, the scrape of that familiar voice burned along Brendan's bones, turning his blood to ice. Squaring his shoulders, he bowed his way beneath the doorway, allowing no glimpse of anything less than perfect confidence to cross his face. Máelodor wanted a groveling, terrified prisoner. Instead he'd find a mage as skillful and determined as himself.

Brendan entered the gloomy room, a sulking fire burning to a few dull coals in the hearth, shutters drawn over the narrow window. The stuffy warmth caused sweat to bead upon Brendan's forehead and cling stickily to his back.

His host rose stiffly from an armchair. Leaning heavily upon a staff, he stepped out of the shadows.

Son of a bitch! Bile chewed its way up Brendan's throat as he tried not to show by even the flickering of an eyelid his complete repulsion. Was this the price for manipulating the forbidden magics? Would this have been his fate had he continued to work the dark arts?

It had been less than a year since he'd last seen Máelodor, and in that time a horrible change had overtaken the master-mage. As a *Heller*, he had always possessed the ability to call upon the power of his fetch animal—even to take on certain characteristics of that animal—but as the *Unseelie* magic consumed him, the line between animal and man was blurring in unspeakable ways.

He'd lost all his hair, his scalp and forehead rough and crusty, except for the patches that had been replaced by glistening gray-green scales. His nose had flattened so that the nostrils were mere slits on either side of a narrow bump of cartilage, his mouth no more than a lipless grinning slash. His eyes protruded beneath scaly ridges that must have once been eyebrows, the slitted irises bearing a fevered intensity.

Yet, the trade-off was obvious. Máelodor's power throbbed the air, his personal wards impenetrable. If he'd been strong before, now he was damn near invincible. The strength needed to bring him down would need to be equally formidable.

"No greeting for an old ally, Douglas? A man you once called comrade? Friend?" His eyes blazed. "Uncle?"

"Let's not get carried away," Brendan replied smoothly. "Father may have honored you with his friendship, but you were always just poor old Simpkins to the rest of us. A dreary functionary with a flair for the dramatic. I see nothing's changed."

The backhand rattled his teeth in his head. Disgusting and disgustingly strong. A bad combination.

"Respect your elders and your betters, boy. A shame your father didn't beat that lesson into you along with all the others. He might still be alive." His hand shot out, grabbing Brendan's chin, squeezing hard as he turned Brendan's face this way and that. "You've more and more the look of Kilronan. The favorite son, weren't you? How he loved you, the deluded fool."

Brendan wrenched away, coming up hard against the servant Oss's chest.

A slow, ugly smile parted Máelodor's mouth in a black gape. "Touched a nerve, have I? Do you grieve for the old man still? Do you wonder how he died? I can tell you if you ask nicely. I can tell you how they all died. All but you . . . and me. Sole survivors of *Amhas-draoi* vengeance." His voice dropped to a cold, snaky hiss. "The only two left who dared to dream for all *Other* and were punished for their vision."

"It was madness, and you know it. Any war begun by the *Other* will end in our destruction."

"Is that why you betrayed us?" Máelodor pushed himself into Brendan's face, the grotesque snake-man features stomach-turning. "Or was it to save your own cowardly skin?" Clutching Brendan's shirt at the shoulders, he ripped it away, exposing the crescent-and-arrow tattoo sloping down over Brendan's collarbone onto his chest. "You were one of us. Trusted. Valued. A leader to those who envied our abilities. And you threw it all away." He shrugged away with a flip of his fingers. "A shame in the end your treachery earned you nothing. And now you'll lose everything."

Oss's fist shot out with inhuman speed. The kidney punch exploded along Brendan's nerves. With a cry, he landed on his knees, his gut on fire. The follow-up kick to his ribs knocked him onto his back, the air driven from his lungs.

He slammed his mind shut before the retaliatory crack of power seared the air between them. He'd not fight back. Not while Elisabeth remained in danger. He'd bide his time. And hope there was enough left of him when the moment came to make Máelodor regret laying a finger to him.

The albino stood over him in readiness for another blow.

"Enough, Oss," Máelodor demanded. "Where are our manners? He's a guest."

Oss dragged Brendan by the shoulders into a chair, where he fought back the wave of cold nausea rolling his insides. Forced himself to meet Máelodor's gaze with a stoic, measured stare.

"Isn't there someone else awaiting an audience? Douglas, you'll be interested to meet him as well, I believe."

Oss stalked to the door with a gesture to someone lurking about in the passage.

Rogan entered, his eyes searching the room, lighting for a moment upon Brendan with a grimace before settling upon Máelodor in his chair. He was not as successful at hiding his shock, but it was a reaction quickly schooled, though Brendan noted the harper's gaze never rested squarely on the master-mage; rather, it darted here and there in nervous agitation.

Máelodor ushered him forward with an imperious wave of his hand. "I'm told you've brought us a gift."

Rogan nodded as he pulled a leather pouch from his coat pocket. Turned it over in his hand to shake it. Into his palm dropped the Sh'vad Tual.

Its facets shimmered at first silver and ivory and palest gold, deepening to amber, then bronze then orange and coral, and finally black. Light flickered within it, a rippling, angry movement as if something fought to escape. The faint ringing of bells stirred the heavy air of the room, a chime deepening to a sonorous tolling that throbbed Brendan's temples.

Images flashed through his consciousness. A hidden glade. A toppled stone. A man with hair like flame. A sky dark as blood. And always a constant overlapping of voices in a language like music or running water or the earth as it cools in the night.

Rogan hurried forward to present the stone to Máelodor, whose smile now stretched to his ears—which, like his nose, had receded into his skull until they were but holes on either side of his head. "Arthur's return is finally at hand. The race of *Other* will once more hold a place of authority and respect. No more will they be treated like creatures of the devil and chased into the corners of the world like vermin." He looked down on Rogan as an emperor upon his subject. "For such a treasure, you have my eternal gratitude and may ask any price."

Rogan swept a deep, theatrical bow. "You are generous to such a humble foot soldier as myself. I would rejoice to see that glorious and celebrated day."

What ridiculous drivel. Brendan would laugh at the Irish blarney spewing from the old harper's mouth if his ribs didn't hurt so much. He restrained himself to a simple scoffing grunt that elicited matching black looks from Máelodor and Rogan.

"As you shall. As we all shall," the master-mage answered, his gaze locking on Brendan. "And you shall help me, Douglas. For without you, Arthur's rebirth would be naught but a castle in the air, would it not?"

"It may have been my idea originally, but it's long passed through my hands and into yours." Brendan found it hard to concentrate as the tip of Máelodor's tongue darted out and back. "I no longer take responsibility for your mania, and I'll not help you achieve anything but a slow, painful death."

"So brazen in your threats. Since you're the one bound and bleeding, I'll allow you your petty confidence. I've found it's always the bravest whose destruction proves the most . . . enjoyable." His attention turned back to Rogan. "I believe you've brought a young woman with you." His gaze slid toward Brendan. "Douglas's bride. I would see this rare beauty who has stolen the heart of our once prince of *Other.*"

Rogan shifted uneasily, his lip curled in a lecherous sneer. "The woman's locked away as insurance against Douglas using any of his tricks."

Máelodor's eyes narrowed. "We are safe enough. Douglas's powers are great, but in this, as in much, he is unequal to me. Oss, retrieve the young woman."

Again Oss left the room, returning with Elisabeth, her face ashen, hands clutched in her skirts. She shrank from Máelodor, her terror seeming to excite him, his hand curled around the knob of his staff, a new light entering his fevered gaze.

Brendan willed a thought across the divide, a thread of reassurance and hope against the desperation and fear boiling in her dark eyes. *Hold on, sweet Lissa. This is not the end.*

She stole a quick glance his way, a flash of surprise and dawning comprehension. Then, as if taking command of herself, she straightened in a regal pose of defiance, head lifting so that her flame-red hair rippled and curled down her back. The pulse fluttering in the perfect curve of her throat was the only hint she was less confident than she looked.

Máelodor's tongue darted over his lipless mouth, his nostrils flaring. "She is ripe for a man. I can smell her need. What do you think she would do to spare the man she loves? How much of herself would she sacrifice?"

No, Brendan mouthed silently, jerking in his seat,

Máelodor's threat bearing the force of one of Oss's punches.

Rogan stepped forward. "Master, I've brought you the stone of Arthur, and now I would claim my price if you'd be so generous." His gaze fell on Elisabeth. "I want the girl."

Brendan's eyes never wavered from Elisabeth's face. He saw the jump of her pulse, the way she bit her lip, the turning of her wedding ring round and round her finger. He committed these things to memory as he did her honeyed, freckled flesh, the velvet in her dark eyes, her body's luscious curves.

He'd told her once. She was home for him. A refuge from the darkness within him. A balance against the hunger for power that, had it continued unchecked, would have left him as misshapen and malignant with evil as Máelodor.

The mage rubbed his hands together, a wicked gleam in his eyes. "A steep price indeed. I would like to taste the flesh of this traitor's woman. Have her screams bleed into the dying mind of her husband. Let Douglas know the true cost of his betrayal."

To her credit, Elisabeth didn't faint, though she swayed dangerously, and her face grew chalk white.

Máelodor goaded him. It was obvious in the sneer as he taunted, at the coiling probe of his mind as he sought to discover the effect of his words. Brendan bit down until his teeth ground together, emptied his expression and his thoughts of anything but bored indifference. Any show of emotion and Máelodor would never let Elisabeth go.

Rogan interrupted the seeking thrust of Máelodor's mind just as Brendan felt the first crack in his mental barriers. "Surely you'll be too busy, now that the Sh'vad Tual has been restored to you. Old vengeance will surrender to new ambitions as you prepare for the coming of the king. Give the woman to me as payment, and she will warm my bed nicely. Douglas can still know as death comes for him that his bride is pleasuring his enemy." The men's eyes locked. An instant's meeting before Rogan dropped his gaze.

A silence followed when only Máelodor's wheezy breathing broke the mounting tension. Brendan curled his fingers into his palms, his spine so tight he felt it might snap, his brain on fire.

Finally, Máelodor turned away to hobble back to his chair. "So be it. Take her. She is yours."

Rogan grabbed Elisabeth's arm, propelling her out of the room before Máelodor could change his mind.

Brendan and Elisabeth had time for only one last look. He spoke his good-byes to the wind and saw her no more.

They were shown to a chamber at the top of the stairs. Locked in together with much laughing and ribbing and rude comments. Despite his slimy threats, Rogan never touched her. Only when food was brought to them that evening did he advise her to take off her gown and climb under the covers and stay quiet—no matter what.

She did as she was told, stuffing a pillow around her head, but still the vile filth leaked through.

". . . banged her till she wept and then rode her once more . . ."

". . . udders like melons and an ass . . ."

". . . rogered the redheaded slag . . ."

Embarrassment and anger burned her cheeks, but she pretended to sleep until the door closed behind the guard, and they were once more alone.

She flung the covers off, glaring at Rogan. "We did nothing of the kind, and frankly I feel sordid even hearing the lies."

"You keep that to yourself unless you want to end as Máelodor's plaything," Rogan growled. "As long as they think I'm screwing Douglas's whore, you're safe."

"Safe? You call this safe? Locked in a room with my kidnapper while steps away a crazed snake-man threatens to torture my husband before he brings a dead myth back to life to begin an all-out magical war? Have I left anything out? Any other dangerous, threatening, or otherwise horrific detail?"

Instead of growing angry, Rogan laughed, which was like throwing oil on the fire. "No, I think you've summed it up nicely."

She leapt out of bed, ignoring the fact that she was in naught but a chemise and petticoat, not even stays to add an extra layer of armor. She felt like a turtle out of its shell. "You find this amusing? We trusted you, Rogan. Helena trusted you."

He sobered instantly, and for a moment she thought he might strike her. "Helena will understand once she sees Arthur in the flesh. Once she understands what his presence will do for us."

"And when she sees Máelodor in the flesh? There's a sight to inspire loyalty. The man's a monster—literally!"

"He does what he must for the good of all *Other*. Just as I do. This is about creating a future for our race that does not rely on *Duinedon* benevolence, but our own superiority."

"Killing thousands of innocent people makes you superior?"

"You're *Duinedon*. You don't understand."

"I'm human. As are you. I understand war. Death and grief. You tell me how we're different."

That was their last conversation. Elisabeth subsided into silence, curling up on the bed with the blankets dragged about her shoulders, hands over her ears, though it did little to drown out the sounds of violence from below or the crude laughter of men hard with violence and stupid with drink.

Through it all, Rogan sat at the chamber window, looking out upon the dark, lonely valley, a pipe clamped between his teeth, smoke wreathing his head, shoulders hunched at every sound of breaking glass or stifled groan.

When Elisabeth finally fell into an exhausted doze, her dreams returned her to a sudden storm and a dazzling boy holding her tight in his strong arms. Only this time, instead of the tongue-lashing she remembered, he kissed her, his mouth upon hers, firm, demanding, his heart a steady safe drumbeat beneath her palm while the rain burned her cheeks like tears.

A rooster pulled her awake, the chair by the window empty, the sky low with clouds. An ominous waiting silence hanging over the cottage as if someone had died. She squeezed her eyes shut. No. Not dead. He couldn't be dead.

Squashing the thought as far down in the back of her mind as she could, she opened her eyes, fear battling lack of sleep fighting with self-pity. The result leaving her surprisingly numb, as if she were watching events happening to someone else like a bad play. The defenseless heroine at the mercy of dastardly villains.

If only she could walk out at the intermission.

She rose from bed, splashing her face with water from

a basin upon the washstand. Searched for a clean linen to wipe the dirt from her hands and cheeks.

Rogan's coat lay draped upon the chair back. Hoping to find a handkerchief, she rifled his pockets, smiled as her fingers closed around the cold butt of a pistol.

This heroine was defenseless no longer.

The chamber door opened, whirling her around, the pistol concealed within her skirts.

A hand upon the knob, Rogan raked the other through his hair. "They've gone."

No need to explain. She knew who had departed in the night and why. "When did they leave?" She heard the difference in her voice. Bolder. Confident.

Amazing what a weapon did for a girl's self-confidence.

Rogan, on the other hand, didn't seem to notice anything different. And, in fact, didn't seem to be noticing much of anything. Dark shadows smudged a tired face, his mood sullen and glum. It was hard to feel sorry for him—extremely difficult, actually—but Elisabeth couldn't help sympathizing with his obvious self-pitying moroseness. After all, she'd felt the same way until moments ago. "They rode out a few hours before daybreak."

"And Brendan?"

Rogan closed his eyes for a brief, frightening moment. "Máelodor knows how to break a man slowly."

Rage burned away her sympathy. She wanted to throw herself at Rogan and tear him limb from limb. Call him every name she could think of. Possibly make up a few. This was his damn fault. But indulging in hysterics would gain her nothing. She needed Rogan. Now more than ever.

"Do you know what direction they took?"

"No, and if Máelodor's smart, he'll not stay long to the

main road but leave his escort and move quietly. He's been clever enough to stay hidden this long. He knows how to move without being seen."

"But you can track him."

His brows shot up, the first real interest he'd taken in the conversation. "Me? To do what?"

"Rescue Brendan."

He laughed. "Am I looking like a fool?"

She lifted the pistol in both hands. "No. Like a mage-chaser."

That definitely gained his attention. He went still, sucking in quick a breath. "Now, Miss Elisabeth. I kept you from Máelodor as I promised Douglas I would. More than that's beyond me."

She cocked the hammer. At this range, there was no way she could miss. "The countryside round Dun Eyre can be a dangerous place. Brigands and housebreakers abound, and it's important for everyone to know how to handle a gun. Even the women."

Rogan gave a humorless chuckle, though his eyes remained wary as he fingered a bruise upon his cheek. "If you handle it as well as you do a poker, I'm inclined to be on my guard."

"I handle it much better, I assure you." Her smile was thin as a dagger as she fought to keep her arms straight under the awkward weight of the pistol. The dratted thing was heavier than the gun she'd fired back home. If Rogan didn't surrender soon, her arms would droop like limp noodles. "Will you help me or not?"

He sobered, holding his arms out as if warding her off. "I'd not wanted you mixed up in this. You've got to believe me. You or Douglas. All I want is justice. For me. For

Lyddy. For all the folks like us who've been treated as less than human by the likes of you magic-lacking *Duinedon*."

Elisabeth felt the fear drain out of her, replaced by a crystal-bright clarity. She'd never killed anyone before, yet she knew without the hint of a doubt she would shoot Rogan unless he complied. But if Madame Arana's scrying glass had spoken truth, her plan would work.

Rogan would help her.

She would be there when the tomb opened.

When Arthur emerged.

When Brendan died.

twenty-five

Brendan fell against the roots of an enormous sycamore. He peered up into the dizzying heights of leaves and branches through eyes swollen to mere slits and crusted with dried blood. Cradled his smashed hand close against his ribs.

Gods, he was a damned mess.

On the bright side, at least he'd never annoy Elisabeth with Mozart anymore.

They'd been walking for hours, the trees growing closer together the farther they penetrated, the leafy canopy closing over them until the very air shone green and gold. Moss clung thick to the trunks while thickets of brambles clawed his arms and left long cat scratches upon his cheeks. And yet, there seemed to be no end in sight to the great cathedral of overlapping branches, as if they'd stepped back to a previous age before the land had been cleared for field and farm.

Hidden watchers slid between the dappled shadows.

A faint and gossamer chime stirred the humid air. The *Fey* protected this primordial forest and made it their own. He could only hope they would be on his side when the time came.

Someone dragged him back to his feet, thrusting him forward. He arched against the touch upon his lashed and bloody back, clamping his mouth shut upon the groan of pain churning up through his gut.

Shoving a hand in his pocket, he found Daz's tiny bit of looped twine. He smiled through parched lips as he slid it onto his finger as he might have done Sir Archibald's ring had Jack ever handed it over before Helena had claimed his undivided attention.

Brendan shook his head. Poor, bloody, noble Jack. Spent the past year playing nursemaid. Turned his back for a few hours and *bang* . . . and with Roseingrave of all people.

Both Brendan's minders gone at the very moment he'd needed them.

Concentrating on the path ahead, he didn't notice the shiver of mage energy beneath his skin at first. A prickly, scratchy feeling as if he'd fallen into a patch of nettles. Not surprising if he had. He'd spent more time on his hands and knees than upright, thanks to a strained knee and a spiteful guard. But no, there it was again. A fluttering of magic against his brain. This time brushing past him, turning leaves, dimming the light as if rain approached.

He lifted his face to it, letting the touch of it sink into his flesh, know him and return to its sender. What harm in offering himself up to the tracing? Any not of this company would surely come as a friend.

Unfortunately, Máelodor must have felt the brush as well.

The group stopped as he lifted a hand, his fingers flicking, his curse a mumbled slither of words on an oily breeze.

Immediately, the link was severed, the comforting presence withdrawn, leaving Brendan more alone than he'd ever been.

He forced himself to limp along through gritted teeth. His painful progress slowing as he hoped for a renewal of the encouraging presence.

It never came again.

The forest folded round him in a tangle of green so that every step was a stumbling lurch, mist threading the wood, a ringing in his ears growing louder and more insistent. He couldn't think. Couldn't focus. The bells were all he heard. He began to hallucinate. A face within the trees. The flash of a leg. He blinked: Was he losing his mind or was that Killer's black-and-white fuzzy body keeping pace off to their right? Impossible, but at least it offered him comfort to think the little dog kept him company even if it was a mirage conjured by delirium.

They emerged into a clearing, the mist here clinging thick and gray and wet over the ground. A slab of toppled granite lay upon its side, smaller stones scattered amid the bracken. And something else: a power ancient when the earth was young. A well of magic so deep and immense, it seemed to push to the center of the world. It wrapped itself around him, burrowing beneath his skin until he saw the flux and flow of mage energy in the air, on each trembling leaf, each scratching limb, every glistening drop of water.

He stood dazed, letting this river of *Fey* power surge around him.

It was as he'd hoped.

Arthur's tomb had been built upon a thin place, a spot where the deeper *Fey* magics surfaced and the two worlds touched. A source of enormous power if one were skillful—and desperate—enough to tap the melded energies.

He was both.

Máelodor stepped forward, the Sh'vad Tual raised high before him.

For Brendan, it was now or never.

Rogan's honey tongue had been almost as helpful as his tracking abilities. As Elisabeth waited in the shelter of the cottage's doorway, he persuaded the two guards left behind not only to saddle two horses but, in a display of Irish impudence, to sing every verse of "John Barleycorn" backwards. They willingly complied and Rogan and Elisabeth had trotted out of the yard with the awkward, off-key caterwauling *"wan and pale both looked he till"* wafting behind them.

An hour and a half later, at Rogan's insistence, they left the horses behind and entered a deep, overgrown copse. Clouds flattened gray black across the sky as they pushed into a strange biting wind, as if January's chill had touched down within this isolated corner of the county.

"I'm not certain how you managed to palaver me into doing this, Miss Elisabeth. Perhaps you've a bit of the *leveryas* in you," Rogan joked as he pushed aside a heavy branch for her.

She ducked beneath it, yanking her skirts away from the snagging twigs. "You wanted to go after him as much as I did. It just took the right spark for you to see the light."

He dropped back into his slow, loping stride. "And what do you plan on doing if we do find them in time? I'm thinking these barking irons of ours won't be more than a fly bite to that great hulk of an attendant."

"I haven't the vaguest notion, but something's bound to occur to me. It's gotten me this far, hasn't it?"

This far, being the middle of nowhere following a vague hazy trail of mage energy. For a moment, doubt assailed her. Could she trust Rogan? Could he be leading her away from Brendan? She pushed aside the thought. She'd not go down that road. The vision had shown her she would find Brendan. And find him she would.

The path forked. A narrow winding branch to the left heading down to a stream cut. A wider avenue uphill into deeper wood.

Rogan paused, head up. Eyes trained on a point invisible to Elisabeth as he scanned first one direction, then the other, in a slow, measuring manner. He really did resemble a bloodhound, with his eyes sunk into the folds of his long, angular face, and gangly limbs ending in oversize hands and feet.

She dropped onto a broken log as she waited, torn between relief at the rest for her weary feet and irritation at any delay. After a few moments, she began chafing her hands. Tapping her foot. Trying not to seem impatient when every inch of her jangled with nerves.

Rogan's power couldn't fail them now.

Impatience finally won over her aching feet. "Which way?"

Rogan remained unmoving in the middle of the trail, hands clamped to his side, eyes fixed and staring.

"Rogan?"

No answer. Instead, his eyes rolled up in his head as he began to convulse.

"Rogan!" She ran to him, grabbing him as he fell to the ground, his body curled into a ball, seizures raking him, his jaw clamped shut, low animal moans coming from deep in his throat. Was it poison? Had his heart given out?

She grabbed him to her just as the shuddering stopped. As he went limp, his final rattling breath collapsed his chest. Black oozy liquid dripped from the corner of his mouth.

Tears stung her eyes as she looked up into the canopy of sycamore and maples, oaks and ash. Whispered a prayer for the harper's passing.

"This is dark magic. Máelodor's handiwork."

A man's voice behind her shot her heart into her throat. She spun around to see him standing half within the trees. Where had he come from? She fumbled the pistol up to aim it at the stranger. "Who are you? Show yourself."

He stepped into the open, and she nearly dropped the gun in shock. He was completely naked. Not a stitch of clothing. Not even a strategically placed fig leaf.

He seemed completely comfortable with the situation, and in fact chuckled as if he were used to such a reaction. For some reason his lack of embarrassment overcame the awkwardness of the situation, and she was able to maintain—albeit with difficulty—her composure, though it was hard not to gape. "I said, who are you? Answer, or so help me, I'll blast a hole right through you."

He inclined his head, though it had the solemnity of an old-fashioned courtier's bow. Difficult to pull off nude, but he managed it. "Do you not recognize me?"

She studied him more closely—from the waist up. Medium height and lean—not a spare inch of fat marred the compact muscles. His hair was black as night, though here and there a few silver strands shown through. Premature silver, since he didn't look more than in his mid-twenties. His eyes were brown, his gaze amused and wary at the same time.

A grin pulled at the corners of his mouth, eyes twinkling. She'd seen that tongue-in-cheek amusement before, but where—

"Mop with legs? Fur ball? Blasted mutt? Anything sound familiar?" he asked.

Unfortunately it did. Frighteningly, jaw-droppingly familiar. A dog that had changed into a man. Or was it a man that had changed into a dog? No time to ponder details. She'd add it to the tottering pile of strangeness her life had become and mull it over another day.

"You're *Other*," she whispered.

"I am not." He drew himself up with a huff of insulted dignity. Impressively done for a naked man. "I am of the *Imnada*."

He pronounced it with such solemnity, Elisabeth half expected a clap of thunder to follow.

"Who are they? I've never heard of them before."

"No." He knelt beside Rogan's body, began tugging at his boots.

Like a puppet with cut strings, the harper's body rolled limply, limbs flopping. For some reason, that finally brought everything crashing down around her. Rogan was dead. Brendan was missing. She was keeping company with a naked, shape-shifting dog-man. Her head began to spin, and she found it difficult to catch her breath. "You can't—I mean, Rogan—"

Killer glanced up. "Does not need them anymore, though if you are uncomfortable with my taking them, I will remain as I am." He sat back, awaiting her decision.

Astonishment must be doing things to her. All she could think of was how incredibly polite he was being. That and how very, very undressed he was.

Heat crawled into her cheeks. A bit late, but perhaps it was a delayed reaction. "I suppose if you must, you must. I mean, you . . . you can't be comfortable like that, can you?"

She tried looking everywhere but at him, which was hard to do. There wasn't much else to look at other than trees. A muscular, handsome, gentleman in the buff was a hard thing to ignore.

"Cold doesn't bother me as it does most humans, but you would be more comfortable with me clothed, I think. You look a bit . . . dazed." Again the teasing smile, dimples carved into his cheeks.

"Can you blame me? I'm talking to my . . . my . . . pet."

"Neither you nor Douglas would have trusted a companion in human form."

As he hastily appropriated Rogan's clothes, Elisabeth averted her gaze and tried not to remember how many times the dog had been in her chamber as she'd dressed. How many revealing conversations she'd had with him curled in her lap. Yikes! She'd scratched his stomach, for heaven's sake. "So what's your name? I can't keep calling you Killer."

"That's as good a name as any."

"Why show yourself to me this way?"

There was a silence as if he was pondering his response. "It's a risk, but one I felt necessary. Until now, we've chosen to remain unknown to the race of *Other*, but events no longer allow for such choice. We're not so unwise as to think a war between races would not pull us in as well, however much we've barricaded ourselves away."

She heard the rustle of fabric, a colorful oath that had her smiling despite herself. He might be a shape-changer, but his cursing was all human. "How did you find us? Last I saw, you were gnawing on a man's leg."

There was a bark of quick laughter. "So I was. I tracked you along the coast as far north as Balbriggen before I lost your trail. Then, just as I found you again, the mage storm blew me off course. It took me longer than I'd hoped to make land."

"So you're saying you—"

"I am a shape-changer." His tone said, *end of discussion.* "You can turn around now. I'm clothed."

He had taken only Rogan's breeches and boots and had wrapped Rogan's body in his coat, laying him out beneath the sky, closing his eyes, hands crossed upon his chest. As she watched, he appropriated Rogan's knife and pistol.

"Can't you bury him?" she asked.

"Had we the time, I would burn him as is proper, but this will have to do."

The light dimmed as a strange gray twilight filtered through the leaves, the wind died, the birds fell silent as if the world waited for what was to happen next.

Killer lifted his head, eyes closed. Elisabeth almost expected him to sniff at the air like the dog he had been—or was—or . . . something. She'd worry over this new revelation later.

"We must go," he said. "Quickly."

"Go where? Rogan's dead." She swallowed around the lump in her throat. "He was the one who could follow Brendan's trail. I'm lost."

"But I am not. And together we can save Brendan before Máelodor uses him in the summoning."

"Uses him—"

"Later. For now, we must go." He held out a hand, again with that strange formal gallantry. She took it, feeling the cool roughness of his palm, the strength in his wrestler's body.

And followed him into the wood.

Brendan reached out, sensing the ley lines running outward beneath the earth from the toppled slab like spokes upon a wheel. Feeling his way along the potent river of mage energy as a sailor might take readings to chart his depth. Here and there dipping deeper as he wove his magic into the pattern. Carefully. Skillfully. Too much and one ran the danger of losing one's very humanity in the fierce hurricane storm of *Fey* power. The trick was to manipulate the streams of mage energy in ways that channeled its might, yet did not diminish it.

He hoped to the gods that, after so many years lying dormant, his skills remained, or this would be an extremely short-lived attack.

The spell he finally called upon was one he'd found in a Greek grimoire, the parchment translucent with age, the writing faded to near-illegibility. Father had bought it from a bookseller in Venice during one of his extended tours of the Continent, but it had been Brendan who'd spent a year transposing and translating. Six months mastering the unfamiliar technique. He could still smell the musty aromas of age and ink and old paper that made up the Belfoyle library. Feel the fragile softness of the pages beneath his fingers. See the light spread and shrink over the shine of polished oak floors in the long days devoted to unraveling the secrets contained within.

This must be what they meant when they spoke of one's life flashing before one's eyes.

As he stretched with his mind and his magic, he uttered the words of the spell beneath his breath. *"Esemynest agesh kavesha. Hweth d'esk mest."*

Immediately the magic rose within him like a spring tide. Easing the pain of his injuries, healing the numerous wounds he'd incurred last night under Máelodor's maddened gaze.

Brendan closed his eyes as his body renewed itself, the rising pressure spilling over, dazzling his eyes, crackling along his arteries, sparking new and wild pathways in his brain.

As he felt the power crest, he released it with a sure flick of his fingers, casting it out like the thrust of a sword. Honed to a steel brilliance, the spell cut the air on a whistle of wind and buried itself in Máelodor like a dagger to the back.

The mage screamed, high and thin, his mouth gaping black, his face paling to a sickly gray. He whirled around, losing his balance as he fumbled with crutch and peg leg and the uneven ground. The Sh'vad Tual dropped from his hand to roll free, its fire extinguished.

Brendan's guard grabbed for his pistol, but Brendan was faster. He tore the weapon from the man's hand, pulling him close as he fired into him. The man jerked and grunted before falling to the turf with a dull, wet thud.

Máelodor's response came swift and certain. A savage explosion of ripping power, severing veins and crushing bones. The hiss of his slithered words a mutilating combination of *Other* force and *Unseelie* atrocity.

Brendan panted through his teeth against the pain

unleashed by the dark magic, forcing his mind to focus on the ley lines, on the healing energy centered in the tomb. But even as he struggled to hold on to the *Fey* power, it ran between his fingers like water. His spell unraveling beneath the blacker, stronger, fiercer demon spell.

Shielding himself against the worst of the curse, he groped his way toward the Sh'vad Tual. Reaching for it, he dodged Máelodor's fanged and venomous bite. And never saw the deadly bull-like fist of Oss until it blindsided him, striking him in the head. Rattling his teeth. Breaking his focus. The mage energy draining out of him in one sucking whirlpool rush.

He lay upon the turf, staring up into a sky riven with cloud and fire and a sweep of circling birds. There was a fraction of a second when he saw the slit-eyed malevolence of Máelodor and the blur of his descending staff.

He rolled aside, but not before the tip of the staff scored a bloody gash along his upper arm. Immediately, his fingers numbed and his arm went dead as the poison entered his bloodstream. And time and chances wound down.

twenty-six

Máelodor lifted the Sh'vad Tual high above his head in both hands. *"Mebyoa Uther hath Ygraine. Studhyesk esh Merlinus. Flogsk esh na est Erelth. Pila-vyghterneask."*

The stone ignited in a wash of color. The words of the dark spell beating against Brendan's brain. Each syllable pounding in his chest like the tolling of an enormous bell.

Fire and light poured out over Máelodor's hands and down his body. Sparkling over his skin and clothes in drifts and eddies before burying themselves into the ground at his feet.

Brendan cried out, the visions cascading through his mind. Arthur, his face black with sweat and blood and dirt, his sword broken as he fell. Aidan's lifeless body one of thousands beneath a crow-filled crimson sky.

"Klywea mest hath igosk agesha daresha!"

Mage energy blazed up through the trees in a tower of blue-white fire. The ground rumbled and lurched as the sky darkened to a false midnight. As a storm's tempest raged, wind whipped the leaves, bringing down cracked and splintered limbs. Blinding and choking him with a gritty, throat-scouring dust.

Brendan covered his head as he curved into the shelter of a fallen log. Opened his eyes on a world gone suddenly still.

Where the giant slab of mossy granite had leaned was now a doorway, the shine of silver light spilling from an exposed cavern, the chime of faery bells high and bright and floating clear upon the air.

Slowly lowering the stone, Máelodor motioned with a jerk of his head.

Oss stepped forward, even his blank features tinged with the shade of fear. Ducking inside, he disappeared for a moment before reappearing with a strange shake of his head and a spread of his palms.

"What?" Máelodor's response cracked across the silence like a whip as he pointed to Brendan. "Bring him to me."

Oss's gaze fell on Brendan like the first spade of grave earth.

The man dragged him stumbling to Máelodor. "What mischief is this, Douglas?"

Brendan's lip curled with animosity. "You'll have to be more specific. Mischief is my middle name."

"The tomb is empty. You had the stone. What have you done with the High King's bones?" Máelodor demanded, spittle forming at the corners of his mouth, his eyes alight with madness. I'll have your answer or Oss will slice off a finger one at a time."

The servant pulled a knife from his belt, grabbing Brendan's wrist, though he felt no pain due to the advance of the poison in his bloodstream. In fact, he barely noticed anything as he pondered this new and wild hope.

The tomb was empty. No bones. No Arthur. Máelodor had failed.

"Arthur's not dead," he whispered, his mind beginning to haze, his limbs sluggish as the serpent's venom crawled through him with needling agony.

"What?"

Oss's knife cut into the flesh of Brendan's pinky. Brendan watched his blood dripping down over his wrist with clinical apathy. "Arthur lives. Not a tomb. A portal. To *Ynys Avalenn.*"

How he knew, he couldn't say, only that once he said it, he knew it as truth.

Blood slicked the back of his hand as Oss withdrew his blade. Brendan clutched his hand to stanch the flow. It seemed the sensible thing to do.

"A portal. A way between worlds." Máelodor rubbed his chin in speculation.

"It's over, Máelodor. Without Arthur to inspire them, the *Other* will never rally to your cause."

"Are you certain?" Máelodor's transformation seemed to progress before Brendan's eyes. New scales covered the man's entire head; long white fangs grew to either side of a flickering tongue. "So I will not have our last great king to lead us into battle, but there will be a reckoning. The *Duinedon* will fall. And, bones or not, this portal is the key."

The clap of his hands came like thunder. As he began the chant that would unlock not a passage to *Ynys Avalenn* but the *Unseelie* abyss.

His gaze fastened on Brendan. "And you will help me, son of Kilronan."

The blast of demon magic ripped into Brendan, the

burn along his muscles like acid. Shredded glass pulled through narrow veins. And then something else. A peeling away of his soul. A tearing anguish, as if his insides were being flayed to a million pieces. He screamed his agony to the boil of storm clouds as Máelodor slowly inexorably drained him of power and life.

In the end, finding their way to Brendan had been laughably easy. Or would have been had Elisabeth been in a laughing mood. After all, it hardly took magical tracking or canine smell power when the ground rumbled beneath one's feet. The sky darkened to a sickly orange-green before being swallowed by rolling storm clouds, and the wind carried a stench of charred flesh and rotting bodies.

She crouched at the edge of the grove with a stomach-tightening swirl of terror and nausea. Magic infected the air, a sulfurous greasy stench, a black slithering coil of hate and madness penetrating her mind with a dark desperation. All of it emanating from the monstrous creature standing in the center of the clearing. Máelodor had grown unusually tall and thin, his twisted, snarled limbs gangly, his head hooded and scaled like a cobra's. Eyes lidless and red with death. Mouth fanged and bloody. Bearing enough humanity to make the monstrosity of him all the more grotesque.

Her hair stood on end. Every impulse screamed at her to run. To flee this place of ruthless savage power. To pray for a quick end.

Killer gripped her hard until she had to bite back a cry, but it was enough to snap her free of the panic.

Brendan lay upon the ground, the fingers of one hand plowed deep into the soft earth, his other hand held close to his chest, his face bone-white, his body seeming to thin and pale before her eyes.

His eyes met hers. The wild gold of his gaze dimmed to a sinister black.

A blast of thought beat against her brain, overpowering for a split second the pounding rhythm of demon blood. And she knew what she must do.

Lifting her pistol, she took dead-eye aim. Cocked the hammer.

"Wait!" Killer shouted as she pulled the trigger.

With a roar of fire and smoke, she shot Máelodor square in the chest.

Heard the snap of a twig. Felt the chill of a shadow across her shoulder.

An explosion burst behind her eyes.

She knew nothing more.

Máelodor's death would have been too much to hope for. Engorged as he was on *Unseelie* magics, it would take more than a pistol shot to kill the master-mage, but it had been enough to disrupt his concentration. To sever the soul-devouring link between them.

Brendan would die here. There would be no return from this place. For some reason, the idea did not terrify him as he thought it might. Instead, it filled him with a calming sense of purpose. If this was his inescapable fate, he need not fear the struggle with his own blackened soul. The dark magics he'd loosed would serve their master one final time. And die here with him.

The *Unseelie* hovered in the prison of between. Howling, razor-clawed, fangs and jaws clacking, their greasy, fetid charnel-house stench burning his nose and throat. Not yet anchored to this world by ties of the flesh but no longer imprisoned within the abyss, they hovered in a crimson, smoke-filled sky.

Lightning split the sulfurous air, thunder deafening. The storm broke over him, rain like knives, pinning him to the slick, churned mud. He willed his body to respond. Dragging himself to his knees, then his feet. Already his mind fragmented as Máelodor's poison ripped him apart. But he knew what he had to do.

The spell formed unbidden in his head before lying like acid in his mouth. *"Una math esh gousk——"*

A kick to his side interrupted the flow of words.

Brendan rolled away as Oss drew back to level another rib-crushing blow, but even that small movement almost caused him to pass out. Something was definitely broken. Probably a lot of somethings.

Brendan looked calmly into Oss's chillingly blank eyes, but just as the final blow should have descended, a huge snarling blur of fur and teeth barreled into the muscle-bound servant, knocking him to the ground, ripping into his throat with bone-crunching, blood-spraying gusto.

End this, Erelth! Now!

The words formed like a shout in his head. No time to understand. No time to question. Brendan completed the spell, its power searing his vision, ringing in his ears and firing his mind.

Throwing open every chamber of his mind, he drew the power of the thin place into his body before casting it wide in a battering, unstoppable flood of mage energy. If one doorway could be forced open, so could another. And in such a way that both sides must confront one another. Must clash.

Wind froze to ice. Ice shattered. The chime of bells became the clang of shields and the cries of the dying. Smoke burned his lungs. Ash clung to his lips.

Battle was joined in a maelstrom of fury and rage and madness as *Unseelie* and *Fey*—Dark Court and Light—raged and swarmed the air of the grove like an evil tempest.

Máelodor fought to control his army, but the demon swarm once freed was deaf and blind to all but a wild killing frenzy. They turned on him, rending him limb from limb before the *Fey* swept down upon them. Brendan's last view of him was as a headless corpse tossed back into the abyss to be imprisoned alongside his erstwhile allies.

Lifting his face to the storm, Brendan let the rain scour clean the poisonous fog.

And for one moment saw a flame-haired king lifting a sword above his head. His shout carrying a ring of command, his gaze like silver steel as he beat back the challenge.

Arthur. The last great king of *Other*.

Leading the armies of the *Fey* as they drove the *Unseelie* of the Dark Court before them.

The shine of his armor. The golden crown upon his brow. The bloody stain of a crimson sky. The storm blurred them until, like looking through rain upon glass, he saw nothing clearly. Heard only the rush of wind and the ring of bells.

And a voice sounding clear above the din. "You have done well, heir of Kilronan. Now you may rest."

Elisabeth woke to birdsong. The drip of water upon the leaves. The cleansing wash of a gentle rain upon her face. Her head throbbed. She winced, probing the goose egg at the back of her head. Whose side was Killer on anyway?

Crawling from beneath the overhanging branches, she stumbled to her feet, her gown clinging wet and muddy to her legs, twigs and leaves scattered over her bodice and caught in her hair. No sign of Máelodor or Oss or whatever had stripped the trees bare and churned the clearing to a sea of mud and broken branches. She didn't think she wanted to know.

The shape-changer knelt beside Brendan, his face grave, Rogan's knife in his hand.

All weakness burned away. "Stay away from him, you filthy, damned dog!" she shouted as she half ran, half tumbled across the clearing.

Killer looked up, his dark eyes heavy with sadness. "You're awake."

"Stay away from him, do you hear?" She grabbed Killer's knife arm, trying to wrestle the weapon from his hand. Easily accomplished. In fact, he handed it to her.

"I am not your enemy," he said evenly.

"Aren't you?" Blood soaked Brendan's shirt, pooled viscous and dark beneath him. There seemed to be no part of him without injury.

"The blood on the knife is my own." Killer held out his arm, which bled from a gash across his forearm. "Blood from us can be powerful medicine. I offered mine to Douglas as a way to hold his soul within his body." He shook his head. "But it is not enough. Máelodor stripped much of his essence away, and what the mage did not claim was summoned by Douglas in opening the portals between worlds."

Elisabeth gathered Brendan's hands in her own, his fingers cold, the tips blue. Strange—he wore a silver and pearl ring that glowed softly in the strange twilight of the grove.

Elisabeth had never seen it before. "Brendan? Can you hear me?"

"Dying . . . not deaf." His smile broke her heart into a million jagged pieces.

Killer stood abruptly, his body rigid, hackles raised. "There is one chance yet. A slim one, but it's worth a try." To Brendan, he said, "Hold on. This may hurt."

Bending, he lifted Brendan in his arms as easily as if he were a baby. Carried him across the grove toward the cave, where white light spilled like water and a strange shimmering glassy melody rose and fell as if the wind had been given voice.

"Why did you hit me?" she asked, mainly as a way to keep from thinking. Thinking was not a good thing right now. Thinking would lead to uncontrollable weeping, and she refused to have Brendan's last image of her be tear-streaked and blubbery. No. Not his last image of her. That meant he was dying. That there was no hope left. That Máelodor had won.

"The mage would have sensed your conscious mind and attacked it as he did with Rogan," Killer explained. "I let him believe I was the shooter. Magic does not work on me in quite the same way."

Before ducking beneath the toppled broken slab that served as entrance to Arthur's tomb, Killer sought her eyes with his. "Do you come?"

She returned his questioning look with a determined glare.

"Then take hold of Brendan's hand and do not let go. That should keep you safe in the between of worlds."

She'd no time to ask for an elaboration before he stepped into the wash of white light, the color blanched from his face and body, replaced by a strange blue-silver glow that crackled over his skin and clothes. Quickly she grabbed Brendan's right hand, squeezing it as if she were stepping out onto a narrow cliff ledge above a raging sea. A roar filled her ears, her body buffeted in rip currents of air and water, leaping flames and grinding earth. And together they crossed the threshold and entered the cave.

From the outside, it was no more than a granite slab lying at a crooked slant against a shorter, stouter stone, barely large enough for a full-grown man to stand upright.

Inside, the narrow mouth opened into an immense cavern, the walls rising around her glimmering with an opalescent fire. Water ran over folds and ridges in the rock before being channeled into a marble bowl at the base of the opposite wall. In the center of the cavern stood what looked like an altar or a sarcophagus. Long. Narrow. Its side separated into intricately rendered panels depicting the lost king's life from birth within a Cornish fortress to defeat at the hands of his traitorous son. Carved into its lid, a dragon coiled round a sword protruding from a rock. The details wrought so well one almost saw the twitch of a tail, the gleam of steel.

Arthur's tomb. The resting place of the last great king of *Other*. Fantasy come to life.

She'd no time to be awestruck before shadows surfaced within the cave's strange shimmering mother-of-pearl walls. They moved within the rock like figures seen through thick, wavy glass or beneath murky water. As she watched, they took on definition and then form as one by one they stepped from the walls to ring the chamber. Nine gray-robed women, silver diadems upon their brows, each one so beautiful she was almost painful to look upon. Elisabeth gazed on them only in quick snatches and only through downcast lashes.

Killer didn't seem to have the same reaction to the faery women. He looked upon each one of them in turn as if searching their expressions for the slightest hint of sympathy. But none weakened or spoke or moved to assist them. They were still and white as marble, gazing as though staring into eternity.

Killer stepped forward, laying Brendan down at the foot of the tomb, Elisabeth kneeling beside him with a clamped hold of his hand, willing her life into him.

Standing tall, the shape-changer scanned each woman in turn. "You can feel its call or you would not have shown yourselves. Douglas bears a token of *Ynys Avalenn*. He is known to one among yours."

It seemed as if minutes ticked away with no one moving, Brendan's grip upon her hand weakened, his eyes growing opaque, breathing becoming shallow, so that his chest barely rose and fell. "Help him!" she shouted to the women, her patience snapping.

They looked through her, remote in their apathy.

"You're *Fey*. You can save him!" Frustration and fear burned through her like lava. She'd never been so angry in her life as she was at these stone-faced women. "What's the good of being immortal and all-powerful if you won't use your power to save a life? You're a bunch of cowards. Deceitful, false-hearted, conniving, hypocritical—"

"Not helping . . ." Brendan whispered while Killer muttered, "Why don't you tell them how you really feel?"

"—treacherous scum!"

"Enough." The smooth, vivid voice echoed through the chamber before rattling around in Elisabeth's skull. The throbbing in her temples moved down into her neck and shoulders.

Two figures stepped out from behind the phalanx of silent attendants to approach Elisabeth and Brendan.

A woman with long blue-black hair, but for a thick streak of silver. A face unlined with years yet shrewd with ancient, immeasurable wisdom. She wore a gown of deepest azure blue beneath a surcoat of beaten silver scales. From a wide leather girdle at her waist, a sword hung ominously.

Even as statuesque as she was, her companion dwarfed her. His head crowned in hair that glowed burnished red and gold. His face set in bleak and battle-hardened lines. His sword, he clenched still in a scarred fist, black stains splashed up and down the blade.

A prickling shiver ran over Elisabeth's skin before settling low in her stomach. This might be Arthur's tomb, but if she wasn't mistaken, this was Arthur in the flesh and very much alive.

Killer stepped forward, his expression respectful but not submissive. "I have brought you Brendan Douglas of the House of Kilronan. He carries a talisman of the *Fey*. One you cannot ignore."

The woman's gaze was like a bolt of lightning. "The ring allowed you to pass into the between separating our worlds, but do not presume, shape-changer. We owe this one nothing."

Meanwhile, Arthur knelt down beside Elisabeth, laying a hand upon Brendan's shoulder. "He is dying."

As if she didn't know that already, she wanted to snap, but didn't. After all, one didn't snarl at dead myths come to life. And there was real sorrow in his solemn voice for all that he stated the obvious.

"There is nothing we can do," the woman replied, her voice cold as the first breath of winter frost.

Arthur shifted to meet her eye. "There is a way, Scathach."

Scathach? This was the warrior-queen and head of the *Amhas-draoi*? Elisabeth held her breath. Brendan was under a death order. If this woman so chose, she could fulfill it with one fierce hack of her sword. There was no one to stop her.

"Impossible," the woman said, dismissing Arthur as if he were a child.

A sly smile curved Arthur's lips. Despite the centuries that had passed since he'd lived among men, his humanity remained. No *Fey* could match that look of boyish mischief. "I am proof it's not impossible."

"There is a difference. You are a man conceived in magic. Your life among us was fated as soon as you drew your first breath in the circle of your mother's arms. Douglas is fully human. To bear him to the summer kingdom is not wise."

"He will die otherwise."

"Then he will die. That is the way of mortals. And as he is the last of the Nine, it is right that his death should signal the end."

Elisabeth glanced at Killer, but he remained placidly awaiting the outcome of this back-and-forth, his dark eyes unfathomable. Come to think on it, between the two of them, Arthur seemed the more human. Perhaps he was. She didn't know anything about the *Imnada* other than the tiny bits she'd gleaned in the last few hours.

She decided to address Arthur, as he seemed the one most likely to be swayed by emotion. "Please. He may have been a part of them once, but he risked his life in the fight to stop Máelodor. To prevent a war that would destroy the *Other*—your blood kin. Doesn't that count for anything?"

The three of them stared back at her with varying degrees of surprise, but no one had any answer for that.

Brendan had never been so cold in his life. Miserable Irish weather. He blinked. No, not the weather. He needed to keep his wits. At least a little longer, but it was difficult. He wanted to close his eyes. Wanted to sleep, but something screamed at him that sleeping right now would be very bad. Why? He tried concentrating, but he couldn't remember. Not why he should stay awake. Not why he seemed to be in a room with candles blazing and all these people staring at him. Not why Elisabeth looked so sad.

"Stay with me, Brendan," she called from down a long tunnel.

Was he going somewhere? He didn't think so. He couldn't even move. Not to touch her face. Not to caress skin he knew would be soft and warm. Lifting his arm was too much trouble, and his left hand felt as if someone had shoved a stake through the center of it and twisted.

"Fate decrees our path and our end."

The voice. Those words. Both in his ears and in his mind as if spoken and thought simultaneously. The memories and the pain flooded back. A shame. He liked not knowing and not feeling a lot better.

"And this is the fate of the heir of Kilronan."

Not him. Aidan. It was his brother who had been fated to die here. As one of thousands. It had been Brendan's intervention that had kept that from occurring. His fate had thus been to change fate. He would have argued that point, but he'd no energy to talk.

A man's face loomed over him, a face carved in solemn lines. His hair shone as red as Elisabeth's, and his eyes glimmered like pools of silver light. "I would bear him company as he passes. As I would any warrior of my circle who fought so bravely."

Elisabeth held one hand while Arthur took the other. Even numb as he was, Brendan felt the warmth of the king's touch flood through him. The pressure of his grip digging Brendan's ring painfully into the side of his finger.

Ring? He'd no ring. Yet, there it was, in place of Daz's bit of dirty string. A narrow twisting band of pearl and silver. It shone against his waxen skin. Glowed in the milky dancing light of the cavern.

His vision narrowed as darkness rushed toward him. Voices rose and fell. Questioning. Quick. Sharp. He couldn't hear what they said, but he understood the surprise and the confusion underlying the speech.

And then there was another.

Someone he felt he knew. Familiar. Beautiful and sensual and smoky-smooth. A narrow face. Long, shimmering corn-silk hair. A gown of purest white. Eyes vast and endless as stars. He knew her. Somehow in some part of him, she was extremely important.

A hand cupped his face, the fingers cool against his skin. "He will come to *Ynys Avalenn* as my guest and my charge."

"Are you certain, Sedani?" Scathach sounded troubled by this decision.

"He bears my gift and my blood. I will honor the pledge I made. I can do no less."

Arms lifted him. Hands gentled him.

"Wait!" Something was placed round his neck. Lips

touched his in a kiss of farewell. "You promised you'd not leave me again. I'm going to hold you to that."

Light filled him, banishing the shadows crowding his vision.

"I love you, Brendan" wrapped him in a peace he never thought to feel again. The sound of bells became the rush of water became silence. He drew a final breath of soft earthy air as the portal closed behind him.

The world he left already no more than a hazy memory.

"It was the only way. He would have died had he stayed behind," Killer said as the last of the gray-gowned attendants faded into the cavern walls. One minute there was a coterie of beautiful crowned women and the air was alive with liquid silver and the dance of a million flickering stars; the next, there were no figures and the rock hardened dull and gray and empty.

"My brain knows. My heart isn't convinced," Elisabeth replied, hugging her arms to her body to ease the tight, breath-stealing pain beneath her ribs.

Arthur shifted awkwardly, as if he wanted to offer reassurance of some kind while Killer loomed protectively, his presence—strange as it was—comforting.

"I didn't even get a chance to say good-bye," she said weakly.

"You spoke it in your heart."

She gave Killer a curious glance, eliciting a self-conscious dropping of his head. "I'm able to read minds—a telepath of sorts. Sometimes I can act as a conduit between two others, but only if the two sending are strong. Your thought was sent as clearly as if you'd spoken it. I simply . . . helped it along."

Instantly she felt herself redden. "You can hear everything I'm thinking?"

"No," he hastened to assure her. "Only when I concentrate and only then if the thought is clearly pathed."

Her stomach unclenched. Imagining Killer seeing her thoughts as he'd seen every other part of her would have tipped her over the edge. She was barely hanging on now.

She placed her hand upon the cold marble of Arthur's sarcophagus, tracing the sword as it entered the chunk of rock. It helped to feel the solidity of it when everything else about this place and her life remained pure fantasy. "Do you know how often I heard the story of Sir Archibald Douglas and his faery lover? I can't wait to see the look on Aidan's face when I tell him I've met her in person." She giggled, slightly hysterical.

"Sedani's honor will compel her to do all she can for one of her line, no matter the generations between." Arthur's gaze followed the track of her hand, though whether his mind was on her or the oddity of staring at his own tomb was impossible to tell. Those strange silver eyes gave nothing away.

"And Scathach? She didn't approve of Brendan accompanying her to *Ynys Avalenn.*"

It was Killer who answered this time. "Scathach may have her reservations, but she knows what is owed to Douglas. The *Amhas-draoi* have been shamed. Máelodor came too close to succeeding in opening the gates to the abyss. Had the Dark Court been freed to hunt on the mortal plane, it would have been disastrous not only for your world but the *Fey* as well."

That future didn't bear thinking of, so she didn't. Instead, Elisabeth turned her attention to Arthur. "Will you return as well? Or are you"—she scanned the cavern with dismay—"trapped in our world?"

When Arthur smiled, it was like the sun breaking through the clouds. He seemed to beat with a light all his own. A majestic charisma that made one want to be near him just to bask in that aura. It was clear how such a man could grow to be a legend. And how the legend could forever inspire. Immediately the shoulder-crushing weight of her grief lifted. She wouldn't say she was happy, but she wasn't as close to smashing her fists against the stone in desolation either.

"I'm not trapped," he answered, "but the Sh'vad Tual did work its magic. The portal was opened and I was summoned, if not in the way the mage intended."

Killer put a hand upon her shoulder, his voice growly and rugged as a dog's bark. "We must go."

Understanding, which she'd held back through stubborn will, hit her all at once as if the cavern's walls had just collapsed on her. "Brendan's really not coming back, is he?"

Killer and Arthur exchanged wary male-to-male glances, but it was the shape-changer who was brave enough to answer. "It is"—his brow furrowed as if searching for the right word—"doubtful."

Arthur added, "Mortals taken into *Ynys Avalenn* soon forget their former lives. How they came to be in the summer kingdom. Even their names. They know only what the *Fey* wish them to know."

"You didn't forget," she charged.

"No, but Scathach spoke truth. I am a man more of magic than earth. Different from most mortals."

"You and Killer here should have a lot in common, then."

She knew immediately she'd put her foot in it, though neither said anything and the moment passed.

Killer's arm slipped round her shoulders as he guided her out of the cavern. Around downed limbs and toppled trees. Over rocks that looked as though they'd been uprooted and flung across the grove. And here and there, though she hadn't noticed them before, strange piles of gelatinous black ooze that shone greasy in the fading light of dusk. To the east, mountainous chains of storm clouds fragmented, spitting lightning as they broke apart.

Only after they'd walked for a little while did she rouse herself enough to notice Arthur had vanished.

She was alone with Killer.

Brendan was gone. He had left her. Again. And this time he would not—could not—come back.

twenty-seven

The group of them crowded into Helena's parlor. It still bore awkward signs of intrusion. Cushions had been hastily stitched, though the sofa bore a tear no amount of needlework could fix. A long, ugly scratch marred the piano's top, as if someone had taken out his frustration upon the instrument. The rest of the house was in much the same state, though a setting to rights still continued, the servants unusually quiet as they hastened about their work.

Her mind sluggish and numb, Elisabeth stared into the fire until her eyes watered. She'd felt this way since returning here to Duke Street. Arriving on the doorstep like lost baggage, silent, expressionless, and empty.

Thank heavens for Killer or she'd not even have made it as far as the tiny Cornish village they'd stumbled into that long-ago afternoon, the inhabitants abuzz with talk of strange violent storms, skies gone red, then black. Of strange creatures in the winds, the ring of sword upon shield, and ghostly battle cries. It had been his quiet authority that had secured them lodging, food, passage onward toward the coast, where they could take ship for Ireland.

She'd been too numb at the time, but now she wondered how he'd managed. A half-naked man and a stunned and bedraggled woman arriving from out of nowhere. They were lucky they hadn't been arrested, or worse.

He'd left her on the dawn of their arrival in Dublin. She'd awakened her last morning shipboard to an empty bunk and a curious captain. What could she say: *My companion has turned himself into a bird and flown away?*

She kept to a stubborn silence then and all through the days that followed when all were wise enough not to ask. A word and she might shatter. A touch might crumble her to dust. She remained too raw. Every nerve screaming. Every night's dreams holding a diamond-clear image of Brendan's body beneath a bloody sky.

It had taken Aidan's arrival to unlock her voice. His familiar features, his embrace firm and warm and smelling of cheroot smoke and brandy and soap and leather that released the knot choking off her breath.

The dam broken, she spilled all in a rush of grief and pain and fear, her face tight with tears that never fell. As if crying might seal the truth in stone and wash away all remaining hope. Only one secret was not hers to tell—that of the existence of Killer and the *Imnada*.

To any who pressed, the credit went to Rogan, who'd seen the light too late and died saving her. Madame Arana studied her long and hard, but Elisabeth held to her story and no more was said. Small questions swallowed in the greater crush of Máelodor's annihilation and Brendan's passing into the summer kingdom.

Mr. Ahern perked up as if awaiting his moment. "String. Ring. Ring. String. Rhymes, you see. That was my idea. Hide old Archibald's ring. Keep it safe." He pushed his spectacles onto his forehead, his rheumy, bloodshot eyes bright as a child's. "I'm glad it helped. Have to say, I wasn't certain it would." Elisabeth shot a guarded glance at the older gentleman seated on a salvaged wing chair, his fingers busy turning a broken shard of Wedgwood over and over. "Rings are tricky. Read of a ring wrought by the *Fey* once. Poor devil put it on, immediately burst into flame. Another changed the fellow that wore it into a tree. Got felled in a storm the following year and used for firewood, unlucky sap." He pulled a piece of twine from his pocket. Laid it on the table in front of him beside a cherry pit, a small gray pebble, a playing card.

Madame Arana paused in threading a needle to lay her ever-present embroidery down in her lap, the lines of her aged face deeper, the turn of her mouth sharper. "Come, Mr. Ahern. Let's go see about tea, shall we?"

He beamed at her. "Do you have some of those little yellow biscuits? I love little yellow biscuits."

"I'm sure we can find some," Madame Arana answered, the pair shuffling out of the room arm in arm.

"Should we set a place for Brendan? He should be home soon," Mr. Ahern's words floated back to them.

Jack cringed while Aidan closed his eyes, muttering something under his breath Elisabeth very much doubted was "Sweet, adorable old coot."

"It's my fault," Jack said. "If I'd stayed with Brendan instead of going with Helena . . ."

Elisabeth couldn't help but steal surreptitious looks at Brendan's cousin, his burnished blond hair and piercing blue eyes, the sleek courtier's flawlessness from the elegant cut of his coat to the polished shine of his boots. If she wasn't mistaken, Jack O'Gara was supposed to be inhabiting a family mausoleum in Wicklow, the victim of a highway robbery last year. Not swigging claret and shooting sidelong, wary glances back at her.

As she watched, he tossed back another gobletful as if it were water. Poured another from the rapidly dwindling decanter. Was that his third or fourth?

"Slow down or we'll be mopping you up off the floor," Aidan scolded, unable to take his eyes off his cousin. "I see death hasn't done much to change your habits."

Jack paled as he bowed his head. "We went over this, Aidan. I wanted to go to you immediately. Brendan wouldn't allow it. Said he didn't want to put you in danger."

"And you listened to him? That's the first time you've ever done as you're told."

Jack flinched again. Downed another drink.

Aidan dragged on his cheroot. Slumped into a chair, his face drawn as if he'd not slept in days, his hands jumpy as he stubbed out the butt. She knew just how he felt. The muscles strung rack-tight, the jittery, scratchy-eyed, stomach-rolling exhaustion when sleep was the last thing you wanted to do.

"I want to go home, Aidan. Will you take me?"

He turned to her as if he'd forgotten she remained in the room, his gaze flicking down to the wedding band gleaming on her finger. "Of course. Cat will be delighted to have you."

"No, not Belfoyle. My home. Dun Eyre. I need to leave. Now."

"But surely, your things, you'll want to—"

"Now. I can't stay here another minute." Her throat burned with unshed tears. "Please."

"Go, Aidan," Jack said. "I'll explain things."

Aidan clapped a hand upon his cousin's shoulder, a smirk tugging at the corner of his mouth. "Ever hopeful you can charm the uncharmable Miss Roseingrave?"

Jack waggled his eyebrows. "Let's say returning from the dead has its advantages."

The door was shut upon the Duke Street town house, leaving Elisabeth and Aidan standing beneath a high blue spring sky. A letter carrier ambled up the street with a bag upon his shoulder. Two ladies gossiped as they strolled. A hackney drew up, a man in starched shirt points and a tall beaver hat emerging with a glancing nod in their direction. The world turning in the usual way as if nothing had happened.

None knew how close they'd come to a devastating otherworldly war. None knew what they owed one man who'd traded his life so that they might continue to live in ignorance.

"Look at me, Elisabeth." No reassuring smile graced the Earl of Kilronan's face. Instead his brows drew low, a savage darkness invading his gaze. "My brother's risen from the ashes once. If he's able, he'll find a way back."

"You believe that?"

"Don't you?"

She smiled through watery eyes. "I wish I could."

Dun Eyre
Eighteen Months Later

Elisabeth rested her hands upon the keys of the pianoforte. Ventured a few unlikely notes. She'd unearthed the sheet music from a drawer where it had lain dusty and forgotten. Her proficiency at the instrument yielded nothing like the flood of long-buried emotion Brendan's skill could evoke. Music had flowed from his fingers until listeners felt it in their bones and their blood, a brilliant ferocious gift. It picked them up and carried them with it. Lit him up inside like a lamp, shone from his eyes.

Her chords flowed one after the other. The tune identifiable, but there was no magic. No beauty. No brutal magnificence to stir her soul. It was just music.

She lifted her hands from the keys, leaving Aunt Pheeney's words dangling overloud in the sudden silence. ". . . too thin and too quiet. It's unhealthy."

Not the first time she'd interrupted her aunts discussing her as if she weren't there or as if grief made one deaf as a post. She'd not cared at first, but after months of sneaking glances and gallons of warm milk, their concern began to grate. Couldn't they see she was perfectly, absolutely fine? So she didn't choose to leave Dun Eyre as often as she used to. She enjoyed the sense of peace she felt in simply being home. Taking long rambling walks through the park. Riding across the high fields. Spending hours with Mr. Adams going over the accounts. Reviewing articles. Visiting with the tenants.

She'd even begun organizing her grandmother's old greenhouses, spending long hours with seedlings and cuttings, peppering the gardeners with questions on soil improvement and irrigation, and reading Repton's views on landscape design late into the night.

She found she enjoyed the peace and satisfaction of dirty nails and muddy skirts and a face even more freckled from sun. And if it tired her enough to bring sleep at night, all the better, though she wouldn't tell Aunt Fitz or Aunt

Pheeney. They already treated her as if she were a convalescing invalid—or a prime candidate for the asylum.

"You should have asked her first," Aunt Fitz muttered.

"She'd never have agreed if I'd asked," Aunt Pheeney's stage whisper carried the length of the salon.

"Still, you might have—"

"You know, I *can* hear the two of you," Elisabeth called out.

Aunt Pheeney fluttered up from her sofa, a puzzled look dancing over her round features. "What's that, dear? Did you say something?"

Elisabeth rose from the pianoforte to join her aunts by the fire. "I said the two of you are about as subtle as a herd of stampeding oxen."

She ignored Aunt Pheeney's hand pressed in motherly fashion against her forehead, the offer of a shawl against the December chill, the suggestion of an extra pillow behind her, "as that chair has always been uncomfortable."

Aunt Fitz merely regarded her steadily from half-lidded eyes before picking up a letter from a tray by her chair. "There's something for you just come from Belfoyle."

Aunt Pheeney snatched it from her sister, handing it to Elisabeth with a suspiciously satisfied smile. "Open it. It might be important."

She hated the unbidden skip of her heart. As if somehow miraculously after all this time word would come that Brendan had returned.

Tearing open the wax seal, she scanned the page. "It's from Cat," she said, though she'd a strong feeling her aunts already knew that. Had probably set it up in a flash of inspiration. She could hear them now: *We'll force her out of her shell like prying open a crab.*

Well, she liked her shell, thank you very much.

"Cat's asked us to join them at Christmas. Sabrina and Daigh MacLir will be there with their daughter, and Jack O'Gara's been invited. Even Miss Roseingrave and her grandmother are expected."

"Oh, it sounds absolutely delightful. Nothing like a houseful of family to make a holiday sparkle," chattered Aunt Pheeney, grinning like a Cheshire cat. "And having little ones about makes it even better. Isn't it Lord Kilronan's boy's first Christmas? I saw His Lordship just the other day. He looked proud as a peacock."

Elisabeth felt the lump in her throat drop into her stomach. A child. Brendan's child. She would have liked that, but as with so much else, it had not been fated. She'd not even been allowed that much of him.

She chided herself for her weakness. Her maudlin droopiness. It had been long enough. She needed to move on. To stop hoping. To forget. Just as Brendan had.

"We'll begin to lay out your clothes this afternoon. Perhaps a trip to Ennis next week." Aunt Pheeney's cheerfulness was almost painful. "You know what Bacon says: 'Riches are for spending,' and I saw the loveliest velvet in Nicholas blue the last time I was there. And there was a fabulous picture of a morning robe in the latest *Ackermann's*. Let me see if I can find it."

She began rummaging through a stack of magazines and papers beside her chair, looking so pleased Elisabeth couldn't bear to disappoint her. And why not order a new gown? It would go with her new resolve. She would lock away her time with Brendan as a glistening, beautiful memory to last her a lifetime.

"There's a letter from your uncle in London as well,"

Aunt Fitz said, her gaze narrowing. "He writes to say Gordon Shaw was married last month."

Elisabeth frowned. It had been six months since Gordon had arrived at Dun Eyre, looking as smug as ever as he asked her to reconsider a marriage between them. Six months since she'd sent him away, wondering if she was giving up her last chance at a husband and a family of her own.

"I'm happy for him," she said as Aunt Fitz continued to regard her steadily. "I am. We would have made a horrible hash of things had we wed." She rose, dragging her shawl close around her shoulders. "Excuse me." Chin up, she forced herself to walk sedately from the salon. "I've just forgotten something in my room."

Twin pairs of worried gazes bored into her back. The buzz of whispers trailing behind her. "Told you not to throw that at her . . . a shock."

"Needed to know . . . not coming back . . . over . . ."

Once out of range of her aunts' custody, Elisabeth dashed up the stairs, through the upper corridor, to the long gallery, where she sank onto a sofa, her breath coming in short, heaving gasps as she fought back foolish tears.

How long she remained there before her aunt found her, she couldn't say. One minute she was alone with the portraits for company, the next Aunt Fitz was beside her, an arm around her shoulders, a hand smoothing her hair as she'd done when Elisabeth was a child.

"I don't know why I'm crying. Had we married, Gordon would soon have been miserable and I—"

"Would have found yourself married to a man you did not love. Young Lochinvar still holds a tight grip upon your heart."

"I've tried so many times, Aunt Fitz. I tell myself every morning: I shall make this the day I finally stop believing he's going to come back. Then I dream of him, and it's so vivid it's as if he were in the room with me. I see that his hair needs trimming and he's thinner. I see a scar upon his cheek that wasn't there before. He takes my hand, but he never speaks. And when I wake, I can smell his scent on my pillow and feel the heat of him in the bed beside me. I know he's not returning. It's been too long and my hope is gone, but I'm afraid if I make myself forget, he'll stop coming to me. I won't even have my dreams."

They sat in silence, each lost in her own thoughts. Elisabeth felt herself relax in her aunt's quiet embrace, her muscles slowly unwinding, her breathing slowing to normal.

Aunt Fitz gathered Elisabeth's hands in her own. Her gaze lifting to the portrait of her parents. "You remind me of your grandmother."

Elisabeth wiped her face, sitting up to gaze at the woman in the portrait's dreamy features, her wistful smile soft as a spring rain. No one had ever compared Elisabeth to her before. Her grandmother had been tiny, wispy, faded, and quiet. Everything Elisabeth was not.

"She too retreated into dreams when she lost the one most dear to her," Aunt Fitz explained.

"Grandfather?"

"You never knew him, he died long before you were born, but the two of them loved deeply. Perhaps too deeply, for his death seemed to kill a part of her. From that time on, she was never the same vibrant, beautiful woman we had known. She became as much a wraith as any spirit."

"Brendan once called him a prune." Elisabeth brushed away a tear.

Aunt Fitz laughed. "He could be, but he also loved his wife beyond reason. It's rare to find that kind of bond. And almost impossible to set aside. But no matter how hard you try, you cannot follow where Brendan's gone anymore than my mother could follow my father. And there is a risk in living only in dreams."

"So you're saying I should wake up now?"

Firmness in her gold-flecked eyes, Aunt Fitz nodded. "It is time."

He stood upon a hill above Belfoyle, his hand upon the ward stone, its power pouring through him in pulses of coruscating light.

Breán Duabn'thach, it whispered in the tongue of the ancients, accepting him as its own, though he'd the feeling it had hesitated, as if unable to comprehend this strange mixture of man and *Fey* that he'd become.

From this ridge Brendan could look down upon his home, seeing it laid out before him like blocks upon a child's quilt. The folds of the hills, a stream becoming a river as it moved inland, cabins and houses connected by lanes and tracks and roads bordered by a low stone wall, the walls of the house, its towers rising above the trees, and beyond it, the sea moving slick and gray in the distance, the sound of the surf amplified by the low, dirty clouds scudding overhead.

Closing his eyes, he inhaled the cold, damp air, feeling it in every freshly healed bone. Flakes drifted frozen across his cheeks, clung to his eyelashes. He opened his eyes to see snow falling softly over the meadows and fields, bleaching the world to gunmetal gray.

All but for a lone rider. The horse's glossy chestnut coat

drawing his eye. The rider's blaze of red hair clamping a fist around his heart. A vision and a name he'd clung to when all else had grown ragged and faded in his mind. A woman he'd traveled between worlds to find again.

Elisabeth.

He'd finally come home.

Snow swirled in the wind, drifting out across the gray waters of the sea. Gulls floated on the updrafts, while others dove into the chop. Surfacing to swallow their dinner. Elisabeth lifted her face to the cold, letting the sting of ice burn her cheeks. Inhaling the crisp bite of winter wind. Her horse sidled with impatience, but Elisabeth held the long-legged chestnut mare still as she scanned the horizon, a ship's sails bright white against the cloudy sky.

She'd ridden out alone, the laughter and noise and constant need to play a part finally wearing her down. She needed space to breathe. To be alone with her thoughts and last night's dream.

It had been as real as life. Brendan looking over his shoulder as he stepped from a circle of weathered stones. Swinging up on a rangy, flea-bitten gray with a wild eye and chopping gait. His gaze lifted, and it was as if he looked straight at her. Over time. Over distance. And she'd jerked awake, heart crashing, blood pushing through a restless body. Somehow she knew this would be the last such dream. He would not come to her again. She would lose even that small comfort.

The snow intensified, the tiny, drifting flakes becoming a curtain of white, the ground disappearing beneath a feathery blanket. Her horse pawed the ground, its breath clouding the air. Perhaps she should return to Belfoyle's warmth and company. Let Sabrina's daughter crawl into her lap for a story. Smell the sweet baby scent of Aidan's new son. Wrap herself in the love of family, old and new.

She reined the chestnut in a circle, headed back toward the warmth of the Belfoyle stables. The horse dropped into a slow, surefooted canter, the cliffs sliding past them on their right, the sea a foaming, white-capped silver froth rimed in black at the far edge of the world. The wind and the snow mixed with her tears to blur the track before her, but instead of slowing, she gave the chestnut its head, the lengthening pound of its stride matching her heart beat for beat. Her hat flew off. Her hair fell free from its pins in the tear of wind and snow.

And then there was another. A rider pushed his way through the storm toward her.

She dashed the tears from her eyes as she leaned over her mare's withers, refusing to allow an intruder into her solitude. And then refusing to lose the unspoken challenge as the horse swept down on them.

The ground flew beneath her, the mare giving and then giving again, but still the newcomer inched his way closer, eating the distance between them. Elisabeth steered for the far hedgerow, but he was on her, the horse's nose pulling even, then just ahead. The rider turned his face toward her, and his eyes glowed bright as suns.

She couldn't breathe. Her heart stopped. She heard nothing but the sound of the wind. Saw only a swirl of storm clouds. Felt nothing beyond the slowing of her mare as the man leaned over to take a rein, bringing both horses down to a trot, then a walk, pulling them up as she slithered from the saddle and into his arms.

His lips warm upon hers. His embrace like steel bands

pressing her close, his voice a lilting purr in her ears. "No tears. No tears, my love."

"Are you real or a dream?" she whispered, unable to believe. After all, how often did one's wishes come true?

Brendan took her by the shoulders, pushing her to arm's length, and she got her first good look at him. There was the scar on his left cheek. The unfashionably long hair brushing his shoulders, the leanness of his once muscled frame.

"Not a dream, Lissa," he answered. "Not this time."

Her eyes widened. "You sent them. It was you all along."

"It was the only way I knew to keep you from forgetting until I could find a way back to you."

As she drank him in, other changes sharpened into focus. A new sculpted beauty to his fallen-angel features as if he'd been riven in sharper lines, deeper colors, all earthly softness cut away, leaving only the forged steel of his *Fey* heritage. The very air seemed charged with his presence.

She frowned. "You're not the same. I don't mean the clothes or the hair, but something else. You don't feel the same." She placed a hand over his heart. "In here."

His fingers laced with hers. The bones broken and bent, they curled into his palm. The flesh stretched and silver with scars.

Her eyes swam with tears. She couldn't seem to stop their flow now that she'd begun. As if a year and a half of grieving had been loosed. She wanted to tell him everything, all that had occurred in the past year and a half, but managed only a sobbing, "Your hand."

His smile held self-consciousness and a small tinge of embarrassment. "The *Fey* kept me alive, but even their healing has limits. And that came at a price. I'm not sure if I'm exactly who I was before. I feel less human. Less solid. And yet, not of their world either. Like I'm standing between. A foot on each side of the divide."

"Like Arthur."

His brows rose, his lips curled in a crooked smile. "That's a comparison that could go to a fellow's head."

She stood on tiptoe, tasting the cool firmness of his lips. Snow slid over the carved lines of his face. Melted upon his collar. "They warned me you would forget. That, once within the summer kingdom, there was no coming back."

"Not so long ago, to forget my past would have been my greatest desire. But they say be careful what you wish for. Losing those memories meant losing you. I couldn't do it. I loved you too much to give you up without a fight."

His gaze slid into the cold ice of her heart until she ached with the pain of its thawing. As if she could finally breathe without the stab of his loss. "But how?"

"I had this." He pulled free a gold chain, the rainbow sparkle of her opal catching fire in the gray light.

She laughed through her tears. "You said it was just a stone. Nothing magic about it."

"It was given in love, and that's a magic not even the *Fey* truly understand."

She burrowed against him, hearing the steady rhythm of his heart, the slow rise and fall of his chest, his hand running up and down her back, and she shook with horrid, wretched weeping.

"Ah, my sweet. Don't cry. It's over. I'll not leave you again. I'm home. For good. I promise."

"Is that a promise you'll keep or one you'll break?" she sniffled.

"All this way and that's all the welcome I get? I can leave again if you like."

He tried to walk away, but she grabbed hold of him. "No!" Looked up to see the teasing laughter in his eyes. "You're a right bastard, Brendan Douglas." She wiped away her tears with the back of her hand.

He put an arm around her, wrapping her close as she reached out to touch his hair, his face, his chest. Reassuring herself he was real.

He tipped her chin up with his bent and crooked fingers, his smile breaking her heart all over again. "Aye, Mrs. Douglas, but you love me anyway."

Fantasy.
Temptation.
Adventure.

Visit PocketAfterDark.com, an all-new website just for Urban Fantasy and Romance Readers!

- Exclusive access to the hottest urban fantasy and romance titles!

- Read and share reviews on the latest books!

- Live chats with your favorite romance authors!

- Vote in online polls!

www.PocketAfterDark.com

Hungry for more?

Pick up a bestselling Paranormal Romance
from Pocket Books!

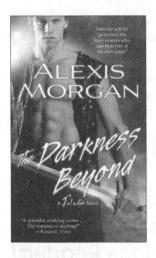

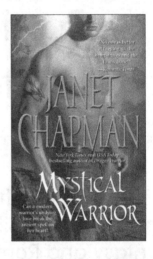

Printed in the United States
By Bookmasters